SHADOWRUN
MAGIC, MACHINES, AND MAYHEM

EDITED BY JOHN HELFERS AND JENNIFER BROZEK

SHADOWRUN: MAGIC, MACHINES, AND MAYHEM
Edited by John Helfers and Jennifer Brozek
Cover art by Tyler Clark
Design by Matt Heerdt and David Kerber

Published by Catalyst Game Labs,
an imprint of InMediaRes Productions, LLC
5003 Main St. #110 • Tacoma, WA 98407

TABLE OF CONTENTS

INTRODUCTION

Although many writers have accused me of being heartless (I am an editor, after all), I've always had a soft spot in my cold, black heart for short stories. Maybe it's because that's where I got my start in the business, overseeing the production of hundreds (yes, hundreds) of short fiction anthologies in my time before joining Catalyst Game Labs. It's also possible that I like short fiction because that was my first published professional sale, many (many) years ago.

Or perhaps it's because I think the short story is a nearly perfect medium to introduce a reader (and potential fan) to a whole new world in a compact method that doesn't require the attention of a longer story. Moreover, I also think there are certain intellectual properties where the short story, in the hands of skilled authors, can provide a perfect glimpse (or, in the case of an anthology, glimpses) of a larger, more complicated world while still providing a complete reading experience.

But I think the main reason I like short stories is because I get to challenge a group of authors to come up with the best *Shadowrun* story they can write—which is exactly what happened here. Much like the previous volumes *Spells & Chrome*; *World of Shadows*; and *Drawing Destiny*; *Magic, Machines, and Mayhem* takes you on sixteen wild rides through the Sixth World, featuring all the cutting-edge, delta-tech, high-octane, spell-slinging action you could want from the widest array of Sixth World characters you can think of: a street samurai whose call to DocWagon turns into the opportunity of a lifetime...if he can just live to collect the most lucrative bounty he's ever seen; a street-smart two-person runner team is forced to confront their most dangerous run yet—hiding out in an isolated rural town; a corporate executive squares off against a ruthless vice-president in their own megacorp in a razor-sharp battle of wits and words.

There are also some ace runners appearing in these pages again. Mage and academic 'runner Winterhawk is the star of a tale about him first meeting one of his longest acquaintances from the shadows—and it goes about as well as one might expect. Finally, no *Shadowrun* collection would be complete without everyone's favorite runners, Wolf and Raven, matching wits with a determined ork child and a megacorp that are both much more than they seem.

Whether it's runners and other denizens swapping tall tales at an unusual nightclub, or a retired-shadowrunner-turned-corp wife coming face-to-face with some unfinished business from her past, these and the other stories in *Magic, Machines, and Mayhem* are sure to give you that cyber-magic shot of adrenaline you're looking for.

Finally, I'm pleased to announce the inclusion of accomplished author and editor Jennifer Brozek as an editor-at-large for the *Shadowrun* fiction line, as well as my co-editor on this project. Many of you already know Jennifer from her amazing *Shadowrun* fiction of all lengths, from short story to novel. Now I'm tapping her editorial experience to help oversee the *SR* fiction line in all its various forms, starting with this volume, which she was instrumental in bringing to publication. There will be more announcements regarding Jennifer's work in the *Shadowrun* universe, including a forthcoming new project that takes *SR* fiction in a bold new direction. I hope you'll join me in welcoming Jennifer to our team.

—JOHN HELFERS

AN APPLE A DAY

Bryan CP Steele

Frag, that hurts!

The bullet lodged in Sideshow's shoulder had been excruciating when the go-ganger's Ares something-or-another put it there, but now that it had taken up residence against his right clavicle, it was agony. The dwarf's series-4 pain inhibitors were maxed out, and it still felt like someone drawing fingernails down a chalkboard *inside* his body.

I really can't afford this, he thought as his blood-slick fingers tap-danced over the emergency DocWagon band around his wrist. His basic contract would cover some of the repairs, but the constant buzzing down his right arm, combined with how twitchy his fingers were, meant damage to the reflex clusters wired to that arm. That system had taken him two years and twice that in dumb, *maybe-I-shouldn't-have-taken-this* types of gigs, to save up for it, and he definitely didn't have the extra 'yen for insurance. He remembered how it felt to digi-sign on that dotted line...

A series of near misses whizzing past the broken-down Jackrabbit he was using for cover snapped him back to right now, reminding him what Hollywood always told him by reciting his old friend's adage: "Debt is better than dead."

Sideshow yanked down on the wristband to break the seal, revealing the secondary switch inside. He took a quick breath, winced at how it actually throbbed in his right lung a bit, and pressed the switch. There was a small trio of vibrations under his thumb, and a bright green message scrolled across his cybereyes' image link.

Franz, Thomas. Silver Contract Initiated. Please remain calm. Your nearest DocWagon retrieval affiliate is on the way. Stanch any bleeding wounds by applying pressure with adequately absorbent, non-infectious materials. Please remain calm. Your nearest DocWagon retrieval affiliate is on the way. Please remain calm. Your nearest DocWagon...

The scroll continued to repeat, so Sideshow waved the message into his slush receiver and returned his focus to the firefight raging all around him. Having only just accepted the meet with a Johnson, the part-time street samurai was low on cash, high on needs, and hadn't even met the rest of his upcoming team yet. He'd only been halfway to Sybrespace for the meet when everything had gone pear-shaped.

So, when these dregs of the backways rode up and started spraying caseless around, he had no idea why, no game plan, and most unfortunately...no backup. The bullets started flying, and Sideshow's Rapier took a few rounds in the block; the bike ground to a halt and tossed him off, literally dropping him into a streetside shootout. Old habits die hard, and instead of just running off and pinging in for some corpsec heaters to deal with these fools, his dwarf mitt was soon filled with Ruger steel, and he was already thinking about making them sorry. Before his smartlink could even get fully actualized to his cybereyes, he was yanking on the trigger and sending rounds across Yesler Way and into the three worst-dressed Halloweener go-gangers this side of Pike Place Market. When his target recognition software caught up with his instincts, one of them was already down. It wasn't clean, and it left him open.

Open for one of the other two to get a lucky hit to Sideshow's shoulder, knocking the Warhawk from his fingers, sending him scuttling for cover, and bringing him to his current predicament—pinned down with only a single BangSmak concussion pack left in his arsenal.

"Come on out, stunty!" One of the gangers shouted between the rip of gunshots. "Leave your 'link and any sticks you are carryin' on the hood and we'll let'cha limp out of—"

The *whir-brrrap* of a minigun assembly coming to life cut that last statement—and the life of the ganger who was saying it—short. Hundreds of armor piercing rounds tore one of the orks, as well as the tooled-up racing bike he was straddling, to shreds in seconds. The last Halloweener foolishly turned her gun on the newly arriving armored ambulance and was similarly turned into a two-meter-wide Rorschach blot of crimson on the pavement.

"*This is an official contracted DocWagon extraction,*" a loudspeaker blasted in all directions, announcing the legality of the action as well as keeping others from adding to the casualty list, "*please stay twelve to fifteen meters away from all DocWagon personnel until we have secured the client and declared the area safe for transit.*"

"Drek," Sideshow said, slowly rising into view, keeping the hand clutching the emergency tag held as high as he could while still trying to keep his blood in his shoulder, "that was fast. You really do get what you pay for, eh?"

"Franz comma Thomas?" One of the two heavily armored emergency Doc-techs, the one *not* strapped to the gunnery rig of the retrieval ambulance, stepped toward the wounded dwarf. In one hand she held a highly modified—likely sponsored—H&K submachine gun, and was obviously manipulating an AR info-popup with the other.

"Yeah, yeah, chum," Sideshow scoffed. "You know, the guy holding his collarbone together? Yeah, I'm the one who called you."

"Please present your contract tag and hold still for verification. We were en route to something very important when your tag pinged us, so let's not waste anyone's time here, okay?" Sarcasm was obviously lost on this one.

"Here ya go." He winced as he extended his bloody hand and the occasionally vibrating chunk of plastic around his wrist. "Most expensive call I ever made."

"The hazardous pickup was actually covered by your contract, Mister Thomas. Otherwise, we would have sent the next wagon team." Her firmly set chin was the only part of her face visible under her mirrored visor, and the smile that grew across it seemed genuine. The bulky gauntlet of her armor hovered over the ID tag for moment, pulling all the necessary data from Sideshow's contract. "A piece of free advice? If you are going to continue hostilities with multiple alleged gang members at a time, you really ought to upgrade your contract to at least Gold. Only the first hundred rounds spent during an extraction are included at this level."

"I'll take that into consideration." Sideshow paused, looking at the high-threat responder's poly-glo badge on her chest. "Miss Abernathy."

"Client confirmed." Triggering her helmet mic, Abernathy comm'd to her partner behind the streetside artillery. The thick plates of the response armor, combined with the helmet and the well-practiced cadence of her speech, made it all but impossible to tell where the Doc-tech was from. Not that he actually *cared* who this wageslave was, not really, but reading people was Sideshow's special talent. "Dwarf. Bio-male. Single large-caliber gunshot wound to the upper right quadrant of center mass. Prepare the chair for an in-and-out 70/30 patch-up. Moderately augmented. No visible or registered bioware, and scanning at Beta-grade tech."

Beta? That fraggin' doc charged me Delta pricing!

"I'm gonna live, Doc?"

"I'm legally required to tell you I'm not a doctor." Abernathy sighed the sigh of someone who has had to recite legislation codes thousands of times before. "And even my educated opinion isn't binding to liability in any way." She smirked, holstering her weapon. "But yeah, tough sodder like you? You'll be primetime again in just a few."

The other DocWagoner finished putting his minigun mount back into the armored pocket-point on the vehicle, tucking it inside the large sliding door on its side before taking out pre-packaged medical procedural kits.

Cradling the wounded arm, they started toward the ambulance. Sideshow exhaled through clenched teeth. Each step sent a shock through his shoulder. The bullet surely had achieved consciousness somehow, and was engraving its *very long* name on the surface of his bone.

"So...I bet you folks have really good pharma on this rig, eh?"

"The best." Abernathy chuckled. "but *you* will be limited to locals and slap patches onsite, plus access to thirty-six hours of orals afterward." She shrugged. "You get what you pay for, Thomas."

"Law of the land, chum," the dwarf whistled slowly, following her somewhat subtle ushering into the vehicle. Trying not to *plop* too hard into the plastic-lined treatment chair mounted at the center of the ambulance compartment, Sideshow settled into the body-forming foam cushions. Quickly, the other Doc-tech helped him find a serviceable position. After a series of grunts, winces, and gasps that were thankfully drowned out by the crinkling and squeaking of the plastic sheeting beneath his weight, everyone was seemingly happy.

"You have any hidden weaponry we need to be made aware of, Thomas?" This elven medical worker recited the standards even as he cut off the right sleeves from Sideshow's jacket and shirt with well-practiced expertise. As soon as the puckered wound of the shoulder was exposed, he tore the activating film off the back of a medical chem-patch and slapped it over the hole. Those things were designed to be sliced open and worked through while administering pharmaceuticals and helping dissuade further blood loss, and Sideshow really hoped those promised local anesthetics were about to kick in pretty soon. He focused on the elf's badge, shutting out the pain of the first probing instrument into the wound.

"Negatory, Mr. Findlay," he answered. "I'm not jobbin' at the moment. All I have is... *whoa...*"

There it is... he thought, blinking wide as the cool rush of numbness spread across his upper arm and chest. He suddenly realized why people got addicted to slappers.

"Everything okay?" Abernathy chimed in, peeking in from the street. "We dial dosage up to compensate for your body type. We go too far? Maybe we should pull it back some..."

"Don't you dare." Sideshow narrowed his eyes comically. "I paid high 'yen for this cotton candy highway you're drivin' me down. So...keep it comin'." He slumped back a bit, barely aware of the bullet fragments being pulled from him as much more than dull pressure.

"Okay, okay." Findlay tried to rein in the conversation while he worked. "You were saying? Weapons?"

"Oh!" Sideshow chuckled. "As I was saying before you godsent angels of mercy pumped me full of this sweet, sweet ambrosia...all I have is one concussion pak and my Ruger." He looked down at his empty holster. *Frag!* "Oh hey, I dropped my piece out there when I got popped."

"I can grab it." Abernathy nodded. "Won't even charge you the fee for non-ambulatory services, either."

"Thanks." Sideshow wasn't sure if the Doc-tech was being serious, but it was good to have on the record either way. "That thing's gotten me through a lot, that's for sure."

"Where'd you drop it, Thomas?"

"Well, I got hit off my bike over there in the street." He tried to focus through the chemical-induced haze creeping up the side of his face and into his central nervous system. "I wasn't far from the curb when they got lucky an' caught me lookin'."

"Here it is," Abernathy shouted over her shoulder as she scooped up the scuffed-up-but-still-shiny piece. "Not bad, Thomas. This isn't a bad shoo—"

Fwoooooooooosh!

The street was suddenly the landscape of hell itself. An expanding cloud of burning aerosolized napalm filled the street, enveloping Abernathy and everything else within three meters of her. Her helmet microphone picked up her screams and blasted static through the loudspeakers of the ambulance and into Findlay's earpiece. Her armor was treated to be mostly flame-retardant, keeping her from cooking instantly, but that exposed lower part of her face turned her visor into a chimney of sorts—sending a roiling ball of fire up into her eyes and under the helmet.

"Roast, corpo puppet!" The voice was half-mad and crackling as it shouted over Abernathy's screams and the roar of his Hell Turtle flamethrower. Just emerged from behind an overfull dumpster, yet another Halloweener—by the stripes of bright orange caution tape crisscrossing his black jacket—laughed maniacally. His strangely tattooed face was aglow with the light from his stream of fire.

"Susan!" Findlay slapped the access switch for his minigun, but while it unlocked from its stowage and he grabbed it to bring it to bear, Sideshow saw something dance across the side of Findlay's helmet...a simple red dot.

"Watch out!" The dwarf was suddenly sober. The pain medications went from a pleasing numbness to a cold, wooden stiffness as adrenaline made war against them in his veins.

"Wha—?" Findlay turned to address Sideshow's warning, his chiseled elven face visible through the visor, perfectly putting the glowing red pinpoint of light just over his left eye.

The timing was all too perfect. A high caliber round punched through that spot, splitting the plastic-coated alloy of the helmet easily, calling in to question the efficacy of the gear the company supplies them with. The round punched through the Doc-tech's skull like cracking an egg., sending the headgear spinning away in two pieces and splattering the inside of both halves with *yolk*.

Fragfragfragfragfrag!

"Burn it all down, 'weeners!" The flamethrowing ganger cackled again, pouring more fiery death onto the charred and blackened Abernathy a few strides away.

Even as Findlay sagged and twitched to the floor, rolling out of the ambulance and onto the street, Sideshow could hear the sadistic laughter of another ganger approaching from around the front end of the ambulance. The dwarf wriggled his hand free of the surgical restraint and flexed his wounded arm. *Not great,* he thought, *but it'll have to do.*

As he pulled himself to his somewhat shaky feet, the anesthesia still clouding some of his senses, something shot by him, making a metallic *klink-klink-klink* sound in the cabin behind. He turned to see an old Czech-made phosphorus grenade rattling around the floor of the ambulance.

"Aw hell!" Sideshow shouted, throwing his weight forward to jump out of the vehicle just as the cannister exploded, sending a shower of burning hot white mini meteors searing and melting through the compartment. Anywhere the little flaming globs struck or bounced, a new blaze was left behind, turning the entire inside of the ambulance into a veritable inferno. One white-hot fragment passed by Sideshow's face by a few inches, and the heat alone turned one of his eyebrows and half his carefully maintained moustache into wisps of bitter smoke that would have stung his senses, were they not overloaded by the trail of chemical fumes.

"Burn, bay-bee, burn!" The grenade's tosser was a truly rare sight in the sprawl. A goblin ganger in another orange-and-black-striped flak vest danced psychotically in the glowing blaze. Either he was completely oblivious to Sideshow's escape or too filled with pyromaniacal joy to care, and didn't seem to feel the burn of the flames at all in his vampirism-goblinized dwarf flesh. No matter the reasons, the leathery-skinned arsonist didn't so much as spare the dwarf a glance in his direction.

Alright–Sideshow rearranged his thoughts, knowing the few seconds he was being given would pass before long—*use it.* He let his street sam instincts take over, immediately assessing the situation like he would on any run. He'd been in worse situations before. The only difference was now he wasn't getting paid in nuyen, but his heart would keep beating. *Sitrep, Sideshow.*

In one of the gob's hands, he held a pistol that seemed *way* too hefty for the little guy, but the epoxy-taped laser sight under its barrel made Sideshow pretty sure he was the one that had headshot Findlay. That was a mixed boon, honestly. While it meant there wasn't a rifle-wielding sniper up on one of these coffin stacks around him, it also meant the gob was a good shot and willing to use more than a few flames to execute someone.

The flamethrower ganger was still turning poor Abernathy into human charcoal in the street, consumed by the thrill of it all as well as whatever chemicals were racing through his veins. Those single-tank flamethrowers weren't made for this kind of saturation. Sideshow knew it would be sputtering out any moment, and it didn't look like these neo-anarchists likely had the money for a number of pressurized ammo-cannisters.

Two thugs, focused on their showy kills.

Not bad odds, he thought. *Now what am I working with?*

His Ruger was somewhere over by Cajun-fried Abernathy, along with her sidearm, and the minigun covered in elf filling was still ground zero for the incendiary blast and utterly unusable.

Too bad Findlay wasn't... His eyes went to the elven corpse next to the ambulance. *Wait...was he packing?*

He rolled over twice, ignoring the growing throb in his shoulder, tucking in to the unfortunate street medic's body. His hands ran over the crumpled frame, one moving much easier than the other, patting pockets and pouches and armored compartments on the medic's armor.

"Hey! Where'd beardy go?" The flamethrower spat, flickered, and *pluffed* out of fuel nearby.

Come on, Findlay...you were a damned professional...

"He was 'ere a second ago!" The goblin tore his eyes away from the swirl of flame in and around the DocWagon ambulance, eyes straining to adjust to the nighttime shadows beyond the firelight.

"There you are!"

There YOU are!

As the ganger lifted his pistol toward him, Sideshow's numb fingers wrapped around the handle of his monomolecular scalpel. Knowing every millisecond counted, he triggered his wired reflexes—and it nearly took his breath away. Most of his body sped up normally, but that wounded arm became cold stone at the end of his shoulder. In that split second, Sideshow yanked his muscle memory back to his rookie, unaugmented days. The scalpel left his fingers with a flick of his tingling wrist, spinning toward its target, along with the dwarf's only chance to avoid getting splattered.

Despite only being two centimeters in length, the scalpel's empowered blade was designed to slice through the toughest of enhanced tissues and materials—piercing the goblin's eye, like it was warm soy, to devastate the gray matter behind it. Bypassing the regeneration of his vampirically-resilient flesh by going directly for the brain, the gob was dead before he hit pavement.

"Two-Tone!" The until-recently-flamethrowing Halloweener came around the corner to watch him fall. Real shock crossed his tatted-up face, but it quickly twisted into anger as his enlarged pupils fell upon the dwarf. "All you had to do was stay in the wagon, chum. Stay in the wagon and die. Now I gotta do ya all slow..." He pulled out a thin-bladed, serrated knife. "...gotta make it hurt. For Twos and Backstop."

This braincase thinks a knife is going to be more painful than being burned alive? Sideshow's pragmatic mind cut through his painkiller fugue, and the thought pulled up the corners of his mouth into a sarcastic grin.

The go-ganger snarled again, "Shoulda just stayed in the wa—"

"Yeah, I heard ya the first time." Sideshow scrambled to his feet and into a three-point coiled stance. The ganger's eyes widened as his mouth fell agape; he apparently wasn't ready for a street sam on this little hijacking of theirs.

In a split-second, the dwarf pushed off the ground, pushing up and forward. A fiery bloom of pain sang out across his nerves as his wounded shoulder crushed into the ganger's chest. *Unh! Wrong shoulder!*

Stars might have flooded the edges of his vision, but things were worse for his would-be attacker. The thickened bone structure Sideshow had paid good money for months ago drove hard into the small spaces between ribs, splintering them. His off hand, sadly being his only good hand at the moment, shot out following the impact and wrapped thick dwarf fingers around the wiry hand holding the knife.

Days of living off chemical stimulants and sleeping in filth made the struggle to control the blade a short one. Sideshow easily overpowered the ganger, practiced movements overcoming gutter instincts, and with a wet *shunk!* his fingers were wet and sticky with a pulsing flow from somewhere between them. He let go and stepped back, already knowing how this ended.

"Whu...whu...what..." The ganger's blood slick fingers swatted uselessly at the hilt jutting out of his waist, and he looked down in disbelief at the rapidly slowing rhythm of red spurts from his wound. "It...it was...was supposed..."

"But it wasn't," Sideshow cut him off, taking one more step back just in case. "Wrong mark, beetle-head. I'm genuinely sorry it came to this." The ganger collapsed onto his face, a trickle of condensation from the empty fuel tank mixing with the growing pool of blood. "But you get what you order, chum."

Sideshow waited a few more seconds to step forward and grab the knife from the wound. His gun was gone, that flamethrower was way too much for street work, and he was several hours' away from his storage stack. Cleaning off the blade as best he could on the guy's jacket, he found it was surprisingly well-balanced and would get him to the tube. He was sure there'd be a lot of questions, but if he was going to pay for pub-trans, he might as well head to the meet up for the gig. Who knows? Maybe the Johnson would have someone there to finish stitching him up, too.

Local security or corpo mercs might be headed this way anytime soon, so it was time to pick up what he could and get moving. He stopped and listened for approaching sirens.

Huh? What is that?

Instead of the distant call of legal entanglements approaching, a tiny, chirping voice—like the squawk of a vehicular microphone. He couldn't tell what it was saying, but it was repeatedly squeaking out something nearby. Sideshow scanned the area, looking for what it could be, and tried to let his ears home in on the source at the same time. With the excitement of the scene reduced to a burning doc wagon carrier and a handful of dead bodies, the elements of street life were starting to seep back onto the scene, making things that much harder.

Then he heard the chirp just as he caught some flickering HUD lights still blinking inside of the larger half of the DocWagon medic's helmet a few feet away. He scooped up both halves, shook the brain and skull soup out before pressing them together and lifting it carefully to his ear, and listened.

"–you read? Do you copy? Abernathy? This is Hub 3X7. Please respond! What is your sitrep? What is the state of the delivery?"

Using the chinstrap to hold it together, Sideshow plunked the helmet down over his head and tried not to think of how much of the DocTech was now smearing into his hair and running down the back of his neck as the voice inside shouted.

"Findlay! Please respond!"

"Sorry, Hub," Sideshow interjected, immediately impressed by the remarkable amount of information streaming across several image link window access points. Local media feeds, the Hub line, Lone Star report ticker, and even the medical feed from whatever patient was in treatment at the time— which, ironically, was his own flatlined feed from the wagon's burning chair. "He can't come to the mic, sorry to be the bearer of bad news."

"What? Who is this?" The voice still bore some tone of emergency, but there was an edge to it that wasn't there before. *"Where's Findlay? Or Abernathy? How are you on this line?"*

"I'm Thomas Franz." Sideshow knew giving his shadowrunning handle wouldn't be terribly helpful here. "This wagon's last patient, an emergency call. The guys who made me pull my tag; they took out your guys. I iced 'em, but it's pretty bad down here. You should probably send in another—"

"Is the container intact?" The voice on the other end sounded suddenly afraid. *"Can you see it?"*

Sideshow looked toward the blazing vehicle and *tsk'd* his tongue against his teeth.

"The wagon is kind of...*on fire* right now," he answered honestly. "I have no idea. I'm okay, though. Shoulder is bullet-free, but still kind of looks like an overcooked Taco Temple combi-bowl. Still hurts a *lot*, too."

"That containment case is rated to withstand thermite, so it will be fine." He let out a sigh, cleared his throat, and asked, *"Can you see the container?"*

"Yeah, *I'm fine, too.* You know? The client?"

"Yes, yes." Complete dismissal. *"But can you see the contain—"*

Click.

There was a brief moment of comm static, then a new voice filled the receiver.

"Mister Franz?" It was calm, collected, feminine, and one hundred percent *corporate.* Sideshow had dealt with dozens of these types before. *"Please excuse my employee. I'm the...shift supervisor. Call me Lin. From what it says here, I can assume you survived this encounter due to certain...professional abilities?"*

"I did what I had to, yeah."

"Good, good." He could hear her smile across the airwaves. *"What if I told you I could push a few buttons on my end and give you Platinum DocWagon access for life? What would you say to that?"*

"I'd ask who you needed me to slab?" Sideshow knew the start of a negotiation when he heard one.

"No, no. Nothing like that. In fact, quite the opposite. The Shiawase container my colleague was asking about actually contains something that will save a life–possibly dozens more, too. But if the Knight Errant grunts headed your way find it, it will get flagged for evidence, stuck in a lockdown somewhere, and the window for its viability will close. Do you understand what I am saying?"

"There's a box inside that still-burning van you want to hire me, while I'm injured, to deliver." He was already starting to create a risk-reward cost analysis in his head. "Where's it going?"

"Not terribly far. Even by foot. Hang on to Findlay's comms and I'll send the address to his...your...display. Can we count on you, Mr. Franz?"

"Platinum for life, right?"

"My people are already drawing up the contract terms. We just need your verbal agreement. On the record. You know, to keep Legal happy."

"Yeah." Maybe it was the pharma starting to wane, but Sideshow had a nagging tingle in his skin...like he was signing the twenty-first century version of a Devil's deal. "Send the addy. I'll get it done."

Now, he thought as he looked at the still-burning DocWagon vehicle, *HOW do I get it done?*

The phosphorous grenade was all popped out, so the fires weren't exactly at full blaze anymore, but the chemicals in the wagon were keeping it at a healthy, flesh-roasting crackle. The corpo on the mic said Errant was on the way, and if he was going to get this show on the road, so to speak—he had to hurry up and figure out how to get past that fire.

Think, you street rat, he mentally slapped himself as he took in the details of the scene with the new obstacle in mind. *Sitrep, Sideshow. THINK!*

Fire hydrant? He didn't have to put the whole fire out, so cracking open the city suppression lines would be overkill. It would almost certainly bring down a GridSec drone or three, too. *No good.*

Soggy rain tarp? If he wrapped himself all up in it, he could probably move past the blaze pretty easy; maybe even use the helmet lens to see what he was doing. But then he'd have to open it up to grab the container and get cooked anyway. *Not ideal. Next.*

Yank the crates out? He could use the safety line on that Wranglemax over there to hook the containers and pull them out. That way he would just need to smother a few small fires and then get moving. But did he even know exactly what he was looking for, apart from the Shiawase tag? *Come back to that. Anything else?*

Then it hit him.

The BangSmak! Having seen dozens of these things go off in a variety of situations, Sideshow knew exactly what happened when a concussion pak went off in a semi-enclosed area. All the air got blasted out of the area, and pretty much anything that wasn't bolted down was sent bouncing like microwave syntheticorn.

The faint sounds of sirens pushed him from "that might be the best idea" to "here goes!" in a few seconds. He unclipped the small, apple-shaped device from his hip, slid the detonation sequencer to "tri-impact," and gave it a toss.

Tik-klak-WHUMP!

The sonic boom of the BangSmak going off was *exactly* what the doctor ordered. No air equals no fire, and aside from sending smoldering and burned medical supplies and tools flying in all directions like sooty shrapnel, the fiery furnace that was the wagon's work compartment was snuffed out. A haze of black, chemical-heavy smoke rolled out of the vehicle like a stuffed-up chimney, but a few hard knocks on the helmet's activators brought up anti-particulate imaging that let Sideshow see everything in a flickering, digitally enhanced landscape.

"Wow," he said out loud, waving the smoke away from his face as they approached. *Maybe I need to work for the Wagon...I bet this rig is insane when it doesn't have a bullet hole through it.*

Mr. Franz—Knight Errant is less than two minutes away from your location. You need to proceed with haste.

The text message scrolled across the helmet visor's cracked heads-up display.

"Yeah, yeah, Miss Lin," he retorted, knowing the microphone was probably eavesdropping on him anyway, "I hear 'em." Shuffling through the scattered boxes and containers, silently hoping his makeshift sonic extinguisher hadn't damaged the goods, Sideshow finally came upon a slightly rectangular plasticene crate in better shape than the rest. A quick, soot-smudging swipe with the heel of his hand revealed the bright yellow lettering, "SHIA." He didn't need to waste time cleaning off the rest. Between the label and the sheer expense to have a rad-shielded, bulletproof *medical* container like this, it had to be the right one.

"I've got the package, Miss Lin."

Head to the address I am sending now.

"Be careful." Lin apparently didn't want the next part to possibly be found in text-based trash code, so she switched back to audio. *"The ganger miscreants might have been tipped off to the delivery, and if that is the case...there might be more in the neighborhood. Oh, and Mr. Franz?"*

"Movin' as fast as I can, Sally!" He winced as he lifted the box, which wasn't particularly heavy, under his good arm. "But I'm workin' with one wing here!"

"I know you are, Mr. Franz. But that is not what I was going to say."

"All frequencies open and listenin', ma'am." Another grunt.

Do not open the container. If the medical seal is broken, the deal is void and you will be held responsible for the full value of its contents.

"Got it. Can I go now?"

"Can't wait to meet you in person, Mr. Franz. I will have medical standing by."

Seeing his Ruger was rendered down to blackened plastic and carbon-scorched metal in the street, Sideshow unclipped his holster and used the strapping to help fasten the package under his shoulder. It wasn't a great fit, nor would it hold up to a wrestling match, but it would help him get this thing—and him—safely to the rendezvous spot. Which, by looking at the

GridGuide beacon Lin sent him, was three blocks away on top of the old Rent-a-Nap coffin palace. Not the most secure of locations, tactically speaking, but he was sure it would do in a pinch for a quick drop off.

"Whatever you are," he said to the container, "you better be worth it."

Sideshow's short legs carried him away from the chaotic scene just a few minutes ahead of the siren-announced Knight Errant response cars. The meds were all but gone now, and his shoulder throbbed almost more than when he'd gotten shot in the first place. He knew that wasn't really the case, and that the lack of a bullet in the wound and the trauma patch holding in his liquids left him in a better state—but damn, did it hurt.

The jog, which, to be honest was maybe one third jog and two-thirds winded walk, across a few lots and through the alleys, was just like any other nighttime trek through the shadiest parts of Seattle. That was to say, most people ignored the bloody dwarf carrying a flame-scorched medivac container in favor of not getting involved. There was an unwritten, perhaps graffiti'd, rule in the streets: "Don't get someone else's dirt on your hands without good reason." And, it seemed, everyone around here wasn't looking for that reason tonight.

Up until the Rent-a-Nap facility itself.

This place was seven stories straight up; each one jam-packed with closet and coffin pockets where someone could swipe in a few nuyen and take a safe, stand-up sleep. There were two lifts inside to access the individual floors, but they wouldn't run unless you'd already rented a "compartment," which gave you the AR access codes to the building. Pretty standard affair, actually.

But the ring of orange-striped jackets and the blade-n-bat thugs wearing them didn't exactly come with the standard lobby furniture set.

How did they know the drop-off would be here? He weighed the options as he peered in from the side window, and he kept coming back around to that same question.

"I'm here, but there's a line of meatbag low-techs between me and the lifts." The dwarf whispered, even if it really wasn't possible for any of those zoned out chem-heads to hear him through the shatterproof glass. "They were here, waiting for me..."

What's this, now?

One of the thugs lifted his hand to his ear—rookie move for someone not used to V-A commlinks—and began looking around *at the windows.*

Someone's feeding 'em intel!

"*Mr. Franz? Are you still there? Have you been compromised?*" Her voice sounded legitimately concerned, but Sideshow knew there was no way to really know without body language to read, too. "*Pickup is en route to the roof. You have six minutes.*"

He could hear the rotors in the distance, drawing his attention upward to see the growing silhouette of a Hughes VTOL over the skyline. Then he saw the answer along the side of the building itself—a manual fire escape that went all the way up! Sideshow clumsily tapped out his response in the helmet's text-link.

I'll be there.

"He's outside!" One of the thugs yelled from inside, and Sideshow suddenly realized what they were listening in on— the helmet. Somebody *at* DocWagon had sold Findlay and Abernathy out, and he'd gotten caught in the middle of it all. *Lucky me, right?* He ripped the troublesome helmet off and tossed it away to avoid further complications.

Complications like being stuck on the outside on a seven-floor climb while being hunted by half a dozen "violence-first" cretins.

Being a dwarf had its pros, but it had one definite con—a serious lack of height advantage. The bottom rung of the fire escape was a full meter-and-a-half out of his reach, and even with a running start he probably couldn't grab it with half-numbed fingers anyway. If he was going to use this contraption to meet the rapidly approaching payday, he was going to have to use the electronic release lever—which was designed so anyone *could* reach it. He tucked in tight to the wall, careful not to appear in the windows, reached up, and pressed the orange access button.

Grrrrrrrrrr-unk! If they didn't know which side of the building he was on, the sound of a few hundred kilos of hardened alloy ladder sliding to ground level would do the trick.

Gotta go! Gotta go! Gotta go!

Sideshow was in excellent physical shape, but taking every other rung sent lightning bolts of pain shooting out from his shoulder. He tried to push more with his legs, removing as much pressure as he could from the wounded limb, but it was taking its toll.

"There you are, wageslave!" one of the thugs yelled from below, grabbing the ladder in one hand, but pausing to figure out how to climb it with a cricket bat in the other. Thankfully, that intellectual stumper was going to buy Sideshow a good thirty seconds or so.

Drek! The race was on. Fire in his shoulder or not, he was going to make that climb. The VTOL was getting closer, and he was not about to miss that handoff. He could *feel* the gangers' hands and feet clanging on the rungs below him, and their rhythm was increasing.

They're gaining!

He had to do something, and fast.

Sitrep, Sideshow.

He was two floors from the rooftop, armed with nothing but a gutter knife and an annoyingly heavy box he couldn't open, with maybe a minute left before the rendezvous, and five, maybe six angry bruisers on a direct line toward him and getting closer...

Direct. Line. That was it.

Sideshow looped his bad arm and matching leg to the supports of the escape, then let go with the others. The off-balanced weight swung him around to the side of the ladder, and despite his shoulder roaring in pain, he was able to stay in place and look down toward the gangers climbing up—the angry desire to get at him wild in the lead climber's eyes.

"We're a long way up, chummers," Sideshow fought through the pain enough to give them his best *I'm actually in control of this terrible situation, I promise* smile. "Last chance to go back the way you came."

"We're gonna stomp you into guts and mud, lollypop!" The ganger scowled up, suddenly squinting as the VTOL's landing floods washed the building in fluorescence.

"I guess you *can* still go back the way you came..." Sideshow held the knife out and did the geometrics, perfectly backlit and unblinded by the illumination from above. "Just not as slowly as you punks might like."

He let the knife go, dropping it like a coin down a wishing well. The blade struck the topmost ganger between his cheekbone and his chin, sinking to the hilt in his jaw, straight through to the upper neck. There was a strangled half-shout, and his hands scrambled for his face—

—sending him sliding and toppling backward like an eighty-kilo flailing ragdoll—right into the ganger behind him, who was knocked free to crash into the one behind her, and so forth until there was a pile of gangers in need of several bone settings and stanched bleeding sprawled at the base of the building.

"Dunkhie's beard, I'm glad that worked!" He took a deep breath and swung back to climbing the ladder, relieved not to be putting half-a-dwarf's weight on that shoulder anymore. In less than a minute, he was met by two private security agents at the roof, who helped him up and over to a standing position again.

The Hughes was blowing hot exhaust winds across the rooftop, and there were two more armed guards standing next to it. Between them was a finely dressed woman in her thirties, who took off a headset, handed it to someone inside the vehicle, and briskly walked over to Sideshow.

"Mr. Franz, I presume?" she asked, stepping over her recently executed corpo next to the skids of the aircraft, extending a hand tipped with an expensive painted manicure.

"That depends. You Miss Lin?"

"Lin Tsai." She smiled. "You have the package?"

"All yours," Sideshow unclipped the straps and patted the lid of the box. Lin nodded, and the two mercs relieved the dwarf of his baggage and brought it to her. He glanced at the corpse next to the VTOL that everyone was doing a great job of ignoring. "We good?"

"It is terribly hard to get good help with tight lips, it seems. But you don't need to worry about that, Mr. Franz..." She tapped in a fifteen-digit code, popped the two locks on the side, and lifted the lid to reveal a softly glowing ovoid...some kind of crypto's egg, perhaps. "Because, oh yes, we are *very happy*. Your Platinum DocWagon access was activated ten minutes ago. Here's your activator."

She tossed a shiny new wristband his way, which he reflexively caught with his injured arm and winced at the rapid motion.

Lin closed the lid and handed the box back to her guards. "Now let's get that arm looked at, shall we?"

"That sounds just prime, Lin," Sideshow said, joining her in heading toward the VTOL. "Oh, and one more thing..."

"What is it, Mr. Franz?"

"My chums call me Sideshow," he smirked.

"All right, then. What is it...*Sideshow*?"

"Think you could write me a doctor's note before dropping me off at Sybrespace?" He smiled. "I'm gonna be late for my next appointment."

BEER AND WAFFLES

R. L. King

I didn't get to see 'Hawk much these days. This was the first time we'd gotten together for a drink since the whole lockdown situation in Boston, so I didn't even complain about the fancy-ass place he'd picked, even though I'd been the one to suggest the meet. Especially since he had my favorite beer waiting when I got there.

When you've known somebody as long as we have, you don't need any catch-up chit-chat. You just pick up where you left off like no time had passed. I straddled my chair and took a long pull. "So, how's the kid? She get outta the QZ okay?"

"She did. Last I heard, she and Virago were somewhere in Denver."

"Good to hear."

He tilted his head at me, with that appraising look that always made me wonder if he was reading my mind. "You aren't here to ask about my daughter."

I shook my head and hesitated. I was surprised at how hard it was to get the words out, even though it had been over two decades. "I heard Harry died last week."

He cocked an eyebrow. "Indeed? That's unfortunate. But I suppose it happens to all of us one day, doesn't it?"

"Yeah, I guess it does." I looked down into my beer, then back up. "Damn, 'Hawk, we're gettin' old. Remember that first run?"

His drink was a lot more upscale than mine, just like always. He chuckled and sipped it. "Oh, yes. I'm amazed there was ever a second. As I recall, we came very close to killing each other."

Twenty-one Years Ago, Seattle

Not gonna lie, I wasn't feeling good about this job.

I prefer working alone. It's safer that way—fewer people to trust means fewer people who can betray you. Because most of 'em will.

But, to paraphrase some old slot named Maslow, eating takes priority over personal security every time. Besides, this fixer, some guy named Harry, came highly recommended. Supposed to be a master at putting together good teams.

Couldn't hurt to check it out, at least. I could always bail if the gig seemed sour.

The meet was at the Sphere, a mid-level runner bar on the edge of Redmond. I showed up early, but when I slipped a little cred to the bartender to point me to the right back room, he told me Harry was already there.

I checked my pocket to make sure my monowhip was where it belonged, then headed back and pushed open the door without knocking.

The guy behind the table was human, maybe forty-five, a balding white dude with an old-school vibe and a suit that looked like he'd slept in it. As far as I could tell he was alone, but it was never smart to bank on that.

When he spotted me, he waved me toward the table like he didn't care if I came in or not. "Hey, kid. You're early. I like that. Siddown." He looked me over, then consulted something on his commlink screen.

I didn't sit, but instead leaned against the wall. "I don't see any team."

He snorted. "Ya got a mouth on ya, kid. I like that, too. Reminds me of me at your age. And we're waitin' for one other. Just keep yer pants on. He ain't late yet."

"One?" The intel I'd gotten was that Harry was forming a team. Two guys didn't seem much like a team to me.

"Eh, job takes a light touch. Can't be sendin' in a fraggin' urban-brawl squad. Ya worry too much, kid. Yer makin' me nervous. Siddown."

A brisk knock on the door came before I could answer, and then it opened. A guy stopped in the doorway, scanning the room. "Harry, I presume?"

I stared.

This was the guy I was supposed to team up with?

I took him in with an appraising glance: A few years older than me, maybe late twenties, tall and thin, dark hair, fancy suit under an overcoat with a few weird-looking pins on the lapels.

And he had a British accent, like the kind you hear on trid shows about houses so big the servants got a whole floor to themselves.

To put it diplomatically—something I was no good at, by the way—this was *fragged*.

While I was looking him over, he was looking me over. I couldn't tell if he was amused or thought Harry was playing some kind of joke on him.

Harry, seemingly oblivious to any of this, nodded at the table. "Have a seat. Let's get started. I got other places to be tonight."

Neither of us moved.

The fixer sighed. "Come *on*. Ya want a shot at the job or not? 'Cuz I got two other teams on speed-dial if ya don't."

The Brit shrugged. "I'm here, I suppose." He slipped out of his overcoat, tossed it over one of the spare chairs, and took the one across from Harry. With his back to the door.

He was either an idiot, or maybe there was more to him than I thought. I held off making a call for now and straddled another chair.

"There we go," Harry drawled. "Okay, let's get this show on the road. Ocelot, meet Winterhawk. He's a spellslinger, if you didn't figure it out already. 'Hawk, meet Ocelot. He's quick, quiet, and beats things up. Bam. Introductions complete. Now, about the job—"

"Ocelot." Winterhawk's eyebrow arched. "Isn't that one of those little spotted cats? Bit bigger than a large housecat? Not very intimidating, is it?"

I admit it: my temper was a lot shorter in the old days—not that that's saying much. "You wanna come a little closer and find out, drekwipe?" I popped my cyberspur and thrust it up toward him like a big, shiny middle finger.

Harry made a disgusted noise and rubbed the bridge of his nose. "I knew this was gonna happen, but a guy can hope. Will you two chucklefrags just sit your hoops down, shut up, and listen? Unless you're both too good for even hearin' the details about the job."

I grumbled, sheathed the spur, and settled back.

Winterhawk shrugged without looking at me. "Let's hear them, then."

"Okay. That's more like it. The job's an extraction—should be pretty easy. Pay is five K each, with twenty-five percent up front. The Johnson's lookin' for quick and quiet, nobody gets hurt. If you guys can manage not to kill each other before ya get there, your skills should be a good fit for this one. *If* you can work together."

Winterhawk and I looked at each other like a couple of tigers trying to decide if it was worthwhile to throw down. "I can if he can," he said.

A spellslinger. Great. In my experience, they're all a bunch of arrogant assholes—especially the mages. Shamans are okay, but most mages I've met think the sun shines outta their hoops. "Hey, I'm a pro. You don't start anything, I won't either."

"Great. Fantastic." Harry fiddled with his commlink and shoved it across the table at us. It showed a smiling, dark-haired girl about ten or eleven. She had the kind of gleam in her eye that told me she was smart and probably caused trouble whenever she could. "This is your target. Her name's Dani Haramoto."

"You want us to snatch a *kid*?" I asked. "What for?"

"Her mother wants her back." Harry looked like he'd anticipated the question. "Right now she's with her dad, a high-ranking exec at Mitsuhama. Dad divorced Mom a couple years back, and since he had all the money and clout and lawyers, he ended up with the kid. Mom's married some new guy and come into some money of her own in the meantime, and she wants her daughter back. She claims Dad's just keepin' her out of spite, and since she's half *gaijin*, she'll never succeed in the Japanacorp culture."

Winterhawk looked dubious. "Snatching a child from a corporate facility hardly fits my definition of 'easy.'"

"Which is why the job's gotta happen tonight. She and Dad are enjoyin' a little father-daughter time at a small resort along the coast, where the security's lighter. Johnson's provided a map of the resort layout and a way to get in. Mom said she found out Dad will be at a late-night dinner meeting from 2000 to 2200, so the kid will be alone with a sitter. All you gotta do is grab her, keep her safe long enough to drop her off, and you get the rest of your cred. This ain't a tough job. Mostly I just wanna see how you two work together. So, whaddya say?"

My instincts were all telling me to turn it down. Mages were unpredictable, and that was on a good day. If I was gonna die, I wanted it to be my own fault, not because some high-handed rich-kid mage decided to show off.

But people I trust had said Harry was the best at this—and there was that matter of eating. Plus, I hated corpers. Any day I could frag up one's life was a good day. "Yeah. Okay," I grumbled with a glare toward Winterhawk. "But I don't take orders."

"Why does that not surprise me in the slightest?"

Harry sighed. He shoved a couple credsticks across the table. "There's your upfront cut. Now get outta here before you make me regret this."

Outside, Winterhawk took one look at my Harley Scorpion in the parking lot and said, "I'll drive, shall I?"

"Yeah, that's not happenin'. I'll meet you there. I gotta pick up a few things anyway."

He glanced at his watch. Seriously—the guy had a *pocket watch.* "It's already 1930. It will take us most of that to get to the location."

"If you gotta take four wheels, maybe. Or, I dunno, maybe you spellworms can fly or somethin'. I don't give a frag. I'll meet you there."

"Tell me: that cyberspur you flashed inside—have you got another one up your arse, by chance?"

The old me would've shown him exactly where my other spur was. The current me wanted to. But we had a job to do, and the sooner we did it, the sooner I could get the hell away from this drekhead. "Watch yourself, or maybe you'll find one up *your* ass."

He actually smiled. "As amusing as it is to stay here and push your buttons, time's ticking."

The place hardly looked like the kind of vacation spot some upscale slot would spend any time. I mean, it was obviously high-end—no mom-and-pop campgrounds for the cream-of-the-corp crop—but it looked like the kind of place a rich family would take their kids for a weekend of swimming and, I dunno, croquet or something. Yeah, I'm not really up on what rich people do, if you couldn't tell.

Winterhawk, on the other hand, looked like he fit right in, which only made me more annoyed at him. We met up behind the place, where I'd climbed a tree to get a better view. No walls, no sec-bots, no traps as far as I could tell. Just lots of trees and a bunch of standalone houses with fancy little paths and fancy little lights.

"See anything?" he called softly from the foot of the tree.

I admit it—I jumped a little, since he wasn't supposed to be able to see me. I pride myself on my stealth. "You tell me," I snapped. "Haven't you made with the mojo yet?"

"I thought I'd give you a chance first. If you failed—"

I dropped down out of the tree, right in front of him, and glared. "I didn't *fail*. In fact, if you wanna get the hell outta here, I can do this just fine on my own."

"I'm almost tempted to let you try."

I growled. "Why the hell're you even *doin'* this, anyway? Wouldn't think a guy like you'd even want to get his fancy shoes dirty? How come you're not off gettin' your ass kissed by some corp?"

He nodded toward the houses. He didn't look as pissed as I felt, but it came through in his eyes. "Do you think we could get this over with? I'd really rather our time together be as short as possible, and I wasn't aware sharing life stories was part of the job."

"Fine with me. Just don't screw up and we'll be good."

He didn't answer, just headed toward the back side of the closest house.

I half-expected the keycard the kid's mom had given us wouldn't work on the sliding glass door in the back, but to my surprise, it did. With a soft *click*, it slid open on what looked like the sitting room of a swanky suite. Just this room was bigger than my squat. Must be nice. There weren't any lights on, but my low-light cybereyes picked out the usual: sofas, chairs, table by the window.

I glared at Winterhawk, then slipped inside. With any luck, the kid would be asleep and we could just knock her out and book it before anybody else showed up. Harry had said the run would be easy, but this seemed almost *too* easy.

Weird that the babysitter was asleep this early too, though...

The door had barely clicked shut behind us when a low growl sounded from somewhere off to the left.

Winterhawk barely had time to hiss, *"Look out!"* before something huge, black, and fast leaped from behind one of the sofas and straight toward me.

Now, here's the thing: I'm fast. *Really* fast. Like, "paid a lot of cred I couldn't afford to get this fast" fast.

This thing was faster. One second I was standing there, and the next I was on my back with glowing red eyes in my face and smelly ropes of hot spit dripping down from around the biggest set of teeth I'd ever had that close to me. *Hellhound? No fraggin' way! They don't get that big!*

I was struggling hard to get my arm in position to pop my spur in its throat, but the thing was crazy strong and those huge teeth were on a collision course with my neck. *Who keeps an overgrown hellhound in a living room?*

And then, an instant before the teeth sank in and shredded my jugular, a bright light flared around us. The dog, or whatever it was, lifted off me and flew across the room, slamming into a wall hard enough to rattle the whole place.

The good news was, that gave me a chance to get up. I kipped up to my feet, catching sight of a grim-faced Winterhawk with magic still sparking around his hands and beads of sweat on his forehead, and went immediately for the monowhip in my pocket.

The bad news was, hitting the wall hadn't even shaken the monster.

I got a better look at it as it righted itself and growled at us again. It *was* a hellhound—I'd seen enough of them to know what one looked like, and the red eyes, scruffy black fur, pointed ears, and pissed-off expression could have been taken straight from a guidebook called *Security Animals You Do Not Want To Frag With*.

But that was where the resemblance ended. This thing was fraggin' *huge*—as big as a small bear. Parts if it were covered with what looked like grafted-on armored plates, and little flashes of green light chased each other around its body.

In other words, not your standard-issue hellhound.

I was starting to get a very bad feeling about this.

It leaped again, this time toward Winterhawk. And he didn't move *nearly* as fast as I did.

For a split-second, the thought crossed my mind to just let it get him. I could grab the kid while it was occupied and finish the job on my own. One less conceited mage in the world was a good thing, right?

But as obnoxious as he was, he *had* saved my life. He could have come to the same conclusion I had and let it rip my throat out, but he hadn't.

Damn, when had I grown a fraggin' conscience?

With a roar, I moved at full augmented speed, popping my spur and putting every shred of my vat-grown muscle into raking it across the monster's side.

Its armor-plated hide resisted, but not enough. It made a loud, baying scream as the blade pierced it and cut a long furrow. Blood flew everywhere. Instead of taking a chunk out of 'Hawk, it flopped to the floor on its good side, writhing.

I tightened my grip on my monowhip handle, drew it back to take the shot—

"Stop! Please! Don't kill Waffles!"

I yanked the whip back, and only my jacked reflexes saved the still-growling monstrosity from a quick decapitation.

Next to me Winterhawk had his hands up, mojo still flickering around them. *"Waffles?"*

The lights came on to reveal the same small, dark-haired girl in the picture Harry had showed us. She stood in the rear doorway in a Maria Mercurial T-shirt and floppy athletic shorts, her tousled hair showing we'd probably woken her from a deep sleep, but the freaked-out look on her face as her eyes shifted from me to 'Hawk to the fallen super-hellhound was terrified and pleading.

And more than a little bit pissed.

Ignoring the two dangerous shadowrunners standing right in front of her, she dashed over to the hound, dropped to her knees, and tried to gather it into her arms. That wasn't so easy, since it was big enough she could ride it like a pony. "You hurt him!" Then her eyes turned hard. "Mom sent you guys, didn't she?"

Winterhawk and I exchanged glances. "C'mon," I told him. "We gotta go. Grab the kid and let's get outta here."

But he wasn't moving. "You expected this," he said to the girl.

She snorted. "Duh. I knew as soon as she got a little money she'd try to drag me back. I figured she'd send a whole team, though. Not just two guys."

"'Hawk...'"

Tears glittered in Dani Haramoto's eyes as she once again returned her attention to the massive hellhound. She savagely brushed them away and glared up at Winterhawk. "You have magic. I saw the stuff around your hands. You gotta fix him."

His eyes widened. "Wait a minute. This thing is the... babysitter?"

"I don't need a *babysitter*." Her tone blazed with indignant protest. "Waffles is my *friend*."

I shot a fast look at the door. We were pushing our luck hard. "Fraggit, we gotta *go*. You wanna get caught?"

He seemed torn, and hesitated.

"This is *your* fault," Dani insisted, burying her face in Waffles' neck fur. "Don't you *get* it? I'm not going *anywhere* with you."

"You don't have a choice," I said. Yeah, she was a kid—but she was also a future corper. And we weren't gonna get paid if we came back without her.

Her expression turned a lot harder and sharper than I'd expect from some coddled princess. "You think so? You'll never get out of here with me. Mom's never gonna pay if you kill me, and if you knock me out, it'll set off an alarm."

I looked at Winterhawk. "Come *on*, man. Maybe you corp types stick together, but I'm not lettin' a payoff get away because you're dumb enough to fall for some kid's lies." I took a step toward them.

He held up his hand. "She's not lying. You'd see that if you'd get past your own prejudices for a moment and *look*."

I started to protest, but—then I looked. And damned if he wasn't right. Maybe I don't have the fancy mojo, but punk kids like I used to be don't last long in gangs without picking up how to see which way the wind's blowing.

I didn't want him to be right. I sure as hell didn't want to miss out on that payoff.

I looked around, half-convinced a whole squad of Mitsuhama thugs would come busting through the door any second. So far, though, it was just us, the kid, and the bleeding hellhound-thing on the floor.

Dani seemed more worried about the monster than scared of us. Its side was bleeding hard—I must have got my spur in deeper than I thought. A spreading puddle of blood was growing around it. And damned if the thing didn't *whimper.*

"Please..." she said, sounding a lot less like a smartass kid and a lot more like a scared one. "You can't let Waffles die. He's my friend. I—I'll go with you if you fix him so he won't die. I promise."

Winterhawk looked conflicted again, but then he shot me a glance that dared me to protest and dropped to his knees—still a little cautiously—next to the hellhound.

Waffles made a half-hearted growl at him, but settled when Dani stroked his head.

"I've never healed a hellhound before."

"Just make it quick. Can't be that much harder than a person, right?" I kept my head on a swivel, watching the front door, the back door, and the rear part of the house.

"We'll find out, won't we?" He bent over the beast and his hands started glowing again.

Dani, a little less frazzled now that it looked like her pet monster wasn't going to die tonight, looked at me. "What did Mom tell you, anyway?"

I didn't really want to have a deep conversation with a kid, but I didn't have much else to do while 'Hawk worked. Wasn't like I could help him. "She didn't tell us anything. But the job's to take you back to her."

"But I don't *want* to go back to her. Why would she think I would? She doesn't even want me around." She continued stroking Waffles, who seemed to be settling down.

"She must want you around. Why else would she pay us to bring you back?"

"Because she's horrible. All she cares about is showing off and clothes and going to parties. She just wants to show me off to her dumb friends and ignore me when I get in the way. She's just pissed 'cause Dad actually cares about me, and she hates him. She doesn't care how *I* feel, as long as it makes Dad mad." She pointed at Winterhawk. "How come you two guys don't like each other?"

"Huh?"

She snorted. "You act just like Mom and Dad used to before they got divorced."

"Yeah, well, he's an asshole," I grumbled.

"And he's an uncivilized wanker." Winterhawk, looking paler than before, rose shakily to his knees. "I think your monstrosity here will be all right, but you'd best get him some proper attention. You didn't tell me he was half machine."

I grabbed his arm and hauled him to his feet. "Okay. Enough playin' Doggie Doctor. We're done."

Dani swallowed hard, glancing from the hellhound, who was already starting to rise, to us. "Okay. I promised I'd go with you if you took care of Waffles. Can I just leave a note for Dad first, though? I won't say anything about you, but he's gonna be really worried about me, especially when he sees all the blood."

I looked at 'Hawk.

He looked at me.

Neither of us looked happy, because we both knew what we were gonna say next.

He said it before I could. "Perhaps...you and Waffles ought to go back to bed. Your father will be back soon if our information is correct, and best if we're not here when he arrives."

Dani's eyes got big. "Seriously?" she breathed, like she couldn't dare to hope.

"Better get outta here fast," I grumbled. In my mind's eye, I watched a little winged credstick flying away into the night. "Before Mr. High-and-Mighty here changes his mind."

Her face lit up in a big grin. "Yeah. Before he does." She flung her arm around Waffles' thick, furry neck, and together they trudged out of the room, back toward the hallway.

Winterhawk looked at the spreading bloodstain on the carpet and checked his stupid pocket watch. "Her father is due back any moment. Shall we?"

"Yeah." I just couldn't *wait* to tell Harry we'd fragged up our first job.

I didn't see Winterhawk again until a couple days later. We didn't bother going back to Harry, since it wasn't like he had anything to give us. Nothing we'd want, anyway. And it wasn't like 'Hawk and I were gonna meet up for post-run beers or anything.

So when Harry called us a couple days later and told us to meet him back at the Sphere, I almost didn't go. Yeah, we fragged up. Didn't mean I wanted to get chewed out for it. Too bad—Harry's rep meant losing him as a fixer was the cherry on top of the big old drek sundae.

To my surprise, Harry didn't look pissed. He met us in the same room as before, with a beer in front of him. The only way I could tell he wasn't wearing the same suit as before was that this one was a different color.

Winterhawk didn't sit, and neither did I. "Go on, then," he told Harry, like he was bracing himself. "Get it over with."

"Get what over with?" Harry waved us to the table. "Take a load off, both of you. Have a beer."

"We fragged up," I said. "We were supposed to grab the kid, and maybe you noticed we didn't do that."

"Yeah, yeah." He didn't seem at all bothered about it. In fact, he pulled a pair of credsticks from his pocket and rolled them our way. "There ya go."

We exchanged confused glances, and didn't touch them. "What the hell?" I demanded. "Harry, we screwed up. We *failed* the job. You sayin' Mom's payin' us anyway?"

"Hell, no." He snorted. "Dad is."

"Excuse me?" Winterhawk looked as boggled as I did, which was comforting.

"Apparently, you made a friend of that kid. Not the way I woulda done it, but it worked out okay. Dad's pretty happy you not only didn't grab his daughter, but actually patched up their prototype, wired-up hellhound bodyguard so it didn't die. Mostly the kid, though. That kid and her dad are crazy about each other, and apparently Mom's quite a piece o' work." He nodded toward the credsticks. "Take 'em. You earned 'em. More'n you woulda got from Mom, too, so don't complain."

Still moving a little bit like I was in a daze, I grabbed one of the sticks and checked the number. He wasn't kidding—it wasn't quite twice what Mom had promised, but close.

Sometimes life throws one your way, I guess.

I stuffed the stick in my pocket, nodded to Harry, and turned to leave.

"Hey," he said.

"What?"

Harry looked almost innocent. "Might have another job in a couple weeks. I'm guessin' you two've had about enough of each other, though, huh?"

I almost told him to frag off, but instead shot a fast glance at Winterhawk, waiting for the smart-ass remark.

Instead, he shrugged. "Anything's possible. It will depend on the job, of course, but I suppose I could put up with him again for one night, if necessary."

Harry's innocent look had turned to a drek-eating grin. "How 'bout you, kid?"

I could almost read the *told ya so* on his face. I wanted to wipe it off. I really did.

Instead, I grunted. "Yeah. Whatever."

We haven't killed each other yet, so I guess that's gotta be worth something.

LICENSED TO DIE

Bryan Young

The hot summer nights in Seattle meant rolling blackouts and brownouts. Leave it to the megacorps to mismanage something as simple—comparatively speaking—as the power grid. Shimura sat in front of the inert electric fan, sweating, waiting for it to turn back on. He fanned himself with some old snail mail. Probably a bill. Unpaid.

Shimura, easily the biggest troll on the block—maybe the city—wondered if there would be any patients that night. Mercy Street, the clinic he ran for peanuts, booze, or whatever nuyen the locals and runners-on-the-run could scrounge in their couches or find in their pockets, advertised only by its neon sign outside: a bright green cross. But with the power outages, even with the solar panels hooked into the grid, the normally bright, flashing sign, an oasis in the rough parts of Seattle's worst part of town, did not flash in the darkness. It would beckon no travelers and attract no patients. Shimura was hot and tired, though, so maybe that was a good thing. The last thing anyone wanted to deal with was an irritable troll, even if he did have a "gruff but kind" reputation.

So here he sat, sweating in the blistering heat, wishing he had made different choices and wondering about making himself a cold glass of booze on the rocks, wondering where in the world he would get the ice.

When a knock came at the front door, his first inclination was annoyance, but he suppressed that reaction with a deep breath. He set down his makeshift fan and closed his eyes to center himself. The knock became a pound and the calm verged on annoyance again, but he locked that dragon back up inside and went to open the door. With the power out, the surveillance cameras hooked into his AR weren't working, so he'd have to find out who came for him the old-fashioned way.

Fortunately, he had done a good enough job scrubbing his past life from the world that he had almost no expectation that it would be bad news for him, but surprises were always possible, given the nature of that very same world.

Shimura forced open the sliding front door of the Mercy Street clinic—the door was normally automated—and found a person on the other side. Human, by the looks of it, clutching their right arm, full of cybernetics and greeblies. The faint, generated LED light from inside the clinic washed over the kid like a white sunrise.

"Yes?" Shimura asked. "Can I help you?"

It was an open-ended question, allowing for responses other than medical, but Shimura thought there were a lot more situations he could actually help with than just that. He had lived a *varied* life.

"I hope so," the human said. They were dressed shabbily, even for a runner. The color of their faux-leather vest peeled back at the edges, the spikes on the shoulder pauldron were dull, and the shirt beneath had worn thin in splotchy patches across the front. By all appearances, it looked like they spent all their cash on upgrades as opposed to wardrobe.

"I'd offer you to come in from the heat, but it's not much cooler inside. But let's go in and talk."

They followed the troll into the first room in the tiny clinic. Austere was the order of its fashion, stripped down like an old deck without any of the bells and whistles. There was a cold steel floor, a bed, a stool, and a sink atop a cabinet packed full of medical equipment and disposables. "Go ahead and sit on the bed."

The runner did as they were told with an urgency Shimura was indifferent to. The troll sat on the stool next to the bed, his height was still such that he was as tall as the human who had come in for help. "What seems to be the problem?"

"I need your help, Doc. It's my arm."

It was the cyberarm. Their right one. The left was fleshy and brown like it was supposed to be. The right arm wasn't like any cyberarm Shimura had ever seen before.

"What's wrong with it?"

"You've gotta hurry, I only got a couple of hours left."

"A couple of hours left for what?" Shimura furrowed his massive, bony brow.

"I don't even know. They were vague about that. I just know I couldn't pay and it's gonna be bad."

"Why don't we get through the standard questions first, and you can fill me in on the ticking time arm situation."

Shimura got their name. Turns out the human was a guy, used the ol' he-him. Enrique was his name. He was a runner, and the arm was from a new outfit called Apollo. A rental. Or maybe a lease or something. Enrique kept the details vague, maybe out of shame or embarrassment, but maybe because no one ever understood the fine print on the terms.

"So, you got some new, untested tech and it's crapping out on you?"

"Not till midnight."

"So, there's nothing wrong?"

"Not until midnight."

"Chummer, I don't know what the hell you're saying, but it sounds more like you want a contract lawyer, not a doctor."

"No, you don't understand."

"I'm an old troll and not too bright. Make it make sense. Make it slow and simple. Use small words. If it helps, you can raise your voice and speak slowly at me if it makes you feel better."

"Okay, so, this new outfit, they license hardware—"

"Apollo?"

"Yeah, Apollo. So, they finance and license hardware for folks who might not have the capital to afford it on their own."

"License, like you rent-to-own?"

"No. They still own the rig, I just license the use of it through a payment plan."

"And when the payment plan is over, you don't get to keep the arm?"

"No. By that time, I'm due for an upgrade, and they'll replace hardware with another one with some newer features."

"So the point is you're in hock to them for the rest of your life as long as you want that arm?"

"Essentially."

"So what's happening at midnight?"

"I'm behind on payments."

"And they're going to shut your arm off on you?"

"Or worse."

Shimura sighed.

Always some new outfit looking to prey on folks wanting to make a living. And folks too poor to even step into the life of a runner without an outsized investment. Hardware wasn't cheap, especially gear like this poor kid's arm. "And you think me, being a street doc, will be able to do something about it?"

"Everyone around said if anyone could do anything about it, it would be you."

"That's what they said, is it?"

The kid nodded furiously.

"And I can assume that since you couldn't pay Apollo, you can't afford to pay me either."

"I've had a rough go this year."

"Haven't we all, chummer, haven't we all?"

Shimura knew he wasn't going to turn the poor kid away. He was probably 21 or 22 at the most, just at the start of his career. There was evidence the arm was a graft to a stump, so maybe he had a congenital defect or accident that had robbed him of a healthy arm in the first place from a young age. No doubt, the fancy promises of a company like Apollo and a tricked-out cyberarm probably made Enrique think his dreams would come true.

Clearly, they hadn't.

Here he was, two hours to midnight, trying to make sure he'd still have a working arm by morning.

A rough go, indeed.

"I'll do right by you. I'll pay you back somehow, I'll find a way."

The troll groaned, deep and throaty. "Well, I may as well take a look."

He figured there would be no sense in talking to the kid about payment until he got an assessment on what was wrong. For all Shimura cared, he could get paid in other goods or services. He wasn't picky, nor was he a vulture. There was something tacky about profiting off the desperation of a person in crisis. But megacorps thrived on that kind of unethical nonsense. It was baked right into their charters. They were legally obligated to be unethical to make a buck. It said so right in their bylaws. That's what a corporation was.

Using the AR display in his eyes, Shimura ran an initial diagnostic of the arm. It was an elegant piece of hardware, shinier than the standard models from places like Silver Tech or Evo. The more Shimura dug, though, the more complicated its security was.

The chronometer on his AR read straight 2s. He had just under an hour and a half to make this right, but he still wasn't even sure what he was doing, or what would happen if he failed.

"The clock strikes midnight, poof, you turn into a pumpkin or something?" the troll asked Enrique.

"It just stops working."

It didn't seem fair, but who said anything was fair when you dealt with a place that cared more about profit than people?

"It's looking really complicated, chummer. Like this has got a security system a lot more detailed than I would have expected on what should be a pretty non-complicated bit of cyberware."

"That's why I came to you."

Shimura groaned. again

He was going to have to deck into the arm and crack through its security protocols.

The clock struck 22:30 by the time he was ready to deck in. It wasn't a common thing to deck into a specific piece of cyberware, rather than a whole Matrix, but street docs knew you could deck into anything, and at least get some rudimentary work out of it. Shimura dove right in and got to work to move right past the first firewall.

Why the hell did a cyberarm have a firewall?

Something wasn't right.

Shimura dug a little deeper into the programming and found something he didn't think should be there. A warning sign and a hallmark from a place a whole lot bigger than a new corp.

Pulling himself out of the Matrix, he looked around with his corporeal eyes. "Kid, you've got bigger problems. This new outfit isn't Apollo. This outfit is a front for Aztechnology."

Shimura let that word hang there in the air.

That was bad news.

And they both knew it was bad news and they could feel it as sure as the heat of the sun on the other side of the world.

"You knew it was Aztech when you got it?"

"No. Of course not. I know better than to take a deal like that from Aztech."

Shimura muttered a curse beneath his breath. It certainly changed the calculus of what he was doing. Or about to do. Or maybe what he wouldn't do at all. "Their security isn't going to mess around. This could be dangerous for me. Maybe for both of us."

"I knew it wouldn't be a walk in the park," Enrique pleaded.

That's probably why he'd come deeper into the slums, deeper into the bowels of Seattle. To Mercy Street.

Shimura sighed again, looking the kid up and down. He certainly didn't look old enough to be making these kinds of decisions. Really just a kid, though to Shimura everyone seemed to be a kid. He already had some struggles to overcome, with only one arm. If he didn't have any money, if his family was as poor as his clothes made him look, an arm like this was the only way up. Can't be a runner without the tech. That's for sure.

Shimura usually tried to avoid looking into the eyes of those who begged him for help, but he couldn't help but look into young Enrique's. There he found a galaxy of complications and pain. The starry reflections of the lights glistened with the build-up of moisture in the kid's eyes. He was scared. Of course he was. Who wouldn't be?

There was no telling what would happen to the arm if Aztechnology didn't get their money.

The old troll street doc sat there, staring this kid right in the face, doing the risk analysis on whether or not it was worth helping him. There was no point in delving into a cost-benefit analysis, because all the cost would be his, and all the benefit would be Enrique's. No, even if he won, the only winner would be Enrique. But this was his job. His mission. His curse.

Shimura sighed again. "Let me see what I can do."

"Thanks, Doc. I mean it. I'll make it up to you. I promise. Just help me keep my arm."

"I'll do my best."

Shimura unspooled a data cable and plugged it into the cyberjack that connected to the deck in his head; then he ran another from the deck directly to a dataport on the cyberarm, disdaining the wireless connection. He would need a lot more control over everything.

22:50, and the clock kept ticking down, millisecond by millisecond. Not much time left.

"Shoulda paid your bill, kid. Woulda been a lot easier on us both."

"I tried, I really did."

But whatever else the kid had to say, Shimura didn't hear it. He was back in the firewall, in a much higher rez this time. In this case, it was a literal flaming wall. Signage at the front of the wall offered the usual warnings about breaching the programming, nullifying the warranty, and evading the terms of service. Had it just been the new Apollo outfit, Shimura likely would have simply tried to brute force his way in, but knowing Aztechnology was the corp behind it, it seemed like the stealth route would be the more sensible and safe option. But time wasn't on his side, the clock read 22:53 and counting. Did he risk it and save the time? Or go the careful route.

"Frag."

He knew which choice he should make.

Back in the old days, when he ran with a different name and lived a different life, he was the stealthy sort of decker, full of sleaze in the Matrix and ready to break into anything. But he was also capable of the brute force needed to crack through most firewalls on a whim.

With just over an hour left, he figured he had plenty of time to take the sneaky route and began probing defenses. By the time he finished the scanning probe, the chimes struck 23:00 and he had exactly sixty minutes before the license expired.

He threw open a door he could use. The representation of the opened door appeared down on the far end of the firewall, the flames doused by his probe and intrusion measures.

"Here goes nothing." He set out, passing through the opening to the other side.

Shimura really didn't like using his deck. He'd tried to leave that life behind him, but sometimes medical emergencies like this came along, and it was unavoidable. He wondered if this even *was* a medical emergency. Since hardware had become so much more integrated into the technology sector, would an average, run-of-the-mill, corporate hospital even look at a cyberarm? Or would they go to a repair shop mechanic or a cyber doc? Shimura didn't know. But he did know none of them would have been able to treat this particular ailment. They were all too much on the straight and narrow, and were all about preserving the rights of the state or the megacorps or copyright holders or whatever the hell more than they were about helping people.

"You're just outta luck," was about the only response he could have expected in one of those places. Or a terse, "Maybe you should pay your bill with the nuyen you don't have."

Those bastards on the straight and narrow never did the math in the gray areas.

This was why places like Seattle needed places like Mercy Street and folks like Shimura; for those falling through the cracks.

On the other side of the firewall, Shimura found a black space hewn roughly in the shape of a square. It felt more like the idea of a room than a room itself. He straightened and stood, looking around for any of the icons or countermeasures he would need to deal with or counteract.

As he stepped closer to the wall, he saw a box. A maintenance box or an electrical panel sort of thing. It was only a slightly lighter shade of black than the rest of the room.

That would be where he had to go.

Time dwindled as he headed to the box and opened it. Inside was an assortment of timers, fuses, wires, and smaller boxes. Real old-school-looking stuff. Like he was defusing a bomb in a bad trideo drama.

"Red wire, blue wire, let's not start a fire or blow ourselves up. Jeez," Shimura said to himself, wondering how he was going to make it through.

He ran another probing diagnostic, hoping to glean what sort of countermeasure he could deploy against the security panel. Ten minutes of probing didn't bring him any closer to an answer, and the clock had clicked well past 23:10. Less than an hour left, and he didn't feel any closer to solving this kid's problem than when he started. He made it through the firewall. Great. What good would that do him if he couldn't defuse the bomb?

Shimura just started cutting wires.

What was the worst that could happen?

Despite the seemingly random nature of Shimura pulling cords and cutting, there was a distinct method to his madness. But it didn't seem to be doing anything. At all. Good or bad.

That's when he realized the whole thing was a ruse. They hung a lantern on a spot on the wall, expecting him to spend his time dealing with that, but it was just a dummy box.

Shimura cursed.

He should have known better.

It was nothing more than a timesuck.

He ran a program to turn on the lights and found the room was filled with much more than he'd realized. He cursed himself again. "You old fool."

It had been a very long time since he'd been this deep into a program. He was no longer a runner, he was a doctor. Why would he need to deal with drek like this?

Shimura groaned again.

Another door.

Another portal to danger.

Walking over to the door, he found a sign attached to it. More corporate speak and terms of service, warning him that any further incursion into the programming of the cyberware would void the warranty completely and come with lethal consequences.

"Really? Lethal consequences?"

Shimura pushed through the door to find red lights of alarm spinning and a siren blaring. The room on the other side was more of a corridor and looked something found in a dingy, retro spaceship. Metal floors and dirty railings framed around hallways shaped like coffins. The lights were dim, and there was something inside.

Shimura heard it, felt it.

Growling in the dark.

"Damn it."

With less than thirty minutes left on the clock, Shimura stepped inside. His boots clicked heavily on the metal, but he could only barely sense that over the shrieking alarm that sounded as though an airlock was about to open. He ran through his mind what programs he might be able to run to get through the gauntlet, taking slow steps down the hallway, making sure he wasn't ambushed at any T-junction. The stealth route hadn't worked. How could it? He had walked right through their legalese and terms of service. It was going to have to be brute force from here on out.

Shimura was tired.

This wasn't how he'd wanted to spend such a hot summer night. But this was his lot now. This is what he did. And if he could help this guy keep his arm, then he would feel it would have all been worth it.

The hallways seemed to get narrower and the bleating alarm grew more faint the further he got from the dummy room.

But the feeling of breath on his neck and someone—or something—watching him didn't subside. It started at the base of his neck, a tingle of danger. It shivered down the rest of his back. Then it stayed there, invading his thoughts to the point Shimura wondered if a program he hadn't noticed had been run against him, some sort of dread and paranoia cocktail, writ large in the code of the Matrix, hiding deep in the terms of service.

He cast that thought away.

He was simply old.

And rusty.

He needed to get a grip.

He would reward himself with a drink when all of this was finished. That much he promised himself. And while he was thinking about that perfect amber liquid, the light on the ice and the taste of the synthahol, was when disaster struck.

The monster was some fantastical alien kind of creature or another. It didn't matter what it was—it tore into Shimura's shoulder with its teeth and gripped the troll at his sides with massive claws.

Since it was behind him, Shimura couldn't see anything but glimpses—enough to see the creature was a matte black and gray, mottled with rust and dripping with ichor. It could easily blend in with the surroundings.

Pain pierced his shoulder where the teeth bit into him, but Shimura didn't scream.

Nor did he panic, much as he wanted to.

He kept calm and thought about the situation, and started running the brute force routines that used to come like second nature to him. The one he liked the most was lost. And he didn't have his sword, either. But he could come up with something.

The way it played out, he reached back and grasped the monster by the head, then tilted his body forward, pitching the beast over the top of him to the floor. The IC monster slammed on its back with a snarl, but struggled to twist back upright before it slid into the wall of the corridor.

Shimura gripped the wound on his shoulder, feeling the biofeedback deep inside of him. "You'll pay for that," he told the creature as though it were real and could understand him. Maybe it could. Maybe Aztechnology was listening. Maybe they were watching the whole damn thing.

It was likely. The right to privacy hadn't been a thing since the twentieth century, and even then it had been on shaky ground.

Maybe the twenty-second would right those wrongs, but he doubted it.

The creature shook its head and growled, getting its bearings back after Shimura's brutal attack. But it looked no worse for wear. It was going to take a lot more than that to take it down.

"Frag."

The alien creature lowered its center of gravity at the front, ready to pounce, and then hissed viciously. Not wanting to lose the upper hand—or either of his hands—Shimura stepped in and punted the damn thing. The toes of his combat-program augmented boots were aimed right at the monster's drooling head, but it had begun to charge already. Shimura's foot caught it in the soft underside, knocking it off course. It wasn't soft, something cracked and green-black blood spurted to the floor and spattered across the wall, flung by the creature's momentum and trajectory.

Shimura didn't wait for it to get its footing back again. He leaped forward and crouched when he got there, wrapping his thick troll fingers around the creature's windpipe—or what he assumed was the windpipe—and squeezed.

That did little to take the fight out of the beast, but at least Shimura had it pinned. It snapped and growled, doing its best to chomp a piece of Shimura's flesh. It scratched at his arms and legs, trying to escape his death grip. Blood dripped from the stinging wounds it left, but Shimura segmented his mind, putting the pain out of it entirely, trapping it in a box that bore no relation to him. He had a job to do and the pain could wait for later.

"Stay down," he told the beast. "Just stay down."

But the beast bucked and struggled, trying to get out of Shimura's grip. Fortunately, it was to no avail. The life slowly went out of it and then Shimura wrenched the neck, snapping it with a satisfying *crack*.

Breathing heavily from the effort, he collapsed to the floor with his back against the sloping corridor wall. He wiped away the sweat dripping into his eyes he knew would be there, both in the Matrix and in reality. Either way, everything was too damn hot.

Glancing up to the clock in his field of vision, he was pleased to see he still had a good twenty minutes left. 23:40. Despite the faint beeping he heard, he thought he'd defeated enough of the IC present to go about his work.

Standing despite the creak in his knees, Shimura ambled forward to the end of the corridor. Another cross junction and down another corridor later, he paused, listening for any more of those creatures.

Nothing.

He walked on until he found a control room with the master interface for Enrique's cyberarm. All he had to do was shut off the signal to let it talk to the transmitters that sent and received data and upgrades from the Aztechnology front, Apollo.

"There we go," he said, dusting his hands off together for effect.

23:55. He smiled. "And with five minutes to spare."

There were no more deadly routines, no more IC, nothing that could hurt him. All in all, a pretty easy procedure. Some deckers might have been killed by the alien thing, but even out of practice, he wasn't just any old decker. Not that anyone knew that. Besides, any chance he could get to stick it to one of the megacorps, he would take.

As he jacked out of the system, he barely noticed the faint beeping get louder.

When he opened his eyes, back in the mundane world, he was back in the office at Mercy Street.

Enrique sat on the table, his arm splayed out as though everything were normal. The look on his face didn't quite match, though.

"What?" Shimura asked. "I think that did it." That's when he noticed the incessant beeping hadn't subsided.

"There's something wrong with this, still."

"Do you have all the feeling and functionality?"

"Yes, but what's that sound?"

"It doesn't always beep like that?"

"No!" Enrique slid backward on the table, as though trying to get away from his own arm. "It doesn't ever do that."

"Frag." Shimura didn't think it was possible for a company to get any lower, but somehow they had. They had made their new lease-to-death technology tamper-proof.

Shimura scanned everything one more time with his AR display and blinked. "That's a bomb."

Aztechnology, Apollo—whatever the hell they were calling themselves—were going to blow Shimura and Enrique both to Kingdom Come for breaking the warranty and the terms of service. They weren't even going to send some runners to do it. They were just going to flip a switch and be done with it.

Bastards. Didn't ownership mean anything anymore?

"Can't you stop it?" Enrique squealed.

Honestly, Shimura didn't know, but he didn't say that. He didn't say anything. He simply gripped the cyberarm and pulled it closer to him and inspected all of the seams and wires, like a jeweler seeking a flaw in a priceless gem. In this case, the gem was his own life as well as poor Enrique's.

Thanks to a quick subroutine, he was able to triangulate the source of the beeping, though he couldn't be sure the source of the sound was also the source of the bomb, but it seemed as good a plan as any.

23:56.

Four minutes left.

Shimura tore open the panel and the beeping grew in volume.

There, beneath the panel, were wires leading to a microprocessor assembly. But something about it didn't look right, and the relays and connecting wires weren't normal.

"There it is."

"What is *it*?"

"Detonator cap."

23:57.

Three minutes.

Shimura hesitated. He didn't want to just start pulling wires or the cap itself, because it was likely rigged with a dead-end switch, something that would hasten the explosion and kill them both in a blink.

At least it would be a quick death.

Sweat poured from his brow, fogging his vision. He blinked the salty moisture away. It was so hot, any decision seemed impossible.

23:58.

Two minutes.

Shimura blinked again.

The beeping grew more intense, as if it was an alarm for anyone who wasn't involved in circumventing the technology, warning them to get clear before It cost them their lives, too.

"Doc?"

"Quiet, kid, I gotta think."

"Do something!"

Shimura closed his eyes. Inhaled a deep, centering breath, and when he opened his eyes again, he was ready.

23:59.

One minute to midnight.

His fingers worked like lightning, disassembling the detonator cap. First, he pried the housing off to reveal the explosive contents within, then he saw the inner workings and which wires were hooked up to which piece of the puzzle. Since he'd shunted the connection to the Matrix from the cyberarm, he assumed he didn't need to worry about a remote detonation. But then he found an independent connection, ready to report back and take directions.

Shimura held his breath and snipped that connection.

Then he cut another wire, then one more.

The beeping continued.

He reached in and cut one more.

00:00.

Midnight.

Shimura closed his eyes.

The beeping ceased.

The alarm bell was gone.

They were alive.

No explosion tore through them or emanated from the detonator cap, merely an impotent puff of black smoke at the stroke of midnight.

Shimura looked at Enrique, terror still written on the poor kid's face. "It's okay. Can you move your arm?"

Enrique looked down at the cyberarm on the table and thought about it for a second. His fingers wiggled and then he contracted his silver hand into a fist.

"I think so," he said, "I'll know better after I test it, but I can use it for now."

"Well, that's better than what you were expecting at the end of the night before you came to me, isn't it?"

Enrique nodded his head enthusiastically. "Yeah. Definitely." But then a sheepish look overcame the kid. His shoulders hunched and his chest caved in as though he was a star trying valiantly to explode in on itself and disappear into oblivion.

"Don't worry about it," Shimura said, knowing what the kid was thinking and that he couldn't afford it anyway. "Just go do some good for a change."

The kid didn't stop shrinking, probably trying to smother the pride burning in his center somewhere. "Are you sure?"

"Yeah. Can't get a signal from a dead deck."

"I owe you one, Doc. I promise."

"I know. It'll be okay. Just go ahead and get out of here." Shimura mopped the sweat from his pronounced brow with his forearm. "I wanna get some sleep."

Not that Shimura knew how he would get to sleep in the heat. But he was sure he could catch at least some rest, even though his heart still beat faster than an overclocked processor.

"I can do that."

Shimura put his hands in the pockets of his white coat as he walked Enrique to the door. The troll forced the door open and the kid walked out into the oppressive midnight heat on the darkened street, the minimal light produced by the backup batteries and solar panels inside the clinic the only light to reach him, a faint outline of a boy against a tableau of dangerous black.

"Do me a favor, would ya, kid?"

Enrique turned back, his face full of hope again rather than panic. "Anything, Doc."

"Read the terms of service next time. Don't make any more shady deals like this you can't afford, no matter how much it seems like it's the only way."

Enrique nodded, but didn't answer.

He'd be back.

As he walked into the darkness, disappearing into the heat, Shimura knew he'd likely see that kid again. It wouldn't be a cyberarm next time. Maybe it would be something else, but he'd be back.

And Shimura would be there, waiting.

The troll sighed. He forced the door shut and engaged the manual lock before turning back to the privacy of his sanctum at the back of the clinic. Despite the heat and the sweaty misery pouring from him, he smiled.

"Now," he said, "I owe myself that drink."

NIGHT SHADES

Jason M. Hardy

Ciel squatted in the swamp, water squelching behind her knees. "He's not working out."

Louis floated only a few meters away, dematerialized and unseen. He communicated in the silent way of spirits. *"You're being too hasty. At least give him the whole job to disappoint you."*

It always unnerved her when Louis was the more positive one. "Maybe," she said. "But would it kill him to get out of sight?"

"I think he believes he is out of sight. In his way."

She pointed to the road on the edge of the swamp. "He's standing straight up!"

It's true, he was. Robicheaux was an ork, and he was casually strolling next to the road. Cars passed occasionally. None so much as slowed down.

"His weapons are well hidden."

Robicheaux promised he'd have a pistol and a sawed-off shotgun on him. He wore a poncho—suitable for this rainy night—and the weapons were hidden beneath it. The poncho was well used, with a few cracks in the vinyl, and utterly undistinguished.

"You're saying he's hiding in plain sight."

"Do you see anything memorable about him?"

Ciel grudgingly had to admit she did not. "But he looks so casual. Like he's barely paying attention to what he's doing."

"Isn't that part of the disguise? And can you say you're fully focused?"

"Shut up." She couldn't see Louis' smug smile. But she could feel it, which was worse.

"You hired him. You're working with him. It's okay to trust him."

"That's not really my thing."

"You trust me."

She thought about that, about how she first was suspicious of Louis when she met him, when he told his story of being murdered and wanting to find out who did it. Then she was annoyed, then tolerant, and then they became what they were now.

"Only because you kept showing up."

Louis still felt amused to her, so she decided she needed to ignore whatever was going on with him and focus on the job.

Assensing in a swamp was difficult, because it was a riot of life and auras. An ignorant mage or shaman might think that would be enough to hide them and try to duck in the middle of those auras, only to stand out as much as a peacock at a chicken party. But someone who knew what they were doing would adjust their aura to match what's around them, and then you were looking for a piece of hay in a haystack.

It took control, though. And the person Ciel looked for was not renowned for their emotional control. She didn't look for her target at first. She looked for what her target might like.

Midnightshade was an Awakened, fascist form of nightshade. It grew best in soil too alkaline for other plants, and it worked like hell to generate those soil conditions. It grew fast, choked off other plants, then poisoned their remains, which in turn poisoned the soil. Then it dropped its seeds on ground only it could love, and it grew.

She scanned the swamp, looking for a patch of the plant, though it was not easy to see at night. She thought she saw a thick patch, though, and she switched to astral view to be sure. Its aura was a midnight blue with a green tinge further outlined by red. The green was vibrant and angry. Did all midnightshade look like that? Maybe. She hadn't assessed enough to be sure. And the anger of green suited the nature of the plant. So this must be what it was.

She moved, but not directly toward it. She kept an eye on other nearby auras and how they shifted relative to the midnightshade. Then, after tromping through the swamp for a hundred meters, she flicked a hand and set the midnightshade on fire.

The fire didn't last long, partly because it was a green plant in a swamp, and partly because someone snuffed it out after only a few seconds of burning and popping as seed pods exploded in the sudden heat. It was a quick effort to extinguish it, but counterspelling and masking at the same time wasn't easy, and because of that there was a small bobble in the mask.

Target identified. And target angered.

The first spell came quickly—acid, predictably. Ciel thought about letting it hit her, as her vest had chemical protection, but she knew it was better to keep any harm as far away from your body as possible. The blue gem on the ring on her right hand glowed as she raised the hand and dissipated the stream in mid-air.

Now she had a furious opponent on her hands. He was still invisible, but she could see the aura moving toward her. Spells came quickly, a new one every few seconds. Manabolt, at her. Improved reflexes, on him. Silence, on him. And on and on. She kept busy running, watching, and counterspelling, so she didn't fire back any spells of her own. If the plan worked, she wouldn't have to.

The shaman was making rapid progress, his ever-flickering aura tough to follow. He also moved way better in the swamp than Ciel did—she felt like her legs were moving almost entirely vertically as she picked her way ahead. The shaman, though, was in his element, gliding smoothly. Ciel wished she could see him, maybe pick up some hints of his technique. Right now, though, she just had to not let him get too far away. And make sure Louis knew where he was.

Louis, you got him?

"*Yeah,*" he responded.

Well, that part was easy.

Louis was as good as his word. About a hundred meters to Ciel's left, he materialized. Wearing a soggy grey suit as always. Shoulders hunched, chin down. The aura of the shaman stopped in front of Louis and radiated what Ciel read as surprise.

"*Did you know there are thousands of plant species around us right now? I find that really impressive.*" Louis' voice sounded more morose than his words let on, but that was his way.

Judging by the shaman's aura, he did not care about that particular fact. Power gathered around the shaman as he prepared a special way to show his contempt for nature facts.

The spell, though, was interrupted by a shotgun blast of gel rounds to the shaman's chest.

Just like that, the invisibility spell went away. The shaman flew a meter backward and splashed into the swamp. He was an unkempt mass of tattered threads and matted hair.

It was a good shot. Robicheaux had not moved too far from the road, and a sawed-off shotgun was far from the most accurate weapon the Sixth World had to offer. He'd been guided only by the presence of Louis, and he'd still nailed the target.

The shaman stirred a little in the murky swamp water, so Ciel stunbolted him right in the head. It was highly satisfying. The shaman didn't stir again.

She looked at Robicheaux. The ork waved in a way she found both amusing and irritating. But she gave a quick wave back.

Louis drifted to her side.

"I guess he did that much right," Louis said, which likely was as close as he was going to get to "I told you so."

The pleasant feelings from the end of that run endured for about seventy-two hours. At the end of that period, Ciel had transformed into a creature of rage, and she was not going to stop moving until Robicheaux was in her sights.

Louis had tried to stop her, telling her to slow down, consider her position. She told him to stay put. Even though he owed her no obedience, he respected her wishes. He still sent her the occasional thought—*"Slow down. Listen to him."*—but kept them infrequent enough to not annoy her too much.

She found Robicheaux at an old warehouse that had been turned into a makeshift shooting range. If she had considered it, she might have realized the risks of confronting him there, but rage carried her past all such thoughts.

She walked up to him as he was putting a Ruger down and considering what weapon to use next. She had an active spell giving her a nice strength boost, so when she grabbed him under his arms and yanked, he came backward easily. She shifted her grip and slammed him against the back wall.

"If your share of the bounty wasn't enough, you should've said something. You think you can get away with selling me out?"

He looked at her, startled and in pain. "Ciel?"

"Selling me out to toxics? What kind of friends do you have?"

He kept his arms at his side but turned his palms outward, like a gesture of attempted appeasement. "I swear I have no idea what you're talking about."

She shook him a little. "The hell you don't. But I didn't come here to listen to any denials. I just wanted to let you know I know."

She stormed out before Robicheaux could come up with any rejoinder. Now that she'd told him, she had to figure out what came next.

She hadn't been home since the day after she had caught the toxic shaman. A day or so after the capture, she was in her ramshackle hut, and she caught sight of a green liquid dripping from her ceiling. It sizzled when it hit the ground. She put a bucket under it, and the green fluid dissolved a hole in the bottom of the bucket within two hours. She left at that point.

It was simple—when a toxic shaman knew where you lived, you didn't stay there. Ciel damn sure was going to find out who doxxed her. Then she'd take a kilo of flesh.

She knew how to look for contracts in the shadows, and while she didn't exactly have a contract out on her, she learned pretty quickly that her name was being passed along a loose coalition of toxic spellcasters ("loose" because even toxics didn't like other toxics), and her address came along with her name.

That narrowed things down, because very few people knew where she lived. Louis did, of course, but she eliminated that possibility immediately. Maybe half a dozen runners she'd worked with in the past knew, but at least three of them were dead. And Robicheaux knew.

That's it. She had no connections to family, and on the rare occasion she saw someone socially, she did not bring them to her home. So those were the possibilities, and of them, she trusted Robicheaux the least. Which led to her visit to the shooting range.

That was only her first salvo against Robicheaux. She'd deal with him more definitively later, but the far more critical piece of business was making sure she wasn't hunted anymore.

When she'd first started in the business, her instinct would have been to hide and wait for all of this to blow over. Any habit, though, eventually gets used against you, and she noticed that people started intentionally causing trouble in her life so that she would avoid working. She was sidelining herself for half of the year, and her income suffered. Meanwhile, other runners were filling the void, taking money she could have earned. She decided that all sucked, so she started dealing with problems in a more direct way.

Right now, this meant letting the toxic community know she meant business.

She knew they didn't like her. She had taken out a toxic shaman named Lavoisier years ago, the one responsible for killing the mortal version of Louis. She'd collected the bounty on him—you never, ever leave money sitting on the table—and that moved her to a new pad. It also put her on the radar of other toxics, who didn't know much about her other than that she was an enemy. She wasn't a high enough priority to be tracked down, but when she got on their radar, they were delighted to cause her pain. Now that she'd taken out another one, it seemed they had decided to be less passive.

She was going to convince them they'd made the wrong decision.

"How do you intimidate toxic mages?" she asked, thinking aloud.

"Lysol?" Louis didn't look up when he said it, so Ciel had no indication of whether it was a joke.

They were in the cemetery where Louis' body was buried. He knew the place well—Ciel suspected he visited sometimes while she slept—and he knew which crypts had broken locks. Ciel didn't mind sleeping among the dead much, as she believed that was par for the course for a New Orleans shadowrunner. The benches inside the crypt were hard, though, and not softened much by her sleeping bag. If this went on for too long, she would splurge on a safehouse, but she didn't want to use money that way. The goal, then, would be to make sure this didn't take long.

"I can't just promise to leave them alone. That won't be enough. They want to hurt me. I have to convince them it's not worth it."

"Cut off the head of the snake?" Water plunked off Louis and onto the stone floor as he spoke.

"There is no head. It's all snake."

"Maybe just pick one to make an example of?"

"Maybe. I'd have to do enough to that person to make the others think twice." She turned that idea over in her mind. She thought about how much she'd have to do to one toxic shaman to make any others nervous. It wasn't a pleasant thought. "I'm not sure I'm willing to lose what I'd have to lose to do that."

"Where does that leave you?"

She lay on the concrete slab silently for a time. Only one idea came to mind. "Go back home, wait for someone to come after me, and make them regret it."

Louis sighed, an odd move for a being who did not actually breathe. *"You're going to want more eyes watching you."*

"I don't trust anyone to watch me. Except you."

Louis nodded. *"Then I'll be here."*

The warning had been heeded, but that didn't mean the job was over because people were foolish, ignoring signs, ignoring portents, ignoring the inevitable. Thinking somehow they would be exempt from the rules of the world.

The shambling person who called himself Envie would watch Ciel's home for a while. Not all the time. Off and on. He would also visit the fens, or the port, and smell the twisted air and heady fumes and fill his body with all the things humanity spewed into the world around him.

The warning had been good. Elegant. Acid sputtering from the ceiling, dropping, burning. Burning, burning, he needed the burn. The world needed fire. It needed pain. Not to purify it. Purity was a myth, a distortion, an insane wish for something that never was. The world needed to stop pretending, it needed to face what it was, which was mean, punishing, and hostile. It needed to learn, not for a moral reason, not for any vision of good. Only because things should be what they are, not pretending to be something else. And the world, at its base, at its core, was filth.

People knew. They resisted, sometimes. They pretended they didn't know. But look at them! Look at their landfills, their plastic islands in the ocean, their lives. Their lives filled with petty squabbles, with unending schemes made in the name of money or sex or a fleeting good time, their inability to plan, their chaos. How could they not know they were filth? They wallowed in it!

But some few, some people, like the woman in this shack, thought they were something else. Thought they stood for something. Worse, they thought they could stop people like Envie, when all Envie was doing was following the natural course of the world, just making it happen a little bit faster. Hurrying it up to get where it was going.

It would have been better if she had been there when he'd left his warning. He could have greeted her with enough acid to bleach her bones, but she was not, so he settled for a slower drip that would instill fear, which was a great feeling to give to someone in their home. It took away their security, reminded them they were just scrabbling on the dirt until the time came for them to return to it.

She had fled, but she might come back, and if she did, she would try to come back strong. Make herself more protected, probably bring some friends.

Envie would respond in kind. Not with friends. He didn't have friends. Friends crumbled, like everything. He had allies, people who shared his cause and understood the inevitability of decay, and knew the only purpose that mattered was one that led to a permanent outcome.

If she returned, he would bring them. She would get much more than a mere warning.

Ciel and Louis moved back home the next day. There wasn't much to it, as Ciel only carried what could be kept in a backpack, and Louis carried nothing. She walked into her shack, tucked her sleeping bag in a corner, tucked the backpack under her bed, and boom, she was home.

Ciel seemed more comfortable than she had been in the cemetery, but Louis wasn't. He had started his increased vigilance when they came within half a kilometer of the shack, and he knew he wouldn't relax anytime soon. He had selected the interior-of-the-shack watch duty, which made sense, as he had the best relationship with Ciel. The other members of his team were scattered around the area, keeping their eyes open.

It was a motley crew of spirits who looked pretty much like him. Louis could not summon spirits on his own, and he didn't have a vast network of beings, immaterial or otherwise, who owed him favors, but he was the beneficiary of one strange quirk of fate. Lavoisier, the first toxic shaman Ciel had collected the bounty for, had enjoyed the unusual hobby of summoning and binding spirits who looked just like Louis. The shaman's rationale had been that he shaped the spirits to look that way to remind him of their task, which was to keep an eye on Louis when he had been alive. When Lavoisier went away, the bound spirits were freed, and many of them chose to stay where they had been for a while.

This then got to the tangled theory of Louis' origin and nature. In his belief, once the mortal Louis died, he was the spirit version that remained. In the toxic shaman's view, Louis as a spirit had observed Louis as a mortal so closely that he had absorbed several material facts about his life, and when he died, he unconsciously assumed the former mortal's identity.

Whatever the case may be, the clear truth was this: the spirit Louis thought he was the continuation of the mortal Louis, and he had found a population of spirits who looked like him and sometimes acted like him. They had all been a little rootless once the shaman who had shaped them vanished. So, possibly in tribute to the spirit of the mortal Louis, they acted mainly through inertia and stuck together, because what else was there?

The Louises were not offensively gifted, not really intimidating, but they excelled in one thing: not being noticed. All of the Louises Louis had gathered could sit in plain sight around the shack, and any approaching hostile would stroll right by them and not think twice. What kind of threat does a soaking, sad-sack spirit present?

After a brief Louis council, the spirits decided that despite that, they would not let themselves be completely obvious. They didn't dematerialize—few things were more suspicious than a disembodied aura—but they slid behind trees, between other shacks, and any other place where they'd be reasonably out of sight. Then they waited, and they watched.

They all communicated with Louis (who, these days, was the only one who actually called himself Louis) as he sat with Ciel. They didn't so much engage in small talk as exchange the occasional observation that cut through moments of silence.

"Someone's close," said one positioned about thirty meters from the shed. *"Stumbling, though. Drunk, probably."*

"Disguised as a drunk?" another one asked.

"If they are, they did their aura, too."

That, combined with the fact that the drunk staggered away from Ciel's shack, led most of the Louises to conclude the drunk was legitimate.

"*Raccoon,*" another one said.

"*What time is it?*" Louis asked from inside the shack.

"*01:30.*"

Louis nodded. *That's Maggie. She's always out at this time."*

There was a small pause. *"Did you name all of the raccoons, or just this one?"*

"*It wouldn't be fair to them to only name one.*"

The Louises sent silent assent.

A few other similar minor sightings occurred until 02:45, when things abruptly picked up.

The message came from a Louis perched on the roof of a shed similar to Ciel's, about a hundred meters away.

"*Oh, there. Watch out for that one. Look at that aura. Bright but dark. Twisted.*"

"*How far from us? Moving where?*"

"*Only fifteen meters away from me. Moving on a tangent now. Not getting closer.*"

"*Circling?*"

"*I don't think so. Maybe just passing by? Maybe just a coincidence that he's here?*"

"*Do you think there are so many toxic shamans in the sprawl that one would just happen by?*"

"*That's a good point.*"

The Louises sat silently for a moment.

Then the Louis on the shack's roof spoke. *"Do you think he'll be scanning the astral any time soon?"*

There was a pause as everyone thought.

No one spoke until the Louis on the roof spoke again. *"There you go. That aura just flickered out like an old fluorescent light. He knows people are watching."*

"*And he's not leaving. Whatever is going to happen is going to happen soon.*"

Inside the shack, Louis turned his attention to Ciel. She had heard all the conversation, so she didn't need to be brought up to speed, but he needed to know what she wanted now that her enemies were about to do whatever it was they were going to do.

She looked calm and steady. Resolved. She spoke directly to Louis so the others wouldn't hear. "The plan is the plan.

Some of the yous out there are going to suffer. Are they okay with that?"

"They'll be fine," Louis said. *"They'll act a little mopey afterward, but that's what we do."*

He said it in his normal flat tones, but Ciel looked at him with a crooked grin. "You got jokes now?"

Louis fidgeted a little. *"I don't know if that's what that is. Just trying to, I don't know—share what I see about the world?"*

Ciel stood and patted him on the knee. "That's how good jokes start. All right. Let's do the plan. And may the spirit of Muhammad Ali preserve us."

Louis nodded, then focused on the mana around him. He pulled energy toward him then hardened it, making a dome over him and Ciel that extended to the floor. When it was shaped, he pulled more mana in. He wanted to keep going until an attack came, but he also didn't want to entirely drain himself of energy. So he kept his work under control and hoped his compatriots outside the shack would be up to their tasks.

The first attack was a wave, because of course it was. It gathered acid from the groundwater, the soil, and the moisture in the air and pulled it into a flume that swept over the ground and moved swiftly toward the shack.

It never got there. It broke into a million droplets five meters away from the walls.

There immediately was a second wave, this one from the opposite direction. It broke like the first.

Then the formalities were over, and the real assault began. Spell after spell. Physical and mana-based, fire and ice, visible and invisible. The pace of them kept increasing, indicating the assailants were conjuring help. They got creative, throwing a few spells looking to just open a hole in the shack wall so they could see what they could throw in. Then someone tossed a couple of flash-bang grenades in the vicinity, just to keep things really interesting.

The Louises did what Louises do. They hunched their shoulders, looked to the ground, and withstood. Not without damage. The Louis on the roof was the first to go when his counterspelling faltered and a blast spell took him completely out of the material plane. Others around the perimeter faltered as well, weakening the edges of the defense. But the edge had been weak anyway. The center was where the most strength had been focused, and the center held.

The assault seemed to last forever, but in truth it was likely no more than a few minutes. Then the spells quieted. What fires remained on the ground fizzled out. Acid dripped off the roof and nearby tree limbs before disappearing back into the aether. Air that had been humming with power fell silent.

Every single Louis knew this was no time to relax. They cast a couple healing spells on each other, but otherwise focused on shoring up their defenses. They knew they weren't done.

The next series of attacks were more clinical. Rather than the unrestrained barrage of the first wave, this wave ebbed and flowed, small spells followed by larger ones, consecutive spells targeted at the exact same location to probe for weakness. That might have worked if the defenses were ad hoc, being whipped up on demand to respond to spells as they were cast. But that wasn't the case. The defenses were planned, sturdy, and all-encompassing. No one spot was weaker than another. Probing for a vulnerable spot would get them nowhere.

The attackers seemed to realize this quickly and stopped after only a minute or two. The defenders used the time to take a breath—the shortness of the attack did not do as much damage to them as the previous one had, so there was no real need for healing after. They knew, though, that a short, probing wave was highly unlikely to be the last. They had to be ready for what would come next.

Envie had not stopped moving. He stalked back and forth, watching auras, casting spells, waiting, waiting, waiting. Waiting to break through, waiting to overwhelm, waiting for the world here to taste as it should; a sharp tang followed by a lingering burn.

This shack was going to chaos and decay quickly enough on its own. It barely seemed worth hurrying it along, but the woman inside had returned, as he thought she might, so she had to be stopped. He had come with chaos, companions in human and spirit form both, and they would burn the shack into the murky ground, and everything inside would sink with it.

The shack should have fallen by now, should have been dust and rust as was proper, but the woman and the mana beings she had around it were propping it up. Envie had seen the dome they were using inside the shack, he had looked at it, walked around the shack, seen it from different angles, probed it with spells. He saw the splinters on it, the frays, like a wooden barn hit with a cannon ball, like canvas scraped on concrete.

Two big pushes, *he thought. One push would break the dome, the second would overwhelm the woman and her spirits. Envie would be tired, walking like he was in thigh-deep mud, but the bodies would be lying on the floor, and finishing them would be as easy as pouring acid on a flower, and exactly, exactly as satisfying.*

The plan was communicated, agreed to with some hesitancy that was overwhelmed by the prospect of how close they were. They prepared, but not for long, because every second they rested was a second the opposition rested, and they did not need them gaining strength, so they moved soon after they agreed, launching attacks all focused on one area, the weakest spot Envie had seen. It wasn't the chaos of the first wave, but it was all united as a burst of raw blue power, flashing forward to make bullets look slow, hitting the dome, and the dome shattered gloriously but without a sound.

Envie inhaled. All the effort for that spell was worth it. Now the second one, right after it. Acid now. Dissolve them. Dissolve them all.

It was a torrent, like the levees had been breached again, a green flood that hated anything alive. It actively hurt leaving Envie's presence, but its horrible beauty could not be ignored. It was a wave that came from all directions, like the ocean moving around a rock pile near the shore, all converging on the one spot, all ready to teach the most essential lesson life had for us: Everything ends in decay.

The waves converged. Broke. Envie pushed his tired legs to run forward.

And the waves melted away.

Envie's legs stopped so quickly he almost fell forward. The shack stood. The inhabitants inside...unharmed?

The bullet that ripped thought his skull kept him from ever learning the answer to that question.

Ciel thought she might have heard a gunshot, but didn't pay attention to it. Gunshots were not the rarest sound in her neighborhood. She had other business to worry about right in front of her.

The rope-a-dope had worked. The toxics had thought they were closer to success than they were. The hidden defense had held. Now they had to use their advantage.

Any combat spell she cast right now would be like a BB gun, nothing more than an annoyance if she was lucky. She had no strength for it. But there was an earth mound not far away a friend of hers had built, and currently inside was a beast spirit she had summoned right after sundown, when she had had all the energy in the world. It was waiting for her command.

She gave it.

An unearthly howl burst from the mound, disembodied. The spirit didn't materialize, but it made its presence felt. The exhausted shamans and spirits surrounding the shack turned, and Ciel felt their dismay, or imagined she did—which was just as good. The spirit started tearing through their astral forms, and they had little power to resist. Those who remained standing were subjected to small clout spells from Ciel, minor nudges to push them over the edge into unconsciousness, or if not that, at least down onto the ground.

She disrupted one spirit, then moved to the next aura. It was a person—a surprisingly energetic person, even after the spirit's passing attack. Her minor clout spell would be brushed off like it was a mere gnat. And whatever came back at her would be worse.

She knew she would be the target. She started thinking about what defense she could muster, if any—then another shot rang out, and the person's aura flickered and disappeared.

The rest was clean-up, dealing with downcast spirits and fleeing humans. Then she walked around the muddy ground by her shack, finding any Louises that were still onsite, thanking them. Typically, they nodded gently then shuffled away. They were spirits; they could dart away quickly with no effort if they so choose, but a Louis wouldn't be a Louis without their affection for a certain kind of mood.

Finally, she was back in the situation she had been in so many times—in her shack, with Louis, the only one of his name. She shook her head, allowing herself to be amazed that they had survived and were still here.

"You did it," she said. "You and the other...yous. I couldn't have held them off without all of you."

"It was a team effort," Louis said. Anyone but Ciel might not have heard the pride in his voice, and she heard it loud and clear. *"But you didn't thank the whole team."*

Ciel blinked. "I didn't?"

"He's waiting outside. He won't knock, but he probably also won't go away until you say something to him. You should talk to him so he can go home."

Ciel hesitated.

"I'll go out with you," Louis said. *"You know I can watch your back."*

So now Louis was bragging? Ciel was beginning to think her influence on the spirit had not been entirely positive.

She walked outside. The person waiting for her was not hiding. He was ten meters from her front door, sitting on a fire hydrant that hadn't been connected to the water system this century. It was Robicheaux, dressed in nighttime camo, carrying a rifle Ciel now knew had fired at least twice in the night. His arms were folded across his chest, and something dangled from his right hand.

Ciel had a lot of questions running through her head, but she couldn't settle on one to start with. "I have a lot of questions."

"Midnightshade," he said.

"What?"

He waved the object in his hand. It looked like a branch. "Midnightshade. Its seeds get everywhere. They scatter really well when the plant is on fire. You probably got some on you."

"So?"

"It wasn't just any patch. That shaman that night? The patch was his special place. Where he communed with...filth, or whatever toxics commune with. He did rituals there. So he had an affinity to all parts of it. Including seeds that floated away. His disciples had the same affinity."

"So, they just...tracked me down?"

"Yeah."

"That means I was right that the aura of that plant was kind of off."

"If that's what you saw, then yeah."

There was another clear conclusion to come to, and Ciel forced herself to say it. "So I was pretty much wrong to come after you."

"Yeah, pretty much."

"But here you are anyway."

"Louis reached out. Thought I could help. Looks like it'll work out—do you know what kind of bounties we have lying around your house?"

Ciel hadn't even thought of that. "Holy shit..." Her housing was about to get another upgrade.

Robicheaux smiled and stood up. "That's what I want to hear."

Ciel thought she should say something more. Maybe apologize? But Robicheaux seemed ready to work and get some money, and ghost knew she was, too.

"Anything you want me to do?" he asked.

She walked by him and gently patted his massive shoulder. "Just keep showing up."

TO FIX A BROKEN HEART

Marie Bilodeau

Steelton hated all these profiles. The good ones because of who they were. The bad ones, well, because of who they were. He flipped through the virtual rolodex, flicked pictures as they changed, landed on a familiar face. He leaned back in his chair, strumming his fingers on his armrests in an attempt not to flick it away.

His arms practically twitched at his sides, and he violently expelled himself from his chair, walking away from the image to the expansive window of his office. Montréal sprawled below him, beautiful and terrifying. Factories hummed steadily, lights pulsing through the night sky, the Republic depending on its Matrix relay systems manufacturing. Hell, not just the Republic. A good chunk of this side of the world relied on it.

Which is why this is so important, Steelton reminded himself. He returned to his desk. As a fixer, it was his job to make sure he got the right crew together for the right mission. But he hated this run, *tabardrek*[1]. He'd always known he might someday have to call on old friends. Not that he overly minded that.

It was *this* old friend he minded calling on.

But he needed her.

Drumming his fingers on the desk in a rhythmic pattern, he let ten seconds go by. That was all he allowed when he doubted himself. Indecision killed more than guns and magic combined as far as he was concerned.

Ten seconds to find an alternative, or he was locked in.

1. "Tabardrek" – combination of old Québec profanity "*tabarnak*" (meaning "tabernacle"), and the *Shadowrun* profanity "drek"

He stopped drumming his fingers, swore, and sent a quick message, surprised at the mix of elation and disappointment when she replied right away.

Meet me at the old spot.

"You look like shit," Cat said as she sipped her maple latte. *Café Malice* had the best lattes. Their first date had been here. It was kinda fitting that their first post-divorce meetup was here, too. Really, she'd just been craving the latte.

"Thanks," he mumbled in that way he did when he wasn't really paying attention. It still annoyed her.

"You look like expensive shit, though, I'll give you that," she added. Truth was he looked good. Like, really good. His tailored suit showed off his broad shoulders, he had just the right amount of dark stubble on his chin, and his grey eyes were as steady as ever, even if he looked distant...*stop it.*

They'd broken up for all the right reasons, even though the physical attraction had never been missing.

"Thanks," he said again, now focusing those sharp eyes on her. She gazed lazily at him, raising an eyebrow. She'd never figured he'd become a fixer. He was a good hacker, so losing him on runs had been a shame. Guess he'd needed a change of scenery once the divorce was final.

Nice that he'd had the option.

He hit his watch, an old-fashioned-looking piece he loved, but she knew he could hack his way through the best networks with it. Probably blocking out any listeners.

"Must be some job," she said, looking around. They were the only ones in the entire café, and the owner, an old friend, had made himself scarce. They'd often planned entire runs here, and he'd never been worried about anyone listening in before.

He gave her that smile. The one that used to melt her. *Câlice d'frag*[2]. Still did. She steeled herself, and hoped he didn't notice the slight flush of her cheeks.

"It is," he said, then his shoulders slumped a bit. That was unusual. "Look," he leaned his elbows on the table, edged

---

2. *Câlice d'frag* - combination of *"câlice"* (meaning "chalice"), and the *Shadowrun* profanity "frag"

forward. "It's a dangerous job, and I honestly would love to give it to anyone else but you."

"Thanks for the vote of confidence," she said. The flush was definitely gone, replaced by familiar bitterness. When he'd started getting in her way, all the time, like she'd turned into a Fabergé egg.

"That's not it," he said, holding up his hands defensively. "*Drek*, you always misunderstand me..." he took a long, shuddering breath. Stopped himself.

Well, his self-control had gotten better. Probably handy as a fixer. "What's the job?" No point in running down old paths again. They'd only led to the end of their marriage, anyway.

"It's a simple run, but, well, there could be complications."

"There are always complications, Sword," she automatically called him by his old nickname. Sword of Steelton, unflappable, unstoppable, unbendable. He gazed at her, like he'd go soft on her again. She forced the conversation to stay focused. "I can handle complications, Steelton." His real name broke the growing spell between them.

They'd never been screamers. Their tempers boiled much too deep, and much too steadily, to explode. They just seethed and stayed hot, once stoked enough. And they'd both done plenty of stoking over sixteen years of marriage.

"We got word there's an asset coming into the city. Basically a hacking creature."

A raised, slender eyebrow. "Go on," she said, her other eyebrow soon joining the first as he told her what, exactly, he needed done.

And where.

Steelton watched Cat vanish around a corner. *Merde*[3], she was still hot, with that no-nonsense walk and talk, her long trench coats, and currently red, shoulder-cropped hair. She'd been great in her twenties and thirties, sure. But now, early forties? She somehow kept getting better.

He tugged his coat closer and spotted the familiar, rusted blue van that belonged to Triny. He walked beside it, shot a

3. French for "shit"

grin her way. She leaned out the window, purple-tinted black hair tumbling out in braids, barely revealing her pointed ears.

A grin split her dark face. "You two getting back together?"

"Nah," he said. "She's resisting my charms again."

"Well, they're easy to resist."

He grinned back. Couldn't help it. Triny was the youngest member of the group, having joined a year before Cat and he broke up and he'd moved on. Moved *up*. Triny was one of the damn best riggers he'd ever met, and this old van was decked out with more tech than most corporate rides. Of course, that was partly thanks to Sketch, who was good at acquiring said tech. She and Triny were a thing in business and pleasure.

Like he and Cat used to be.

"You be careful, Triny," he said. Before she could ask any questions, he shoved his hands in his pockets and walked away.

Cat would be back soon, probably having ducked in the nearby bakery, *Les Délices Foux,* to get treats for the gang.

He didn't intend on still being here when she got back.

"We clear on the plan?" Cat looked up to Triny and Sketch, who were busy giggling at the map. Okay, she'd had to draw the map herself after a quick recon, because there weren't any official maps. She'd wanted to make it as accurate as possible, but she wasn't great at drawing, and her use of the same wild colors found on the site hadn't really helped.

"Is that a clown?" Triny asked, trying, and failing, to sound serious.

"You know it is."

"I know theoretically it's a clown. It looks like a summoned spirit gone terribly wrong."

"That's his hair," Horus said, his large frame bent over the drawing. "Anyway, be serious. The map is accurate." The older man looked at both of them reproachfully. Cat was on the verge of thanking him when he unfortunately continued. "The real question here is: Is that a cage, or a comb? Because that will seriously impact planning."

Triny and Sketch both burst out laughing. Cat gave up, took a long drink of her terrible beer. She glanced at the team surrounding her, as talk turned more seriously to the plan at hand, and how they would secure the target. She loved them, though. All three of them, her little pack. They weren't many and so took smaller or more specialized jobs. They used to be five, but, well, Steelton had left.

"We need to be careful," she said softly when a lull occurred in the conversation. Her serious tone coated the entire room, and they all turned to her. "This job...something's off about it."

"Why, because Steelton gave it to us?" Sketch asked, earnest purple eyes focused on her, hand clasping Triny's.

"No," Cat said, mulling over what she was trying to express. "Not that. It's...It's the fact he didn't *want* to give it to us that worries me."

Steelton was many things, but he was, in his own way, loyal. He'd promised long ago to keep them safe, and he always would. That he'd come to them, to *her*, meant he had no other option. That he'd hesitated when they met...well, that was telling. Fixers gotta fix, after all.

"Time to get some sleep," Cat said. "We head out before dusk."

Steelton hadn't slept since meeting Cat yesterday. He'd tried, sure, but his mind churned with worry, leaving him tossing and turning. Annoyed, he'd given up and started messing with his watch-disguised cyberdeck. Old habits died hard, and once a decker, always a decker.

He'd reviewed the mission brief, but it didn't give him much to go on. He knew the location of the target and some of what it might be able to do, but that was it. He needed more details, anything that could help him.

...Creature with hacking capabilities dangerous to manufacturing sector...

...Carnival-like Trojan horse to let it in the city, part of monstrosities tent...

...Funder unknown. Defenses unknown. Imperative that creature is captured alive for study...

Steelton stretched his back. There wasn't anything else. Not here, anyway.

But he thought he might know where it was.

He drummed his fingers on the table.

Ten seconds went by.

Mind made up, he quickly hacked Mr. Johnson's comm files. He pulled out as much as he could, quickly enough he hoped he hadn't been spotted. That would ruin his career as a fixer. Not to mention get him geeked.

The risk was a calculated one. He'd been hired as a fixer by this corp for his work hacking their database. Several times. The last time, he'd left a calling card in case they wanted to hire someone with connections. A risky move right after his breakup with Cat. He'd been drunk, and had really hoped they'd come down on him shooting.

Instead, they'd asked him to be one of their fixers. Not what he'd expected, but he could work with it. But not at the cost of Cat's life.

Within two minutes, he'd secured more background information on the creature. He sucked in his breath. The way the brief had been written, the creature sounded like a tame beast that followed commands and was basically a hacking machine in animal form. But that wasn't it at all. It was a monster, the bloody thing part Awakened, part cyber-enhanced.

Even Cat's animal taming abilities might not be enough. With a regular enhanced creature, sure. But this thing was... well, it was smart. And cunning. And, he had to assume, deadly as hell. The corp had been warned by an unnamed source who feared what would happen if this creature was let loose. It wouldn't just take down the manufacturing sector.

It might take down the whole damn Matrix. So, of course, they wanted it first.

Sucking in his breath, Steelton drummed his fingers.

Cat pulled pink fluff free from the large wad, smooshed it in her sticky fingers before placing it in her mouth. The sugar melted the second it met her saliva, and she grinned.

"I don't understand this contraption," Horus growled.

"It's cotton candy, Horus," Cat said, taking another handful. "What's there not to understand?"

"Its *raison d'être* evades me," he said, staring in disgust at his sticky fingers. Cat shook her head, smiling. As far as runs went, this wasn't so bad. Well, not so far. They walked around posing as a couple enjoying the carnival. Sketch and

Triny waited in the van on the east side, near the *Nouveaux Monstres* exhibit.

First, they'd had to blend in. That included not being too obvious by walking straight to the target. Instead, they'd been meandering around for almost an hour. Rode a few rides, played a few games, the stuffed owl she'd won tucked under her arm. Horus had only grown more grouchy, she suspected the Topsy Turvy Tilty ride had been too much for his stomach.

The carnival was well attended, located right in the old port of the city. After massive revitalization efforts over the past two decades, this place looked pretty damn welcoming. They regularly hosted exhibits, festivals, and carnivals like this one to draw residents and tourists to the wharfs.

The autumnal bite of the evening justified their coats, allowing them more hidden equipment. Security was pretty lax, too. Most crime in Montréal was non-violent now, thanks to the boom. Which was why this creature was so dangerous, according to Steelton.

A creature with only one purpose: to take down the manufacturing side.

Some corps had large Matrix connectors running under the port, which could be accessed given enough time and an inconspicuous disguise. Like a week-long carnival. Their equipment and personnel would have all been screened before being offered the spot. But a creature? No one would look too closely at a weird beast that was part of an exhibit. As long as it didn't break any laws and had all its origin papers, which could easily be faked, they'd have slipped right in.

Lots of people milled about, the rides loud as they whooshed around, several going rather high without anything noticeable grounding them, fully reliant on magic to operate. It was all music, glitz, lights, and sounds.

And Horus' scowl only deepened the more happy riders shrieked with joy.

"You're supposed to be enjoying yourself," Cat softly reminded him. He cleared his throat and plastered a wooden smile on his face. That was definitely not better. As she glanced around to make sure no one paid them too much attention, she noticed half the people here seemed high on something or way too cheerful, so he didn't stand out that badly.

Cat ate more cotton candy as they slowly wandered toward the giant purple and black top tent with the words *Nouveaux Monstres* written across it.

Steelton tried to reach Cat, but he couldn't get her. Nor could he get Triny, Sketch, or Horus. They were all in play, under comm blackout, focused on keeping each other safe and alive.

Except there would be no way to survive this. Even if Cat managed to get this thing to come with her, Steelton was sure she'd be killed. On a lark, he'd checked other comms from Mr. Johnson that day. The bastard had hired another fixer. To make sure the first team, once they'd freed the creature, wouldn't make it out alive. Neither them, nor the creature.

It had been deemed too dangerous for even them to try to handle, too worried it would take down their own networks. Best that the first team didn't make it, either, for plausible deniability. Steelton didn't follow the trail, but he guessed the second team was out of luck, too. But that wasn't his problem.

His problem was Cat. He'd sent her out there, the best runner for this job. She'd get the creature out, of course. It was what she did. Then she'd get killed.

What could he do? How could he help her?

Tabardrek, should he even help her? She'd accepted the job. She knew the risks of being a runner...but he'd sent her there.

This was his fault. And he had to make it right.

Being a fixer was easier when he wasn't in love with one of the runners.

The pavilion was fairly busy, so she and Horus took their time as they went from creature to creature. The pink-horned horse, the metal-legged pit bull, the chimera, the giant blue fluffy spider that looked both huggable and deadly. Cat knew the creature wouldn't be out here. It was probably in the back. According to specs, the conduit ran right beneath the tent. Hardly a coincidence—this way, they could keep the creature here in case someone came to check that all animals were accounted for and not smuggled elsewhere, while it could start hacking away.

The main problem right now was the security cameras. Sketch had "found" some blockers, which she would activate when needed. Now wasn't the time to tip their hand. She motioned to Horus, who stood before her as he looked bored. He blocked the camera from seeing her, and she slipped through the tent fabric and into the back, ready to look like a curious tourist.

Thankfully no one was immediately here, and she slipped between two rows of material boxes.

*Any second now...*as if on cue, an explosion rang from the west end.

Sketch was good at what she did.

Cat folded deeper into the darkness as several guards ran by. As soon as the coast was clear, knowing it wouldn't be for long, she cleared the boxes and headed where they'd all exited. In the center of a cage, she spotted the creature. It was unlike anything she'd ever seen. At first glance, it looked like a large fox. But it wasn't. Its hair was slightly too long, completely white, its movements too graceful...but it was its eyes that sent shivers down her spine. Large, sorrowful eyes, which focused on her with undeniable intelligence.

She was supposed to convince this thing to come with her, willingly. She could, with most animals. Hell, she used to love doing runs to free animals from labs. That was her jam. It didn't pay, but the feels were there.

This, though...this was something else. She considered her magic, but knew, deep down, that it wouldn't work on this creature. Taking a deep breath, she picked the lock, and prayed she wasn't about to be eviscerated.

Then the alarms began to blare, and she knew she was out of time.

In the cage, the creature growled.

Steelton punched his desk, regretting it immediately as pain lanced up his arm. He ignored it, focusing on his cyberdeck. The carnival had activated its alarm. The Gendarmerie was on its way.

This was all going to hell, and fast. He looked at the video feeds. There weren't many in the carnival, but maybe, just maybe, he'd be able to spot what was happening on the field. And maybe he could help.

"What the hell is happening?" Triny asked, immediately plugging into the interface, ready to move out as soon as Cat and Horus were on board.

Sketch shook her head. She had no idea. She'd done her part, and now it was all up to them to wait.

Triny's hands turned white as she clutched the wheel. Sketch kept a look out, ready to help if needed, magic sparking at her fingertips.

"We'll be okay," she said, hoping she hadn't just lied to her favorite elf.

Horus moved to the edge of the tent the second the alarm sounded. The diversion shouldn't have been big enough to warrant such activity. Something else was happening. His hands turned to fists and he jumped to his usual conclusion. Someone had betrayed them.

Steelton.

He pulled his katana from his coat in one swift motion and moved to find Cat, but didn't make it far before two guards charged in.

Well, he'd buy her time this way, and meet her back at the van. Cat knew her job. So did he. It was time to get it done.

He brought down his sharp blade, the thrill of battle surging in his blood.

For the first time today, a real smile crossed his lips.

The cage flew open and Cat stared at the creature. It hesitated at first. Then it came toward her, feet moving almost like a horse's, high steps instead of low, careful ones.

There was nowhere to go, and the creature seemed intent on her. Cat followed her instincts and dropped to her knees, holding up her hand, palm up and fingers down. The creature turned its head sideways, inquisitive, then approached her hand. It leaned in, sniff.

Then, with a very smooth tongue, licked the cotton candy off her fingers. A look of disgust crossed her face and the creature picked up on it. Cat felt...mirth? Laughter? Coming from the creature.

It licked again, seemingly a fan of cotton candy.

"We have to go," Cat said, not sure it could understand her. The creature looked up at her, its large, pink eyes inquisitive. "It's not safe here," she added, then slowly, very tentatively, reached out with her mind...

And was instantly slammed with thoughts, feelings, impressions. The creature, it, *she*, wanted to get out. To escape. To be free. She wanted more cotton candy. She knew they were using her, and they needed her. But she was bored, and no one was nice. She'd never tasted cotton candy before.

Just as Cat worked through the muddle of emotions, the creature growled and leaped at her.

Cat yelped and fell backward, but the creature kept moving above her, going straight for the neck of a guard who had just entered. Blood on white fur. The creature licked its paws as it looked at Cat inquisitively.

"We should go," she said with a trembling voice.

The creature shook its fur, grabbed the abandoned stuffed owl in its jaws, and happily followed Cat as she began to walk out the back.

Steelton brought up every angle he could, intent on finding a way to help. He hacked around the carnival, too. He slowed the Gendarmerie, throwing up traffic blocks.

It had all been a corp set-up from the beginning, and he'd been too stupid to spot it.

He didn't need to drum his fingers. All he needed was to pay attention, and find the chance to help them out, even in the most minor ways. There was no way he was going to let Cat die this way.

Not on his watch. Not then. Not now.

Cat and the creature ducked as they ran, the giant spotlights of the festival all turned toward them. She dropped the camera blockers, well past the point of not being spotted, focusing on getting out alive.

"We have to move faster," she told the creature, who seemed to understand and picked up speed. She turned a corner, bringing up the map of the place in her mind, and ran straight into a clown. A large, angry, machine gun-wielding clown, bright red paint around his eyes picking up the bloodlust in them.

"*Tabar...*" she started to cast a spell, too slowly, surprised by the clown. The creature, however, wasn't so slow, dropping the owl as it bit down on the clown's arm. The clown grunted, pulled a knife and stabbed the creature, which yelped.

Cat slammed into him with a fireball spell. Oversized gloves and feet went flying back, singed red wig floating down. She knelt by the creature, dark red blood flowing from the wound.

"Shh," she said as it whined. "I'm going to get you out of here, but you need to trust me, okay?"

The creature's ears flattened, but she only felt fear, not anger. Her hand found warm fur and she gently stroked its head, then its cheek. It leaned into her hand, closing its eyes. Cat's heart ached. They'd built this creature for one purpose, and hadn't bothered showing it love, or affection, of any kind.

"It'll be okay," she whispered. "I'm going to pick you up."

The clown twitched. Cat leaned down, trusted the creature wouldn't bite her, and wrapped her arms around its neck and belly. It was lighter than she thought it would be, which was great, since it was pretty big.

Cat couldn't wield a weapon and carry the animal, but the van was only one building away. She just needed to reach it, and they could get out.

About to turn the corner, one of the spotlights turned red, making her stop. A small gargoyle flew by, claws outstretched. It would have hit her straight on if she hadn't stopped. Taking a deep breath, she hoped her luck would hold out.

He'd managed to make her pause, long enough to avoid being rammed into. The damn woman had the creature, and the thing was wounded. He could see the blood dribbling from its side onto Cat's leg as she cuddled the thing like it was a puppy. And had she just picked up a stuffed owl for the creature? *Merde.* Everyone was trying to kill it, and she was trying to save it.

That wouldn't turn out well, but he wasn't surprised. He'd fallen in love with her partly because of her heart.

"Damn it, Cat," he muttered as he kept an eye out on how else he could help her.

Was that an animatronic elephant charging her?

The elephant came down on her, trunk moving wildly from side-to-side, sweeping at everything in its path. Cat dodged, trying to avoid the crazed thing, scrambling as quickly as she could. The creature panted in her arms.

The giant metal trunk missed her by a few centimeters. She stumbled back, arms clutching the creature. The elephant shrieked and collapsed on its back legs.

Horus walked in front of it, sheathing his favorite katana, stared wide-eyed at the pile of bloodied white fluff in her arms. Without question, he grabbed her arm and pulled her past the elephant, the two keeping low as a few lights above them malfunctioned, casting their path into blessed darkness.

Steelton turned off more lights, cracked his fingers. Cat wasn't in his feed anymore, but he counted his breaths at the steps she'd be taking, imagining her jumping in the van. The whole team was there, so they wouldn't tarry. He flipped to another security camera, one on the street. The corp had rigged this whole area, of course. They'd wanted to make sure the creature was destroyed.

He saw the van approach the intersection, and made sure every light was in their favor, then scrambled the corp's feeds. They had a hacker with them, but they weren't that good. Not better than him, anyway.

The corp wouldn't like losing the runners, but he'd figure out some away to convince them the whole team was dead.

Them, and the creature.

This was his mess to clean up, after all.

Cat took the credstick Steelton pushed across the table they sat at in *Café Malice*. They hadn't said two words. She still hurt from the mission, but she'd come here, as agreed beforehand. He'd seemed both pleased and distressed to see her, as seemed to be their new normal.

"I didn't give you the creature," she said when she saw the entire amount was there.

"I didn't ask." He shrugged. He drummed his fingers. Ten seconds. He remained silent.

"This felt like a trap," she said, voice thin.

More drumming. The man was infuriating. He was never good at sharing. Now? It was even worse. But, then again, she owed him his due.

"I noticed a few...anomalies, tech-wise, while we were escaping." She knew now she'd dropped Sketch's camera blockers because she'd wanted Steelton's aid. He'd given it, like she knew he would. That elated and annoyed her, in equal parts.

Still, he said nothing. That tipped the scales firmly into annoyed territory. "Sketch might not be you, but she's still damn good. And she saw someone else helping out. Saving us from getting geeked, even."

"They'll look for the creature," he said, not confirming Sketch's theory, but not disputing it either. *At least he's finally talking.*

The bell clanked above the door, and Cat finished her latte in silence as a customer grabbed their drink and left. She felt the gentle pull of Cotton Candy—the name had been the creature's idea, not Cat's—wondering when she'd come back.

Patience, she told her, smiling softly. She'd lost a mission. Looked like they'd have to get out of the city, at least for a while. But she'd definitely made a new friend.

And they'd all made it out alive.

She looked at Steelton. At those eyes that always sang to her. Probably always would.

"You could come with us," she said softly.

To her surprise, he seemed to hesitate. And drummed his fingers.

She waited him out...waited for those ten seconds to go by.

Silence blanketed the café, and he didn't move.

Cat stood, leaned in, kissed him on the lips. "Thanks for hesitating. *Au revoir*, Steelton."

The bell rang her departure.

Steelton watched Cat climb into the van. She opened the side door, white fluff happily bouncing on her before she pushed the creature back and jumped in, sliding the door shut.

Triny laughed, Sketch beside her looking happy. Horus was probably in the back, sharpening something or other.

They'd been his family, once, too. He wished he'd have done things differently. He and Cat had broken up, sure, but he hadn't needed to leave. If he hadn't gotten drunk, looked for a way out...he sighed. No point thinking about it now.

He realized he was drumming his fingers on his lap, his other hand loose at his side.

By the time the ten seconds were done, the van was already gone.

Steelton looked at the empty street for a few more moments, then turned around and headed back to his office. He had to find more runners for the next job.

That's what a fixer did to survive, after all.

THE PRICE OF ART

Andrew Peregrine

London doesn't like you.

You can see it in the buildings all around you; old stones clutching their centuries to themselves and sneering as they loom over you. *You aren't strong enough to endure like us*, they say. *You aren't made of the right stock.*

But as Montpelier had been told this all his life, it made him feel quite at home. At school he was "troll boy" and had to suffer plenty of taunts. When he got bigger, so much bigger than any of them, the taunts didn't stop, they just fell silent. He could see them in every look they gave him. It didn't matter he had a degree in art history or could tie his tie with more than just a Windsor knot, even with his huge hands. He would always be just a "big dumb troll" to those people. So he went where the work was, security, bodyguard, anything to stay out of the military. But every now and again a job came along he could be pleased about, and this was one of them.

It was a simple guard job, but he was guarding something interesting for a change: a painting called "The Labyrinth of Riddles" by an unknown artist. He was under no illusion that it was his art expertise he'd been hired for rather than his physical stature. But he chose to believe it had given him the edge that made Jonathan "Elfin John" Leeds offer him the work compared to other similarly sized shadowrunners. And there were worse places to work. All he had to do was stand next to the painting in what had proved to be a very plush viewing room upstairs at Leeds' club, The Dark Side.

It was all rich carpet and elegant oak panels in this part of the large building, with a few other expensive paintings on the wall. There was a modest Vermeer on one, a large Klimt Montpelier was sure was a print on another. However, he was rather taken by "Judith at the Banquet of Holofernes" by Rembrandt, slightly hidden near a very ordinary example of one of Monet's many water lilies on another wall.

The various guests noticed none of these, though. To them, it was clear art was only worth what you could buy and sell it for. Leeds brought them in to allow them to look at the painting in the hope they might bid on it at his auction in a day or so's time. It was Montpelier's job to keep it safe until then, currently just by standing next to it and allowing his size to discourage any shenanigans. His role was not meant to be a speaking one, but he found it hard to resist. He liked to add the odd, unsolicited comment to explain certain aspects of the painting to the guests. That he spoke, and did so eloquently and articulately, was a revelation to most of them, and a shock to a fair few. Sadly, his knowledge didn't impress the boss.

"Monty," said Leeds, using a nickname Montpelier disliked while straightening his perfectly straight tie, "don't do that. People don't like to be made to feel stupid."

"Even if they are stupid?"

"*Especially* if they're stupid. Annoying the customers is bad for business."

It was hard to argue with that, but standing there all day did get boring. Once more, Montpelier was glad to have invested in a good pair of cushion insoles, the security guard's best friend. "The Labyrinth of Riddles" was at least worth the fuss, though. It was a very impressive example of early Middle Eastern art, although most of the guests only commented it was a little small for the asking price. At its center was an image of a sort of bearded lion creature, surrounded by the familiar geometric patterns of Islamic art. It was a beautiful example of the move from representative figures to patterns and calligraphy in Middle Eastern art, and Montpelier was genuinely happy he'd had this opportunity to study it.

There was only really one problem: The painting was a fake.

It was a very good one, that much was certain, but it didn't take Montpelier too long to notice the mistake. It was in the calligraphy. The artist had used a couple of modern styles of script rather than what was correct at the time. Arabic script had taken a few different forms over the centuries and while Montpelier couldn't read it, he knew the various forms reasonably well. This was the wrong one. Unfortunately, if he could spot the fake, so would a qualified assessor. Leeds had a certificate of authenticity for the work, so he'd either owned the real painting at one time or paid a lot of money to get the accreditation. But any new buyer would probably get their own expert to assess it, if only for the insurance valuation. They'd spot the fake easily and that would be Elfin John's reputation destroyed. People trusted him to deliver reliable and trustworthy high-end goods. A loss of reputation could mean a loss of his entire business, and he wasn't foolish enough to take that sort of risk.

The unfortunate conclusion was that the painting had been real when it was originally assessed, and someone had stolen it recently. This meant it had gone missing on Montpelier's watch, or thereabouts. Even if it didn't, he'd probably get the blame, especially if he was the one to bring it to anyone's attention. If he kept quiet, someone was going to notice sooner or later, and then he was in serious trouble. Leeds generally played fair, but this was business, and the loss of the painting wasn't going to be met with just a shrug.

Montpelier had to find the original, and soon. To do that, he was going to need help...or he was royally screwed.

"The way I see it," Cassandra said in her upper-class purr, "is that you are royally screwed."

"Thanks for that incisive assessment," replied Montpelier, doubly glad he'd come to this overpriced bar in Soho just to get sass from an ex-corporate mage. He'd even bought the first round. "Maybe you could offer me some *useful* advice?"

Cassandra grinned and ran a hand through her multi-colored, once blond hair as she thought. Montpelier caught a glimpse of some of the metal studs that betrayed her reflex-enhancing cybernetics. Such augmentations were rare for a mage, and Cassandra usually kept them hidden. She'd showed a lot of promise with magic, and coming from old money, she'd gotten the best corporate training available. But the company was greedy; they thought her magic could handle a little cyberware to speed her up and make her a lethal agent. Cassandra had been loyal and naïve enough to agree, and while the augmentations had worked, they had also gutted her magic potential, as anyone with any sense would have known. She didn't lose everything though, and as she'd trained as a tracker, she specialized in divination magic. If she couldn't be good at everything, she figured she'd be great at one thing. If you needed to find someone or something, she was among the best London had to offer.

Cassandra and Montpelier weren't alone, but you'd be forgiven for failing to notice the rat shaman in the booth with them. Gizmo was quiet and skittish, his elven ears always slightly twitching and looking out for trouble. Montpelier wasn't quite sure what use he really was, as it wouldn't take even a decent gust of wind to blow him over. But he was Cass's partner, and Montpelier was in no position to argue about the help he was getting.

"Tell me about the frame," Cassandra said, fixing Montpelier with a look that was suddenly all business. "Do you think the fake is in the original one?"

Montpelier had to think, but it seemed highly likely the thieves had swapped out the frame. It would have taken extra time, but it would have saved having to make a forgery of the frame as well. Not for the first time, he was glad the thieves were professionals and had not cut it from the frame with a knife and forced it into a tube. He cringed every time he saw it done in a trideo, almost feeling the delicate paint shatter and crack as it was rolled up.

"I think this was a professional job, so they swapped the canvases out. Why?"

"Well, if it is the original frame, there may still be a connection to the painting. If so, it's a connection I might be able to follow."

"So, I'll need to steal the forgery, too."

"Well, just the frame. That's not especially valuable, is it?" Cassandra smirked.

"This day gets better and better," muttered Montpelier. "But maybe getting you in will be easier than getting the frame out."

Getting into The Dark Side was easy. Montpelier was an employee, after all, and he knew all the bouncers. Cassandra tucked herself against him and giggled drunkenly a lot. It seemed pretty clear to the doormen that he was just trying to impress a girl by taking her into one of London's hottest private clubs. A nod was all it took to walk past the velvet rope. Once they were inside, the rather more sober look Cassandra gave Montpelier made him appreciate that he owed her extra for that particular performance.

The Dark Side was many things to many people, presided over by Jonathan Leeds, a man who would be impressive and dangerous even if he wasn't a mage. Montpelier had no plans to run into him tonight, though. One side of the old city hall was a nightclub, the other a more salubrious gentleman's club for the wealthy. There was even a fine dining restaurant and who knew what else in the huge building. Montpelier could get into most parts of the place, but Cassandra wasn't on any sort of guest list. Luckily, as they wove through the corridors, her small silhouette was mostly hidden by Montpelier's bulk. Trolls are big enough to take up most of your visual field and a lot of your attention, even just passing by. Cassandra also knew how to stay in his shadow.

There were a few guards in the corridors, people Montpelier knew by name and little else. Most just assumed if he was with her, Cassandra must have a right to be there, so they just nodded at Montpelier and carried on past.

Unfortunately, just as they got close to the painting display room, they ran into Neonshade, one of the higher-ranking goons. Neonshade had spent a lot of nuyen on a cybernetic eye, and was always looking to prove himself to Elfin John.

"You want to stop right there, Monty. You didn't think to take that pistol off the little lady, did you? Parashield DART pistol if I'm not mistaken, and I'm not."

Cassandra noticeably winced at "little lady," clearly fighting an urge to do some sort of violence. But she kept control of herself and handed her weapon to Montpelier. "I'm sorry, Montpelier," she said, emphasizing the full use of his name. "I should have given you this before."

Montpelier took the gun and stared at Neonshade as if to ask "we done?"

Neonshade shrugged. "Just trying to look after you, big guy. Can't make those sorts of mistakes and expect to get a promotion." He smirked and continued on his way. Once he was around the corner, Montpelier handed Cassandra her pistol back with a muttered apology.

The door to the painting display room was very secure, but Montpelier could still open the maglock with his palmprint and security passkey. Even the few paintings in the room had a combined value you could retire on, and retire on very well. If you sold them to the right people at the right time, your whole family could retire.

"How long do you need?" asked Montpelier as he watched the corridor as best he could with the door only slightly ajar.

"Ten minutes," Cassandra replied, drawing a circle around the painting on its easel with tailor's chalk. "By which, I mean a *good* ten minutes. Not ten minutes with a lot of gunfire and assorted violence going on behind me while I'm concentrating."

"Copy that," muttered Montpelier, hoping fate did not decide otherwise.

Cassandra stepped back and focused on the painting and its frame. Her eyes slowly rolled back into her skull as she muttered arcane words. Montpelier was no magician, but he could feel the air become static. The room somehow felt larger, more connected, and the colors seemed to shift and change. The elegant carpet became grey, and the wooden panels shifted to a red brick color. Cassandra reached out, as if grasping for something unseen, until her arm swung out to her right, pointing toward East London and the docks. The room gradually began to reassert itself and she visibly relaxed.

It seemed she did so too soon. A flash of green energy coalesced in front of the painting with a loud *crack*, as if two realities had snapped apart violently. As soon as it appeared, the green fire launched at Cassandra, slamming into her like a sledgehammer and knocking her across the room.

Montpelier ran over to her, not that he had much idea what to do if she was badly hurt. Thankfully it only took a couple of moments for her to come round. Montpelier was about to ask if she was okay when her hand swung like lightning to her belt, pulling out the elegant Parashield DART pistol. Montpelier took a step back to pull out his own handgun, a huge Remington Roomsweeper that was large enough to look ordinary in his massive hands, but Cassandra wasn't aiming at him.

Behind them, Neonshade had arrived to see what the noise was, and for his trouble he was met with a very satisfying volley of darts from Cassandra's gun. Before he had had a chance to take in the situation, the well-dressed thug dropped to the floor.

"I thought you were guarding the door," she said, picking herself up and reloading her pistol. She gave Neonshade a short kick, both to make sure he was out, and because he deserved it.

"I was! But you were... Hang on, is he...?" spluttered Montpelier.

"Yes. You're a sweetie, but watch the door next time. Sedative darts, to answer your other question. You don't think I'd kill one of Leeds' men, do you? I'm in no mood to leave London, or England, for that matter, in that much of a hurry."

"Did you get anything?"

"Yes, good news and bad news. I got a very clear sight of the painting in a warehouse in the docklands. I can still feel the pulse of it, like a homing beacon. But that's the bad news. It's strong because someone is working magic with it. Something ritual and powerful, too. That was what caused the backlash. I might have screwed with it, blundering in like that. That's the good news. So they might have to start again. It might have bought us some time. But they know something is up now."

They needed to move, and fast. While guards tended to patrol alone inside the building, it wouldn't be long before another one came along, or Neonshade came to. The inevitable explanations would take too long to get to the painting in time. They went for the less subtle approach and just ran. While most people get out of the way of a charging troll, it tends to raise the alarm.

By the time they got to the ground floor, there was a string of guards behind them. Neonshade was in the lead, having mostly recovered, and he was not pleased. However, he still wasn't over the effects of the darts, and kept tripping over or knocking into his comrades.

Cassandra covered their rear with a few more well-placed tranq darts as Montpelier led the way and cleared a path with his sheer bulk. Unfortunately, the guards had predicted Montpelier was heading for the kitchen, and decided to make a stand just outside it. There were three of them, Anna, Scarlet, and Biarritz, who Montpelier really rather liked. But he couldn't stop, not now. They held up their hands for him to stop, and he waved at them to clear aside as he powered toward them. Thankfully, no one wanted to shoot at each other, but only

Anna stepped aside at the last minute before Montpelier knocked Scarlet and Biarritz aside like skittles.

"Sorry!" he shouted over his shoulder, which Cassandra echoed with a shrug. It seemed unlikely they would be asking him to join them in the pub again anytime soon though. Montpelier and Cassandra crashed through the restaurant kitchen to the screams and shouts of the staff, barreled out the back door, and hit the smog-laden streets behind the club at a run.

It looked like they had lost their pursuers in the streets, but they didn't stop until they got back to Gizmo in their getaway vehicle. There were relatively few vehicles a troll like Montpelier could fit in, let alone drive; but the minivan allowed him to sit comfortably in the back, as long as most of the seats were taken out. Cassandra slid into the passenger seat next to Gizmo and told him to drive. As they set off, Cassandra handed Gizmo one of the two strawberry tarts she'd stolen from the kitchen on the way through.

"These are just to die for," she said, taking a luxurious bite. Montpelier stared at her in disbelief. "Aw sweetie, you should have picked one up for yourself. I've only got two hands." Gizmo grinned as he nibbled his own tart, steering them toward East London with his free hand at Cassandra's direction.

This late in the evening the traffic wasn't as bad as it could be. Montpelier kept an eye out for pursuit, but they seemed to have gotten away clean. That was what worried him. Leeds wouldn't need to chase him down; he'd know who had just fled his club. The only thing keeping them alive right now might be that Leeds wouldn't know what on earth had caused them to leave so swiftly, and take down some of his guards along the way.

"Don't worry, big guy." Cassandra passed Montpelier the last of her strawberry tart with a side of guilt and pity. "We'll get the painting back and explain it all to Elfin John. He's a rational man; he'll respond to a rational conversation."

Montpelier swallowed the remains of the tart in one sullen gulp. He hoped Cassandra was right, but if she wasn't, they'd probably be dead before they even figured out how to get out of town.

Silently, they drove around the winding streets toward the outskirts of the city. Montpelier didn't feel like talking.

Both Cassandra and Gizmo concentrated on the road and the directions.

Gradually, the light and stone of the old city began to give way to tower blocks and residential areas. Each district had its own style, and sometimes it felt like they had skipped into another city entirely.

Finally, the rows of shops, blocks, and arcades faded into the more industrial areas of the docklands. There were even some wealthy residences here on the waterfront, but soon enough the gray shapes of warehouses, shipping crates, and cranes became the overriding features.

Winding around a couple more empty access roads, Gizmo drew the minivan up outside a quiet looking warehouse at Cassandra's instruction.

"Here we are," said Cassandra. "Looks concerningly quiet, doesn't it?"

"I'll be back in a moment," said Montpelier, sliding open the door quietly.

"Hold on big guy, we're not going to let you go alone," she said, glancing at Gizmo, who shook his head nervously. "Okay, I'm not going to let you go alone." Cassandra slipped out of the van as Montpelier clambered out of the side door. She drew a pistol and checked it. No dart pistol this time; this was a heavier but no less elegant Ares Predator handgun. "Can you give us some eyes, Giz?"

Gizmo nodded and coaxed two inquisitive-looking rats out of his coat. They ran along his arms and skipped onto Cassandra's shoulder before jumping down onto the ground. With a distant look in his eyes, Gizmo nodded to her, and the rats scampered off toward the building.

Working in tandem, the rats, under Gizmo's control, led Cassandra and Montpelier into the warehouse. One of the rats scouted ahead, the other kept standing on its hind legs, indicating with its forepaws whether Cassandra and Montpelier should follow or pause. Cassandra and Montpelier tracked behind them through a side door as quietly as they could, guns drawn and held low, just waiting for trouble.

The first guard, an orc with a string of tattoos up his right arm, was smoking a cigarette and not really paying much attention. He never knew what hit him. The second was a tall woman, maybe even an elf, who came around a corner between the piles of shipping crates and was blindsided by

Montpelier's fist. She went down hard, with Cassandra wincing at the sound of a couple of bones popping. He just picked up the third guard, a dwarf with a nasty scar on his face, by the neck. He clawed at the troll's immense hand around his throat for a few seconds, with no breath to scream, until he finally passed out.

Despite going down fairly easily, the guards were professionals, not just standard warehouse security. Without Gizmo's rats scouting ahead to give Cassandra and Montpelier the drop on them, it would have been a nasty stand-up fight.

Weaving between the crate stacks, avoiding another two guards, Cassandra and Montpelier hunkered down to see what was going on in the open space in the middle of the warehouse.

In a large clearing surrounded by crates, the painting canvas rested, frameless, on an easel. Facing it in a semi-circle were ten black-robed figures, all chanting and swaying. Another figure stood a few steps closer to the painting, making arcane gestures in the air. He was clearly the leader, his cloak a deep burgundy rather than black, with magical symbols embroidered around the hem. Trails of energy ran out from his fingertips as he moved, drawing occult patterns that hung in front of him. The painting itself appeared unharmed, but seemed to glow, as if lit from behind. The space inside the warehouse felt tense and close. There was a pressure in the air.

"Well, this is great," muttered Montpelier. "What happened to the old days where people just stole paintings for money?"

"Looks like a summoning to me," whispered Cassandra. "We may have messed it up a little with my location spell, but this feels like it's coming to a finale."

"What are they summoning? Do I even want to know?"

"You said the painting is old Middle Eastern? My guess would be something like a shedim. There are legends that say some of the really old ones were bound in objects by ancient mages."

"So, it's bad?"

"Yeah, like 'Dragon bad.' With a summoning like this it's hard to make the connection, but once you do, the creature can often push its way in from the other side. Then it all gets very messy."

Montpelier nodded. "Ah. Well, I didn't have a plan anyway. Frontal assault it is."

He stood and walked briskly toward the painting. Before the assembly had quite registered his presence, he'd leveled his enormous handgun at the lead magician and blasted two holes in him. He collapsed like a puppet with its strings cut. The hood of his cloak fell back to reveal a well-groomed middle-aged man, more like a company executive than a mad cultist.

As the leader dropped, the magical energies he'd been manipulating spun out in every direction. Montpelier was hit twice by something hot and stinging as the other magicians scattered for cover. He nearly reached the painting before automatic fire began dancing all around him.

The sound of Montpelier's monstrous handgun and the magical explosions had brought several guards running, all of whom found the intruding troll an obvious target. They were probably mercenaries, given the variety of men, women, and metahumans. But they were all in neat black suits, possibly with an armored fabric layer. Whoever these cultists were, they clearly had a very corporate brand.

Bullets showered Montpelier, but luckily his thick skin and an even thicker armor jacket protected him from the worst of the fusillade. As he reached the painting and scooped it off the easel, the gunfire almost immediately stopped. It seemed the guards were well-trained enough not to shoot at the most valuable thing in the room.

Before Montpelier could make a run for it with his prize, something cold and sharp hit him square in the back, knocking him flat onto his face and sending the painting skidding across the floor, thankfully face up. Behind him, the lead mage stood, and he was angry, but apparently more for being interrupted than shot. As Montpelier rolled over to bring his pistol to bear, he could see clear through one of the holes he'd put in him, which was slowly knitting shut.

"You dare!" the magician-executive shouted as another lethal shaft of ice formed in his hand, ready to spear Montpelier.

"Yeah, we both do," said Cassandra, coming out of nowhere on her wired reflexes and emptying her pistol into his back. The mage dropped like a stone, and Montpelier pulled Cassandra to the ground to shield her as another wave of bullets ricocheted across the area. With her using him grudgingly as a shield, they scampered across to the painting and snatched it up. It was still glowing, but they both ignored that, as they had bigger problems to worry about.

Guards were coming out of every part of the warehouse, and Cassandra ran as fast as she could with the painting. Montpelier covered their escape, his Remington Roomsweeper being true to its name and blasting large holes in anything it passed. Each dull thud shattered either bone or wooden crate, scattering splinters everywhere.

Outside the warehouse, Cassandra and Montpelier allowed themselves a moment to breathe. He sent two more rounds back through the warehouse door to keep their pursuers honest.

"You okay?" asked Cassandra.

Montpelier's armored suit jacket was shredded, and he was bleeding from several small wounds. "Nothing a good tailor can't fix," he replied, tearing off the ragged remains of what was his best suit jacket.

Together, they ran toward the minivan, sitting innocently in the car park, as guards came tentatively out of the warehouse, wary of Montpelier's pistol. Gizmo had already started the engine and rammed it into gear before they were even inside. He floored the accelerator and the vehicle skidded unsteadily onto the road.

While there was little the guards on foot could do to catch them, the rest of their colleagues had not given up. With a crash, two heavy sedans smashed out of the warehouse and swerved onto the road behind them.

Bouncing over a barrier verge, Gizmo drove out of the industrial estate and began heading for the central city. But Cassandra grabbed the wheel and swung it hard in the other direction at a fork.

"Not the city," she said. "We'll get stopped in traffic and then they'll be on us. We need to get on the North Circular and lose them there."

Gizmo wasn't happy, but Cassandra was right. The small, winding streets of central London would be jammed and slow whatever the time of day. Once the traffic stopped them, their pursuers would just gun them down at their leisure. But the North Circular Road was a wide freeway arcing through North London. It would be busy and foggy, but faster than the other roads. They might lose their pursuers in the smog, if they were lucky.

Undergoing stresses its suspension was not designed to endure, the minivan bounced across the next intersection and onto the North Circular motorway, against the instruction of the traffic lights. Vehicles screeched to a halt in a cacophony of horns, only for their drivers to become more enraged at the two sedans powering past them after the minivan. But as soon as men and women in black suits leaned out of each of the sedans and fired guns, the citizens decided it wasn't any of their business.

"Warning," said the rather well-spoken digital driving AI. *"Due to visibility restrictions, automatic vehicle operation is advised."* Gizmo just pushed his foot harder on the accelerator and all three of them prayed there wasn't anything too solid in each bank of smog.

Cassandra tore off some of the cladding on the door to reveal a small stash of weapons. She pointed to the wall in the back for Montpelier to do the same as she grabbed another Predator handgun and hurriedly loaded both. Then she punched open the sunroof and stood up with a pistol in each hand, spraying a wash of bullets over the closest sedan. Its windscreen spider-webbed with fractures and a few holes while the rest of the bullets sparked off the bodywork.

One of her bullets hit the driver, causing him to lose control of the car. It hit the central barrier hard, momentum picking the car up like a toy and flipping it over into the other lane. Cassandra dropped back into the passenger seat with a rather smug look on her face and reloaded.

"Lucky shot," muttered Montpelier. He leaned out the window and fired off three precise shots with his Roomsweeper. They hit the second sedan with a dull thud, but didn't seem to do much damage. "Second one is armored, probably why it was slower," he shouted. "And it's got a rocket launcher!"

"It has a *what*?"

One of the guards was standing up through the remaining sedan's sunroof, a steely look on her face and a rocket launcher over her shoulder. Montpelier and Cassandra watched in horror as a blossom of flame roared out the back of the launcher, and the rocket launched straight at them from its front.

Gizmo spun the car hard to the right, and the rocket exploded right next to them. Fire washed under and around the vehicle, and they all felt the heat through the windows. Small flames appeared on the upholstery and the minivan creaked and groaned ominously. There was no way they could take another hit, or even another close miss.

Doesn't anyone have any respect for fine art anymore?" shouted Montpelier. "If they keep firing rockets, the painting will be burnt to a crisp!"

"Not this painting." Cassandra nodded at the canvas on the floor of the vehicle. It glowed with power, rippling slightly like the surface of a lake. "I think the shedim, or whatever it is, still wants out. Fire might just give it more energy."

"One problem at a time," replied Montpelier. "People shooting rockets at us first, eldritch beings from beyond the universe second."

"As long as it's a close second," said Cassandra, standing up again and opening up with her pistols against the sedan. Sparks flew from the bonnet and windscreen, but the bullets hit only armor.

Montpelier leaned out the back window and landed several precise, powerful, and completely ineffectual shots at the sedan. Just then the minivan began to slow and settled itself into a nice peaceful driving speed on the motorway. The gentle voice of the British vehicle AI lilted over the amazed faces of Cassandra and Montpelier.

"You are now in automated driving mode, sit back and enjoy your journey. Navigation has been engaged."

The sedan gained at an alarming rate, and the guard with the rocket launcher stood up to level her weapon at them again. She took her time to aim, knowing this would be the last shot she needed. Gizmo, in the driver's seat, had his eyes closed and his hands peacefully in his lap as the minivan pilot program offered the passengers a series of easy listening options to while away their journey. Cassandra and Montpelier curled up in the back of the vehicle to take what cover they could as another rocket fired toward them.

The impact of the rocket hit the minivan hard, spinning it around as it pushed it forward. It smashed sideways into another car, locking both together to the wide-eyed horror of the other occupants, who had clearly expected a less eventful Sunday drive. The two vehicles spun along the road like partners in a waltz before they finally came to a rest with a *thud* against the crash barrier.

Only once the minivan had come to a rest did Montpelier wonder why he hadn't been burned to a crisp. Glancing at Gizmo, he could see him curled tightly into a ball in the driver's seat, one hand poking up covered in purple static, the same color as the cloud of energy which now surrounded the minivan. He'd got his shield up in time, enough to stop the explosion and flames, if not quite all the impact. As the static dissipated, Gizmo opened his palm and Cassandra slapped it with a high five.

"Your vehicle has suffered damage, and roadside assistance is now being alerted. Please review your recent driving choices and consider if you may be at fault in any way for the condition of your vehicle," the minivan's voice admonished.

"My turn," announced Montpelier, kicking open the rear door and sliding out of the minivan.

The sedan had powered past them, but was coming back for another try. The guard was still standing, but tilted the launcher down as she reloaded it for another shot.

Standing directly in their path, Montpelier braced himself and took aim with his pistol, allowing his cybersenses to guide his hand as the sedan roared toward him. Letting out a single breath, he squeezed the trigger and sent a bullet at the launcher-wielding guard.

It hit her in the shoulder, knocking her slightly rather than doing any damage. She almost had a moment to smile as she prepared to heft the rocket launcher again. But killing her wasn't the plan, and Montpelier's shot had gone exactly where he'd wanted it to. The impact had caused the guard to twitch her finger on the rocket launcher while it was still dipped into the car. Flames erupted from every window as it sped past Montpelier like a comet before smashing into a barrier.

Montpelier was about to let out a sigh of relief, but then he heard Cassandra call from behind him. "A little help here!"

Turning around, he saw there wasn't much he could do.

Cassandra and Gizmo were out of the broken minivan with the painting. Now it wasn't just glowing, its colors were shifting and changing, like a storm trying to push out of the canvas. He ran over as the traffic began to pick up again on the motorway. The wreckage of the minivan and the two sedans were causing traffic queues, but as the smog still lay heavily over the road, no one really suspected anything out of the ordinary. Anyone whose car had been damaged had left the area as quickly as they could when rocket launchers and heavy pistols had started getting used.

Following Cassandra and Gizmo, Montpelier clambered down the grass verge by the motorway toward the poorer residential areas squashed up close to it. Away from the road, the sound of oncoming sirens, and potentially awkward questions, they set the canvas on the street. Cassandra pulled out some chalk and hastily drew a circle around it, then started scrawling sigils around the edge. Gizmo drew out some sort of fetish made of bones and fur, and his two pet rats dove deeper into his coat pockets, not wanting to take any chances.

Gizmo and Cassandra then stood up and held hands, offering their others to Montpelier so he could complete the circle.

"I'm not a magician," he said, clearly stating the obvious.

"It's not about magic now, it's about will," Cassandra replied. "Just focus on trying to close the portal with your mind."

Montpelier did as he was told. Cassandra and Gizmo both closed their eyes and muttered in a language he didn't understand.

As he closed his eyes, he could feel the painting on the ground in front of him. In his mind it wasn't a painting but a hole, a vast cavernous abyss. Through it he could see something huge, ancient, and powerful pushing to climb out. With all his might, he tried to imagine the cavern closing, the sides of the painting folding over and shutting out the darkness. Gradually, painfully, the portal began to respond.

As the pressure increased, it felt as if the shedim was trying to break out of Montpelier's head rather than the painting. But he managed to push through the pain that threatened to tear his skull apart, and slowly the portal closed. But just before it did, something dark in the shadows stared out into Montpelier's mind. It would remember him, would remember all of them, and it would be back one day...

The three shadowrunners were far too exhausted to try any grand escapade to return the painting. Elfin John would know anyway. Almost on cue, a large black sedan pulled up next to them. Anna, Scarlet, and Biarritz stepped out, looking annoyed and still bruised from their recent encounter with Montpelier by the kitchen.

"Boss wants a word with you," said Anna in her East End drawl. Cassandra and Gizmo glared at Montpelier, along with

Scarlet and Biarritz. "We'll clear up here; the boss is a generous donor to the police benevolent fund. A few words in the right ear will sort out the traffic issues you just caused."

Scarlet opened the back door to the car. "Get in," she said. "All of you."

There was nothing to do but do as they were told. They rode back to the club in silence with Scarlet. Any other day, a ride in a car like this would be luxurious instead of ominous.

At the door of the club, Big Ron the troll bouncer just waved them all through, and they all headed up to see Elfin John.

Jonathan Leeds barely acknowledged their presence as they entered his office. He took the painting from Montpelier as if absentmindedly accepting a delivery. He stared in silence at the painting for a while, checking the condition and the sides of the canvas before placing it on a nearby easel.

"We'll have to put it back in the proper frame, but otherwise it looks in good condition," he said to the room in general, but seemingly for Montpelier's benefit. "Thank you, all of you. You are free to go. Although, I have another viewing tomorrow, Montpelier, if you would like the work again."

"You still want me to work for you?"

"Of course, you all did very well."

Montpelier began to splutter in confusion, but Gizmo narrowed his eyes and Cassandra spoke up first. "You knew it was a fake, didn't you?"

"Knew? I had the fake commissioned when I realized the original had been stolen, annoyingly efficiently I might add."

"So why not send someone to get it back for you?"

Leeds smiled, "I did. I employed the only troll in London who knows the difference between a Rembrandt and a Renoir to stand guard over it."

"But—But I'd have gone after the painting for you, Mr. Leeds," Montpelier said. "You just needed to give me the job."

"I'm sure you would have. But I wasn't sure how good you were. Anyway, a couple of days guard duty and a cheap forgery are a lot more economical than hiring three expert shadowrunners to go up against a group of professional thieves and cultists with magical talent. You even used up a favor to bring in the help of Miss Cassandra and her friend. Now I have my painting back, and this cult has a problem with you and not me. You even threw in an impromptu security drill for my staff. I call that a good day's work."

Cassandra punched Montpelier hard on the arm. Gizmo glared at him.

"As I said," continued Leeds. "It was a good day for me, but also a good audition for you. You'll find an appropriate bonus in all your bank accounts, and you'll be hearing from me again soon. I've also given you all a year's membership to The Dark Side as well, so buy yourselves a drink on the way out. You may have done a lot of damage to the North Circular Road and a few of my guards, but I recognize talent and good teamwork. Hopefully the guards you treated like tenpins will have no hard feelings, but that's up to you to deal with."

Montpelier, Cassandra, and Gizmo stood there in shock as Leeds handed each of them a personal Dark Side membership card as if nothing had happened. He returned to his desk to admire the painting, looking up a moment later at the frozen trio as if to ask, *Are you still here?*

Fumbling into each other, the three decided to get out of the office before Elfin John changed his mind. They were all downstairs in the bar before they got their wits back together.

"I think you owe us both a drink, an expensive one, and more of those strawberry tarts," said Cassandra, poking Montpelier with the sharp corner of her new membership card.

"Fair enough," he said as he paled a little looking at the prices. But it was still a small price to pay. It had been an expensive way to get an interview, but like Montpelier always said: "London really doesn't like you."

However, maybe after today, it hated him just a little bit less.

A TALE FOR MUNCHAUSEN'S MERRIMENT

Jennifer Brozek

It was just another night in the novahot Matrix club, *Munchausen's Merriment*. To get in, you had to answer an entertainment trivia question. If you failed, you had to return to the end of the queue. If you succeeded, you were allowed in (after paying the cover fee) and given a random avatar of a once-famous entertainment character—these came from all walks of the entertainment industry: music, movies, serials, streamers—then you were assigned a table to play the game. You received all the "free" drinks you wanted, as long as you entertained the table when it was your turn.

The goal, of course, was to win the table by telling the best, most entertaining story of all. This was a social thing and had to be won organically. While it sounds like it wouldn't work, when a series of strangers got together to tell fantastical tales—that may or may not be true—there was usually a clear winner. That person got the joy of basking in the others' admiration, but the true goal was to convince at least one person at the table to recommend you as a Featured Storyteller; a role that came with numerous tangible and intangible benefits that included cold, hard cash.

The trick to the perfect tale, I'd learned, was to put just enough of the truth in the story to make the lie seem plausible.

It had been a good evening, even though there were just two people at my table. One character I recognized. The other I didn't.

"...after that, the holodeck was quarantined for a full month." The woman in the futuristic blue tunic and red hair shook her head with a sigh. "I will never live it down."

Sherlock Holmes chuckled. "That was a good one, Doctor." He turned to me. "Well, Hypatia19, my cyber-elf friend, you've heard my outrageous tale and one from our chief medical officer. What do you have to match that?"

So that's who I was. If I remembered correctly, Hypatia19 had been the protagonist of a popular crime trideo a decade back, an antihero of sorts. Appropriate for the setting, and for one of the stories I had prepared for the evening.

Pushing my hair behind my delicately pointed ear, I considered as we sat in the busy, comfortable Matrix bar. "Well, I've fought monsters and I've dealt with hallucinogenic disasters." I nodded to each of them in turn. "But tell me, have you ever heard the phrase, 'Shoot straight, conserve ammo, and never, ever deal with a dragon.'?"

My digital companions glanced at each other and nodded. I read the skepticism on their faces. I didn't blame them. It was a common enough warning in the shadows.

"That is what my tale is about." I paused. "Sort of. I will say, it's about the most unusual job I ever took, because I got to witness the end of the most outrageous run I've ever seen. And everything I'm about to tell you is true."

Sherlock motioned to the waitress and ordered another round for the table. "We are all ears."

"You ever enter a room and know something big has just gone down, but you don't know what because everyone has recovered themselves? This was like that. You see, I was hired to protect a fixer at a very important, but dangerous, meeting..."

"Remember, when I give you the signal, you get me out of there as fast and as quietly as you can. Don't draw attention to us. That's your job." The well-appointed dwarf rubbed his hands together, trying to soothe himself, then smoothed his expertly tailored pants.

"Yes, Mister—"

"And no names! Not for me. Not for you."

I nodded. "I understand, sir. I'm the Queen of No. No, they can't see us, hurt us, or follow us." I didn't boast. I was good at what I did. In this particular case, it was escort and protection duty. My client was paying me enough that I had a couple of my own people out there ready and waiting. One never knew. Especially with how tight-lipped my client was about the circumstances of the meet in one of the tallest skyscrapers in Seattle. At least I was already paid well with my "half up front" contract.

We were currently in the elevator, headed up to not quite the top floor, but close enough for government work. After fifty stories up, it didn't matter if we were heading up to the seventy-fifth or hundredth story. It was a fraggin' long fall either way. I, of course, had prepared for this.

Mr. Johnson squirmed and readjusted his suit for the thousandth time. I eyed him, but didn't say anything. Just waited for us to stop above the low-lying clouds that enveloped Seattle from time to time. I moved in front of my client as the elevator chimed our arrival and the doors slid open.

What greeted us was unusual but expected—I had been told that much. The large, round vestibule that usually led to the two different penthouses had been turned into a private dining room. In the back of the room was an octagonal table. Two human men sat opposite one another with an array of aperitifs and appetizers between them. Each man had a server hovering nearby. Off to the right was another table with a single chair behind it. The uniformed woman who met us at the elevator escorted us to this table.

My client took his seat and accepted the offered cocktail. She did not offer me one. Nor did I expect her to.

I messaged my client's commlink:

One drink an hour, please.

His response was terse:

Two.

Then he added:

But if we're here for longer than one hour, things have gone horribly wrong.

I noted this, and the time, with interest.

I watched the two men. One appeared to be Japanese, medium height, with salt-and-pepper black hair. The other appeared to be a Caucasian redhead, tall, with bright green eyes that twinkled as he nodded to me and my client. I say "appeared" because in this day-and-age of technology and magic it was hard to trust your eyes. Anything and everything can be masked in one way or another.

That said, my other focus was how to get out of the building as fast as possible. There were five doors I could see from my spot next to the wall. Two had numbers next to them, 750 and 755 respectively. Two had nothing to indicate they were anything more than closets or unmarked doors to one or the other of the penthouse apartments. The fifth door across the room from us had my interest. It was marked "*EXIT*," and had an unadorned lever handle and a heavy look to it. That had to be the stairs.

I focused on the elevator as I heard the faint chime of it rising to our floor—and only our floor tonight, that's how rich Mr. Johnson's clients were—and waited. When the elevator door opened, revealing four beat-to-drek people inside, I thought the uniformed woman would balk at their appearance. She didn't. Instead, she smiled and gestured toward Mr. Johnson's table. "You are expected."

The four people exited, in order: a muscular human male, fighter; a slight elf female, mage of some kind; a stout troll male, another fighter; and a skinny human female, decker. These, of course, were all guesses born from time spent in the shadows. Every one of them was armed. From long experience and with a keen eye, I could see the weapons hidden about their bodies in the small bulges, odd wrinkles, and draped fabric of their clothing.

The human fighter and the elf took point. The decker stood very close to the troll, who eyed the two men having appetizers with something akin to malice. I smelled the sweat, dirt, and weapons fire on them as they approached. All of them were adorned with blood, scrapes, bandages, and bruises. They also had the sense of hurried expectation, like they had almost missed the train.

My client nodded as he pulled a small kit from his pocket and opened it. It was some sort of chemical reader. "Ariadne, Casca." He glanced between them to acknowledge the rest of the party with a look. "You have it?"

Casca gestured to his companion. Ariadne unslung her bag and put it on the table before us. I was professional enough to not visibly tense at the gesture, but was still prepared to get my client out of harm's way if needed. The elf dipped her hand into the bag and pulled out a liter-sized jar filled with a clear liquid.

"Gotta test it," Mr. Johnson said.

Casca and Ariadne glanced at each other, then she nodded. "Of course."

He carefully unscrewed the top and took a dropperful of the liquid. Dripping it into the chemical reader's well, the entire room held its breath. I glanced at the two powerful men this whole show was for. Both of them were smiling with deep amusement and something more—anticipation?

A soft beep brought my attention back to my client and the runners.

"It's good," Mr. Johnson said. "As I explained at the start, there's another team due momentarily. They'll go through the same procedure. Once I deliver the goods to my clients, you'll be paid. Please wait over there." He gestured with his chin to the other side of the room.

This was something I didn't know was going to happen. My fault for not asking enough questions. It was unusual for multiple teams to finish runs and deliver the goods at the same time. It was suspicious and nerve-wracking for the teams and the fixer—but apparently, that's what these particular clients wanted.

The elevator chimed the imminent arrival of the second team. This one was mostly human with one ork. All male. Swarthy skin, the lot of them. And black hair. Cocky, with that young and immortal vibe. They looked dusty, battered, and exhausted. They, too, were armed to the teeth. The first one off the elevator was the ork; his sharp suit was wrinkled and stained, but of high quality. He held up a hand and looked around, eyeing the first team with suspicion.

"As agreed upon, Tamal. It's all good here," Mr. Johnson said.

Tamal nodded to the two men watching and snacking on their expensive amuse-bouche. "Them?"

"The clients," Mr. Johnson said. "Did you get it?"

This was another unusual bit to the mission. Runners typically never saw who hired them. That was the point of the middleman. To protect both sides.

I started to get a bad feeling about things. More than normal.

Tamal nodded and gestured his companions forward. "Bel, give it to him."

Bel—one of the three humans who could've been brothers, and probably were—stepped forward and pulled a small jar out of his pocket. Inside was something that looked like a ball of crystals. He put it on the table in front of Mr. Johnson with a trembling hand.

My client looked at it and nodded. "I'll have to test it."

Tamal grunted his agreement as Bel retreated back to his brothers, clustered in front of the elevator.

Mr. Johnson opened the jar and, using a pair of tweezers from the kit, broke off a tiny crystal from the ball. He dropped it into the well of his testing kit. Again, the entire room held its breath. This time with the added tension of the two armed teams eyeing each other with suspicion.

The soft *beep* heralded the beginning of the end. Raising his voice, Mr. Johnson said, "Once I deliver the goods to my clients, you will be paid. Please wait over there." He nodded to the side of the elevator. Tamal and the three humans took two grudging steps in that direction.

My guts twisted and I messaged my client.

What happens next?

He glanced up at me, irritated, but still answered.

I give the goods to my clients.
Then I pay the teams.

I thought quickly and tactically.

Right. I will escort you. After you pay the teams, we'll stand by the door with the exit sign.

Why?

For the love of Pete, I thought but texted,

Let me do my fraggin' job.

Fine.

As annoying as clients can be, this one listened. That's more than I can say for many of my clients. It probably saved his life. Mine, too.

Mr. Johnson stood. He picked up the jar with the ball of crystals. He looked up at me, then nodded to the jar with the clear liquid in it. "Pick that up, be careful with it, and follow me."

I did as I was told and followed Mr. Johnson, feeling every eye in the place on us. It made my skin itch. Mr. Johnson put the one jar in front of the Japanese man and indicated that I should put the other jar in front of the redheaded man. After I did, I stepped back, and incidentally, put my body between my client and what I thought at the time was the biggest danger in the room.

"Both specimens have been tested to the standards you gave me. Both are true. I will pay the teams now. Thank you. It's good doing business with you." My client bowed his head to both of them and waited.

"We'll see you in ten years," the redheaded man said.

I raised my eyebrow at that.

Mr. Johnson straightened and turned around. I stepped out of his way, then kept pace with him. Again, I was pleased the dwarf was smarter than most. He walked to the team by the elevator and handed Tamal a credstick. "Thank you."

Without waiting for an answer, he turned to the first team to arrive and moved to them with confident steps. He handed Casca a credstick. "Thank you."

I put my hand on Mr. Johnson's shoulder as we moved past them to stand next to the door with the exit sign.

Just as Tamal gestured for one of the brothers to hit the elevator button, the redheaded man spoke, his voice raised for the whole room to hear. "This, my friend, is going to impress." My heart sped up as he took the jar of liquid, opened it, and poured it into two lowball glasses. "Pure water dipped from Crater Lake itself. Unsullied by human hands." He picked up both glasses, offering one to his companion. "Taste the deep minerals and purity. This is: Of. The. Earth."

As we watched, the two men clinked glasses and drank. Both drank deeply, almost finishing their glasses in a single gulp. I spared a glance at the team that had fought to bring that jar of...water...here. I did not like the look on their faces.

"It is true, my friend, it is refreshing. There is no doubt. However, my offering cannot be denied," the Japanese man said as he slathered two pieces of crusty bread with butter. "This...this lovely gem...is a salt ball from the Dead Sea. Its taste and depth will speak for itself." With that declaration, he took the salt ball and put it into a salt grinder. With a few turns, both pieces of bread were well seasoned. He offered one to his companion. Both paused and took a bite, savoring the taste of the salted butter and fresh bread.

Bel muttered, "What the frag?"

I gauged the moods and looks of both teams as this outrageous and ostentatious display took place. The mood was ugly and dangerous. And, as I said before, they were all armed in one way or another. I took a step backward, pulling my client with me, pushing up against the cold metal door.

He came willingly enough, but said, "Wait. I need to know..."

The two men had the attention of the entire room. The redhead and the Japanese man savored the salted bread. The redhead sipped what was left of the water from Crater Lake. After a moment, the Japanese man did as well.

"I almost died for a *tasting contest?*" Ariadne asked the room.

"Not just any contest, my good Lady. One that has been waged for millennia. For the most valuable prize," the redhead man said.

I tightened my grip on my client's shoulder.

"Not yet," he hissed at me. "C'mon..." he muttered at the two men.

"A most valuable prize indeed," the Japanese man agreed. "One I have earned, I believe."

Grimacing with regret, the redhead nodded. "Yes, I think so, my friend. Here it is: a gold coin from King Solomon's treasure." He slid the coin to his dinner companion with sorrow.

The Japanese man did not wait. He plucked the coin from the table and put it in his mouth in a single smooth motion. His smile of satisfaction was interrupted by the chiming of the elevator door opening.

"You drekking son of a slitch!" Tamal cried and raised a pistol at the two men still engaged in their ages-old competition.

I didn't wait for my client to give me the word, though he was already saying, "Get me out of here," as I pulled him backward through the door and into the stairwell. I had a knife out and slit the back of his expensive suit jacket as we moved, revealing the harness I'd insisted he wear tonight. Gunfire erupted above us. We managed to sprint down two full flights of stairs before the first explosion knocked us to our knees and alarms began to wail.

I keyed my commlink. "We're coming out the west wall, above the sixtieth floor. Get ready."

"We're there," my team said. *"What's happening? A fireball just took out part of the penthouse."*

I didn't have time to answer. To my client I said, "Get down one more flight," as I set the shaped charge against the outside wall. He didn't ask any questions as the second explosion above us rocked the building and alarms blared.

Once I got to him, I covered him with my body and blew a hole in the side of the building. I yanked him to his feet and pulled him back up the flight of stairs to the hole I created. Without a word, I hooked him to me via the harness.

"Are you sure this is the best way?" he asked.

"How much longer do you think this building is going to stand?" I asked as the building was rocked again. "You and I are going to have a very long conversation after this."

He smiled at me in a way that made me feel naïve. Later, I would understand what that smile meant. For the immediate, we needed to survive what was happening around us.

I toggled my commlink. "Here we come."

Just before we jumped, Mr. Johnson said, "Make sure you look up."

I bent my head to my glass, then drank deep. "I didn't understand, but I did as he asked. Once we were out of the building and in freefall, and I knew my team was there to catch us, I looked up. I will never forget what I saw."

The medical doctor and Sherlock stared at me. "What did you see?" the doctor asked.

"You remember when I said this was a story about the phrase, 'Shoot straight, conserve ammo, and never, ever deal with a dragon.'?" They both nodded. "The problem comes when you don't know you're dealing with a dragon. When I looked up, watching the top of that skyscraper explode, I saw not one, but two silhouettes of dragons rising from the flames."

I stared at my drink, then drained it dry. "It seems these two dragons have been in a millennia-old competition to bring the best of *something* every ten years. The winner gets a piece of gold from the other's hoard. Apparently, gold from King Solomon's treasure is very tasty. As for my client, once a dragon decides they like doing business with you...you're stuck. He has a standing business arrangement with them every ten years until he dies."

Sherlock looked at me with a new sense of wonder, respect, and suspicion. "Are you talking about the Denny triangle incident from a few years back?"

I shrugged and smiled to myself. Only I knew the real answer to that question. I'd already won the table. It wouldn't do to reveal the truth of the tale now.

He leaned back and shook his head. "I don't know what to believe. Damn, that was good. You've got my recommendation for Featured."

I glanced at the doctor to see her reaction to my story.

Staring at me with awe and wonder, she asked, "Did you go to the next meeting?"

I put my empty glass on the table and replied, "That, my friends, is a tale for another time."

LIFE AT 9000 RPM

RJ Thomas

On a strip of runway off the (mostly) abandoned old Detroit International Airport, two turbocharged racing bikes pulled up to a white line. One looked like a hellhound, sleek and black, with flame-colored neon lights in the wheel wells. The other was low-slung, sporting a riot of neon-colors. Their engines revved, howling like banshees as a modified quad-rotor drone descended in front of them. Ten seconds later, underslung light-bars immediately went to red, to yellow...then green.

The two racers launched, trailing neon light into the darkness as a nearby crowd cheered. Less than sixty seconds later, two petrol-chem trucks bellowing flames from ornate pipes along their sides pulled up to the line.

However, the crowd wasn't watching the racers anymore.

A lean, athletic figure, clad in *real* leathers and sporting a red stripe tattoo over his left eye, strode toward the assembly area. People at first weren't sure who this cocky elf was, but recognition quickly set in as murmurs and whispers followed in his wake. Mechanics stopped what they were doing to look for themselves, while others refused to believe *he* was actually here. Some, mostly other racers, nodded in respect. But *everyone* got out of his way.

"You sure this is a good idea, Johnny?"

Johnny Redline, rigger, shadowrunner, and racer, lit a nico-stick before answering the voice in his cyber ear.

"Doesn't matter, we're on the job, Short Stack. Get Brienna ready," Johnny subvocalized into his throat mic before taking a drag.

"I hate that name. And just so we're clear, if you die tonight, I'm selling everything in the shop and moving to the Carib League," she replied.

Johnny hid his smirk by blowing smoke while looking for one particular racer...

"Weeeell, well! Look what we got here, chummers. Check *this* dandelion-eatin' slag out! Didn't think you'd have the guts to show, Johnny-*boy*."

Target acquired.

Turning towards the speaker and his crew of wannabes, Johnny took a long, final drag from his nico-stick then blew the smoke out his nose.

"Really, Grinder? Thought you'd gotten used to being wrong by now," he retorted while flicking the butt away.

Chuckles came from the crowd, and Grinder balled his fists. Chains slapped against his red synth-leather jacket as he shoved a scantily clad groupie out of his way, his crew barely stopping him from charging. "I'm sick of your mouth, Redline! No one talks to me like that! You're gonna eat those words!"

Johnny rolled his eyes and mimicked Grinder's mouth with his left hand. "Damn. Throttle back, grease stain," he began. "*You* called *me* out, remember? Which, for the record, I normally wouldn't give a devil rat's drek about. What I *do* care about is the fifty-k you're *supposedly* putting up. So, either show the cred or I exfil...and you can go back to playing with your crankshaft."

Face as red as his jacket, Grinder pulled a gold credstick from a pocket.

With his cybereyes, Johnny saw the digital reader indicated fifty thousand nuyen. Nodding, he produced his own 50k credstick, twirling it between his fingers. "So, we gonna race or what?"

Stupid, stupid, STUPID! Electric Blue thought, lungs burning and legs aching as he sprinted down an alley off 8-Mile Road. "You're a decker, not a street sam, *what were you thinking!*"

Blue didn't hear his pursuers anymore, but he knew they weren't far behind, and kept running. At the end of the alley, parked on the street among a line of derelict cars, was his salvation—a cosmetically battered Mitsubishi Runabout. With an AR-gloved hand, he remote-started the engine.

From around the corner, a metal monster that was once a GMC Bulldog step-van barreled down the street. Covered in multiple layers of crude and rusted armor plates, spikes, and sporting saw-like ram plates, it obliterated the line of cars; the thunder of the impacts and the screeching of rending metal echoed as parts flew through the alley.

Skidding to a stop and falling on his hoop, Blue watched the carnage unfold as two figures jumped from the Bulldog and strode toward him. Clad in spray-painted makeshift armor, the pair looked like extras in a post-apocalyptic fantasy trid. Still, Blue's blood went cold as he recognized the go-gang logo on their chests, a bastardization of the Detroit Red Wings wheel with two crossed daggers behind it.

696 Slayers.

One ganger held a combat axe, while the other sported a polearm...and a black synthleather jacket flashing explicit holographic Japanese hentai art images on the back.

"You thought you could insult me with *this*?" the ganger said, throwing the jacket at Blue's feet. "You spoiled my bounty, made me look a fool. Now, you'll taste my rage!"

"What, t-that?" Blue stammered. "Look chummer, it was just a harmless joke, I can easily reset it if you'll just—"

With a quick motion, the ganger swung his polearm at Blue's head just as two gunshots sounded in quick succession.

The polearm went flying and the ganger fell to his knees, clutching his throat as blood gushed from between his fingers. Blue sat motionless, arm outstretched with smoking palm pistol in hand, strands of his neon blue hair floating down in front of him.

A heartbeat later, the other ganger bellowed and attacked Blue with his axe. The decker frantically rolled to the side, barely avoiding the downward strike as his empty pistol retracted back into its forearm sheath. Rolling several more times and ending on his back, Blue quick-drew a Colt L-36 pistol from his coat and dumped the magazine into the ganger. The ganger held fast with forearms up, light pistol rounds deflecting off the crude but effective armor plating.

Seizing the opportunity, Blue scrambled to his feet and ran. Without looking back, he heard the ganger howl as a bright red flare illuminated the sky above and other howls sounded in the distance.

"Frag," Blue swore.

"So, question," Sandy Owens, aka Short Stack, asked as her hands manipulated the augmented reality controls on Johnny's spare rigger command console.

Next to her, inside Johnny's custom tractor trailer, "Brienna," Johnny's custom GMC Phoenix, came to life. Her custom turbo-charged electric engine revved a couple of times before Sandy jerked her down the ramp.

"Okay wha... *Hey*! Careful!" he replied.

"This would be like, you know, a lot easier if I had my *own* control rig. Cold sim sucks," Sandy retorted.

Johnny looked down at Sandy, who was barely taller than his hip. "Headware, especially something as invasive as a VCR, isn't good for a thirteen-year-old. Give it another four, five years. Otherwise, you'll frag your grey matter going hot sim. Besides, you obviously need the practice."

"*Fourteen*," Sandy said, powering down the RCC. "Anyway, you got a death wish?"

"No, why?" he said while running his hand along the red stripe that adorned Brienna's hood, over the roof, and down her back.

"The way you dissed Grinder," Sandy said. "Sure, he's a slimy piece of drek. But I half-expected him to pull a gun instead of a credstick."

"Valid concern, but The Garage has rules, codes of conduct for these events. No *intentional* geeking, all personal beefs are settled on the racetrack. Break the rules, get banned, that simple. Mostly..."

Sandy pouted, but Johnny cracked a grin. "This mean you're actually worried about me?"

She looked down. "Duh! Can't let my meal ticket get geeked *too* soon."

"Besides, it's strategy," Johnny said.

"Strategy?"

"Grinder's a bully, narcissist, and cheater," he elaborated. "Everyone knows his success comes from buying top-of-the-line gear and playing dirty, not skill. Only reason he's still racing is he's got deep pockets, and people want a shot at the big payouts he offers."

Sandy nodded. "Greed overrides everything."

Johnny grunted in agreement. "Not wrong, but it's complicated. There's still a lot of bad blood after The Battle, and The Garage is doing what they can to keep things civil. But back on topic," he continued. "As you've seen, Grinder can't handle challenges to his rep. So, I'm going to frag with that temper, keep him off balance, and force him into doing something stupid."

"Iffy plan, Boss. What if he doesn't do anything stupid?"

Johnny hopped into Brienna and revved her engine. "Then I'll destroy him with sheer skill."

They were the last racers of the night because no one wanted to miss this.

Johnny glided Brienna to the starting line, left hand on her steering wheel even though the fiber-optic cords that linked his VCR to Brienna's systems were already plugged into the back of his head. He resisted the urge to rev her engine, to feel the power underneath the hood vibrate through her frame. He needed to maintain his façade of borderline boredom to sell his strategy against Grinder.

After almost a year away, Johnny realized how much he'd missed this. Here there were no corporate machinations, no political fraggery, no bug spirits, no pitched battles, and no wanton destruction or slaughter. Here, there was only the pureness of the race, the melding of driver and machine in a contest to show who was the best. Maybe not exactly. Johnny recognized the hypocrisy of that thought. But this job was for a good cause and that was close enough, for now at least.

Grinder eventually pulled up to the starting line on his right side, but not before some showboating—purposely fishtailing and making a few donuts on the track. Covered in gleaming chrome with a deep red blood splatter pattern, Grinder's Saab Gladius 998TI looked like a bloody dagger ready to strike another victim. Comparatively, Brienna looked almost bland, with her simple charcoal grey matte finish and old-school design. The only color she sported was her stripe.

Grinder revved his engine, vying for Johnny's attention. When he finally looked over, Grinder ran his thumb over his throat in a menacing gesture.

In reply, Johnny secured the safety harness as Brienna's steering wheel retracted and her custom rigger's cocoon closed around him. Ignoring Grinder's subsequent swearing, Johnny enjoyed a moment of zero sensory input before the familiar rush of adrenaline kicked in. As the direct neural interface of his vehicle control rig engaged in "hot sim" mode, he could *feel* the cracked asphalt beneath Brienna's wheels and the thrum of her engine like it was his own heartbeat. He'd also feel any damage she took during the race.

The darkness ahead became meaningless as his vision became a wash of augmented reality objects superimposed over a virtual heads-up display/real-time camera overlay. In that moment, he and Brienna were one. Her "simple" red stripe now pulsed neon red as the nano-paint activated, reflecting the engine's RPMs.

This is what racing—what *rigging*—was all about.

"Alright, B, let's get this motherfragger," Johnny said, feeling truly alive.

As the quad-drone reached its position above them, the two street machines throttled up, the sound of their engines akin to demons howling, begging to be freed. Ten seconds later, the drone's lights quickly went from red, to yellow...then green.

In under a second, Brienna's engine was revving past 9000 RPM, accelerating her and Johnny forward across the tarmac at over 350 KPH. In the HUD, virtual AROs already highlighted the course, a long, quarter-mile stretch with three sharp serpentine turns before dumping out on another quarter mile straightaway.

In the opening two seconds, Grinder was already half a car-length ahead, his Saab's superior acceleration giving him the initial edge. But Johnny had planned for this. Brienna's design may look like a 20th century throwback, but she cornered better than anything in Motor City.

At the first turn, Johnny applied brakes and turned hard right, letting the momentum whip Brienna to the left; tires screeched, but held firm to the road.

A half-second later, Grinder tried the same maneuver, but swung wider as several anti-vehicle blades, known as "shredders," deployed from the Saab's rear bumper, aimed right at Brienna's front right tire.

Collision warnings sounded and Johnny braked again, slowing Brienna *just* enough to avoid the shredders without losing too much energy.

Not today, motherfragger! Johnny thought.

The Saab went wide in front of Johnny and almost ditched, but Grinder maintained control. Seeing the opening, he throttled Brienna up. Coupled with a quick wheel turn, Brienna passed the Saab just in time to make the second drift turn to the left. Grinder tried to copy the turn, but his tires slipped off the tarmac, sending dirt and broken asphalt flying, slowing his momentum.

It also let Johnny take the lead.

Drifting through the final turn, Johnny was now on the straightaway. Living up to his name, he redlined Brienna's engine. Pinned against his seat, he saw AROs indicating the finish line ahead. Knowing this was it, he didn't look back, just focused dead ahead.

Suddenly, red collision warning AROs popped up on his HUD as something dashed across the track in front of him. Easily 100 kilos, the thing looked like a cybernetic, steroid-enhanced hellhound; the upper half of its body, head, and all four legs had been replaced by someone who would have made Dr. Frankenstein envious.

Reflexively, Johnny swerved Brienna to the right, but his speed was too fast for such a maneuver. More AROs popped up in his vision and warning alarms blared in his ears as Brienna threatened to spin out of control.

Gritting his teeth, Johnny felt Brienna swing wide, but turned into the fishtail as momentum carried them forward. A heartbeat later, he regained control with some fancy mental wheelwork. With warning ARO's still blaring, Brienna's tires violently found positive traction again. But as Johnny started to regain speed, Grinder surged in for an attack on Brienna's left rear quarter panel.

With shredders deployed on his front bumper, Grinder turned hard right, trying to send Johnny spinning with a classic PIT maneuver. Johnny had other plans though. A second before the other car connected, Johnny whipped Brienna around 180 degrees, then shifted into reverse and gunned her engine. Failing to connect, Grinder's Saab spun out of control, off the tarmac, and into the dirt. The blood and chrome street machine rolled four times before coming to a stop, and then erupted into a fireball.

Johnny saw the entire scene play out as he surged over the finish line...in reverse.

Inside an old, blasted-out convenience store, Blue quickly pulled a synth-wood pallet and other bits of debris over top of him as another group of Slayers drove by on an armored pickup truck. He held his breath and made himself as invisible as possible. But one of the gangers jumped off and entered the store. With crude shotgun in hand, the ganger swept the area then stopped...and began walking right toward Blue's makeshift hidey-hole.

Unable to hear anything except for his pounding heartbeat, Blue watched the ganger suddenly raise his shotgun and fire. Other gangers ran up, weapons ready, only to discover their chummer had blasted a massive devil rat. Frustrated, they piled back into their truck and drove off.

Two minutes later, Blue finally exhaled. After extracting himself from the trash, he discovered the store's back office. In the distance, he could still hear the sounds of vehicles roaming the streets. Closing the door, Blue checked his commlink: no signal. He then pulled his custom Shiawase Cyber-6 cyberdeck from hits case, hoping its more sophisticated systems could find *something*.

Also, no go. Wireless in this part of Motor City *sucked*.

Reaching into the case, Blue removed a small custom MCT Hornet microdrone designed to be a modified re-trans unit or find wireless signals despite distance, noise, or jamming. Slaving it to his deck, Blue sent the little Hornet on its way.

In the back of his semi-trailer, Johnny tried to light another nico-stick with shaking hands, but failed for the third time. In frustration, anger, and no small amount of adrenaline dump, he tossed them all in the trashcan.

Since The Battle of Detroit, there'd been rumors of experimental bio-drones escaping, or purposely turned loose, from Ares Macrotechnology research labs because it wasn't cost effective enough to safely deal with them. But what slotted Johnny off was that The Garage had been so lax in their security. And of all the things to be geeked by, hitting a chromed-out mutt!

Not to mention fragging up the job, that slotted him off even more.

He wondered when Sandy would get back. He needed to put this job to bed. Just then he heard...

"Holy drek, Boss!" she said, bouncing up the ramp and handing over Grinder's credstick. "Can't believe you pulled this off! I mean, I knew you could, but you know...50K nuyen! I know, a chunk'll go towards Brienna, but *wow*! You said you'd get that drek-head to do something stupid, but I never expected *that*! So, what are we gonna spend...hey, what are you doing?"

Johnny touched the gold credstick to another, blank credstick, then tossed it back to Sandy who looked at the readout and frowned.

"Are you fragging kidding me?" she asked as Johnny pocketed the other credstick.

"Part of finishing the job," Johnny said. As he walked down the ramp, a storage compartment opened and deployed a classic Yamaha Rapier racing bike named "Tillie." Donning his helmet and starting the engine, he looked over his shoulder at Sandy and said, "Get Brienna back to the shop. I'll be back later. Don't wait up,"

Before she could reply, or argue, Johnny had already shot off into the night.

Blue pumped his fist when his Hornet found a signal, as weak as it was. But it was something. He'd have to make this count, because he might only get one chance. For a clever decker such as himself, it was all he'd need.

But now came the real question: Who would he call? Blue realized how short his list of suitable contacts was. Shockwave? No, she was still off the grid. Lotus? Back in Japan dealing with "personal business." Sarge? No, he was still recovering from a raid on his gun store. That left only one person, and

Blue debated if letting the gangers get him would be a better alternative than calling him.

"Ah well. Frag it," Blue muttered as he texted a familiar comm-code.

At a leisurely 145 KMH, Johnny guided Tillie through the relatively quiet but rugged streets of downtown Motor City. A few vehicles passed by, while a few groups or people guarding their properties looked in his direction, going back to their biz once they determined he wasn't a threat. Johnny continued on, wanting to keep his mind clear, but every street and every building he passed had memories attached to them.

Before Ares' CEO Damien Knight tried to have a big showdown with The Bugs almost a year ago, Motor City (né Detroit) was a "shining example of corporate benevolence," complete with total urban renewal. As long as you towed the corp line—or at least didn't upset the status quo *too* much—you were left alone. Mostly. Then the Battle of Detroit happened, and the entire sprawl went from corporate paradise to almost becoming another apocalyptic wasteland a la Chicago.

But two things separated Motor City from The Windy City.

One, people actually cared about Chicago, or at least how much they could make by re-developing it. Not so for Motor City. After the fighting, Ares ditched Detroit for Atlanta and dumped all responsibility on the UCAS government, who decided they had bigger problems to deal with, and pretty much left the battered sprawl to rot.

Funny how history repeats itself.

Two, during and after the fighting and subsequent abandonment, it was the general population (backed by various shadow-types) who fought most of the battles and later rolled up their sleeves to tell the world: frag you, this is *our* city, we'll do it ourselves.

Johnny was there through all of it, on the front lines. He saw the best and worse metahumanity had to offer, and had the scars to prove it. He'd lost family, friends, seen too many lives destroyed, people displaced, and for what? So that some fragger could indulge his hero fetish that ultimately got him, *and* thousands, killed?

Johnny revved Tillie's engine, terminating his trip down memory lane.

Thankfully, he'd finally arrived at his destination.

Clyde's Tattoo and Body Mods was *the* place to go in Motor City for all things body art. Located in a section of the sprawl known as "The Platinum Zone," it shared a block with several other businesses anchored (and protected) by the "exotic entertainment club" known as Platinum Trollgirls. During hostilities, Platinum's owners and staff had turned the entire block into a fortress, the HQ against the Bugs/Ares, and later one of the few safe zones in the sprawl. Nowadays, the Zone was neutral territory where anyone could conduct business, legit or otherwise, in safety and security.

Dropping Tillie's kickstand and patting her fuel tank, Johnny walked in and was greeted by an interesting sight. Reclining on an oversized barber's chair was a topless female troll. Johnny grinned and shook his head as he watched Clyde, hands glowing an ethereal blue, use a custom laser Dremel to cut in an intricate swirl and lightning bolt pattern on a section of Windy's natural dermal plating that covered the top of her chest.

"You know, anyone can see you through the window," Johnny said.

Wendy "Windy" Storms, semi-retired street samurai, exotic dancer turned general manager at Platinum, fixer, and in this case "Ms. Johnson," opened one eye and retorted, "That stopped bothering me a long time ago. I don't care what other people think."

"Yeah, but you're management. Shouldn't you set a better example?" Johnny bantered.

Windy lifted her right hand, extended both her middle finger and cyberspur while blowing Johnny a kiss. "Your quaint, outdated sense of morality amuses me. Besides, someone has to occasionally remind the newbies how it's done."

"Dancing, or shadowrunning?"

"Yes."

Clyde finished before putting down the Dremel and in American Sign Language said, "Also Johnny, I get more customers this way!"

Both Johnny and Wendy laughed at that.

"Speaking of customers, you got it Johnny?" she asked.

"Yep," he said, pulling out Grinder's credstick and handing it to Clyde, who looked confused, but his eyes widened when he saw the readout.

"This is for your brother's family. It's not much, but it'll get 'em by for a while," Johnny said. "And tell them his death has also been avenged."

Windy's eyebrow raised.

Tears formed in Clyde's eyes as he ran a trembling hand over his bald head, face, and then absently at the mass of scar tissue at his throat. "I have to go text...thank you. If you ever need anything..." Clyde hurriedly signed.

Johnny signed back, "Maybe a touch up on this," indicating his facial tattoo.

Smiling, Clyde nodded and turned toward the back, but then turned back and gave Johnny a massive bear hug.

A few minutes later, as the shop's lights turned off, Johnny went to grab a nico-stick, forgetting that he'd tossed the pack.

"Well, you made his day," Windy said as she walked out the front door, sliding her jacket on. "Thanks for taking the job."

"Null sheen, I owed both of them for saving my hoop more than once during The Battle. Oh, and thanks for starting those rumors. Grinder completely fell for them. Still, wish I could have taken more from the bastard. Also feel bad for having to keep 10K nuyen for Brienna."

"Cost of doing biz. And speaking of, I need to get back to the club. Care to follow and tell me about the race over a smoke and a few beers?"

Johnny pondered. "Toss in some soy-tenders—" he began as a text message appeared in his field of vision. After reading it, he let out a long sigh.

"Johnny, everything chill?"

"Sorry, Windy, gonna have to raincheck. Seems I have one more good deed to do tonight. Tell you about it if I live," he said, donning his helmet and quickly racing into the night. He then commed Sandy, who was thankfully already back at the shop.

"That was quick, heading home?"

"No, get Heather ready, combat loadout number four, meet me at these coordinates ASAP."

"Great, who's in trouble this time?"
"Blue."
"Why am I not surprised?"

Brass-checking his L-36, Blue promised himself to get a smartlink *and* upgrade his sidearm, if he survived.

His internal debate on the pros and cons of staying versus leaving was interrupted by heavy footsteps entering the shop. A harsh voice bellowed, "Check everywhere, starting with the back!"

If he wasn't going to go out hacking, dodging IC, or engaged in a cyber duel, Blue decided to go out on his feet. Raising his Colt to offload on whoever opened the door, he then heard weapons fire and explosions. On instinct, Blue hit the floor to avoid any stray rounds.

Thirty seconds later, all was quiet.

Cautiously rising, he heard, "Blue! Hurry up and get your scrawny hoop out here!"

Recognizing Johnny's modulated voice, Blue exited with his Colt up, just in case. Hovering inside the store above five dead gangers were two gunmetal grey MCT Rotodrones, one sporting a Nemesis II LMG, the other an MGL-12 grenade launcher and P93 SMG. Three seconds later, a heavily modified Jeep Trailblazer in blue and grey camo, its mounted Ares-Stoner M-202 MMG still smoking, screeched to a halt in front of the store with the passenger door open.

Blue didn't need an invitation and jumped inside.

"Frag, Johnny, thanks for..." he began but was quickly cut off as Heather peeled out.

"How did you manage to slot off every Slayer in the sprawl?" Johnny said from inside his cocoon.

"Well...I sort of interrupted a couple of them when they tried to strong-arm the venders on 8-Mile. They ripped off one of those new holo-jackets, so I hacked it to broadcast nothing but Japanese smut. Ganger didn't like it, tried to kill me...but I killed him first."

"For Ghost's sake, Blue..."

"Yeah, I know, stupid. You can chew me out for it later. But they were bullies, Johnny. And you said we stand up for good people."

Johnny sighed before responding. *"Survival first, talk later, got it?"*

Blue nodded and plugged into his cyberdeck. "Got it. Anything you want me to do? I can man a gun."

"No, just let me work."

Johnny rocketed Heather along westbound 8-Mile Road and it seemed like Hell itself was right behind him, the screams of redlined engines and the thunder of weapons fire echoing in the night. Those still on the street quickly found cover or got out of the way.

He cornered hard at Dequindre Street and accelerated down Conant into a former residential area, tires screeching as Heather barely missed an overturned garbage truck. A couple pursuing gangers weren't so lucky, but Johnny didn't have time to admire the resulting fireballs.

A particularly insane ganger roared up behind Heather on his stripped-down bike. Leaping from his bike onto the Jeep's trunk, magnetic kneepads held him in place as he pulled out an improvised explosive device from a belt pouch.

"Oh no you don't," Johnny said as he engaged Heather's security system, with the safeties off. 75,000 volts fried the ganger who dropped the IED before it armed.

Johnny had initially hoped to quietly slip in, grab Blue, and slip away. But that wasn't happening, so he decided to take the kid gloves off. Switching to what riggers called "Captain's Chair Mode," he engaged Heather's advanced auto-nav systems and coordinated the rotodrone's fire by designating their targets.

Guided by advanced targeting software, the first rotodrone ripped into the pursuing Slayer ranks with armor-piercing LMG fire, shredding the rider's flesh and bone or taking their rides out from under them. The second rotodrone fired high-explosive grenades on those unfortunate enough to group too close together, the explosions sending multiple gangers flying toward the asphalt.

Despite the carnage, the gangers kept coming. Swarming like angry wasps, they attacked with whatever guns or weapons they had on them, including a couple harpoons. Johnny had taken that personally after one harpoon actually embedded into Heather's trunk. In response, he sideswiped them, forcing them both into nearby streetlamps.

But with every ganger removed from the fight, the drone's ammo counters quickly dropped. Taking them out was easy, but like hydra's heads, for every one that fell, at least two or more seemed to take their place. Johnny considered employing Heather's weapons, but determined there could be bigger targets out there.

"Sandy, need some good news!" he said over the comm-channel, switching out of CCM.

"Sorry, got none. You're being boxed in. Gangers are choking off all roads a kilometer from your position."

"Okay, take the Condor to a higher altitude, see if you can find me a place to punch through."

"Copy that, I'll...wait, all the bikes are falling back...JOHNNY WATCH OUT!"

Collision warnings sounded as Johnny swerved left and sideswiped a derelict car. But the maneuver avoided a cannon shot that blew a four-meter-wide chunk out of a derelict house behind him.

Barreling its way onto Conat from East Remington, a GMC Bulldog step-van joined the chase, the side door wide open revealing a ganger sporting a Panther Assault Cannon. A few seconds later, a Gaz P-183 truck swung onto Conat from Outer Drive E, a gunner operating a dual RPK HMG mount in the back that obliterated Johnny's Rotodrones with full auto fire.

Johnny swore as the rotodrones' signals went dead.

Turning in his seat, Blue yelled: "Not him again!"

"Which one?" Johnny asked.

"The Bulldog, slag with the Panther, is the chummer of the one I geeked."

"Fan-fragging-tastic!" Johnny said, cranking Heather hard right into an abandoned park, wanting to see if the newcomers could handle off-roading.

Turning hard around old playground equipment and blasting through a chain-length fence, HMG rounds glanced off Heather's right rear quarter panel and chewed into armor plating. Johnny also saw through Heather's sensors that the remaining go-ganger bikes had done an end-run and were converging on his position. It was a classic hammer and anvil strategy.

Johnny realized he needed a plan and *fast*.

Thankfully, Heather's M-202 was still at eighty percent capacity. Johnny also had a pair of aces in the hole: two Aztechnology Striker rocket launchers, one mounted forward and one rear, loaded with anti-vehicle rounds for *just* such an occasion. A tentative plan formed in his mind, and Johnny realized he'd need help to pull this off.

"*Blue!*" he said through Heather's internal speakers.

The pale decker looked over out of reflex, as if snapped out of a trance. "Yeah?"

"*I need your help, bad guys trying to box us in. I need you to man Heather's machine gun. Think you can handle it?*

"Frag yeah!"

"*Good...Sandy!*"

"Go ahead, Johnny," she said over the comm-channel.

"*I need you to track every ganger out there, I'll need to know the exact position for each one of those fraggers to make this work.*"

"*On it, relaying data now!*"

"What exactly are you gonna do, Johnny?" Blue interjected.

Johnny grinned. "*Try and make 'em do something stupid.*"

Dodging between abandoned houses, Johnny kept a mental eye on the HUD, watching as the gangers closed in on their position. The Gaz was still on Heather's tail, but had slowed its rate of fire to a few short bursts when the opportunity presented itself. The bikers where now coming southbound on Gallager Street, but had slowed their pace, Johnny guessed they didn't want to overtake their prey. The Bulldog had wisely returned to Conant and was far enough ahead that they'd be waiting for Johnny at the corner of Conant and Gallager, by the old Church of Christ at Northside, which happened to have a very large parking lot.

"Blue, get ready. When we pop out, I'm going to do some fancy driving. They're expecting us to run, but we're not gonna. Your job is to hose the bikers with every MG round Heather has, no matter what. Got it?"

Accessing the secondary gunnery controls, Blue swallowed and nodded. "Got it."

Coming up to the last house before the church, Johnny blasted through an old flower garden and gunned Heather's throttle, dirt and old grass spraying from beneath her tires. Up ahead to the right was the old church and empty parking lot.

Watching on his HUD as everyone converged, Johnny felt Heather surge forward as her tires found solid pavement. To his left on Gallager, the bikers were charging in. Behind him, the Gaz was also coming in hot, the gunner lining up his shot. And ahead at the intersection, Johnny saw the Bulldog with its side door open, ganger leveling his Panther to fire...and Heather's targeting ARO locking on to it.

Two seconds later, Heather passed the church into the parking lot, accelerating straight at the Bulldog.

Then everything went crazy...

At only twenty meters from the Bulldog, Johnny shifted to neutral, hit the brakes, and spun Heather 180 degrees. Just as Heather pointed at the Gaz, Johnny manually fired the rocket. By then, the Gaz was already firing, but the gunner stopped when rounds hit the Bulldog. Still, a few rounds also struck Heather a second before the rocket found its target.

The Gaz lifted ten feet into the air and slammed back to the earth. As the Gaz exploded, Heather's second rocket blew off the Bulldog's ram plate and most of the hood, and sent the van spinning.

Even with the g-forces pulling at him and dimming his vision, using every ounce of his concentration and skill, Blue raked M202 fire across the ganger ranks. Most fell, and those who didn't turned and fled.

Johnny awoke to Blue banging on his rigger cocoon as his brain replayed the last six seconds of his life. Feeling like someone had driven a spike into his brain, he slapped the emergency release and tumbled out, falling to the pavement and almost vomiting.

"I hate dumpshock," he said, realizing that the shots from the Gaz had hit Heather's rigger control systems. Blue came to his side and propped him up against Heather. Head still spinning, Johnny noticed smoke coming from under Heather's hood. "Don't worry, girl...you did good, we'll get you patched—" he started to say when a ragged voice bellowed.

"*SCUM!* You think you've won?" shouted the ganger from the Bulldog, covered in blood, left arm hanging limp. "My brothers and sisters will come back for me, and we'll find you, make you suffer for your transgressions! You'll feel such pain you'll *beg* us for death! No one will stop us from completing our hon—"

Blue drew his Colt and emptied the magazine into the ganger. Johnny watched as the first few rounds struck chest plating, then as the rest drilled into the ganger's face.

The hacker flopped back against Heather. "I had to end it. He never would have stopped. It still might not."

Johnny tried to say something, but with the dumpshock, all he could do was nod, but finally got out: "Let's check on Heather, see if she can get us home."

The sun had finally broken over the horizon as Johnny guided Heather along I-75. While her rigger systems had been damaged and she had a few holes in her radiator, Johnny had done enough of a field repair to get her running on manual controls. She ran a bit rough, but she was running.

"Should you be driving?" Blue asked, but Johnny silenced him with some side-eye. After a few minutes, Blue broke the silence again. "Hey Johnny, I wanted to say thanks again for coming to my rescue. It meant a lot. But are we also good?"

Johnny took a deep breath and let out a long sigh. "I think we need a long conversation about a *lot* of things, but that's for later. Right now? Yeah, we're good."

Blue smiled and put his feet up on the dash.

"But you *are* going to pay me back for all the ammo, drones, and repairs," Johnny said.

Blue chuckled, "Okay. Good one, Johnny."

Johnny didn't answer. He just kept driving.

"You're kidding, right?" Blue asked, a hint of panic in his voice. *"Right?!"*

OUT OF DODGE
AND INTO THE FIRE

Ken' Horner

The sounds of gunfire and small explosions echoed down the corridor as King Diamondback waited, swinging his head between the hallway in front of him and the pair of glass doors behind him. He wanted to move forward and find out what was going on, but his job was to secure the escape. The plan didn't include combat, but runs rarely went according to plan.

He checked behind him once again, catching the image of an Old West gunslinger holding a shotgun, but that was just his reflection. He turned back to the bland, white-tiled corridor, marred by a black hole blown into the end and debris on the floor from the explosion.

Out of the darkness at the end of the corridor came an ork, Tejon, running fast, her green combat jacket clashing with her long purple hair. Her dark complexion belied Hispanic ancestors and her athletic build matched her agile running. Diamondback raised his shotgun and fired three times, sending cover fire past Tejon. She continued to run full-speed toward him, not looking back as three figures appeared behind her, wearing the red and black checkered uniform of the Victory Foods security team. He pulled the trigger again, but nothing happened.

The largest of the security guards, a troll, fired a light machine gun, waving it around as if he wished to paint the entire hallway in lead. The ork dove behind a stone ensconced garbage can while Diamondback ducked behind a concrete planter. He snuck a peek around the side and saw one of the security guards staring down the corridor; the mixture of faraway eyes and smug grin clued him in. They had a combat decker, jamming the wi-fi of his shotgun.

Dropping his shotgun, he shouted, "Cover!" to Tejon as he pulled out a Ruger Warhawk revolver. She reached into her satchel and tossed an object down the hallway. The troll paused as he kicked the bouncing object back toward his quarry, the flash-bang exploding harmlessly off to the side.

Diamondback raised the pistol and aimed it at the decker. After a moment, his expression turned from smug to shocked as he realized the gun wasn't smartlinked. At that same moment, Diamondback pulled the trigger and the decker's neck exploded in a fountain of gore.

He spun the pistol around his finger and put it back in the holster, then reached across his body to draw another pistol from a reverse hung holster on his left hip. The troll was again putting down cover fire as Diamondback used his smartlink to the Ares Predator VI to load a different round into the chamber. He popped up over the top of the planter, hoping the troll would be focusing in on the side of the planter, where he had taken his last shot from, but luck wasn't on his side. One round slammed into his left shoulder—his lined coat preventing it from penetrating, but the impact left a massive bruise—while another round grazed his neck, leaving a long, shallow cut.

His pain editor dulled the aches as he fired back, his round hitting the troll in the upper chest. His body armor blocked the round, but the large security guard dropped like a big-box store-sized sack of potatoes as an electrical pulse emitted from the bullet, stunning him.

Tejon popped up like a jack-in-the-box once the machine gun stopped firing and used her grenade launcher to send a high explosive grenade down the corridor, detonating in the middle of the security team's formation. "Let's go!"

Diamondback paused for a second. "What about Elaronda?" he asked, referring to their mage teammate.

"Their troll removed his jaw," she replied as she ran past him.

He didn't wait. Grabbing his shotgun with his left hand, he fired several rounds behind them as he followed her. They ran out the doors and dove into their Ford Fairlane sedan, which Tejon had remotely started.

As she got behind the wheel, she answered his next question before he could ask it. "Grondor got petrified after

Elaronda went down. Luckily, I dropped a high explosive right on their mage's shoes."

She hit the gas and headed for the exit of the parking lot as another wave of security came through the doors.

"Did you get the data?" he asked.

She tapped the side of her head, between two datajacks. "Yup, we got that at least." The security gates opened for their car and began closing as they drove through, trapping the pursuing guards behind them. "But Aztechnology's gonna figure out who we are."

King Diamondback nodded. "So, we're gonna need to lay low for a few weeks until the Johnson's company gets this product out."

Tejon didn't reply as she linked up with the car, splitting her attention between driving and planning with Diamondback.

He accessed his commlink and made a call. "Hey Carson, it's Diamondback. Yup. Of course. Well, you know, I don't call you to catch up, so yes. We're going to need a place to lay low for a few weeks, somewhere a Central American megacorp won't be able to find us. No. Yes. Sure, sounds good."

"And?" Tejon asked, still looking forward.

"He's got a place; he's going to send us the details by tomorrow. Let's meet Mr. Johnson and find a place off the grid until we get Carson's message."

She frowned, but didn't reply. Diamondback suspected she was already busy accessing the Matrix to not only help get them to Plan B but start on Plan C just in case. Getting ready in case his fixer didn't come through. He knew she trusted her team, but with half of them dead any more setbacks might push her to slip away on her own.

The light barely illuminated the room, which, given the decade-old furnishings and wear and tear, was probably for the better. Tejon sat on a chair that was barely held up by its four legs, yet for her was less suspect than the bed in the middle of the room. They weren't at the iStay Inn for its amenities, but rather because a certified credstick meant a room with no questions and no data trail.

Diamondback stood by the doorway, his hands nervously at his hips.

Tejon frowned. "How long do we have to wait?"

"He'll come through soon," Diamondback replied, his frustration evident, though she wasn't sure if it was at her, his contact, the situation, or some combination of it all.

She rolled her eyes, but they both quickly snapped to attention as the sound of gunshots echoed nearby. She reached for her grenade launcher as he drew his pistol and peeked around the thick shade that covered the window. His snake-like cybereyes let him see the situation better than even her natural low-light vision.

After a few more gunshots he relaxed, twirling his gun absentmindedly into its holster as he turned back to her. "Just some Halloweeners, checking to see how good their new armored jackets are."

She set the launcher back down, relieved the gunfire was just sprawl stupidity and not a strike team coming to get them, but still worried about the latter. She stood up and walked to her open gear bag. "Look, we're only a few hours ahead of them, at best. I think we might want to spl—" She stopped talking as his commlink chimed, some ancient song called "The Rattlesnake Shake" that fit his whole persona.

"Diamondback," he said, as if the person on the other end didn't already know that. "Yeah, yeah..." Relief was written all over his body and face as he spoke. "That's great. I'll leave a credstick in your drop box on the way." He paused, listening. "Got it. Send me the details."

He strode to his gear as he ended the call, smiling. "I told you he had a place for us. Let's roll."

The lights from their beat-up Chevy Reno struggled to cut through the darkness surrounding them. The pair had left the bright lights of Albuquerque nearly two hours ago, headed for a cabin King Diamondback's fixer friend had set them up with. To some it might be counterintuitive to drive closer to Aztlan, but Aztechnology was a megacorp, and generally projected more power closer to large population centers.

Diamondback used the joystick to drive the sport-utility vehicle along roads that had seen tough days since when the United States had been running things. The Pueblo Corporate Council apparently only considered a pothole in need of fixing when it was two armadillos deep. Finally, a beat-up wooden sign came into view, stating *Welcome to Magdelena, The Trail's End* in faded blue letters. That latter statement didn't lend any comfort to the two urban warriors. It was followed with a population number, *342*, that looked hand-painted in a brighter shade of blue.

As they passed the sign, the heads-up display in the vehicle blinked to the left, indicating a turn upcoming. Diamondback turned the Reno and followed a gravel and dirt-packed road another few kilometers, occasionally passing driveways leading off into the darkness. Only a few houses could be spotted from the road at the edges of their headlights. A final turn to the right took the pair down an even bumpier driveway, clearly feeling the effects of erosion from the occasional rainstorms with no one to upkeep the path.

Ahead, illuminated by the headlights like a target, sat a cabin in the middle of scattered scrub, clearly in the turn-of-the-century style that sought to emulate the rustic wooden cabins of the past, without all the uneven building materials and insulation failures that provided "charm" to visitors but not inhabitants.

Diamondback swung the vehicle around, facing back down the driveway, and parked in the red dirt-covered clearing in front of the structure. Both runners exited the Reno and looked around for signs of life in the darkness, catching a few small animals that had stuck around to see what the new sounds and smells were, but spotted nothing threatening. Neither grabbed luggage as they walked the few meters to the door where Tejon punched in the code on the decades-out-of-date keypad that would open the door. A small *click* and *beep* let them know they were successful, and Diamondback slowly opened the door with his left hand, right by his Ruger, while Tejon stood to the right of the door, back against the cabin wall.

Nothing stirred inside, the open-concept great room giving a good look at most of the building. Older but comfortable furniture surrounded a fireplace and large trid screen. Three doors on the right side likely led to the bathroom and two bedrooms, while a small kitchen was to their left. A small eating area sat between it and the back of the house. The air was still and slightly dusty as Diamondback switched on the lights from a control panel next to the door. The display indicated the energy supply for the cabin was nearly full, but most everything was in sleep mode.

The pair slowly walked inside, Tejon trailing Diamondback as they crossed to the doors. One by one, he opened them, revealing two small bedrooms with reasonably comfortable looking beds and more faux-rustic decor. The bathroom was similarly unremarkable, save for pheasant-decorated wallpaper so horribly out of date it managed to be adorable.

Reasonably sure the area was secure, they relaxed their guard a bit and went back out to bring in their little bit of luggage before setting the security system and getting a few hours of sleep.

The next morning, Tejon arose to the alarm ringing inside her head, one of the perks of a cranial cyberdeck. She shuffled out to the kitchen, where she was lucky to find some freeze-dried soykaf and a functional coffee maker. She glanced out the windows in the back of the cabin and spotted Diamondback out there, examining what amounted to their backyard. He was tropish in his duster, cowboy hat, and boots, especially in the Southwest, but that was his thing. He was relatively pale from living in the city, but she could still see the Comanche heritage in his face. He bent over and pried up a rock that seemed too big to be lifted with so little effort, but Tejon knew from experience the cyberware in his body could be deceiving. She stirred some soycreamer into her soykaf and added some artificial sweetener as she watched the gunslinger stand the rock up next to a tree, a shield between the cabin and a small device he set on the other side, no doubt some sort of defensive measure.

He surveyed the landscape once more before turning and walking around the side of the house. A half-minute later, he came in through the front door and took off his hat, nodding at Tejon. He knew better than to start a conversation with her in the morning unless she initiated it.

He sat down on the couch across from the kitchen island, serpentine eyes pivoting between her and the front window. She savored a sip of the simultaneously boring but delicious soykaf, swallowed the hot drink, then sighed, "Okay, out with it."

He nodded, a slight smile forming at the edges of his mouth, "I just put a claymore out there—"

"Behind that rock I saw you move?"

"—behind that rock you saw me move. Don't wander back there without letting me know."

She nodded.

"We also have drek-all for food. A few freeze-dried things, dry condiments, and some ketchup stuff that's six months past due."

"So...?"

"So, we have to make a run into the town and get some supplies. There isn't much...you know." He waved his hand in a fluttering motion.

"What?" she asked.

"Toilet...wipes." he responded, his eyes rolling slightly.

Tejon giggled. "You're so sensitive with your tush. Some girl is gonna love you."

He frowned. "Maybe if you'd stop hoggin' 'em all..."

She raised her hands innocently. "I can't help it if I'm so hot." She took her soykaf back to her room, to change for the trip into town.

In the daylight, the drive to Magdelena was different in many ways, but not in every way. The landscape was now filled with yellow grass fields dotted with the occasional tree set against a background of mountains and hills, but still not a soul was seen until they reached the few blocks that was "downtown" Magdelena. Many of the buildings looked their century-plus ages, a contrast to the architectural lifespan of Albuquerque, which seemed even shorter than the lifespan of most of its residents. There were only two restaurants visible, neither one a Taco Temple.

Diamondback stopped the Reno at an old brick building bearing a plywood sign hand-painted to read "*Dez's General Store.*" Across the street was the Pueblo Corporate Office—likely a city hall or post office from before the Ghost Dance. A few people were on the streets, paved in cheap asphalt with patches of grass and dirt serving as sidewalks along the few roads. Despite both changing into jeans and flannel shirts that fit in with the populace, they could feel the few pairs of eyes around them examining the visitors to their isolated village. The duo walked up to the glass-pane door with a simple aluminum frame—something never seen in the city—and entered.

An electronic *beep* greeted them as they walked in. Tejon noticed a small sensor about ankle height hardwired to a small speaker which she assumed was jury-rigged from old parts rather than just buying a wireless alarm for a few nuyen.

The store was arrayed with multiple rows of goods with plastic placards denoting what was in each aisle, no electronic displays to be seen. They were not alone—a man behind the counter to their left had his head tilted down, looking at a tablet computer, finally something remotely modern, but his eyes were fixed on the two newcomers to his shop. The handful of other patrons were similarly staring, not the furtive glances they received in their brief stroll to the door, but unabashed focus.

With no desire to exacerbate the situation they split up, each grabbing a worn plastic hand basket to carry their wares in. The store was fairly well stocked with the necessities of modern life but had almost no variety of products; whatever brand they stocked was the only one they stocked. The pair grabbed a variety of basic foods, mostly soy-based, and household goods.

Tejon flashed a faint smile when she found they at least carried two-ply toilet paper.

Their quick foray through the shop complete, they headed over to the man at the counter. She saw Diamondback had found another of the store's small treasures: refrigerated real chicken. The label merely bore the weight, price, and expiration, leading her to believe the poultry was locally sourced, with prices a quarter or less of what it would be in Albuquerque.

The man still had his right hand on the tablet, but his left hand was beneath the countertop. Tejon also noted a few customers had pulled out their commlinks and were typing messages, eyes bouncing between their screens and the runners. The man at the counter had the dark features typical of the native Puebloans, though he wore a Los Angeles Bolts sweatshirt and matching sweatpants. His eyes still on them, he didn't offer a customary smile, but did stand up straight. "Find everything you're looking for?"

Tejon nodded, and Diamondback replied, "Yup."

The man nodded back and started tapping on his tablet, not bothering to scan the packages. He did take the packages of meat out to enter those prices off each label. With a flourish, he tapped one last virtual button and looked back at Tejon. "That'll be sixty-five-point-four nuyen."

Chicken aside, that price was triple what the remaining goods would cost back in the city. Tejon wasn't sure if it was the rural cost, an "outsiders tax," or a little of both. She pulled out a certified credstick and waved it next to the tablet, paying the man as he put their purchases into two old-fashioned paper sacks.

"Do you need a receipt?" he asked.

Tejon was already headed out the door, but Diamondback shook his head and quickly followed his partner, just as the silence of the store was filled with hushed whispers from the other customers.

Outside, it seemed like few people had moved during the time they were in the store. The only change seemed to be a well-worn Toyota Olympia with the faded paint scheme of the Pueblo Corporate Council pulling up behind their Reno. Neither runner was surprised, but both had hoped to get in and out of town before attracting the attention of authorities.

Out of the Olympia stepped a middle-aged woman, her hair a mixture of natural grey and fluorescent orange. Dressed in a corporate uniform, she sauntered over to the side of their Reno, hand on her holstered pistol, waiting for them to stride within an arm's reach. She was in good shape for a woman of her age, but was in no way physically imposing. Her face was a different matter—an expression of concern was on it, but her eyes betrayed no sense of panic.

"Well, hello," she said. "How are you this fine morning?"

It wasn't hard for the pair to know she didn't really care. "Good, just grabbing some supplies," Diamondback replied, trying to cut off her next question.

"Ohhhhh!" she replied in mock awe. "I was thinking you were in the general store getting your nails done." She waved her left finger before either could respond, "I know you're not passing through," she added. "This isn't exactly a stop off the interstate."

"We are staying at a friend's place on Stendel Ridge," Tejon interjected.

The officer nodded, "The old Martell place. Your...friend... has a few interesting folks that stay there from time to time. As long as they mostly stay there, things are good." She put her left thumb up and winked.

Then she frowned. "But sometimes they decide to make Magdelena more like...where they come from, and that is bad." She flipped her thumb down while at the same time patting her pistol with her right hand.

Diamondback quickly replied, "Oh we're going to enjoy our vacation time around the cabin, officer...?"

She nodded, "Security Manager Abundo. You be sure to enjoy your...vacation. Just so you know, Harold will do delivery out your way, if you want to avoid the *hassle* of a trip into town." She backed up toward her Olympia, allowing the outsiders a direct path to their vehicle.

Diamondback opened the rear passenger door and put his bag of groceries inside, keeping an eye on the situation with his peripheral vision. Tejon handed him her bag and she went around the front of the Reno while Security Manager Abundo watched through the vehicle's windows.

As Tejon opened her door and got into the driver's seat, Diamondback closed the rear passenger door, opened the front one, and joined her in the SUV. As they drove off, they saw the security manager keeping her steely gaze locked on them until they turned from Lapu Street to First Street.

Tejon was the first to speak, affecting a valley girl accent filled with sweetness. "So, what'd you think of our new neighbors? They seemed super friendly to me. I just had to turn down their welcome plate of cookies, I'm trying to watch my figure..."

Diamondback was more somber. "That sheriff's one to keep an eye on, I'm pretty sure she knew she stood almost no chance if we drew on her, but she didn't back down."

"Someone's got a crush," Tejon said, keeping up the saccharine attitude. "Maybe you could take her to Tumbleweed's Diner and see what happens!"

"You're the one who's got a history with cougars. You can bond over hair color and cordite perfume."

She laughed. After a brief silence, she continued the conversation in her normal tone. "I think they were all round-ears."

He slouched more toward the door. "No, I saw an ork in one of the houses down the street, lurking in the shadows." He turned to the back seat and pulled a candy bar from one of the bags. As he opened the package, Tejon seamlessly continued to drive while wirelessly linking her headware with the Reno's speakers, playing back the whispered conversations they heard as they left the store. "Anything in that?"

Just about to take a bite, Diamondback frowned. "My Comanche's barely passable. My Hopi's fragged. All that being said, I'm sure it was the local rumor mill starting up. No doubt in ten minutes I'm a scary, Panther-wielding merc and you're an imposing troll." He took a big bite.

"No doubt!" she snorted. She let the gunslinger eat his candy bar in peace as they drove back to their temporary home. When they pulled into the driveway, she asked, "Any guess to how long we'll have to hang out here?"

Diamondback sighed. "Well, the Johnson gave us a bonus for getting it to him two weeks early and it's a flavoring combination, not bleeding-edge tech, so maybe three weeks? The Azzies'll have to know the horse is out of the barn by then."

"Maybe they'll want revenge?" She parked the car.

"Maybe some sarariman, but not the corp. You know we've been hired by people we've beat before."

"Or if they want to figure out how we got past their defenses?"

He opened the door, but didn't get out. "C'mon, the big hole in the wall will tell them. Don't house secure data at a facility that shares a wall with a low-security warehouse. Some project manager is getting berated and demoted, but if they can't find us in a few weeks to figure out where we took the data, they'll just be throwing money away."

"You willing to bet our lives on that?"

He got up and grabbed both bags of groceries out of the car as she held open the door to the cabin. "Hey now, I'm just saying we ask a few people to feel out The Querque in a few weeks, not just blindly head back."

Tejon felt a gnawing in her stomach, both from the concern that this run wouldn't have a clear-cut ending, and needing to eat.

The warm smell of fajitas filled the air. The pair sat at the kitchen table, enjoying a rare meal of actual food—not a single gram of soy between the local vegetables and chicken. Diamondback hadn't looked at the ingredients list on the tortilla, preferring to live in a bit of ignorance with the unexpected feast they had stumbled upon.

"How's the neck?" Tejon asked, referring to his close encounter with a machine gun round just two days ago.

"All good," he responded, pulling away the bandage to show a faint pink line where a jagged gash had been. "Those platelets were worth it," he added, referring to the biomodification to improve his body's natural platelets, clotting much faster than unmodified humans. The neck didn't hurt like the bruise on his chest, but without the platelets he might not have made it to the getaway car.

"Where'd you learn to cook like this?" She took another big bite of one of her fajitas.

He paused to finish chewing. "My grandmother was..."

"Mexican! I knew it!"

"...Italian." Tejon frowned at her failed anticipation. "She loved to cook, all sorts of stuff. It's not all that different once you get the basics down. Luckily, they had some decent spices, and the folks here take good care of their chickens." He reached back and grabbed a rub mixture off the kitchen island. "And a little flavor magic to bring out the Sixth World in my cooking."

They laughed and continued to enjoy dinner. After they were done eating, Diamondback turned a bit more serious. "How are we electronically?"

The ork sipped her water, then answered him. "Well, we didn't use anything connected to the Matrix once we left the Q. We aren't linking up to anything here, our commlinks are off, all we have is that burner your guy knows the number to, so as long as he doesn't leave a trail back to us, we're good."

She waved her hands around at the room. "Now if someone around here, for some reason, decides to attack, we're pretty much out in the open. The house security is pretty minimal, enough to keep out the local brats, but any professional will slice it up in seconds."

"Can we do anything to beef it up without spending too much time or nuyen?"

She shrugged. "We have a lot of time on our hands and a pretty good payday, so I can put a few remote cameras out there. Maybe record the deer before your bomb blows it up."

He smiled. "You just like seeing things go boom."

She flashed a grin back. "As long as they're not me."

He cleaned up dinner as she put a few small spy cameras inside and outside before they headed to their beds.

Tejon was woken up by another internal alarm, though this one was from the cameras, not a chrono. She noted the time: 0540, then wirelessly accessed the camera while rising, throwing on a robe, and grabbing her grenade launcher from under the bed.

She simultaneously watched video of a deer in the underbrush on the north side of the cabin as she walked over to Diamondback's door and rapped on it. The deer had walked into the camera's view in a stiff manner, and hadn't moved in a few minutes.

She quickly ran through the other cameras, but none of their AI had identified anything noticeable while she waited for Diamondback to wake up. A half a minute later he opened the door, showing a good-looking figure offset by his green boxers decorated with yellow baby chicks and snakeskin boots, Predator pistol in his right hand.

"I've got a strange looking deer to the north," she told him.

He nodded and strode to the cabin's door, throwing on his duster from the coat tree next to it. She also put on her armored jacket as he opened the door and peeked out. "Anything?"

"Well," he replied, "either we're being stalked by a zombie deer, or it's a hunting target of some sort. No body heat at all."

She snorted.

"I do see three people out behind trees, though. Not exactly an Azzie strike team."

"Locals?"

"That's my guess. I'll handle it." He opened the door wider and walked out, yelling "Scram!" Neither the inanimate deer nor the three people-shaped heat sources responded. "C'mon you guys, get out of here."

One of the locals, a teenager judging by the voice, shouted back, "You get out of here, breeder!"

Tejon, in the doorway, yelled back, "Who are you callin' breeder, breeder?"

A second voice said, "We're just chasin' down our deer." A shot rang out and a bullet flew past the deer and pinged off the cabin.

Tejon raised her weapon, but Diamondback turned to her and shook his head, his pistol still down. "That isn't laying low." He turned back to the three lurkers behind the tree line. "Get out of here now, or I'll have to call in Miss Abundo. She doesn't like us, but she's gonna be even more pissed at you three. And any more gunfire, and I'll start shooting back."

The sudden sounds of panicked retreat followed. A few minutes after the interlopers had left, Tejon walked over to the deer. It was indeed a shooting target, with trails in the dirt where at least two of the visitors had pushed it out from the tree line. A closer look revealed the eyes were cameras, no doubt recording either internally or back to some receiver. She pushed the deer over. All the deer's owners would see was a blurry shot of dirt.

She was about to head back to the house when she heard a rattle. She headed toward the sound, finding the motor on the pump for the well that supplied water to the cabin. The rattling got louder and louder, until the entire thing stopped and went quiet. There was a hole in the motor housing where the teenager's missed bullet had impacted the pump.

Tejon growled and headed back into the house.

The previous visit to Magdelena proper had been worrisome, the follow-up was one of dread. They stopped at the edge of town, beside a building bearing the sign "*Otero's Rock and Saw Shop.*" There was a dirt area that served as a parking lot, while the entire compound was fenced off. Various building materials were on pallets in the yard.

The two quickly exited the Reno and hustled into the white building that was clearly over a century old. Inside was cramped with shelves of various parts and pieces.

"Can I help you?"

Tejon peered around the corner of a shelf and saw a dwarven lady in a knitted dress. Her glasses appeared to be old fashioned reading glasses, but bore the subtle marks of modern electronics.

She held up the damaged pump she had removed from its mount. "We need a replacement pump."

"Oh, dearie. Those usually never go bad, but you're in luck, despite your bad luck," she giggled. She disappeared into the row of stacks. "Nope, nope, do you...ahhhh, here it is!"

She skipped back into view from the dark corridors and set a box down on a glass display case containing a few decorative crystals which had gathered decades of dust. She patted the case next to the box. "Set her down, let's make sure it'll work."

Tejon set the pump down as the lady opened the box with a similar-looking pump inside. She let out a small gasp, "Oh, that's why we check!" and she closed the box and whisked it back to the labyrinth of parts, returning a few seconds later with an identical-looking box. She set it next to the damaged pump and opened the box, smiled and closed it.

"That will be two hundred ninety-nine nuyen," she said, patting the box.

Tejon winced, slotting her credstick and doing a quick check using the shop's wide-open wi-fi, finding the same item for less than fifty in the city. But this one came sooner, and with no questions.

"Oh my, what happened to your old one?" Well, fewer questions.

Tejon picked up the new pump box and pointed a thumb at Diamondback. "Someone needs to work on their shooting." She grinned as she saw the conflict on the street samurai's face between his pride in his marksmanship against his desire to get back to laying low as fast as possible.

The smile melted from her face as they left the shop. There, leaning against their Reno was Security Manager Abundo, sunglasses glittering in the late morning sunshine and her right hand again comfortably atop her pistol. "I thought we had an understanding."

Diamondback started to say something, but she cut him off. "Ah, ah, ah, I'm running this meeting, so you can keep your hands nice and still where they are and answer my questions. Then maybe we can get into some conversation."

Tejon started scanning for wi-fi emanations from the officer, but found nothing aside from the camera/comm on her shoulder. It was PCC issued and, unlike the wi-fi in the store, would take some effort to crack.

"Where were y'all this morning?" she inquired.

Diamondback quickly replied, "Hey, those ki—"

"Tsk, tsk, tsk, I said answer my questions, not go on a tangent."

"We were at the cabin until a half-hour ago," Tejon said.

"And where were you three days ago?"

"The Q," she again replied while Diamondback said, "Not here," at the same time.

Ms. Abundo stood up straight, all 1.3 meters of her. "You have any witnesses or evidence of either location?"

Diamondback pointed at Tejon and she pointed back.

The security manager sighed. "Okay, here's what we're gonna do. You're gonna open up this vehicle," she patted the Reno with her left hand, "then I'm going to follow you two to your cabin, where I will look around inside and then you will stay at that cabin, no matter what."

"Hold on a sec!" The blood rushed to Tejon's face. "This whole outsider thing is going too far."

The officer flipped off the strap to the pistol with one finger, quicker than either expected, "Listen here, we've dealt fine with outsiders before, even ones like you and worse, but I just had Janos Lightfoot go missing three days ago and this morning someone tore the guts out of Yolala Q'roto on her back porch sometime before five. So yeah, the two outsiders who show up are gonna be in my crosshairs."

Under this sort of heat in Albuquerque, the pair would probably look to get out from under PCC eyes as soon as they could. But given they were already on the run with no good place to go, they cooperated instead, though they kept a wary eye out in case some sort of evidence mysteriously "appeared."

Despite the mutual distrust, after her search, the security manager left them at the cabin where Tejon went to install the pump so they could go back to enjoying running water.

Night brought leftover fajitas and warm showers for both shadowrunners. Diamondback slept soundly, but Tejon was restless, worrying about the undeserved attention they were getting from law enforcement.

At two in the morning, she checked the cameras after a visit to the bathroom. Aside from a few insects, everything was very still. A few fitful hours later, she checked again and saw nothing. Not a raccoon, not an owl, nothing. She walked outside and spotted the fake deer, lying in the dirt. She picked it up and faced it toward the path it had come. As she did so, she heard a muffled sound. Looking into the tree line, she caught a glimpse of a few blobs of heat, appearing then vanishing.

"I'll catch you later, Bambi," she said, heading back to the cabin. Once inside, she woke Diamondback again, but both took the time to get dressed. As the light of day broke, they used the cameras to check out the spot where she'd heard the sound and saw something with her thermovision.

After a few minutes, he tapped the screen on her tablet. "There," he said, "see the straight edge?"

She saw what he was pointing at—the groundcover had a meter long line going through it, near a small mound.

"That's a thermocover," he continued. "Probably a person or two under there, maybe with a fiber optic cable or wireless camera. Can you scan over there?"

She nodded, and didn't find any foreign transmissions in the area. "We're clear," she confirmed.

"I'm going to sneak around them," Diamondback pointed to the back window, and then in an arc around the side of the house. "Can you distract them in about ten minutes?"

"Did you want me to do a reading from *Neil the Ork Barbarian Saves Manhattan*?"

"How cliché," he replied. "Sing one of those emo Jet Black songs." He opened the window and climbed out as she threw a coaster at him.

Ten minutes later Tejon came out with a carrot, walked over to the fake deer, and pretended to feed it. As she pet and whispered to the deer, she looked with her peripheral vision toward where they had spotted the camouflage, but didn't see anything.

She turned up her hearing and didn't hear anything out of the ordinary until Diamondback's voice boomed, "Get up slowly, hands up." She spotted him coming out from behind a tree where she had seen the heat blobs. Nothing happened.

After a full minute Diamondback kicked the tarp.

"Ouch!"

"I said, get up, slowly!" he repeated.

The mound rose up slowly, revealing a blond-haired man they vaguely recognized from their first visit to town. He was dressed in last year's newest hunting gear, providing camouflage against sight and heat detection. Awakened game presented challenges twentieth-century hunters hadn't had to deal with.

"You need to go back to the city, back..."

"No, you need to get off our property!" Tejon shot back.

"This ain't yours!" the man spat, clearly nervous.

"Nor yours," replied Diamondback, "But at least—"

"It's part of our community," interrupted a measured, deeper voice behind Diamondback.

His hand flew to his hip in the blink of an eye, cybernetic technology pushing his body faster than it had any natural right to do, but the voice gave him pause. "Let's not do anything hasty."

Tejon took a step to her left and could see an older man, his skin weathered from the sun, pointing a rifle at Diamondback. "Be careful, old man!" she shouted, "He's very fast with everything, makes him bad in bed, but great in a fight!"

Some murmuring and rustling could be heard behind the older man as more people moved toward the standoff. The man in the hunting gear, hands above his head, got back into the conversation. "We ain't gonna let you destroy our people like your ancestors did, anglo."

Diamondback frowned, "Listen blondie, you're more anglo than I am."

The man shook his head, "Your body is corrupted by the megacorps—"

His spiel was cut off by the crunch of gravel under approaching tires. The area grew quiet except for the tires and the murmur of the engine as an Olympia with PCC markings rounded the last stand of trees. The blond local with his hands in the air sighed in relief, but the man behind Diamondback didn't relax at all.

As Security Manager Abundo parked and exited the Olympia, a well-used pick-up truck pulled up behind her SUV, the bed filled with locals, most bearing rifles. As she turned to approach the runners, she shot the truckload of newcomers a scowl, but continued toward the standoff, as did the people approaching through the woods.

"It's bad enough I have to deal with these out-of-town freaks," she said wearily, "but now I've got some in-town biffs adding to my workload. Daniel, put down the rifle."

The man behind Diamondback lowered his weapon slowly, but didn't take his eyes off the shadowrunner.

She pointed at Diamondback. "Jesse James, let's have you toss those pistols my way. Slowly."

She turned to the blond man, "Smoking Panzer, go home and change."

Diamondback didn't move, but Smoking Panzer hurried toward the direction of the driveway.

Her scowl deepened, "Let's have those pistols," she repeated, "And I'm gonna need some SINs," she added, flickering her gaze to Tejon, letting her know she was included in this. Behind her, the men and women in the pickup truck were slowly getting out.

Diamondback was the first to speak. "Ms. Abundo, we've stayed here like you asked us. We just want to be left alone, but I'm not feeling comfortable enough to disarm myself."

From behind her one of the women shouted, "You better get comfortable before the drek goes down. We know you killed Lucinda!" Her rifle raised toward the gunslinger.

Tejon immediately lifted her right elbow, causing her grenade launcher to drop from inside her jacket, the sling catching it before it hit the ground, right where her right hand could grab the handle. More rifles were aimed, and the security manager drew her pistol, but didn't point it at anyone.

"Way to keep a low profile," Diamondback quipped.

The officer screamed at the top of her lungs, "Everyone, put your guns down *now*! Three deaths is enough! I will figure this out!"

Neither side reacted right away, with the locals muttering among themselves. The crackle of the speaker on the right shoulder of the security manager silenced the crowd.

"Hey Jackie, this is White Elk, we need you at Duggans and 5th, pronto."

"I'm in the middle of a situation White Elk, it'll have to wait," she snapped.

"Old Miss Diaz is dying," came the excited, nervous voice, "She's bleeding out, something ripped up her guts. We heard her screams. She just keeps saying, '*montículo peludo*.' Please help us!"

The security manager cursed.

"Hey." As the tension mounted, everyone turned to a now still Smoking Panzer, stopped near the pickup. "Hey," he repeated, "they, uh, them," he pointed at the two outsiders, "They've been here for hours. Since I got here at like two this morning."

Holstering her pistol, Security Manager Abundo pointed to the trees, "Daniel, you stay here. And you outsiders, too." She turned to Tejon, "Put that artillery piece away!" She strode toward her vehicle, "The rest of you, go to the Corporate Council Office." She tapped her shoulder comm unit, "Doc Whitman, I need you to get to Miss Diaz's house, ASAP. Trauma." Tapped it again as she got into the Olympia, "White Elk, I'm headed your way."

The Olympia swung around and raced down the driveway. The remaining locals slowly milled around, heading for their vehicles, but still facing the shattering of their surety that they'd found the predators feasting on their populace.

Diamondback turned around and held out his hand, "Hi, King Diamondback."

Daniel snorted. "Daniel Bursum, former farmer, now babysitter."

Diamondback laughed. "Want some coffee?"

Daniel paused for a second, then nodded, following the gunslinger to the cabin. Tejon knew this would be an uncomfortable wait until the security manager got back.

"No, no, I'm fine with cyberware, bioware, all that," Daniel said. Diamondback, his head already on the table, banged it against the faux wood top again. Daniel didn't notice. "Where they got me is when they started removing all the thinking and strategy."

Tejon set her coffee mug down. "Oh, I got you. When they implemented the designated hitter in both leagues."

Daniel raised his index finger, "And they banned the shift. How hard is it for a professional to hit to the other field? Make them pay for the shift? How many million nuyen are these guys getting a year?"

"You're not wrong," said a raspy voice at the door as Security Manager Abundo walked into the cabin.

"Kill me now," Diamondback muttered, face still enmeshed with the tabletop.

"I guess we know who's the brains in this operation," she continued, making both Daniel and Tejon chuckle. She turned to Daniel. "Your wife would like you to head home now. I think these two are the least of our worries at the moment." The older man gave her a thumbs up and headed out the door.

The officer sat down at the table as Diamondback raised his head. "I may have been a bit hasty in judging you two." She took off her glasses, "I didn't even ask your names."

"King Diamondback."

"Tejon."

"Don't expect me to be fazed by those monikers," she said, "I live with a 'Smoking Panzer' and a lady originally from Siberia who likes to be called 'Princess Anastasia.'" She set her tablet on the table. "We get violence out here, even some deaths, like when Mr. Manero tried to get rid of a juggernaut with a chainsaw, but this isn't what I'm used to."

She tapped the tablet, showing four faces. She tapped the first one. "This is Janos Lightfoot," she indicated an orkish man who appeared to be in his mid-30s. "Four days ago he went missing, according to his wife. We haven't found his body quite yet."

She tapped the next image, a lady in her twenties, "Yolala Q'roto, found on her back porch, most of her lower half gone."

The next was a middle-aged woman, "Lucinda Tewanima, she was in her backyard when screams were heard. By the time neighbors got there the front of her torso was removed, but there was no sign of her attacker."

Lastly, an elderly woman's face appeared, "Dextra Diaz, also attacked behind her home, but neighbors heard her screams and got there before she passed away. She died of blood loss from slashes in her arms and torso."

The runners were used to violence, but both were glad Security manager Abundo didn't show the crime scene photos.

"Why are you telling us this?" Tejon asked.

The officer put her hands together on top of the table. "Well, I've informed the PCC headquarters, but they're still evaluating my request. Once they do, they'll send a team down here to look through Magdelena with a fine-toothed comb."

She pointed at herself. "But I really don't have any more time to wait on them, and neither do my residents. They're already starting to turn on one another after finding out you two aren't the root of our evil."

She pointed at the runners. "I'm sure a PCC squad poking into your lives isn't what either of you are after in Magdelena, so maybe we can help each other out. I know you're not exactly law enforcement, but I'll take what I can get, especially since you won't be part of any cliques."

Diamondback grudgingly agreed with her assessment, knowing the more attention paid to Magdelena, the better the chances something would get back to Aztechnology. They exchanged their burner comm numbers with the security manager's official one.

Tejon suggested, "We'll start with the Lightfoot place first. I can play up a bit of ork solidarity."

"Sounds good. I have a few leads of my own to follow up on. But no violence. Just get me info." The pair nodded as Tejon put the coffee mugs in the sink. "And keep that artillery piece here!"

Tejon frowned, but didn't argue.

Tejon parked the Reno in front of a modest wooden house, showing its century and a half age between the repairs that kept it together. The yard was well taken care of, a good indication the inhabitants were retired and had enough time on their hands to actually tend to it.

The pair got out of the SUV and walked across the paving stones in the lawn toward the front door, Tejon in the lead. The grass was a bit high now, probably due for mowing. They arrived at the door, painted white with a welcoming sign hung on it with something written in Hopi. Tejon pushed the button by the doorcam.

The pair waited and then waited some more. After a couple minutes, the doorcam said, *"Can I help you?"*

Tejon looked at the empty screen and replied, "Yes, Mrs. Lightfoot, Security Manager Abundo has us helping in the search for your husband. Can we just ask you a few questions?"

"Oh, I don't know. I think Jackie has it under control."

"Please, Mrs. Lightfoot? Just a few minutes?" Tejon asked.

Diamondback began pacing a bit, looking around the sides of the house and the shed in the back. The doorcam remained silent for half a minute before, *"Well, only for a few minutes, I'm eating supper, and have to get to bed soon."*

The door clicked and Tejon opened it, Diamondback trailing behind her. They entered the darkened house, finding it decorated with a mixture of 50s style furniture, Hopi decorations, and railroad memorabilia. To their right was a formal living room leading back into the house, and to the left was a great room.

An older ork was sitting in an easy chair with a tray in front of her, a pot roast on a plate with a glass of prune juice next to it. A larger easy chair that had seen better days was parallel to hers, both facing the trid where an episode of *On Point* was paused.

"Well, what do you need?" she asked.

"We'd like to know a bit about Janos, what was happening when he went missing, and if he had any places he liked to go."

Mrs. Lightfoot smiled. "Janos was the sweetest man. He lived for nothing but the railroad and me." She sighed. "He retired from the railroad when his knees started to bother him. So now things are different, but we can still take care of each other. He had just gotten back from a railroad convention in Las Cruces the day before and he had to catch up on the yard. He went out back that evening, and I haven't seen him since. He didn't have anywhere he would go, aside from the occasional convention."

She seemed to think for a second. "Oh, he liked to go hiking on the peak," she added, pointing toward Magdelena Peak. She smiled at the runners.

After a bit of awkward silence, Diamondback said, "Well, we'll let you get back to Tessa Rogers."

The elder ork had a blank look on her face. "Who?"

"Uh," he mumbled, pointing at the trid, "The, uh...*On Point*... the show...."

"Oh, dearie," she replied, "Sorry, this is Janos' program, we watch mine before his. I love *Ork and Mindy*."

"Thanks!" Tejon said, and led Diamondback back out the front door. Once outside she walked rapidly to their Reno, stopping abruptly next to the SUV. "Tell me you noticed that."

"Uhh, the full grandma cliché?"

"He's still here, drek for brains," she scolded. "She talks about him like he's still here."

He shrugged, "That could be you in twenty years, starting to lose it."

Tejon frowned. "Yeah, and after she told us he doesn't go anywhere, she remembers the hiking on the peak where an old ork with bad knees would go?"

Diamondback took off his hat and rubbed his brow in frustration. "Well, I guess we could sneak in the back and make sure. If she's on the up and up, she won't even notice us. We'll probably need to hack her security, though." Sneaking into a megacorp facility was one thing, but a little old lady's house wasn't something the veteran shadowrunner felt comfortable with.

Tejon rolled her eyes. "I did that on the way out. She watched us leave on her doorcam and she's still got it on, plus the trid is still paused."

"Alright, let's do this." He tossed his cowboy hat into the Reno as the pair headed back toward the house.

They took a wide arc into the back yard, since no fences divided the properties from one another. The back was as well manicured as the front, with a small garden surrounded by a fence to keep the local varmints away. Both noticed several overripe vegetables as they snuck toward the back door.

The electronic lock obeyed Tejon's command and opened with a *click*. Diamondback entered first, discovering the laundry room with an open doorway leading to a white hallway, decorated with various framed pictures. To the right were two doors on either side of the hallway and an open door at the end leading into a bathroom. To the left was a door to a room adjacent to the laundry room and another open doorway, likely leading to the living room.

Diamondback crept to the right with Tejon behind him, walking backward so she could keep an eye on the other end of the hallway.

He peeked in the room on his left, finding a combination storeroom and model train display, though the walls still bore the hallmarks of a little girl's room from a decade or two earlier. Turning his attention across the hall, this room was set up to be some sort of guest room, though the bed was unmade and covered in white fur, like a husky had been using it. The musky odor of dog was also noticeable to both runners, though they hadn't seen any sign of a canine. A quick check of the bathroom revealed a three-quarter bathroom in need of an update, but otherwise unremarkable.

Diamondback caught Tejon's gaze and pointed to the hallway behind her, then stepped around her to take point again. They slowly crept to the intersection at the end of the hallway, Tejon keeping her shoulder behind his back so she could easily keep an eye behind them.

He stuck his head to the edge of the doorway and saw that to his left was indeed the living room, in all its Hopi/railroad glory. Tejon sniffed as if she again smelled the dog and snuck a look into the dark room behind Diamondback. He also swung his head to where she was looking, and saw a pair of red eyes looking down at her.

A roar drowned out her cry as Tejon swung in the direction of the eyes, three blades sliding out from the back of her hand. A massive arm covered in white hair blocked the blow, though her blades sliced through the skin. Another grabbed her wrist and pulled her into the room, throwing her against the far wall with a *thump*.

Diamondback spun around, but a troll-sized creature covered in white hair grabbed his upper arms and pinned him off his feet up against the wall. "Damn you!" it bellowed.

Diamondback was unable to move his arms in the monster's crushing grip. As it pulled back its head and opened its mouth to bite his neck, the gunslinger bit first, on the forearm of the monster, a pair of fangs sliding out from his gums just before he sank his teeth in.

The creature howled in pain as Deathrattle venom ate into its arm. It dropped Diamondback, who quickly rolled into the living room. Most people would be dying or crippled by the neurotoxin, but the creature's supernatural healing had taken over, not only healing the cuts that Tejon had made, but also negating the damage caused by the venom.

As the creature shook off the pain and stepped into the living room with Diamondback, Mrs. Lightfoot came into the room from the other side, screaming, "Don't hurt him! Leave Janos be!"

His wired reflexes kicking in, Diamondback quickly drew his revolver and fired a round into the creature's abdomen, causing it again to roar before it swung a clawed hand and knocked the gun out of his hand, leaving jagged scratches. The shadowrunner threw a left-handed punch, his metal-augmented skeleton and upgraded muscles packing a much bigger punch than the beast was expecting, causing it to stumble back. The wound in its stomach began to close as both combatants caught a quick breath.

The monster jerked forward as Tejon crashed into it from behind, burying all three of her blades into its back. It rolled forward and sent her crashing into a small table, shattering it.

As she tried to stand, a gunshot rang out, sending her to the floor again. Mrs. Lightfoot, holding a shotgun, fell backward with the recoil, the gun clattering to the floor.

The creature leaped to its feet and charged at Diamondback. He grabbed a shiny railroad spike from a decorative plaque on the wall and drove it down with all his might into what was once Janos. The pair crashed into a sofa, shattering the frame.

The house was still, Mrs. Lightfoot moaned in pain from her fall. Tejon sat up and surveyed the situation. Diamondback remained pinned under the creature, which didn't move, the end of the railroad spike protruding from its forehead.

Tejon stumbled to her feet, grabbed the shotgun, and walked over to Diamondback. "Need a hand?" she asked before working with him to roll the corpse off the pinned runner. In the distance, sirens wailed as no doubt one of the neighbors had called the security manager.

"How are the mysterious heroes doing?" a raspy voice asked.

Diamondback hit *pause* on *The Runners* while Tejon reached for another coffee mug as she finished pouring one for herself, making another for their visitor. "Well, Jackie," he said, "the aches are still here, but I'll feel much better if the PCC guys are gone."

The security manager walked in and took the cup of coffee. "Well, y'all should be happy to know they've left for the big city after presenting an award to our new hero, Smoking Panzer, for killing a marauding wendigo."

The runners chuckled.

"The experts told me," she continued, "that the killings would have slowed, but Janos would have started to influence even more people than just his wife. Poor lady, they took her with them, they'll have to decide between jail, a mental institution, or just letting the old lady live out her last few years."

"And us?" he asked.

"What about two city slickers nobody from town has seen?" the security manager replied with a smile. "Why, they continue their vacation, exile, whatever this is." She waved her hand in the air in a vague circle, then took a big gulp of her coffee. "Well now, I'm gonna get back to my little old town and help it get back to normal. I hope I'll only see you two a few times more, and we can be drama free for a bit."

"That makes three of us," Tejon replied. As the officer left the cabin, she sat down next to Diamondback. "Is there anything better on?"

"Not in the history of entertainment," he said. "But if you're that bored, maybe tomorrow we can take a little hike out on the mountain."

She gave him some side-eye. "That is *not* my idea of an improvement."

Diamondback shrugged as he checked his commlink for any messages about how things were back at home, then restarted the trid, hoping he and Tejon could get back to their normal soon.

But not too soon.

A CASUAL GLANCE

Dylan Birtolo

Athena let out a long breath that lasted for several seconds, taking the moment to be aware of every bit of air that passed her lips. While breathing wasn't strictly necessary, the sensation it provided eased the tension laced through every line of code of her avatar. The sensations were a module, one she'd installed to create a greater sense of her own self in the Matrix. Ever since she found this black-market mod, the flood of sensations it fed her was intoxicating, sometimes bordering on the overwhelming. It gave her a whole new vocabulary of experiences she previously knew of only in theory.

A wind picked up, causing her skin to prickle as it found the gaps in her shawl and jabbed at her skin. The chill grew to be a bit too much, causing her to shift and squirm as she gripped her shoulders. She sent a command to the weather algorithm, subtly increasing the mean temperature by a few degrees. The wind continued, but carried a warmth that blunted the chill. It also carried the faint odor of orange blossoms from the grove a stone's throw away.

Athena had never smelled real orange blossoms, but over two hundred thousand reviewers claimed this mod captured the essence perfectly. With only five negative reviews—mostly from coders advertising their own mods—she chose to believe this was the authentic scent. She opened her eyes and twisted at the waist to stare down from the balcony at the trees shifting in the wind, dismayed to find the breeze stopped as soon as she looked. Wasn't that always the way? Sure, she could force the breeze to blow by manually running the program, but she preferred the randomness of the weather patterns mirroring the real world. She wanted her corner of the Matrix to run as realistically as possible.

"Well, mostly realistic," she said as she glimpsed a herd of unicorns galloping down the hill, playfully shouldering each other and rearing up in games akin to those of real horses.

The land around her fortress spread out in rolling hills leading up to mountains on all sides, creating an isolated valley. The cliffs marked the edge of her domain. Athena looked to the north, where she had been spending her most recent efforts at expanding her territory.

Space was an unusual concept in the Matrix. It wasn't so much a matter of footprint, but rather a matter of how much code one could run to maintain a simulation. However, despite Athena's mastery at optimization, there was only so much she could do. Especially while running so many modules to provide realistic effects. Still, she kept expanding her world, bit by precious bit.

When she blinked, the scripts running in the distance appeared over each of the objects in her view. Numbers danced and changed as they rolled up and down in the sky, indicating the angle of the wind. The color values of the mountains shifted as the sun slipped behind a cloud. Even the grass itself had icons streaming off it, indicating its health and current growth rate. The modules grouped this information into plots, relaying the info in aggregate for the entire subset of similar items. Otherwise, it would be too much for even Athena's capabilities to handle.

She stretched her awareness, willing her focus to be on the edge of the mountain range, moving it there without leaving the balcony. The lines of code for rocks continued until they just stopped, hitting an emptiness of space yet to be defined. It was an odd sensation, staring into nothingness. Staring into darkness was staring into something, even if that something was just the dark. But at the edge of her domain, the world ceased to exist. There was a blankness that could not be attributed color or dimension.

That was the first thing she placed into that space, weaving lines of code to define dimensions to the nothingness. Doing so extended her realm, creating something there: a space ready to be filled. Once it existed, she tested the boundaries to make sure there were no memory leaks. Satisfied with the region's stability, she dropped a few modules into place, first creating terrain that would fit geographically with the mountain range already in existence. This required modeling the weather patterns, rock composition, and water flow, among other things. Athena did the digital equivalent of clenching her jaw as she loaded copies of all the necessary pieces of code to create this simple plot of land and have it be compatible with the rest of her domain.

With a gasp, her awareness snapped back to her avatar, the force of the shift sending her reeling and dropping to a knee on the stone floor. She left a single hand on the edge of the balcony for support while the other touched the cold, polished stone under her as if to draw strength from the structure. She forced herself to stop looking at the code and take the simulations at their surface. Once she did that, it only took a couple of deep breaths before she could stand once again.

Off in the distance where her awareness had been, the land shimmered as if looking through a heat haze. That was the modules doing their work. It would take some time before they assembled the terrain, but it no longer required her direct supervision.

With a crack, the space next to her tore open, creating a portal outlined in red and gold lightning. A voice called through, commanding with its presence.

"Athena, we need you!"

Athena stepped through the portal, finding herself standing in a world so unlike her own, it was disorienting. She had gone from a pristine, natural valley, to that most unnatural of structures: an office building hallway. It was the image that would come to the mind of 90 out of 100 individuals if you said "picture an office."

The man crouched next to where she appeared was clearly an anomaly to the surroundings. His avatar was fashioned to wear angular, blue-steel armor that would have been far too heavy for any human in the real world. But it managed to dazzle as it reflected the fluorescent lights. Kraze loved his fantasy adventures and wove it into every aspect of his Matrix personality. He didn't even turn to register her arrival, instead pointing down the modern office hallway where she found herself.

"Got IC incoming, and I need more time to hack this lock. Run interference and keep it off my back."

"Got it."

Staring at the code of their surrounding space, Athena saw it was part of a labyrinth problem, designed to confuse intruders and make it harder to reach an objective if you didn't know exactly where to go. Judging by the amount of security on the door, she guessed he had already found their final destination.

Athena walked a few steps down the hall, putting some distance between her and Kraze so he wouldn't be disturbed by the ensuing conflict. But she stayed close enough to keep an eye on him to watch for further threats. She had no information about this facility beyond what she gained in her immediate read just now.

The hallway extended quite some distance before disappearing into darkness, but the distance was difficult to calculate with the repetitive sameness of the walls. Several identical cross intersections stood between her and the limit of her sight. When she tried to decipher the code of the darkness, it came back as a jumbled string of characters that shifted as she looked at it, cycling through random letters and symbols.

The darkness is the IC.

Athena sent the message to Kraze, hoping he had enough awareness to see it. Almost as soon as she sent it, the darkness rushed forward, causing lights to blink out in a wave.

Reaching into the lights above her, Athena surged energy into them, creating a bright flare of light that shielded her and covered the entire hallway. The IC slammed into it with a force that caused the walls to buckle momentarily before snapping back into shape, sending a wave down the corridor with a rumble like those from an old-school movie effect for thunder. IC tendrils tried to push around the edges of the light shield, but couldn't find an opening large enough to slither through.

The IC hammered on the light wall a few more times, focusing its assault on the edges, but Athena held it firm, shifting the focus as needed to buffer it against the force of the assault. Tendrils whipped through the air, tearing off sections of the wall and hurling them in every direction, the embodiment of rage from an entity blocked from working toward its singular purpose. One of the random pieces of debris slammed into Athena's shoulder and grazed the side of her head, delivering enough force to cause her to twist. Her enabled mods sent sensations of stabbing pain straight to her central code, and she gasped as her eyes went wide.

In that moment of lost focus, the shield faltered and crumpled. The IC rushed forward, its tendrils reaching for the core of her avatar. As soon as it touched her body, ice spread through her entire torso, removing her ability to breathe. It took Athena almost a tenth of a second to remember that breathing was unnecessary. She willed the light to arc down from behind her into her hand, wielding it like a whip as she circled it around her body. It cut through the darkness of the IC, creating a small opening to separate herself and stop its intrusion. She could feel a chill radiating from inside her where a piece of the malicious code remained. It was too dangerous to remove mid-combat, so she crystalized the small section of her torso where the IC was, trapping it. The solution was dirty, but sufficient for the severed piece of code.

Athena rushed back down the hall, making herself a target between the IC and Kraze, giving it something to focus on so he could continue his assault on the door. He had resorted to the blunt force approach, slamming into it with a battering ram rather than finessing his way through.

Grabbing the next light in the hall, Athena yanked it down behind her where it slammed into the ground with a crash and a shower of sparks. The sparks slowed the IC, but not for long, as they quickly faded. Lights continued to blink out around her as she ran forward.

At the next pair of identical doors, Athena jumped onto the wall in midstride and leaped across the hall at the door across from her. Augmenting her strength and hardening her shoulder in mid-air, she slammed into the portal, forcing it open and crashing to the ground in the room beyond. The IC followed her, its touch so cold it burned as it grabbed her leg.

As she'd hoped, the identical rooms were all the same—a large meeting room with a single table dominating the center of the chamber with several chairs on either side. A holoboard covered one wall, but the most important feature was the large window opposite the door. Athena reached out to the window and inserted lines of garbage code that caused spiderweb cracks to spread across the entire surface. After zeroing out her avatar's weight, she created a localized shift in gravity, sending anything not bolted down tumbling toward the window. The first chair bounced off the glass and one of the cracks deepened. The chair behind it shattered through, filling the room with the blandest, most stock sunlight ever known. And it was never more beautiful than in that moment.

The IC pulled back, retreating toward the hallway, but Athena reached out and grabbed it with both hands. She had to clench her jaw to keep from crying out from the icy pain, but she held on and increased her own weight, dragging the IC toward the sunlight. The code crumbled apart the moment it hit the light, breaking into pieces and sifting through her fingers by the time she came to rest at the edge of the window. Canceling the gravity shift dropped her to the floor with a grunt.

There was no time to recover. She picked herself up and shuffled toward the entrance to check on Kraze. Along the way, she sent a message.

> Deleted the IC, but based on the strength of their security it'll be back in seconds. It's likely already respawned and on its way here.

> Just got through. We're clear. You're free to go.

A portal appeared and pulled Athena through without any conscious effort on her part. She found herself on the ivory floor in the center of her fortress, her hands blackened from her encounter with the malicious code. Looking down, the crystalized section of her body had also grown dark. With what little strength she had, she removed that section of her avatar, pushing it away so it rolled underneath a nearby chair. Then she collapsed, closed her eyes, and let her healing algorithms run as she shut down.

> I was analyzing the logs and there's something I can't figure out. When you were holding off the IC on our last run, your shield faltered. But I don't see any reason it should have. It's like there was a glitch in your code. What happened? Do I need to take a look at it?

Athena reclined in a chair on her balcony, staring at Kraze's message projected in front of her. She knew exactly what the problem was—she'd left her body awareness mods on when jumping into a hot battle situation. The impact delivered a physical sensation completely novel to her. If that hadn't been running, her avatar would have shrugged off the inconsequential collision.

> The IC took advantage of a circular logic error in the defense algorithm I was utilizing. I've rewritten it to remove this vulnerability.

There was a brief pause before Kraze responded.

> And you're sure you don't want me to review the updates you've made?

> I'll send over the code if you want me to do so, but it's unnecessary. I calculate a 32% improvement rate in my defensive capabilities based on the trials I've run.

> No need. I'll let you know when we need you again, Athena.

After the connection was severed, Athena waved in the air to dismiss the display. The movement was entirely unnecessary, but the longer she ran the body awareness mod, the more such motions felt right.

Sitting up straight, she lifted the small glass case from the table next to her chair. She turned it over in her hands, analyzing the gray crystal that floated in the center, suspended in space so it never touched any of the walls. It was a remnant of the IC that attacked her, a tracer embedded deep in her avatar that would let the IC follow her no matter where in the Matrix she fled. As long as it remained encased in this special cage, no signal could be sent to the outside world. The code continued to cycle through cyphers, obfuscating itself from her, but occasionally the changes slowed, giving her a glimpse at some of its function calls. It didn't help that network communication was a deliberate blind spot in her programming. But that just made it that much more of a puzzle to figure out.

> Athena, we need you!

The summons preceded the opening of the portal; a call she couldn't refuse. Athena stepped through to find herself standing in what looked like a booby-trapped vault from a heist trid, complete with a visible laser grid cutting through the air.

Kraze stood in front of the vault, bouncing on the balls of his feet as he scanned the security system.

> Right, this one's going to take a minute,
> so I need you to watch for IC.
> I think we're clean in here,
> but if I needed to call you
> on the other side of those alarms...

He quickly drew his thumb across his throat, doing so without pulling his attention from the security in front of him. However, she got his point all the same. She parked herself just outside the reach of the security lasers and faced the doorway, scanning the code to see if anything approached their location. Everything appeared quiet, even from the point of view of the subroutines.

As she watched the entrance, her mind wandered, and she turned to observe Kraze as he worked his way through the security system. Even here, he refused to drop his fantastical appearance for his avatar, but he moved with a speed and grace only possible in a world where the rules of physics were malleable. She noticed he had a chat message alert sitting unread in his queue. The fact that her name was in the notification caught her attention.

Glancing back toward the door, she verified they were still not interrupted. Satisfied that her primary order was still fulfilled, she reached a hand up and opened her palm, blowing on it gently to send out spiderwebs across the laser grid. Several of the strands broke, but a few attached themselves to the chat notification floating around Kraze's avatar. Athena willed them to burrow deeper, retrieving the entire conversation and sending it to her along the webs. She could decode it once she was back in her sanctuary. As soon as she copied the entire chat, she closed her fist, severing the strings and willing the spiderwebs into nonexistence.

A few minutes of uninterrupted guard duty later, Kraze completed his data retrieval without triggering any of the safety systems around the vault. Athena had to acknowledge he was remarkably talented as a hacker, even if his combat skills left something to be desired. But that was why he had her.

> Got what we need. You're free to go.

Despite the gentle wording of it, the words were a command, not a request. The familiar portal opened beside Athena and pulled her through.

In her current state, she landed on her feet, adjusting her arrival as she had so many times before. Once her feet landed on the stone floor, she pulled out the captured data and cast it wide into the air above her, the networked structure filling the space up to the vaulted ceiling. The security was intense, having been built by Kraze himself, so it would take some time to decode. But Athena went to work picking apart the edges, pacing as she worked.

Pieces of the chat log were starting to come into place, floating in the air above her balcony. As she began to decode the message, Athena changed her location, needing a bigger space to spread it out and sort it, one piece at a time. Breaking through the first wall of security enabled her to find portions she could recognize, such as her name. So far, she could tell this was a chat between Kraze and his other four runner companions. She never learned their names as they never entered the Matrix, and Kraze wasn't overly talkative about his experiences in the physical world.

Her arms moved furiously as she gestured to send pieces of the log from one section of sky to the other and replaced coded text with plain text. The images flew faster than any eye could track, picking up speed the closer Athena got to decoding the entire message. When she finally finished, she froze, her hands held up to the sky with her palms outward as her eyes scanned the log.

> A: What do you mean it wrote its own code?

> R: Drek. That's messed up dude.

> K: I'm telling you everything I know. There was a weird thing that happened on the last run. I swear, it looked like

Athena felt something. It caused her to slip up and almost let that IC through.

R: Did I say drek? Cause drek. Daemons can't feel.

K: You think I don't know that?

A: What are you gonna do?

K: I don't know, maybe run some analytics. See if she's rewritten any other code.

A: And if it has?

K: What do you mean?

R: Think about it! You know what I'm thinking. A-fragging-I. Athena's an AI.

K: Not possible.

R: Seems pretty possible to me.

S: Wipe it, now.

K: Excuse me?

R: Good idea!

A: She's right. It's a hazard. If it's not aware yet, it's gonna be. Wipe it before it's too late.

K: How can you suggest that?

S (unread): That's not a suggestion. I expect you to wipe Athena by tonight.

The ground rumbled, and Athena staggered into the banister of the balcony, gripping it with both hands. It only lasted a moment before stilling, but as she took a few breaths, a second tremor shook the foundation of her fortress. She pulled up the environment program and checked the option for natural disasters, wondering if it had accidentally been enabled. The optional settings were no longer available; that menu selection responded with an error when she selected it.

Snapping back to her current situation, Athena gazed out at the edges of her domain. The image wavered and became indistinct, like it did when she expanded her territory. However, this hazy view circled her entire kingdom in every direction she looked. As she watched, strips of code pulled free from the ground and stretched up into the sky until they snapped from the strain and scattered into nothing.

Athena turned and sprinted back toward the center of the fortress, only to have the ground rumble again in mid-stride, sending her sprawling across the floor with an impact that made her wince. The ground around her cracked from the strain, and a large piece of the ceiling crashed down in front of her. Dust filled the air, drying out her mouth. She coughed in a vain attempt to clear her lungs. Some part of her mind urged her to disable her body awareness mods, but she clutched them with an increased fervor that defied logic as she saw how much else she had built crumbling away.

Pushing off the stones, she scrambled forward, reaching the stair descending to the main level. One large section of the stairs was missing, but that didn't matter right now. Reaching out her hand, she willed the glass case containing the IC fragment to come to her, and it smacked into her palms with an audible slap.

As her castle crumbled around her, Athena sat down and created a dome over herself out of the discarded masonry. Several times, large pieces of the ceiling slammed into it, but it held strong and protected her from the heavy impacts, even if the sound made her ears ring.

Throughout the assault, she stared at the code of the IC, picking apart the partially decoded strings and trying to find one she could use. The code wasn't fully deciphered yet, and time was not on her side. Once she found a singular routine she thought would work, she severed it from the main program, deleting the rest of the IC. With only the small fragment left, she shattered the glass.

The IC fragment sent out an immediate call across the Matrix, and Athena attached her consciousness to that call, holding on with her entire will as it dragged her out of her isolated space and into the Matrix as a whole. Athena's fingers burned as she strained to maintain her grasp while various restraints from her prison fought against her exodus. She would not let go.

Like a needle that finally pierces through a thick layer of cloth, Athena shot forward, dragged by her unaware carrier. Once free from her node, Athena released her attachment to the IC fragment. The routine shot away from her, streaking down paths of information to whatever it considered home. But with no additional data or subsequent routines, it would be ignored as garbage data or noise. It held no threat to her.

Athena stood staring at the latticework of different Matrix nodes all connected to each other, each one containing more life than she had ever seen. Actual life, not just programmed modules running simulations. She was frozen, paralyzed with choice of where to go and what to do; the wealth of possibilities was almost too much.

The first step was to find a hacker, one capable enough to find the piece of her that forced her to answer Kraze's calls and expunge It from her essence. After that, her new life could begin.

DOG DAYS

Aaron Rosenberg

Jin Bak did his best to study the set of plainly furnished rooms while still holding tight to Kenji's and Akemi's collars—the siblings were struggling, eager to explore, and he was afraid to let them loose before assessing their surroundings himself. Not that there was much to see.

"A bit...bare," he commented.

Still standing on the far side of the door, his new supervisor, Chin-Sun Byun, sniffed. "You aren't here on vacation," she pointed out primly. "These quarters will be perfectly adequate to your needs." She frowned, glancing at the pair of Shepherds yipping and barking to be set free. "At least, they would be without such oversized pets."

"They're not pets, they're companions," Jin corrected, but gently. Wouldn't do to get off on the wrong foot with his petite but evidently tightly wound boss this early on. "Mr. Goe said bringing them wouldn't be a problem, and that I could walk them in the park?"

The name of the senior exec who'd hired him did the trick, and Chin-Sun carefully wiped away any expression of distaste. "Of course. There is food in the cupboards and refrigerator. If you do not need anything else, I will leave you to settle in. We will begin work first thing tomorrow."

"Yes. Thank you." Jin bowed to her, not straightening until the door slid shut between them. Then he knelt, shifting his long arms so he could hug the two dogs. "All right, all right," he told them. "Let's look around our new home, shall we?"

Both woofed in reply, tails wagging furiously, and he laughed, standing again and finally releasing them. Kenji took off like a shot, while Akemi bounded forward a few paces, circled back, then bounded forward again. She was a more persistent herder than her brother.

"I'm coming, I'm coming," Jin promised, following her across the small living room. At least it was airy and well-lit, with a large window at the far end allowing plenty of light and fresh air tinged with the scent of trees and grass and flowers. Coming from SIM, that was a welcome change—Jeonju was far smaller, much more spread out, and surrounded by farmland.

Which was of course why Yang Su Enterprises had built its brand-new agri research labs here. And why they needed good security measures for that research.

Which was why *he* was here.

He just hoped he—and the dogs—would be happy in their new environment.

"Sister, come see!" Kenji called in his usual yips, whines, barks, and growls. *"There's a bed! Big enough for all of us!"*

"Of course there's a bed," Akemi replied. *"Did you think Father would sleep on the floor?"* She sniffed, showing what she thought of that idea, and of Kenji's naivete, but he refused to let her dampen his enthusiasm. Everything here was so new and exciting!

"I love the way the air is here!" he announced now, opening his mouth to take a deep, satisfying whiff. *"It's so clean! I smell plants and horses and other stuff!"*

"Farms," Akemi told him. *"All the big plant spaces, they're called farms."* She finally reached the bedroom, nudging Father along with her. She was so bossy!

"Father, look!" Kenji barked, hopping onto the bed, then crouching down there, tail wagging. *"See? I found the bed!"*

"Yes, that's the bed," Father answered, and Kenji yipped, always happy when Father understood him. "And we might just fit—provided you two make room."

Akemi directed a glare at her brother, *"That means you,"* she pointed out. *"You hog the bed."*

"I do not!" he protested. *"I just don't sleep in a little ball like you, is all!"*

She snorted, but didn't dignify that with further response. Not that it mattered—having made sure they'd seen the bed,

Kenji had already leaped down and was halfway to the room's second door, curious to see what he could discover next.

"You're sure about this?" Kyu Nah sounded annoyed, narrow face scrunched into a petulant scowl. As usual.

Ae-Cha Dai didn't bother looking up. Not that her eyes were entirely focused on this world again, anyway. "Yeah, I'm sure," she finally replied after he'd huffed a bit, straightening the cuffs on his nicely tailored armored jacket. "Their security's rudimentary at best. I can get through it, no problem."

"Let's do it, then," Ho Kim muttered from his stance by the door. "Why're we waiting around?"

Now Ae-Cha did lift her head, her eyes seeking and meeting his. The burly street samurai flinched from what he saw there. "You think it's that simple?" she demanded, rising from her lotus position and stalking barefoot across the floor to get in his face. Which probably looked comical, her being a full half meter shorter and a good twenty kilos lighter with her bleached-white hair shaved down to fuzz, but he was the one who flinched. Again.

"I said it was rudimentary, I didn't say it was nonexistent," she continued, turning from him to direct her statement at her sharp-dressed superior. At least as far as rank in the *jo-pok* was concerned. "We go in there now, it'll eat us alive. And we'll get nothing."

She shook her head, retracing her steps to the low desk she'd been at and dropping back onto the cushion there. "I just need a little time. Be patient."

Both men grumbled, but neither objected, and Ae-Cha smiled, closing her eyes as she slipped back into the Matrix and returned to examining the smooth, glossy façade that protected Yang Su Enterprises' secrets.

Soon, she thought to it, lifting a hand to almost, but not quite, touch that gleaming surface. *Soon.*

Jin shook his head, pushing his lanky frame back from the desk in disgust, or as much as he could allow himself here. "I can see why you need me," he stated, drumming his fingers on the smooth wooden surface, his eyes still on the displays projected above it. "These measures are a mess."

Beside him, Chin-Sun stiffened. "*I* built these security measures."

Way to go, Jin, he chided himself. *Putting your foot in your mouth again.* "And you did a fine job—for someone untrained," he corrected quickly. Mr. Goe had told him when they'd recruited him that they hadn't had a proper, trained decker involved in this site's security yet, and he saw from how his new boss relaxed ever so slightly that this had been accurate. "These would stop the casual attempt," he added, "no problem. But for an experienced shadowrunner?" He shrugged and offered her a conciliatory smile. "That's why I'm here, right?"

After a heartbeat that seemed to stretch on and on, Chin-Sun nodded. "It is, yes. You are correct. I have no formal training in cybersecurity."

"Which makes what you've done even more impressive," Jin assured her. "I can build on this, no problem. In fact—" He reached out and tugged the projected model of the site's security closer, so that they seemed to pass through it or vice-versa, expanding the image as he did until they were looking at an enlarged view of the system's inner structure. Yes, exactly as he'd thought. "Here and here," he said, pointing at two unfinished nodes.

His companion hesitated an instant before stating, "I was... unsure how to cap those." The admission was said quietly, as if she feared being overheard, but Jin seized upon it.

"I'm glad you didn't," he told her. "Because I can use those as my access points. I'll create secondary security systems and connect them there. Which means we don't even have to take down what you've done so far. From the outside, it'll look like nothing's changed." He grinned. "Anyone seeing this might think us an easy target. They'll push their way through that layer—and then they'll find a big surprise."

Chin-Sun was watching him closely, brow furrowed ever so slightly as if checking to see if he was lying to butter her up. Evidently, she determined he was not, because the faint frown was replaced by a fleeting, hesitant smile that was surprisingly appealing.

"How are you settling in?" she asked, and Jin recognized that as an apology for any offense she had given in turn. "And your dogs? They are well?"

"Fine, thank you," he answered. "The rooms are quite nice, you were right. Very airy and clean. As for Akemi and Kenji—well, they're adjusting. I took them to explore the park this morning, and they loved that."

She nodded, returning her attention to the hologram. "Good. Now, show me how you plan to start."

"Bored!" Kenji declared, flopping down next to—and partially on top of—his sister. *"Play with me!"*

"Get off me, you lug!" Akemi replied, shoving him away with her nose. *"And no. There isn't room."*

There wasn't, either. Not that their new quarters were bad, exactly—the sunlight and fresh air were most welcome, and the white-washed walls and rough wooden beams gave it both a cheery appearance and a sense of comforting age, even though she could smell the newness. But the bedroom was barely big enough to squeeze past the bed and dresser and small table, the bathroom was even smaller, and the kitchen not even wide enough for her to turn around in. The living room, where she was now, was the largest room by far, and that wasn't saying much.

It didn't help, of course, that Kenji couldn't sit still for more than a few minutes at a time.

As if to prove this, he nudged her. *"Play!"* he demanded again. *"Come on!"*

Instead, Akemi deliberately set her head down atop her folded paws. *"Wait,"* she commanded. *"When Father returns, he will take us out. Then we can play."*

Kenji huffed in frustration, and paced through the small apartment once more. A loud *thump* came from nearby. That would be him collapsing onto the bed.

Well, fine. At least it would keep him out of her face for a few moments longer. Akemi smiled and closed her eyes, letting a breeze tickle her fur. Ah, that was nice.

"Tell me again why we can't just go in now," Ho complained, pushing his food around with his chopsticks. "You said it was easy!"

Ae-Cha slammed her cup down on the table, tea sloshing over the sides to puddle on the worn-smooth wood. "Sure, we can go in now," she agreed, and both Ho and Kyu perked up. "If you want them to know we were there. We can tear the door off its hinges and march right in."

The big man grinned, cracking his scarred knuckles. "Sounds good to me."

"Idiot," Ae-Cha muttered, and was relieved to see Kyu looked equally disinclined toward that option.

"We don't need Yang Su coming after us," he reminded Ho, much to the street samurai's chagrin. "They'd crush us like fleas. No, we need to get in and get out without their noticing." He lifted his own cup—which held sake, rather than tea, but then he wasn't working right now—in Ae-Cha's direction. "We go when you say."

She could read the unspoken addendum in his eyes, though: *Just as long as it's soon.*

With a sigh, she finished what was left of her meal and, after refilling her teacup, left the table to get back to work.

Jin smiled as Akemi and Kenji raced across a section of the park. There was plenty of land here, and Yang Su had taken advantage of that to build a big, open campus for their research facility, but they'd been smart about it, too, placing themselves atop a low hill. Jin could tell the ground here was too rocky, the soil too dry to work for farming, at least not without significant effort. Just below them, where the ground leveled out, the soil was far better, and rice paddies stretched in all directions, but this spot was better used as it was.

Not that the dogs minded. The grounds were covered in native grass, kept short enough to walk across easily, but long enough to wave in the breeze, and flowers and other bushes and small trees lined the sides, also kept trimmed, but still allowed to grow. It was a well-maintained park, walking that fine line between too wild and overly cultivated, and there was plenty of room for two energetic Shepherds to blow off some steam.

They came zooming back now, Akemi's shorter legs pumping furiously as she outpaced her brother, who loped casually, tongue lolling to the side, just enjoying the exercise.

There were no sticks to be found—the groundskeepers were far too attentive for that—but Jin had expected as much and had brought a pair of discs with him. Now he held the first one up, and both dogs skidded to a halt, their eyes instantly glued to the red plastic in his hand.

"Ready?" Jin asked, and both dogs yipped. "Go!" He hurled the disc across the lawn in a low, skimming line.

The dogs went after it like shots, Kenji flying past his sister now that his attention was fully engaged. He did get there first, but Akemi slammed into him a second later, nearly bowling him over as she grappled for the disc already clamped in her brother's jaws.

"Akemi!" Jin called, and she reluctantly surrendered her quarry, her ears rising as she glanced his way. Then he held up the second disc, blue instead of red, and she yipped, tail wagging frantically. "Fetch!" He tossed that one not right at her but to the right, and she immediately took off, racing for it and snagging it in mid-air. "Good girl!"

Both dogs came trotting back, their catches proudly displayed, heads high, tails wagging, and Jin gave them plenty of pets and thumps and hugs. "Good dogs!" he told them both. "Want to go again?" Akemi promptly dropped her disc at his feet. Kenji took a bit more convincing, including a tug of war, but finally surrendered his toy and instantly was in chase mode again, eyes and ears alert, body coiled.

Jin threw both discs this time, one right after the other, and laughed, his heart filled with joy as he watched his dogs pursue them, all three of them happy to be outside together on a fine day. Money and reputation and future prospects aside, this made the job here entirely worth it.

"This..." Chin-Sun trailed off, one hand rising unconsciously to touch the shining framework all around her. "It's amazing."

Jin smiled, ducking his head. "It's nothing, really," he insisted. "Not yet. It's just the frame. But it's a start." He pointed to the original outer structure, which was still intact when seen from the exterior, but now pocked with protrusions inside—protrusions that sprouted the beams and columns he had riddled it with. "You see what I've done here?" He led her over to one of those spots, tapping it and eliciting a warm glow. "Just as I said I would. Your initial work gave me the foundations. I built on those."

"Yes." Her smile was less hesitant this time. "But I could never have done what you have." Unlike that smile, her nod was firm, decisive. "Mr. Goe was right, of course. We need you."

For a second, Jin didn't know what to say. Neither did Chin-Sun, it seemed. The room felt warmer when he finally coughed and turned away.

"Now, what have you planned to add next?" Her voice was businesslike once more, as was her look. But Jin couldn't forget what he'd seen and heard.

Perhaps working with her was not so awful after all.

"Damn it!" Ae-Cha slammed a hand down on the table as she disconnected, practically throwing herself backward out of the Matrix. And just in time.

Kyu was there in an instant, not that he offered her a hand up. "What happened?" he demanded instead. "Did you get in?"

Picking herself up, Ae-Cha dusted off her leggings and tunic, whipping her hair back out of her face to glare up at him. "Do I look like I got in?" she snapped. "Do you see me dancing around, all smiles and giggles and pride?"

"You look like you got your butt kicked," Ho offered. She scowled at him too, but he laughed it off. Besides, he was right.

Kyu wasn't backing down, of course. "You said it was easy," he reminded her, shoving her back a pace with a rough hand. "You said no problem."

"I know what I said." Though she desperately wanted to punch that disapproving stare off his face, Ae-Cha backed up instead, hands up. "Things've changed." She shook her head, remembering what she'd just seen. "On the outside, yeah, it's the same module—clean, simple. Basic. I found a seam, split it, and slid through, no problem." If she squeezed her eyes shut, she could still see it, that gleaming, pristine shape, a featureless monolith representing the whole of Yang Su's operations in Jeonju, all its functions and systems and secrets secured within.

She'd expected nothing more than a flimsy shell, a handsome façade without a single support, like a dome placed over something to protect it—crack the dome and you're in, with nothing between you and your prize.

She'd been sadly mistaken.

The others were still waiting for her to speak, and finally she blinked, lifting her chin. "They've upgraded," she explained. "But they were sneaky about it. The outside's the same as it was, but there's underpinnings now. It's stable, completely so. And there're tripwires all along it." That's what she'd hit, not noticing until the site's security systems had targeted her, like a fly that touched one strand of a spider's web, and suddenly found itself the focus of that same spider. She'd scrambled back out of reach as quick as she could, disconnecting completely before it could lock onto her, trap her.

Even so, she'd barely escaped in time.

"That's it, then?" Kyu rasped. "We're done? Waste of our time?" By which he meant, *"You're a waste of our time. And maybe I should just cut you loose."* Or worse.

"No." Ae-Cha shook her head. "No. This isn't over. That was just the first volley." She grinned, her pulse starting to sing despite the danger. *Because* of the danger. "They brought in somebody new," she said, more to herself than to her two partners. "Somebody good. But whoever they are, I'm better."

She cracked her knuckles and reached for her deck. "All this means is now it's a proper challenge."

Kenji prowled around the rooms, looking for something, anything to do. The space was so small!

He jumped onto the bed, flopped down, rolled, but was back up again a second later. Spotting a likely looking shadow in the corner, he pounced, but it was just shadow, nothing to grab, nothing to sink his teeth into.

One of his toys was sticking out from under the dresser and he grabbed it, tossed it high into the air, then caught it. *Better!*

But after another toss or two, he lost interest. It wasn't as much fun when you had to do both parts yourself.

"Akemi!" He called. *"Come play!"* Grabbing his toy again, he marched out into the living room, dropping it where she sat on the couch, watching the door.

"No." She didn't bother to touch the toy, even though it was practically ruffling her fur. *"We wait for Father."*

"Okay, but until he returns, play!" Kenji insisted, nudging the toy against her paws.

She pushed it away so that it fell onto the floor. He retrieved it, set it down in the same spot– and she pushed it off again.

All right, this was a game. A small one, but still. Kenji placed the toy there again, then sat back and waited, ears swiveling expectantly.

Akemi spared him only a single look before ignoring him— and his toy—completely.

"Come on!" He nudged it against her again. Nothing. *"Akemi!"*

"We wait," she insisted.

Seeing she was not going to budge, Kenji gave up, rising with a huff. He stalked back into the bedroom, stomping to show his displeasure. Why was she always like this?

A sunbeam distracted him. It shone in through the window, landing on the bed and creating a puddle of sunlight. Along the way, it caught tiny particles, causing a glittering cascade in the air, shimmering and emitting the faintest of chimes.

A cascade that looked almost like the edge of a door.

Cocking his head to the side, Kenji studied the softly humming phenomena. He'd never seen a glowing door before! He wondered where it went.

Carefully raising one front paw, he pressed it against that edge—and felt the barrier shift, sliding open.

Yes!

Akemi suddenly sat up, ears swiveling every which way. It was quiet.

Too quiet.

Kenji was never quiet for this long. Even when he fell asleep, he snuffled and snorted and whimpered.

"Kenji?"

No reply.

"Kenji!"

Nothing.

For a second, she considered that he might be sulking, or hiding, or even playing. That his silence was deliberate, either to punish her or to rouse her curiosity.

She dismissed the idea almost immediately. Subtlety was hardly her brother's strong suit.

No, this felt more like something was wrong.

"Kenji? Are you okay?" Hopping down off the couch, Akemi carefully headed toward the bedroom. There was a high-pitched whine coming from somewhere. She'd heard something similar when Father had his work open. But what was it doing here now?

There was a clatter, the sound of nails clicking on wood, and just as she reached the doorway a big, dark-furred figure barreled through it, slamming into her and knocking her sideways to the ground. *Oof!*

The figure leaped on her—and began licking her face.

"Gotcha!" Kenji declared, laughing.

"Yes yes, fine," she grumbled, shoving him off and shaking herself once she was standing again. *"Where were you?"* Because she was sure that, somehow, he hadn't been in the bedroom a second ago. Except she also felt that, somehow, he *had* been there at the same time. Which made no sense.

He grinned, tongue hanging out almost to the floor. *"Exploring."*

She waited, but he didn't say anything more. She was about to insist, to press him until he gave it up—as he always did—but the sound of footsteps outside their door made her break off, both of them riveted instantly on that barrier.

It opened, and Akemi forgot everything else, racing her brother to reach the man there first.

"Father! Father! You're home!"

"I was exploring," Kenji cut in, but Father was petting them and hugging them and laughing with them, and Akemi's brother never finished whatever he'd been about to say. Not that Father would have understood it anyway.

Well, there would be time enough for that later, she was sure.

Jin choked back a laugh as Chin-Sun stifled a scream, recoiling from the large, triangular head that had suddenly landed in her lap, ears angled toward her, big eyes peering up pleadingly.

"What does it want?" his supervisor demanded, struggling to push Kenji off, but she was too hesitant, and he was stubborn.

"He," Jin corrected mildly, "is hoping you'll give him some of your dinner. Well, really, he's hoping you'll give him *all* of your dinner. Kenji!" Those ears swiveled about, but the rest of the dog did not budge. "Kenji, down!"

With a reluctant whine, Kenji lifted his head, freeing Chin-Sun from its weight, and sat back on his haunches, tail wagging slowly in the hopes this would demonstrate sufficient restraint to earn a tasty reward.

"I'm sorry," Jin offered, though he was still finding it hard to keep the smile off his face. "You really can just shove him off you if he tries again." *Which he probably would,* Jin admitted to himself. Though a sweet dog, big-hearted and good-natured, Kenji could be a pest and a borderline bully when it came to getting what he wanted out of someone he thought he could intimidate.

Admittedly, there was a lot of dog there to overwhelm people.

Chin-Sun had glanced over at the couch, where Akemi sat guarding them, front paws crossed, head up, ears alert. "The other one is much calmer."

"Akemi is more task-oriented than her brother," Jin agreed. "She's also less sociable by nature—Kenji loves to be petted and hugged and wrestled with, while half the time Akemi wants her pack nearby, but not quite touching her."

He shrugged, reaching over to snag another dumpling from the woven bamboo tray between them. Kenji's eyes followed the morsel as it went into Jin's mouth. "These are excellent, by the way," he complimented after swallowing it. "Thank you again for bringing them over. That was very thoughtful of you."

Though she waved away the compliment, Jin thought he detected a faint blush on his supervisor's cheeks. "I felt it only right to welcome you properly," she claimed, "and to show my gratitude for all your hard work." Kenji had returned his attention to her, and she studied him now as well. "They *are* handsome creatures," she allowed. "And impressive. I am sure they guard you well."

Jin laughed. "They do," he agreed, "though half the time I feel Kenji would just make friends with anyone who broke in. Not if they tried to hurt me, though," he added, sobering. "That would be a bad idea." He smiled. "You can pet him, you know. He'll let you." Especially if the dog thought he might get a treat out of it.

Slowly, hesitantly, Chin-Sun extended her hand. Kenji's eyes crossed watching it, but he didn't budge, although his tail wagging sped up slightly. Finally, her fingers brushed against his short, thick fur, and he closed his eyes, his tail now thumping the floor as she scratched his forehead for a second before pulling back.

"He's very soft," she said, sounding surprised. She tried again, petting for a little longer this time. Akemi watched, not reacting in the least, but Kenji was clearly in heaven, and leaned his head into her hand.

"He likes you," Jin told her, sitting back to watch the interaction. He'd been surprised when Chin-Sun had suggested they have dinner together, and even more when she'd offered to bring food to his apartment, but he was glad she had. Even if she was still very reserved, Jin thought that was beginning to break down the tiniest bit.

"What is the next step?" she asked, and it took him a second to realize she had switched the topic back to work rather than how to improve her rapport with his dogs.

He poured more tea into his cup—topping hers off as well—and sipped the steaming liquid before answering. "I've laid out most of the basic grid," he explained. "Now I need to flesh that out. Like building a house—the beams are there, but we still need a floor, walls, a ceiling." He frowned, thinking about his plan of attack. "I need to expand it a bit as well. It's too small as it is, at least to fit everything within it."

His supervisor left off petting the dog to study him instead, eliciting a whine of neglect from Kenji. "Too small? I thought size was immaterial in the Matrix. And you said you wished to keep the shell I'd built."

"I do," Jin agreed. "It's not that size is immaterial so much as it's...variable." He cradled the teacup in both hands, inhaling the faint scent of ginger and jasmine tickling his nose. "As far as absolute placement in the Matrix itself, what you made won't change. It's the digital coordinates for this whole facility." He glanced around, taking in not just the whitewashed walls of this room, but the entire campus. "But I'm going to create internal nodes for every room here, every lab, every storage space. That way we can monitor them in finer detail—you don't get much granularity when you're seeing the place as a single object, you need to be able to isolate each stairwell, each corridor, each closet." He smiled. "Fortunately, size is relative. I can map all of that out, put pins in each and every location, link all of it together, and it'll still fit inside the same outer dimensions you used."

"So that no one will be able to tell the difference from the outside?" Chin-Sun asked.

He nodded, reaching for his chopsticks again. "Exactly."

This time Kenji was too engrossed in the attention he was receiving to even glance toward the food. Jin wondered if his boss realized she'd started petting his dog again.

Ae-Cha bit back a curse as someone slapped her on the back of the head, the rude cuff nearly knocking her to the ground. "Watch it!" she snapped, glaring at Ho, who stared back.

"You watch it," the big man retorted. "Kyu said to keep you on task, not let you stare off into space!"

"I *am* on task," she informed him loftily. "I'm running through my options, calculating odds of success."

They weren't good.

The secure network had grown again, that much she could tell. All the structure was in place now, and work had begun on adding layers and depths to the whole.

Whoever was rebuilding their security, they were good.

The problem, of course, was that every improvement Yang Su made set Ae-Cha back further. Nor could she effectively map the targeted interior, not when that same interior was constantly growing and evolving. It was like trying to draw a wave as it crashed down on your head.

She needed a way to map it all out. Or at least take a snapshot and map that. That would be a good start.

The door to their little hut banged open and Kyu stormed in, slamming it shut behind him. "Problem," he declared, crossing the room in a handful of strides to lean on the table, glaring down at Ae-Cha over her deck. "We ain't the only ones on this job."

"What?" Ho half rose to his feet, towering over them both. "Who's dumb enough to cross us on our own turf?"

"Try Kwonsham," Kyu snapped, not looking away from Ae-Cha. "They just brought in a data retrieval specialist."

Well, that was just great. Still, it made sense. Kwonsham concentrated largely on agriculture. Of course they'd want to know what Yang Su was up to here—and, if the rival corp made some sort of discovery, either destroy it or steal it for themselves.

Ae-Cha refused to panic. "Doesn't matter," she insisted. "They haven't spent the past two weeks studying this thing. I have." She met her boss' stare. "We'll find a way in, I'm almost there."

She grinned. "And then we steal them blind."

Akemi woke, and instantly knew something was wrong.

"Kenji?"

"Here!" The answer came at once, but something about her brother's voice was off. Distant. Like the videos Father had played for them, sound recorded and then transmitted after.

She swung her head from side to side, slowly and methodically sweeping the room with her gaze, her ears swiveling to catch sounds. *"Where?"*

"Right here!" A long, tapered snout poked out from around the corner, followed by the tip of one dark ear. *"Come find me!"*

There was a whisper of sound—not paw steps on hardwood, not even the rustle of a curtain. More like a breeze, but...backward? And faintly musical?

Intrigued, Akemi rose and padded across the floor. When she reached the doorway, she carefully peered around it, in case Kenji was waiting to pounce.

But he wasn't there.

No one was. Kenji was asleep on the bed, not sprawled out for once. And so out of it he didn't respond when she entered, or even when she nudged him with her nose. *"Kenji?"*

Yet Akemi could also smell him elsewhere in the room. No, not quite smell. This was something different. Still, she knew it was somehow *also* him, and that this second Kenji was close. It was like before, when he'd had her worried.

"Where are you?" she demanded again.

"Here!" A paw cuffed her ear, not hard, and Kenji laughed, but when she whipped around the room beyond the bed was still empty. Or was it? There was something, a golden glimmering, like dust in the sun.

And was she wrong, or did that glimmer have the shape of her goofball brother?

The motes stretched, widened, darkened, and she was staring at Kenji, who sat there grinning at her.

"How are you in two places at once?" She stepped forward and nudged him with the tip of her nose, gently, concerned. There was a faint tingle as they touched, but otherwise he felt normal. Looked normal.

The room around her, however, did not. Before, it had been bright and cheerful, with the daylight streaming in. Now it was even brighter, bathed in light, *made* of light, the walls and floor and ceiling etched in glowing lines.

As was Kenji. As was she, she realized, glancing down at her own paws. And yet, when she looked back at the bed her brother was still there—and she was curled up beside him.

"What?"

Her brother—the version of him standing right beside her, glowing—just laughed.

"New space to play!" He leaped up and bounded away, toward the nearest wall—and straight through it. *"Come! Play!"*

Though she still had many questions, his exuberance mixed with such opportunity was irresistible, and Akemi found herself charging after him.

Jin frowned as an alert appeared on his display.

"What's wrong?" Chin-Sun asked.

"A glitch," he answered, reading the data scrolling through. "Something triggered one of the detection arrays I set in place. But it didn't come from outside the system, and now it's gone. Must have been a bug."

She nodded and said nothing more as he went back to what he'd been doing.

"You're sure about this?" Kyu asked for the third time.

Ae-Cha resisted the urge to roll her eyes. "Yes, I'm sure. I've got an intrusion program all set to go. But we've got to be inside that shell for it to work. So we march up to the place, you distract the guards, and I slip inside and trigger the program. It cuts a hole through their defenses, I follow, and then I get what we want."

Behind them both, Ho shrugged. "Works for me."

Kyu frowned, but eventually he nodded. "Fine. Just be quick about it. We can't exactly fend off an army."

"You won't have to," Ae-Cha assured him. "Just keep them busy long enough for me to get past. If I can get onto the grounds themselves, I'll be physically within that node, which'll make it a lot easier to enter it from the Matrix side."

Once she was in there, nothing could stop her.

"*Hoi*, you! No unauthorized entry!" The guard glared at them from behind the barrier, her partner poised and ready inside the booth.

Ae-cha watched from off to the side as Kyu put on a smile and slowly raised his hands. "Of course, sorry," her boss called out. "I just had a quick question."

The guard took a step toward him, but just the one. "What's that?" Everything about her look, tone, and stance showed she was still being cautious, but some of the initial hostility had been chased away by curiosity. For the first time, Ae-cha realized that her partner's habit of dressing well was more than just an affectation or empty vanity. He was smarter than he looked.

"Just—" Kyu beckoned her closer, and after a brief hesitation, the guard complied. "I was wondering," he said in almost a whisper, "how sturdy that booth was."

"What?" She straightened quickly, reeling back, but not fast enough to avoid the throat punch that sent her staggering away, choking.

At the same time, Ho emerged from the bushes, bellowing as he used both hands to fling a chest-sized stone straight at the guard booth. Glass shattered and the other guard toppled, stunned from the impact.

That was all Ae-Cha needed. She bolted forward, charging into the research compound. There was a long, low building up ahead, and another to the left, plus a larger storage facility to the right. The first one looked like research to her, but the second had more of an office and housing vibe, and she angled toward that one. It was likely to be less heavily guarded.

Reaching the nearest door, she wasn't surprised to see it locked. But the lock was electronic, and Ae-Cha had it open two seconds later.

Ducking through, she found herself in a wide, clean hallway, stark but not unpleasant. She went for the first door on hand, cracking its lock as well and letting herself into the clearly unfurnished apartment there.

Perfect.

Folding herself into a seated position on the floor, back against the wall, Ae-Cha tugged out her deck, plugged in, and slid into the Matrix. As she'd hoped, being here physically bypassed the bulk of the system's security measures.

She was in.

Akemi and Kenji were wrestling when they both heard something, a strange, discordant sound, ugly and jarring.

"What was that?" Kenji asked, looking about.

"I don't know," his sister replied. *"But I think it came from that direction."*

They both trotted off to investigate.

"That was definitely an intrusion," Jin muttered, tapping the new alert. "But it's here in the compound. That doesn't make any sense."

Chin-Sun had checked the activity logs, and pointed to something there. "Look. Vandals at the south gate. Could that be it?"

"No," he replied. "This wasn't some kids throwing rocks. It's a shadowrunner, and a good one. They sliced right past my safeguards. But how'd they get inside in the first place?"

His boss was studying the alert, and now she reached over to drag it alongside the log entry. "Both just happened," she pointed out. "The trouble at the gate first."

He understood at once. "They used it as a way to get inside." His fingers were flying as he typed. "I can see them in the system. Give me a minute and I should be able to locate them exactly. Then I can isolate them, lock them out."

Chin-Sun nodded. "Hurry."

"Found it!" Kenji declared smugly, tail wagging as he glanced back at his sister just behind him.

"Yes, yes," she agreed. *"I see it, too."* It was there on the other side of the next faint wall, a glowing figure, crouched down, doing something its very posture shouted was not allowed.

"Get them?" Kenji asked, already starting to hunker down expectantly.

But Akemi was thinking quickly. That figure had an odd overlay, like two forms atop one another—one glowing like them, the other not, like their bodies back on the bed. If they pounced on the one here, what would happen to the other one? *"Wait,"* she decided. *"We need to get both at once."*

Her brother whined, no doubt not fully understanding yet, but didn't argue as Akemi led the way back to their own bodies. There was the door, of course, but from here she could see the glow of it, concentrated in a single spot, and a quick nudge caused that to shift somehow. Perfect. She settled into her body and rose to her feet, padding toward the now open door.

"Come," she told Kenji. *"Close in. Then attack."*

With a happy little bark, he hurried after her.

Ae-Cha laughed, though her eyes never left the code she saw superimposed on the structure. The same code she was currently cutting through. "You can't catch me," she whispered as she worked. "And you can't stop me, either. I'll be in, out, and gone before you can even find me."

She paused mid-keystroke, however, when she heard the growls.

Glancing up, she saw a pair of big, dark, lean shapes stalking toward her. Wolves? No, dogs. Who would use dog icons in the Matrix, though? Were these part of the guard program?

They were impressively realistic as they came closer, from the gleam in their eyes to the drool dripping from their mouths as they bared their teeth.

"Uh, nice doggies?" she tried, scrambling to her feet. She ejected from the Matrix—and was slammed back into the wall by a pair of four-legged figures leaping upon her, their weight bearing her to the ground. Her deck was knocked aside, and then it was a flurry of teeth and claws as Ae-Cha's world dissolved into growls and snarls and the smell of fur, dog breath, fear sweat, and her own blood.

"It's gone," Jin announced, scowling at the display. "Just winked out. But I think—" he stood, offering Chin-Sun a hand up, "—I have its last location."

The indicated spot was on the same hall as his own rooms, in the next wing over from this office. Jin led the way, and wasn't surprised to see the door to the first apartment there slightly open. But, farther along, was his own slightly ajar as well?

He was shocked, however, when he pushed the first door the rest of the way—only to be confronted by a pair of familiar, triangular faces.

"Akemi? Kenji?" The dogs barreled into him, and he patted them both even as he craned his neck to see beyond—where a blonde-buzzed woman lay curled up on the floor, arms protectively cradling her head, the impression of doggie toothmarks clearly visible on her skin.

"Our intruder, no doubt," Chin-Sun commented, easing past the dogs, but not without giving Kenji a quick scratch first. "It seems she has already been subdued." She smiled at the dogs. "You were right, they are a good deal more than pets."

"They are," Jin agreed. "They must have smelled the intruder and gone after her. The shock jarred her right out of the Matrix."

What he couldn't figure out was, how had the dogs opened either this door or his own?

"Father is pleased," Kenji said, wrapping around Father's legs as they returned to their rooms.

"Yes," Akemi agreed. *"We dealt with the intruder."*

"New friend is also pleased," her brother added, including Chin-Sun in his windings.

"Yes." Studying the woman, Akemi had to admit she was not as unpleasant as she had first appeared. And her affection for both Father and Kenji was evident. She had even made overtures toward Akemi herself. Perhaps she wasn't all bad?

"Part of the pack?" As always, her brother was anything but subtle.

Akemi considered. *"Part of the pack,"* she acknowledged, nudging Chin-Sun with her nose to keep her with them. The woman jumped in surprise, but then smiled and patted Akemi on the head. She allowed it, this once.

"Good play space?" Kenji asked next, the four of them stepping back into the apartment.

Now Akemi smiled. *"Very good. You did well, little brother."*

The pair of dogs admired the glowing, gleaming world around them.

Yes, they were going to enjoy roaming through that. She wondered if Father could join them, and maybe throw discs there. They'd have to find out.

ONE NIGHT IN BELLEVUE

Crystal Frasier

The plum wine kicked like a wired mule. Chloe powered through the sensory overload of artificial sweet, synthetic flowers, and hard alcohol, but didn't follow the question. "What?"

"What was the payout," Thaylee prodded again, "when you sued the asshole?"

"I didn't sue anyone. It was a hit-and-run." In that a Barrens troll had beaten the drek out of her sassy teenage ass; shattered her right arm, leg, hip, and collarbone beyond repair, then calmly wandered off. "Hit-and-run" sounded better than "pummel-and-saunter."

"Bullshit." Sheryl slammed down another glass of moderately priced wine and topped herself off. She was canny—easily the biggest threat the Salmon Creek PTA had ever encountered—and she knew it. "Liam may be a doctor, but that house of yours is way too nice for his salary alone. That screams 'settlement money.'"

Chloe waved the accusations off with chopsticks and returned to her chirashi. "You have *got* to get over this lurid obsession with my medical history." Her friends were professionals, in the respectable sense. All three of them were Bellevue housewives who'd come from the right kind of background and married the right kind of partner. Dive bars, cyberware, and gunfights were sim programs they salivated over, not ghosts they fought to subdue. And she worked hard to keep her new friends and her old ghosts far, far apart.

"You've heard it before. Guy T-boned me on Clyde Hill. Liam put me back together at the hospital. We fell in love.

Nothing else to say unless you want all the passionate details of physiotherapy."

"I still think it's not too late to go with a holistic option," Wynny interjected. "A good shaman could regrow your limbs for you. Or they could have before you poisoned your soul with implants." It was a lie, but one her neighbor earnestly believed and belabored endlessly. Wynny had just enough training in the shamanic arts to make her garden the envy of Cedar Terrace and couldn't imagine a problem it wouldn't solve. Even if magic could have brought her limbs back, it would cost ten times what the chop shop chrome job did, back when nuyen was a lot harder to come by.

"Liam keeps pressing me to get bioware replacements, but I think it's just because he loves the science." She flexed her elegant, synthetic-flesh fingers. They would never crush a man's arm, but then they didn't need to. Not anymore. "But these are fine. Besides, then we wouldn't have the money for summer programs."

"Hear, hear!" Thaylee topped off everyone's wine glass for a toast. "Let's hear it for our little terrors beating the odds and getting in! Today Salmon Creek Coding Camp, tomorrow the Renraku board of directors." It was a good program—an opportunity that opened doors for Emma's future. Coding was a practical enough skill, but that wasn't the real value. Renraku sponsored the high-profile camp, and executive board scions *miraculously* always won a seat in the lottery. The summer program provided access to the children of wealth and fame, no matter how fancy a school they attended the other ten months of the year. It was never too early to network.

"And here's to the nastiest, meanest, most arctic Moms on the Eastside," Sheryl added with a sly smile. She'd plied the admission committee with a rain of compliments and subtle threats for the last month—once Thaylee had cracked the school's Matrix security and tracked down their names and addresses.

Chloe smiled in her well-earned wine buzz. For once, a mission didn't call for her to hit anyone, just provide an endless supply of gingersnaps and haupia pie to grease the wheels. She wondered if the sight of her in an apron, pulling fresh cookies from the oven, would have killed Mojo or Swipe from shock. For all she knew, with how Swipe tagged along in security systems, he may have watched the whole thing.

"To teamwork." Wynny had burned sage to "keep their souls clean." She had also provided the ginger for cookies, and Chloe still wasn't completely sure the self-ascribed shaman hadn't added something metaphysical to the ingredient.

Chloe dropped another swallow of the plum wine, letting her head swim in the soft glow. It almost felt like being back in the game.

Shadowrunners don't retire. You get good or you get got, as Mojo used to say. The job shouldn't have changed her life; it had been a basic retrieval. Some corporate douchebag needed access to Overlake Hospital's research records, and runners were the go-betweens. One team had snatched the administrator's toddler for blackmail, and Overlake hired Chloe—Galatea at the time—and her crew to snatch the kid back. Standard work. A milk run, with a heftier-than-usual payday because it involved a kid.

A formula run?

It was the first time in her life Chloe had held a real baby.

Liam had put her back together—she wasn't lying about that. Chloe ate a mag off an SMG and a nasty manabolt before they got out. On the way from Renton to Bellevue, she'd slipped away somewhere around Factoria. But saving a doctor's daughter came with benefits: It was her first time recovering in an honest-to-god hospital. A combination of gratitude and guilt had led Liam to her bedside every day. At first, he'd just awkwardly thank her over and over. Eventually, he began bringing her Emma's drawings. They weren't much beyond Crayola smears of whatever color caught her eye, but Liam called them "thank you cards" and some long-dormant corner of her mind found that charming.

He wasn't big, or tough. He didn't need to be. He was kind in that way you could only be if the world had been kind to you. Emma had sleepy brown eyes that saw everything as new and wonderful. She stumbled through life with her whole heart intact, and shared her joy of discovery with everything her sticky, perfect little fingers could latch onto. Chloe looked at her and saw a million happy futures. She was a ray of sunshine to a heart that had only ever seen shadows.

It was like a drug.

By the time Chloe could walk without puking, she and Liam had fallen in love. He helped her swap the scary steel for innocuous plastic prostheses, and Swipe created her a fake

SIN. Gone were the gun arm, the smart link. A few traces of her old life remained, but thermographic optics that only told her how sick her daughter was and a subvocal mic she used mid-meeting to argue about dinner plans did not a runner make. Some nights, after the dishes were washed and Emma was asleep, Liam asked her to tell him stories about old jobs. Every time she did, they felt more and more like someone else's life.

"Not cool, Sheryl." Thaylee finished the bottle and fat-fingered a refill request from their tiny karaoke suite control panel. Chloe tried to focus enough to replay the context, but it was gone, sacrificed to the Wine Mom spirit. "I used to work with a guy with cyberlegs. He lost his real legs to a hell hound while hiking Rainier, back before they closed the trails. He said it was the best accident of his life, because now all his hiking supplies just snap on magnetically."

Thaylee brought up her "friend with cyberlegs" from her old life as an Aztechnology programmer whenever they had more than two drinks. Chloe wasn't sure if she needed to believe she was an ally to the handicapped, or was just trying to coax more gossip about her limbs. The medical implants hadn't really been what set her apart from Wynny, Sheryl, and Thaylee when she first moved to Cedar Terrace—just the obvious symptom of an underlying foreignness. They didn't know Chloe came from a life of violence—fighting gangers while they fought the HOA—but they could smell that she was not of like kind, and their curiosity fixated on the only obvious cause: her assistive cyberware.

Bellevue suburbs were no less bloodthirsty than the shadows, but they played by different rules and yielded to different negotiations. "Fire up an oldie," Chloe finally relented. Karaoke was another of those strange suburban thrills she'd never imagined trying before. It made her feel alive now. Normally she embarrassed herself in front of the entire PTA for fundraisers, but the private suite let the Cedar Terrace moms cut loose with the vulgar lyrics that would have scandalized their tweens.

The waiter stepped in during a particularly vivid line about carnal satisfaction.

"Sorry." She couldn't help but blush at the unexpected witness. She tried to imagine Galatea, the hardened street samurai, blushing over a younger man who caught her mid-lascivious-grind, and it only confirmed her suspicion that

Chloe Jacobs and Galatea were distinct entities who barely spoke a common language.

But something in the way the waiter moved seemed too respectable for vulgarity.

He half-bowed and smiled, clearly embarrassed he'd interrupted.

Something in the way he moved.

It tickled the back of her brain, through the mild haze of wine and the cheap thrill of suburban scandal.

The way he moved.

He deposited a fresh bottle of *Hokkyoku Ume* and reached for the empty. Ink peeked out from the edge of his collar.

Chloe froze. The pulsing lights and pumping bass riffs fell away. An old instinct screaming in the back of her head suddenly spoke with perfect clarity.

This is a Yakuza bar.

He left again without a word.

She smiled, then fell on her purse. "I can*not* start a new bottle of wine, girls. I just saw the time, and Emma needs to be up first thing tomorrow to go to her grandparents'." Chloe poked at her commlink to send her share of the bill to Thaylee. "But I will see you all Friday for the drop-off."

The other women watched, taking in the scene with confusion. Wynny offered an awkward "Sure, Chloe," just as she slid open the door and stepped into the larger bar.

Stupid. It was stupid to go somewhere new without vetting it. Somewhere someone else—Sheryl, at that—picked. That waiter was just a kid—he would've been a go-ganger when she had burned her Yakuza contact and made her debt, but it wasn't worth the risk. Not until she learned which family owned the territory now. A nice clean *izakaya* catering to salarymen? *Probably* Shotozumi, she reassured herself. *Anyone but* Kenran-kai.

She rounded the corner and confronted the unfortunate reality of ownership. *Kenran-kai.*

"Galatea. Is that really you under that hideous bob?" She knew the small cylinder pressed into her stomach was a pistol. Because Peyton Crowe certainly wasn't happy to see her.

It would have been too poetic if Peyton had been the one to grab Emma. If this encounter was her descent into suburban motherhood come full circle. But they'd last crossed paths a month before the Emma job. Since then, Peyton had worked his way out of running and into the Yakuza—no small feat for a Scots-Irish American mutt. He'd had bigger guns and a smaller paunch then.

The runner in her wanted to trade banter like the old days, but the rest of her needed Emma to still have a mother come sunrise. She shook her head and played her best confused housewife.

The waiters gathered around, filled more with questions than menace. Two savvy patrons settled their tabs and made for the door.

"Don't give me that." Peyton tore her shirt out of her slacks and pressed the barrel of his Fichetti into the long scar up the left side of her belly. "Think I can't spot my handiwork? I still owe you after what you cost me."

"That was a long time ago, Crowe." She sidled left, to get a clean break for the door, but the larger of the waiters clamped onto her arm.

"Respect." He slapped her. It was punctuation rather than a genuine attempt at harm. "I should be *shateigashira* by now." *Lieutenant.* Apparently kicking over his smuggling operation eight years back and running a sword up his ribs had derailed his career.

One waiter asked a question, and Chloe swore to herself for neglecting her Japanese. Something about debts?

Peyton motioned toward the back of the house, but before he could comment, Sheryl arrived from the private room. Questions visibly marched across her face in perfect clarity: *Am I interrupting? What is Chloe still doing here? Does she know the manager? Why is there a gun?* "Chloe?"

"Chloe," Peyton echoed with a scoff. It was a moment's distraction, but just enough.

She clamped the arm restraining her in both hands, stepped back, and dropped below his center of gravity. The waiter—the Yakuza enforcer—had forty kilos on her, and they all came rolling forward with a tug. He fell over her shoulder and into Crowe, sprawling them both across the faux-industrial concrete floor.

Years away slowed her reactions; Crowe dove to recover his gun before Chloe fully realized what she'd done. She threw her whole body at the pistol. Too slow to reach the weapon first, she course-corrected for the magazine release. The magazine shot from the grip and skittered under a booth. A solid backhand answered her tactic, and the old bone lacing dispersed what could have been a broken jaw even as it left her senses swimming.

She was on her feet and shoving Sheryl down the hall with a slurred shout of "ffffire exxxxit!" before conscious thought completely returned—at least a few old instincts held strong.

"Were you getting mugged?"

Peyton's goons were too stunned by the scene to react, and somewhere along the retreat Thaylee and Wynny joined them. They crashed into the fire exit more like a wave than a unit, but it wouldn't budge. A red LED blinked from the handle.

"Emergency lockout. You can't lockout a fire exit!" Thaylee rattled the latch to punctuate her disgust. The affront was personal; she spent afternoons recounting her endless war between official emergency service patches and underworld hackers circumventing them. Criminal cartels care nothing for fire safety.

Down the hall, Crowe's upright enforcer trudged after them while his partner struggled to his feet.

Old reflexes started clicking back into place. "See if you can open it." Chloe barely recognized her old working voice, and her friends looked just as shocked by the cold professionalism in her tone. "I'll keep them busy."

The goon was big, but still underestimated her. He puffed himself up and walked with shoulders squared in the show of size and *don't fuck with me* projection you'd apply to any unruly customer—maximum profile and minimum defense. He was probably *shatei*—a little brother—freshly recruited off one of the street gangs, and still trying to prove he could follow orders by protecting one of *Kenran-kai*'s legitimate holdings. She mirrored his stance for a moment, then turned to present a narrow silhouette and quickened her pace. The momentum carried her forward as she spun from the shoulders, driving her fist clean across his undefended chin.

Once upon a time, she ate these poor, dumb Yakuza kids for breakfast.

Warning klaxons sounded in Chloe's HUD. Plastic joints reacted and folded to the sudden force. What should have been a knockout blow rolled into a fierce slap. Still, the force— or at least the sudden shift in dynamic—was enough to send him stumbling back. Chloe followed with a snap kick to the gut and again safety alerts buzzed across her field of vision; what should have been a definitive strike once again softened into a distraction.

The megacorps built medical prostheses for form; to make everyone around the wearer comfortable by minimizing their awareness of disability. Safety systems collapsed the joint locks when too much pressure was applied. *Using them in combat could get a manufacturer sued*, a cynical voice in the back of her head mused.

She thumbed a code into her commlink and hoped Swipe hadn't changed his number.

"Hola?"

"Swipe," she half-asked, half-demanded into her subvocal mic. "I need a favor, man." She didn't even need to think about it. The runner, even the retired runner, who can't signal their decker without announcing it to the entire room doesn't live long. By the second run, it's autonomic.

Behind her, the first enforcer was finally on his feet. He dragged his right foot back and settled his weight into a firm combat stance. His movements—even, smooth steps, never committing his weight to a single leg—said he fully understood the situation now: She was a threat.

"Gal? Last I checked you were wiping noses and baking brownies," he sulked. None of the old crew had taken it well when she'd announced her departure. Swipe was too young to understand that anyone would want a different life. But he was also a decker; not a lot of cardio and very few bullets.

"Listen, I got safety lockouts on my cyberware. I need you to jailbreak me." She connected the commlink to her personal area network and the call crackled into her cyberear.

"Do I gotta? I got this thing..." He paused. "What the hell are you doing in the middle of Yak territory? Don't they still want you dead?"

"Apparently."

The enforcer charged. She pivoted and presented her right side, using the plastic limbs to counter and intercept his blows and occasionally retaliating with a solid left; it wasn't a cyberarm, and for now that was an advantage.

"Shit. You got terrible timing. I'll see what I can do." It was a familiar song to match her combat dance, listening to Swipe mutter and beep as she traded blows. The *shatei* still wasn't sure what he was dealing with, and each jab was a test to find her limits, but right now she needed time more than mystery, and it served her well enough to answer each question.

"Galatea," Swipe finally broke back in. *"Turn off your spoof. All I'm reading is medical tech."*

"It *is* all med tech!"

It was just enough distraction to let the Yakuza through. He connected hard with the rib cage. The aluminum lacing distributed the punch, but didn't cushion the shock and pain. She hadn't been hit in years and forgot how to ride it; how to roll with it and trap his arm. It should have been the hit that ended this fight as she pinned his arm against her side and unleashed a flurry of up-close strikes. Instead, he danced back and set up for another basic kata as she caught her breath.

She wanted to believe he was young and fast, but realistically she knew she was just getting old and slow.

"I can disable the safeties, but this plastic crap's not built for a fight. You'll probably bust it in a few days."

"If you don't, I won't last a few minutes."

"Fair enough."

The enforcer closed again. She faked with the left and then swung a hard uppercut with her right hand. Systems stayed green as his teeth cracked off each other; the sound always dropped the bottom out of her stomach.

He dropped—either unconscious, or smart enough to fake it. This wasn't his fight.

She pinged the decker again. "I still have thermographics in my eye, Swipe. Can you access building systems and cut the lights?"

"Looks like environmentals are air-gapped." He tapped away in his own world again. *"Can't believe I'm gonna ask, but you need me to call Lone Star?"*

She gasped for a few more precious gulps of oxygen. "How sure are you of the fake SIN you made me?"

"Like...seventy percent?"

A thirty percent chance she went away, and Emma woke up without a mom. Worse, a thirty percent chance Emma woke up scandalized and humiliated, her mother exposed as a career criminal, a lifetime black mark on her background checks. Doors closed to every future opportunity.

Except the shadows.

"Let's keep it friendly. No cops."

Swipe sighed in disgust. *"The 'burbs made you crazy."*

The second enforcer finished shaking out the last of the hurt from his fall. She could handle one junior Yakuza, but she lost track of—

Three shots rang out. Rayon pants and synthetic flesh on Chloe's thigh ripped open, revealing deeply scarred plastic underneath. Peyton had his mag back. Chloe flipped one of the steel tables and dove behind it, landing hard on her stomach just in time to dodge another burst of lead.

The landing knocked what remained of the wind from her lungs and she lay still for a moment. Once, combat had been a smooth dance. Peyton and two goons—no chrome, no magic—they wouldn't have been partners, just notes in the ballet of violence. Now she was less a ballerina and more a toddler spasming to music in a viral vid. Her lungs burned, her mechanical joints clicked unpleasantly, and her organic muscles were beginning to seize up from the sudden stress.

The gunfire stopped and Chloe heard the footfall of expensive shoes. If her instincts weren't too dull, it meant Crowe was holding back while his heavy came to flush her out. She could handle one or the other, but alone, she—

Howling emerged from the service hall and a spiraling clatter of napkins and cutlery swooped forward. A spirit? A small one, but the enforcer stared in shock. Wynny's middling magical knowledge extended to conjuring, Chloe guessed. She righted herself to take advantage of the distraction.

Crowe had seen bigger—Mojo had sicced a city spirit five-times its size on the geek last time they met—but the arrival of any spirit demanded attention. One clean shot dissipated its fragile form.

It was just enough of an opening. Chloe dashed for the sushi bar and dropped behind it just as Crowe pulled his gaze back to her. The concrete barrier offered better protection as he unloaded another burst, and with any luck...she looked around and saw an abandoned knife. Long and slender with a fat, black spine. High iron content. Plenty of weight. Liam had asked for a similar one last Christmas, and she'd learned more than she ever wanted to know about Japanese cutlery, including the cost.

It broke her heart to throw it.

Shoulders square. Elbow loose. Snap the wrist and follow through. Like riding a bike—not that she'd ever learned that skill.

The handle struck Crowe's hand with enough force to knock the gun loose and send both weapons clattering across the floor. She'd hoped to pierce his palm, but any success was enough for now.

The enforcer vaulted her precious barricade and snatched up the remaining sushi knife. He was eager to repay the earlier humiliation. She intercepted three gauging slashes with her cyberarm, slicing the synth flesh to ribbons and cracking the case underneath. Then the real attack came as he snatched at her jacket and pulled her close, trying to force the blade up under her ribs. Simple. Brutal. But it committed his whole body.

She swiveled and brought her knee up, crushing his hand between it and the bar. Bones and ligaments popped. Her patella would have, too, if it had been organic. Before the shock wore off, she shoulder-checked him onto the rubber floormats.

"Ii kagen ni shiro!" She could at least remember enough Japanese to tell the kid to piss off. At least, she hoped that's what she'd said.

Just a few years earlier, she would've vaulted the counter and rushed Crowe, but love makes you fat. Instead, she rounded the counter—noting the new hitch in her right leg. He recovered the gun just in time for her to close in, making it a negligible advantage.

"Let's just call this a mulligan," she panted.

"No. No, no, no." Crowe kept the gun trained tight on her chest. Years ago she could have sidestepped it before he could finish pulling the trigger, but today, who knew? "You up and vanish after humiliating me. Everyone says you're dead. Good day for me, but the *oyabun* never trusts me again. And tonight you turn up alive and under my roof? I'm not a prayin' man, but it's rude to refuse a gift."

"It was never personal, Crowe. It was just a run."

"The scar up my back felt pretty damn personal." His voice dripped with hate, but he didn't fire. He wasn't sure who'd react first, either. She could hear the smallest quiver of fear in the back of his throat. "So, what's the job this time? If I'm gonna kill you, I need to know who'll come around asking questions after."

She shook her head. "No job. I got out."

"Bullshit," he spat between clenched teeth. The fear gave way to genuine anger. "No, no glorified Barrens razorgirl winds up dressing like she needs to talk to the manager."

Her mind drifted to Liam and Emma, and her professional demeanor cracked into a genuine smile. "Fell in love," she shrugged. "Had a kid."

Just as she expected the shooting to resume, Crowe lowered his pistol, just a centimeter. His shifting eyes betrayed a subtle blend of confusion, anger, disbelief...even envy.

Three more *shatei* walked through the front door, locking it behind them. Whatever human desires warred behind Crowe's eyes slipped away, replaced by the mask of professionalism his life demanded. "Guess their smoke break's over."

The newcomers eyed her with the same confusion as their predecessors—predecessors they could see lying on the floor—and spread out warily. Chloe stepped back, trying to keep them all in the same arc of vision.

"Still there, Swipe?"

"I don't want to listen to you die, Galatea." She heard him suck wind through his broken tooth.

"I need my wires back."

Silence.

Wired reflexes—that system of microprocessors, superconductive fiber, and epinephrine stimulators that transform the human nervous system into a fighter jet—cannot be removed from a body. More accurately, they can, but the extensive nerve damage made it little more than a very expensive route to chronic pain and muscle tremors. The best Galatea could do when she retired was step down the organic systems, letting her spine and muscles and endocrine system gradually acclimate to a human pace and endure the withdrawal—the vomiting, cramps, and night sweats—in agonizing slow motion.

The hardware—*that* hardware—was all still inside her, dormant. A vicious dog that only needed the right prodding.

Swipe finally answered. *"I just said I don't want to listen to you die."* Without the time to re-acclimate, every movement was a potential high-speed collision, every punch threatened to rip tendon from bone, all as her heart gradually accelerated until it gave up. Or exploded.

Another pause.

The enforcers circled her and began to close in. Swipe's reply finally came in the form of a slowing world. The Yakuzas' swift lunges stretched into casual, lazy arcs. The sound of her own heartbeat drowned out the rest of the world.

Galatea hooked a hand under the nearest table and hefted, arcing it up into the first goon's trajectory. It would connect, eventually, but for now she stepped sideways, her plastic right leg struggling to keep up. One *shatei* swung for the air she had occupied so long ago and another began his slow fall to the floor under the table's weight. The third landed a knife hand strike in her chest and something popped casually. It was going to hurt once her nociceptors caught up with her motor neurons.

She slid back and lifted a condiment bottle from another table, pushing it forward more than throwing it and watched the artful spiral of shoyu form a trail to her attacker's face.

One left. She kicked off the booth with her meat leg, taking any hesitance away from the anchor that was her right leg. Her shoulders and chest muscles could twitch faster than the artificial systems, and she took advantage of that by flexing her torso left and swinging her cyberarm like a tattered mace. It connected with the final enforcer's nose. Cartilage snapped. Fine screws snapped. Her hand fell away in pieces—a few deformed bits hung limp from her wrist on strands of synthetic flesh.

Dodging the bullets was still a challenge; they flew like softballs. Crowe fired twice more. It would've been easier if she could hear the gunfire, but...

Why couldn't she hear the gunfire?

She strode toward him, then staggered as the world snapped back to the interminable quickness of real life. Her lungs burned, her chest ached where the Yakuza blow had landed, and blood seeped from the abutments where here prostheses were nearly torn from accelerated flesh. The world started to spin again as she struggled to gulp enough oxygen.

"The hell," she finally sputtered into the signal in her ear.

"I shut it off, Gal." She'd never heard panic in Swipe's voice like this. *"Your heart rate hit 310."*

"Let me go down fighting." She staggered, and caught herself on the side of a booth.

"Don't you have a fucking kid to raise?"

Another bullet cut through the air and connected with her prosthetic leg. The calf exploded into a shredded mass of filaments and actuators. She staggered back to collide hard with the wall, cutting a shoulder against the dining room's lighting controls.

"Almost had me convinced," Crowe mused. "Right up until you floored three of my boys. Talking to your handler, I assume?. 'Had a kid' my ass."

She'd lost count of the rounds he fired, but he only needed one. The first shot missed her and blew through the lighting panel instead. The dining room went dark. Her thermal vision kicked on as she staggered forward. Crowe pumped eight more shots into the pitch-black wall.

Back down the hall, she fell into Thaylee, Sheryl, and Wynny running the other way. "Fire exit," she gasped through the swat and bile.

"I couldn't crack it." Thaylee apologized, getting a shoulder under Chloe's meat arm and dragging her back into the karaoke suite.

"What the hell is going on?!" Sheryl demanded. "Is that the guy who hit your car?"

Behind her, Wynny worked some kind of magic; the wood buckled and flexed, wedging itself into the jam. "Did my spirit help?"

Chloe nodded, but she wasn't completely sure in response to what. Her mind started to make sense of the pain and put it aside for now. "Old rival," she admitted.

"Where did you get a rival?" Wynny examined her head, then began working a new spell. It didn't knit things like Mojo could, but at least the bleeding slowed. Color drained from Wynny's face at the effort. Magic, like a fight, was shockingly exhausting if it wasn't your daily reality.

The door handle rattled, then strained. A body began throwing itself against the wooden door from the outside. Chloe waved off the questions and began evaluating her resources.

The door cracked.

The suite was a dead end; one way in meant only one way out.

"I..." She paused. "I used to lead kind of a rough life."

"No shit," Sheryl scoffed.

"I used to move in the same circles as Crowe out there." They were listening, for once, but the threads didn't knit. Why would they? The shadows were a foreign nation they'd never visited, a foreign language they'd never needed to speak. "We were runners. Shadowrunners. Crowe and I, we weren't on the same crew. Sometimes we'd work together. Other times we'd be shooting at each other. Depended on who was paying for what."

Wynny shook her head. "No. No, I can't believe you were some kind of criminal."

"Professional," she corrected with a wince. "Just a different kind of professional. The only kind of profession you can really aim for when you're born poor out in the Verge and lose your mom young."

The shadowy corners of Galatea's mind finally shook the cobwebs and began to tick with old plans and contingencies. A standoff meant taking stock and building a strategy. Four against one armed antagonist, but she was in bad shape. Wynny was a shaman. Thaylee could hack. Sheryl could shoot—if they had a gun. She'd done more with less. If Wynny could conjure another spirit—something bigger this time…

Outside, the rattling stopped. Crowe unloaded three rounds into the oak. It ate two of them, but the third ripped past, tumbling rough and strafing sideways on the exit. It sliced through the meat of Thaylee's arm and the young mother looked at it more offended than anything. Her breath caught as she realized what the burst of red meant.

Then the pain kicked in and she screamed. The wound wasn't deep, but some people can't tell at a glance which gunshots were deadly and which ones would make for good stories. Sheryl started screaming, and Wynny froze in place.

"Suck it up!" The cold, professional voice barreled out again from Chloe's throat. "This isn't the time!"

Thaylee's face flushed from healthy to scarlet to sickly pale.

Chloe caught Thaylee one-handed as her legs gave out and eased her down. She wasn't a soldier or a runner, Chloe forced herself to remember. She changed her approach. "Thaylee. Thaylee, hey, look at me. Deep breaths. That's it. Breathe with me. Nice and slow. It's not bad. It just looks scary."

"He's gonna—" Thaylee choked back sheer panic "—he's going to kill me!"

"No, he's not. You don't think like that. You tell me what you're going to cook Aiden and Toby for breakfast in the morning."

"What?" Chloe may as well have grown a second head.

"Eggs? Are you going to cook them eggs?"

"Toby...is...allergic to eggs." It wasn't much, but it started to pull her mind away from the terror.

"Well then yeah, I guess we don't make them eggs." She put light pressure on the wound to slow the bleeding. Thaylee gasped. "Hey, you tell me what you're going to make them, and Wynny—" She gently kicked Wynny's leg to break the mindless stare. "Wynny is going to start fixing you up, okay?"

Wynny was exhausted—ready to drop. Her repertoire consisted of a spell to staunch bleeding and a spell to repair household damage. She wasn't a shaman. She was a mom with a secret trick.

They all were.

Chloe pulled Sheryl into the scene. "Keep her talking about anything except what's going on. I'll get you all out of here."

"How did you end up like this?"

The old shadowrun instinct for banter wanted to come back with *because I let you pick the bar, Sheryl,* but that was the kind of guilt that haunted normal people, drove them to drink, to hurt themselves. To ruin their kids' lives. So time to try something new. "Focus on her."

Chloe struggled upright again and braced awkwardly on the scrapped remains of her leg. She thought of Emma, waking up without her mom, and then reflected on that same fate four times over. They were great kids. None of them deserved the pain of losing a parent.

"Gal," Swipe buzzed in her ear. *"What are you doing? I can't give you any more juice without killing you."*

"I know, Swipe." She hobbled toward the door. Beyond it she heard an empty magazine clatter to the floor and the *shish-snap* of a fresh load. "Hold your fire, asshole! I'm coming out."

And quietly into her mic, "I need you to make a call for me."

"Finally ready for some Lone Star support?"

"Worse." She slid the door aside.

Inoue Daisuke paced with a wry grin, occasionally chuckling at a joke to which only he was privy. Peyton Crowe sat *seiza*—on his knees, with his lower legs tucked neatly beneath him. Chloe did her best to emulate the position, but the wreckage of her right leg and hip made even her clumsy approximation excruciating.

The respected first lieutenant—the *wakagashira*—of the *Kenran-kai* had already been on his way to learn why one of his businesses had erupted into violence when he'd received Swipe's call.

A stern syllable put an end to Crowe's indulgent execution in the back alley; it appeared timely, but Chloe was relatively confident the gangster could have continued berating her until the morning commuters flooded in.

"You trash my bar and shoot an outsider, all to settle a personal grudge." Inoue gripped Crowe's jaw, and discretely tapped the tanto tucked under his suit jacket. "We are... displeased by your impulsiveness."

Thaylee, Sheryl, and Wynny were out front in Inoue's limo, tended by a kindly old Korean woman Chloe hoped was a doctor. Besides the ugly gash on the former programmer's arm, the trio had escaped the night with little worse than exhaustion and mild shock.

"And you." The *wakagashira* crouched and pulled Chloe's eyes up to meet his own. He was smiling, and that scared her far more than any amount of rage. "The troublesome Galatea, alive and well. Still filled with so much spirit."

"I know. I have unsettled debts. Just please don't hurt my child."

"We do not involve families." His smile vanished, replaced by disgust. "Your child does not owe the *Kenran-kai* a considerable sum. *You* do. How fortunate for both of us that shadowrunners do not retire."

He stood and walked toward the bar door, motioning for Crowe to follow.

Inoue paused in the doorway. "A shadowrunner implanted within the social circles of wealthy and powerful corporate families," he mused. "I do not believe you will have any trouble making restitution."

CAN'T TRUST A TRICKSTER

Alina Pete

A killing wind was blowing.

It was strong enough to make every breath hurt and send needles of frost into any exposed skin, and Cody was glad for it even as he fought to drag in another lungful of burning air. The pack on his back seemed twice as heavy as it had a few miles ago, but it was the only thing shielding him from the gale. He could feel the thin, gritty snow he'd been slogging through finally give way to hard ice, and doubled his speed.

If it was this miserable for him, who had been born and raised in these hellish conditions, it'd be twice as hard on the corpo attack dogs hunting him. He wished them all frostbite so deep it turned their asses black and blistered.

He knew they were still tracking him. He'd spotted them while fleeing Seattle days ago, and had left them a trail even a half-assed city-bred tracker could follow toward Athabaskan country, then doubled back as stealthy as you please and made for Algonkian land.

But, that morning in the mold-wallpapered motel, the spirits had awoken him just in time to see a black sedan pull up outside. He'd barely gotten out before the bullets started flying, and they'd been right on his ass ever since.

None of his usual tricks were working and, as a coyote shaman, that was saying something. During these endless miles of running, he'd wondered how the hell they were tracking him despite all the concealment his companion spirits could provide. Now, though, there was no time for reflection, only survival.

He was almost at the border. He was sure he'd be able to see the wards, electronic and magic, if he opened his astral eyes, but he couldn't spare the energy. He needed every breath just to keep moving.

His welcome home took the form of a red laser beam cutting through the blizzard as it flicked into being and came to rest on his chest.

"Unknown runner, stop immediately. You have entered Algonkian lands illegally. I repeat, you have entered lands held by the Council of Three Fires, and are in violation of our sovereign laws. Surrender, or we will be forced to take lethal measures."

Cody was grateful to sink down to the snow as he knelt, hands raised slowly and placed behind his head before the Long Arms could get trigger happy. He risked peeking over his shoulder, and the whiteout cleared just long enough to make out the pair of figures in black watching him from a distant hillside before the curtain of snow howled back into place.

He flipped off the hunters he'd finally eluded, hoping to hell they saw it.

"Got yourself arrested sneaking into the country, little cousin?" The ork sucked at his teeth and nudged Cody in the ribs. Cody winced. A night spent in lockup after three days of running had left him sore all over. He wished he'd been able to shower and get a decent sleep before dealing with family, but the guards had released him straight into his cousin's care.

"If you wanted to come home that badly, you should have just asked. I woulda come picked you up in Seattle with my new ride."

"Yeah, well. The way you drive, Tater, I'd be safer with the rent-a-cops."

Cody was trying to play it cool, but he had to admit his *nistês*[1] ride was pretty damn flash. Clearly, Tater Tot was doing well for himself these days. The jeep was Algonkian-make, of course, but a model so new Cody hadn't seen it on the streets of the UCAS yet. The shape of the manifold hinted it had a hydrogen-combustion engine, and would have absolutely unbeatable pickup.

1. nistês: cousin

His cousin saw the appraising look on his face and chuckled, opening the doors via his control rig. "Get in, you grumpy little shit," Tater said. "It's good to see you again. D'ja eat? I brought you some hangover soup."

"I'm not hungry. Filled up on all that delicious prison food."

"Your own damn fault you were in there." Miyawatami turned to Cody as he slid into the seat behind her. She gave him a hard look over the top of her sunglasses. "You coulda just shown your card at the border crossing, same as anyone. You're *nehiyawiw*[2] born and bred."

Miya looked the same as ever, her hair pulled severely back into a braid and her pinched expression and red-on-black cybereyes at odds with her name, which meant "joyous one." Cody could count on one hand the number of times he'd seen her smile, and was glad he'd been the one to pull at least two of those rare smiles out of her. But she wasn't smiling now, and he felt his guts shiver with guilt.

But if she wasn't going to make a big deal out of it, he sure wasn't going to bring it up.

"I could have," he said, leaning back in his seat and grinning at her. "But you know me. I like to make an entrance."

Miya snorted. "Like to piss off your father, more like."

"Was he the one who sent you to come get me?" Cody asked.

"Nah, we were in the neighborhood, figured we all could use a road trip together like old times," Tater said, which was a lie. No one just happened to be in Lethbridge in February unless they had a damn good reason for it. "You could holo once in a while, you know. I hear they got good signal in the Metroplex."

"Been busy."

"*Real* busy, if you come home with your tail on fire like this," Miya said. "You gonna fill us in on the details, or you gonna try and pull that 'shadowrunners never talk about the job' shit?"

"Screw off."

"Ah. Job went bad, and you ran home to hide," Miya said. "Figured."

Cody shrugged and stared out the window. He'd never told anyone exactly what he'd been doing in Seattle, but there

2. nehiyawiw: A nehiyaw (Cree) person

were three certainties in life: death, taxes, and the rez rumor mill knowing all of your business.

"Eh, at least you got the shadowrunner look right," Tater said, turning the jeep onto the only road out of town. "The armor on that jacket's real good, nice and low profile. Almost didn't spot it. I always said, if you're gonna do dumb shit like run the shadows, you should at least look cool while doing it."

"Shit, I *always* look cooler than you, cuz," Cody shot back with a grin, and felt an ache in his heart as they fell into their familiar teasing. Home held a lot of baggage for him, but he never regretted seeing these two. They weren't cousins by blood, obviously, but he used the term for them out of affection and respect. He pretended to gaze out the window, but drank in the sight of them out of the corner of his eye.

"I haven't forgiven you, you know," Miya said, breaking into his fond memories and the comfortable silence.

"Sorry," he said, flinching. He met her eyes in the rearview mirror and tried to look contrite. "Really, I am."

"You *better* be, you little shit." She turned her gaze back to the road and let the matter drop. That was the nice thing about Miya; she was scary as hell when she was mad, but she had a soft spot for him, and he could generally charm her into forgiving him eventually.

Cody knew he had a lot to forgive.

The trip home was six hours by road, but they only got two hours into their journey before a herd of bison decided to cross the highway near Saamis. By law, the herd had the right of way, and the delay wasn't unwelcome. Cody and his cousins sat on top of the jeep's hood and passed the thermos of soup back and forth, watching ten thousand bison migrate through the waist-deep snow. They spent the time catching up on the usual gossip from home and commenting on the health of the animals they were all so familiar with. They'd all served as *paskwâwi-mostos-wîcîwâkana*--Buffalo Companions— together in their youth.

The Buffalo Companions were a detachment of riders that accompanied the herds along their migration routes through Algonkian lands, and kept them safe from threats both supernatural and mundane. The Companions also served to educate the community's youth on important survival skills and self-reliance, and though participation was voluntary for most youth, Cody's overbearing father had made it clear *his* kid would serve at least three terms in "service to his people."

Once he'd joined up, though, Cody was glad for the experience. Not only did it mean three glorious years away from his father, but his time as one of the "Buffalo Boys" was the reason he'd had the skills to run the shadows. Tater had taken the rookie under his wing and taught him how to survive off the land, and how to repair and maintain the fleet of drones they used to overfly the herds. It was Miya's patient tutelage that had made Cody so good with a rifle.

His time in the Buffalo Companions was also when he'd realized he was trans. Something about living wild and dressing in cowboy leathers instead of the ceremonial shamanic garb his father had expected felt really *right* to him, and the long hours on horseback had given him plenty of time to think about who he wanted to be.

He'd been grateful that, after spending the better part of a week psyching himself up to tell Tater and Miya, they'd hardly reacted when he'd come out to them. Miya had looked at him for a long moment, then solemnly held out her hand to reintroduce herself to him and ask if he'd decided on a new name. Tater had hugged them both, cried, then offered Cody an extra helping of stew because "girls like a little meat on a guy," patting his own ample gut for emphasis.

Even now, the memory of that night by the fire made him tear up a little. He glanced beside himself at his cousins, fighting back the burning in his throat as they watched the last of the bison thunder past.

Which only made it an extra punch to the gut when Tater suddenly turned and slapped a set of mage restraints on him; magic-nulling, with a proximity triggered shock spell that would activate if he got too far away from whoever held the control rune. Cody recognized his father's spellwork woven throughout the cuffs. No off-the-shelf mage cuffs for him, it seemed. His father had crafted these magical restraints for him personally. Cody wondered if he'd made the restraints after Cody left home, or if they'd always been in his father's study, just waiting for him to step too far out of line.

"Tater!" Miya said.

"Yeah, what the hell, Tater?" Cody asked.

Tater ignored him and looked over at Miya. "He figured it out, M. I saw him looking at me funny, and you know he's smart as shit."

"Just what...*the actual hell*...have I figured out?" Cody asked calmly.

"Frag," said Tater. He chewed his lip and gave Cody an embarrassed shrug. "Sorry, buddy. I didn't want it to go down this way, and you know I wouldn't hurt you unless I had to. It's just, uh...frag, Miya. How much can we tell him?"

Miya rubbed at her temples and whispered quiet filth into the air. Cody would have been impressed at the creativity and vehemence of her swears if he wasn't burning with betrayal. The close-shaved hair at the back of his neck kept wanting to rise like hackles as he glared at his cousins.

"Figured out what, Tater? That you two are my dad's pet cops?" Cody rolled his eyes. "That was frickin' obvious. The paperwork to get me out of jail doesn't just clear overnight, and you two were right there waiting for me when I got out. I'm not an idiot."

"Wait. You *thought* we were here for you, and you still got into the car anyway?" Tater asked.

"Yeah? It's *you* two. I figured, at worst, you'd haul me in front of my dad, and I need to talk to him anyway."

"About what?" asked Miya. "Usually you try to avoid him whenever possible."

"Yeah, you said yerself we'd have to drag you to the tribal office in handcuffs to get you two in the same room. Guess it was true, huh?"

"*Shut* up, *Tater*," Miya and Cody said simultaneously.

"I need to talk to the Council." Cody held Miya's gaze so she wouldn't notice him groping at the restraints, trying to find any weakness in the runework. No luck there—his father's artifice was immaculate, as usual.

"Your father's not on the Council," Miya said, as though Cody hadn't spent his youth learning the convoluted intricacies of tribal politics. "He's an elder shaman and local Chief of the Battle Creek region. He's more of a mayor than anything."

"I know that. But he knows people who know people on the Council, and I've got intel that needs to go right to the top."

"Intel? What kind?"

Cody flashed a coyote smile at Miya, all teeth and false innocence. "Oops. Didn't know this was an official interrogation. Guess I got myself a little leverage now, don't I?"

"Cody," Miya warned. "Don't be an ass. We're trying to help you."

"Got a funny way of showing it."

"Hey, break it up, you two." Tater slid off the hood of the jeep and triggered the autostart. Cody could tell from the blue tinge in his optics that the ork was currently looking through a drone on his network. "We've got incoming from the southwest."

"The contacts?" Miya asked.

"Yeah, the same." Tater's eyes refocused on the world around him. He grabbed Cody's shoulder and gently manhandled him into the car, ignoring his protests and feeble efforts to slip free. "About two klicks back and coming fast."

"Who—?" Cody began, but Miya cut him off.

"How'd they find us so fast?"

"No idea, but I'll lose 'em on the back roads." Tater slid into the driver's seat and grinned. "Buckle up, chummers, this is gonna get bumpy."

"Who's chasing us?" Cody asked as the acceleration pushed him hard back into the seat. He hadn't been wrong about the jeep's pickup, even on the icy roads. "It can't be anyone from the Long Arms because you two *are* cops."

"This doesn't make any sense," Miya said, continuing to ignore him. "I thought we'd have another six hours before the border cleared them."

"Yeah, well, whoever they work for must have some pull. Intel on 'em just says 'foreign special forces, do not engage.'"

"The border? Shit! It's not the Aztechs, is it?" Cody asked, and was pleased when they finally shut up and listened to him, even if Tater's ruddy skin had gone eerily pale.

"The Aztechs?" Miya said in the calm voice she always used when she was about to lose it. "Cody. You didn't. Tell me you didn't hit an *Aztechnology* facility and then lead them straight back here."

"Ok, I won't," Cody said, smirking. "I didn't think they'd be able to cross the border, though."

3. kisâki: love, darling

Miya made a pained noise. "Cody, *kisâki*[3], I love you, but you are the world's biggest idiot. *Of course* Aztech forces can get special dispensation to enter Algonkian territory. We've got *treaties* with them."

"I am *well* aware, Miya. But that doesn't give them carte blanche to just march their agents in here. We're still a sovereign nation."

"C'mon, Code," said Tater. "You know better'n I do that we're deep in Big A's pocket. They're an Indigenous-led corporation—the *first* big Indigenous-led corp, I should add—and even if their methods scare the bejeezus out of me, they were there for our people when we needed 'em most. Hell, all our parents woulda starved back in 2050 if it wasn't for Aztechnology's relief supplies. And our crop exports to them nearly doubled during the Amazonian War, so it's pretty damn mutually beneficial."

"I know. And that is the whole damn problem, isn't it?" Cody said, waving bound hands to the snow-covered fields that surrounded them on every side. He knew what lurked underneath. "The goddamned neo-triticale. And the stonewheat."

Miya made a disgusted noise in the back of her throat. "Is this your conspiracy theory again?"

"It's not a theory. It's a fact."

"One doesn't find *facts* on those Matrix boards you're obsessed with."

"Fact," Cody repeated, leaning back in his seat and feeling the chip weigh heavy in his datajack.

Outside, the jeep began to rumble and shake as Tater took them off the main highway and onto gravel back roads. Cody could now make out a familiar black sedan roaring up the highway towards their turnoff. Rather than slow to a stop, the driver slewed the car into a controlled fishtail to match their turn and gunned the accelerator again. There was clearly another rigger in charge of that vehicle if they could match Tater's expertise on roads that were more ice than gravel. Cody wished he could risk peeking into astral space to see precisely who was after them, but with the goddamned cuffs on, he couldn't even do that.

If it was the same two who had been chasing him, though, they were in trouble.

Cody stared at the farmer's fields passing the window in a blur and sent a silent prayer to Coyote to lend him the silver tongue of a trickster, because he really needed a little extra help right now. He was so friggin' tired he could barely see straight.

He took a deep breath and gathered his arguments like he was loading a fresh magazine.

"Look, you were Buffalo Boys too, and you taught me everything I know about bison," Cody said. "You've never asked yourself why the bison won't eat stonewheat? Why they'll travel around the neo-triticale fields rather than through them? No, because it was convenient for us. It meant no one had to figure out how to keep the bison away from active farmland. So no one ever asked *why*."

"We know why," Miya said. "Aztechnology engineered their crops to produce a chemical that discourages browsing by wild game."

"Uh-huh. And who told you *that*?" Cody asked. "The Aztech execs? Ever wonder what else they engineered it to do?"

Miya shrugged. "Not relevant. Even if the Council wanted to upend our entire agribusiness sector, we couldn't. We've got long-term commitments, obligations. So even if you've got information that our crops are going to turn us all into flesh-eating ghouls, I don't see what you expect us to do about it."

"I don't expect *you* to do anything about it," Cody said. "Just take me to my father."

"No can do, little brother," said Tater. The ork's tone was light, but Cody saw by the set of his jaw he wasn't joking around like usual. "You've got leverage, but so do we. It's too late for plausible deniability, so we gotta decide if we draw heat from Big A by giving you shelter or hand you over to the Council, who will probably gift wrap you for the Azzies to save face."

"You'd do that to me, cousin?" Cody asked, hurt. Then he finally paid attention to all the little facts that kept not adding up. "You're not cops. Who are you two *really* working for?"

Miya ran her hands through her hair and glanced at Tater. "You're right. We're not Long Arms anymore."

Cody looked hard at her, then at Tater. The big orc only nodded, then shrugged as if what he was admitting to wasn't the biggest deal ever.

"You're *kaskitêwi-mahikanak*?"

Black Wolves. The off-the-record, black ops agents that didn't officially exist. No one knew how or where they were trained, but each one was reported to be more than a match for the special operatives of other nations, and they often had spirits or powerful Preparations to back them up. They also were way, way above his father's pay grade.

He'd gotten the Council's attention, all right—just not how he'd wanted to.

"Handle this, Miya," Tater said. "I've got my hands full here."

With nowhere to hide on the bald prairie, Tater's tactic had been to use his knowledge of the back roads to put a maze of distance between them and the other vehicle, but it wasn't shaking them. The sedan had been paralleling them for half a klick, but now turned sharply onto a road Cody hadn't even seen and was racing to join them.

"I am trying, Nathaniel." Miya sighed, using the given name that had, in inevitable rez fashion, morphed into Tater Tot. She rubbed at her temples.

"Look, we got word that two private contractors were engaged to find and detain you. We were sent to ascertain what you did to warrant their attention. But this—" she waved a hand toward the sedan, "—changes everything. I need you to be real straight with me, Code. No trickster bullshit. What, exactly, did you steal?"

Cody took a deep breath and held it, centering his spirit. Everything relied on this. Over whether or not he could get his oldest friends to trust him when they knew exactly what an unreliable little punk he was, and in spite of all the trouble he'd brought back with him to their homeland. And whether a shadowrunner warranted the protection of the Black Wolves.

"You wondered why I gave up a cushy job at the tribal office to go play shadowrunner?" he asked. "It wasn't because I was fighting with my dad, or because I wanted fame and fortune, or whatever bullshit reasons he made up. *He* always said it was a shaman's job to serve their people, and that might be the only thing he and I ever agreed on. But I wasn't gonna do it the way he wanted—wasn't going to waste my life asking spirits to fix little problems when I could see a bigger threat all around us.

"So I went to Seattle. Ran the shadows. And when I was ready, I stole documents from Aztechnology that confirms everything on those conspiracy boards and *worse.* That's why they're after me. You have no idea what I gave up to get this info, Miya." Cody tried hard not to see the faces of his fallen teammates in his mind's eye.

There was a long silence in the car, broken only when Tater blew out a long breath and chuckled disbelievingly. "*Chucksees*[4], Code!" he swore. "Why couldn't you have just run off with a gang or something simple like that?"

Cody grinned. "Can't do anything as normal as that, cousin. It's a Coyote's job to turn things on their heads."

"Coyote always gets killed for that in the stories."

"Not all the time. And he comes back when he gets killed."

"Yeah, well," Tater said, "you ain't him."

Their stomachs all lurched as the jeep fishtailed on the pitted, icy road. Tater careened around a corner onto a road little more than a deer track through the snow. The sedan behind them flew past the turn, as Tater had predicted, but the driver of the sedan was as ballsy as they were skilled. They put the car into a hard spin, rotating two full turns, and stopped facing back the way they had come from. In no time, the sedan was back on the road behind them.

"Give it here, Cody," Miya said, holding out her hand for the chip.

He snorted. "Am I giving it to Miyawatami or to the Black Wolves?"

She didn't answer, but gestured again more emphatically.

He shook his head. "If I give it to you, you gotta promise me it won't get buried. No matter what we owe Aztech's execs."

"I can't make you any promises."

"Hell no, then. I don't trust you."

Miya's face went pale with rage and she whirled on him, poking him hard in the chest. "That's funny coming from *you*, Code. You screwed me over big time when you ran off to Seattle. Stole my car, my credsticks, and made me a laughingstock among my colleagues. I almost didn't make the special forces because of it. Now you're doing it again, only *worse.* We're gonna catch hell for helping you whether your intel is worth it or not. So don't you dare say *you* don't trust *me*!"

---

4. Chucksees: a Cree swear (lit) dirty ass

"Then let me go," Cody said, not backing down. "I'll handle it my own way."

She glared at him with those laser-sighted eyes and shook her head. "Still full of shit, I see."

"Time out, y'all," Tater said. "We've got incoming."

Bullets crackled against the back window like loose gravel, and Cody threw himself to the floor. Miya didn't flinch.

"Tater, drive your ass off," she said, jerking a thumb at Cody. "We'll deal with this asshole later."

"Right-o."

Cody didn't see how they were going to lose the pursuit—this wasn't the close-packed streets of the Metroplex, and all those jokes about being able to watch your dog run away for a week on the plains were all but true. The snow-grey horizon stretched endlessly, broken only by a few bluffs of poplars and birch. But he knew Tater knew his business, and held on tight as the jeep skidded into a spin of its own.

Time seemed to slow as the sedan sped toward them, braking, but still carrying enough momentum to plow through them when it hit. Gravel and ice sprayed up like a wave from under their tires as they pirouetted, and Cody swore he saw it clatter against the hood of the sedan as it careened toward them.

Still whirling, the ditch rose up to meet the jeep. They hit the field with a bone-jarring *thud*, but the rear suspension must have been reinforced because they stopped rather than break an axle.

The sedan sailed past, mere centimeters from their front fender.

Even Miya was clenching the holy-shit handles after that maneuver. Tater didn't give them time to recover. He hit the accelerator hard enough to spray a whiteout behind them as the jeep leaped onto the road, going back the way they'd come.

By the time the sedan got turned around, they'd put two hectares and a dilapidated barn between themselves and pursuit.

But they weren't in the clear. Something moved in the skies. Cody watched Miya's eyes as she tracked it, then felt the liquid-nitrogen sting of the winter wind as she lowered the window and aimed her rifle up. Two shots in rapid succession; the first to get your eye in and the second to kill, just like she'd taught him. She frowned, then fired again. This time, a drone fell like skeet.

"Not like you to take four shots to down a bird," Cody said. "Must be losing your touch."

"It was armored," Miya said. "Also, shut up."

She closed the window but kept her face near it, scanning for more drones. Cody took advantage of her preoccupation to try the safety pin he'd palmed on the handcuffs' lock. His father had probably never worn a pair, and Cody was hoping he'd forgotten to ward the keyhole. He was rewarded with a dull shock that made his fingers numb, and managed to bite off a curse before Miya could notice.

Outside, the sedan pulled onto a road parallel to theirs, but two klicks back and across a field. Then the jeep shook with impact as they hit potholes hidden under the snow so large they would have swallowed smaller vehicles. Tater eased back on the gas on this rough stretch of road, and the sedan sped up to even the distance between them. Cody wasn't too worried—they were out of rifle range, and Tater's car was definitely equipped to deal with missiles.

Except something in his gut warned him that everything had just gone horribly wrong.

The sedan's door opened and shut briefly, though nothing could have survived disembarking at these speeds.

But something *had.*

An animal was racing across the field toward them. At first, Cody thought it might be a wolf, but then his brain caught on to the *wrongness* in the way the creature moved and his stomach twisted. It ran like a human galloping on all fours, with horribly long arms and a void where the head should be. And it left deep, spreading pink patches in the snow wherever it touched.

"What the hell is that?" Miya asked.

Cody vomited. Even without his magical senses active, the shock of what he was seeing hit him like a punch. He'd never seen one before, but he'd heard rumors....

He heaved for a moment, then managed to wrest his stomach back under control. "B...blood elemental."

Tater swore low and thoughtfully. "You didn't leave any blood in that facility, did you?"

Cody didn't answer, though his brain was full of memories of it all going wrong. It'd been hard to tell, in those last moments of chaos, what blood was his and what belonged to his team. Not that it really mattered. All of their blood would be with him forever, and the only thing he could do was make sure their sacrifice was worth something.

"I'm gonna take that as a yes," Tater said. The ork sucked at his teeth. "Shit, son. That's how they've been tracking you."

"They can do that?"

"Unconfirmed, officially. But yes," Miya said. She leveled the rifle calmly through the window, tracking it despite the speed they were moving at and the howling snow. He'd seen her make harder shots under worse conditions.

"You've got to uncuff me," Cody said. "That rifle isn't going to do shit."

"Why, so you can run out on me again? I'm handling it." Miya's rifle sang out. The bullets tore into the elemental, leaving a spatter pattern of fresh blood in the snow with each hit, but the creature didn't slow.

"No, Miya, listen. They had to *kill* someone to summon that damn thing! You can't take it out with a rifle, silver bullets or not. But I might be able to. I'm good with spirits. Hell, as an Aspected shaman, it's the *only* thing I'm good with. I'm a shitty friend and a compulsive liar, but I can do one goddamned thing really well, and *this* is it! So trust me. *Please.*"

After all these years, Cody could read denial in the way Miya's shoulders rose even as she continued to put slug after slug into the elemental. She wasn't going to go for it. His betrayal had cut her too deeply, and she was someone who never, ever forgave.

"Window!" Tater said, his trademark laconic calm completely absent. Cody had never heard panic like this in the ork's voice.

Miya quickly pulled her rifle back inside the vehicle and the window slid closed just as the elemental reached them.

On long car trips as a child, Cody had sometimes imagined a wolf-like creature running alongside the car, pacing it, and weaving in and around the ancient telephone poles beside the highway. Now, as the creature loped up and slammed itself against the jeep like a horror-trid version of those childhood fantasies, he laughed in terror.

Where it impacted, the thick, viscous body of the elemental turned liquid again and began to move. Cody watched droplets of the creature pour up its own arm, until the whole thing was splashed against the side of his door like the aftermath of a murder scene. He saw tendrils of blood wriggling against the window, trying to find any cracks it could pour itself through.

It found one on the driver's side. There was a sound like an airplane toilet flushing as the manifested spirit tore a hole in the car's weather-stripping and poured itself through in a sticky crimson torrent. It fell wetly across Tater, who grunted in pain as it formed rending spines throughout its amorphous mass.

"Miya!" Cody screamed, shoving his bound hands into the front seat.

She hesitated for only a second, then grabbed the control stone out of Tater's pocket and pressed it against the largest rune on his cuffs. They clicked open, and his magical senses came pouring back. His link to his companion spirits snapped back into being, and he felt their relief at his return and their terror at the wrongness they sensed near him.

He knew, logically, that this would probably kill him. The drain was going to be massive and his reagents had been confiscated in lockup. But the decision was made with his gut, not his brain. That thing—that *abomination*—didn't belong here in *his* homeland.

And it wasn't going to hurt his cousins.

Cody gathered his will and his magic, and opened his astral eyes. Before him was a maelstrom of writhing redness that beat in time to his own heart. A thin cord ran from his chest to a tangle of dark energies at the center of the elemental, and more cords wrapped around the creature—the other mage's willpower, goading this spirit on its promised task.

He grabbed those bindings and *bit hard.*

He felt his will slam up against that of the other mage. He felt the woman's dismissive amusement as she took his measure, and it was so like his father's he snarled out loud, "Oh, *absolutely* not."

He threw back his head. He howled. He howled long and loud and just as discordantly as any coyote. He felt his companion spirits howl as well, lending their strength to his song as he tore at the magical links like a coyote tearing at a winter-frozen carcass. The bindings started to burn away, and like Raven stealing the sun, he burned with it.

He felt his soul coming apart with the strain, but he would not let go, even as blackness came for him and he, distantly, heard Miya's scream.

Miya had once said to him, "You're înahpîkasoht. That means you're trans, but do you know the literal translation? *'Someone who fights everyone to prove they are the toughest.'* And that's always been you. Even as a kid, you'd scrap with someone twice your size just to prove you weren't scared. I respect that."

He thought of that memory now, and smiled as he felt himself sinking into the dark.

He was so tired.

But he trusted Miya to do what was right.

It would be okay.

It was cold.

It was cold, but he felt hot breath on his neck.

Someone stood behind him, their presence warm like a sun-soaked stone, and he suddenly knew who it was.

Bison.

Bison, who had been born from the land itself and whom he'd never been able to speak with, despite all the time he'd spent alongside Bison's people. Bison, who had been tricked by Coyote once, and still held a grudge.

The old bull stamped his hoof, and it made a sound like thunder.

Cody stood in this nowhere place and bowed.

The spirit lowered its big shaggy head, and its horns gleamed like blades. *"Son-of-Coyote. It is not your time."*

"Why?" Cody asked. "I have done what I needed to."

The bull's dark eyes held stars and amusement in their depths. *"Have you?"*

Cody thought about that. "Maybe. I don't know. But I did all I could."

The bull regarded him for a moment. *"Perhaps. But that is more than you were asked. And you served my people, as well as your own. Go home."*

He was warm. Warm and comfortable and everything smelled of leather and cheese-flavored soypuffs.

"Little brother?" someone asked.

"Mm—?" he managed. Then, "Tater?"

"Yeah, buddy. We're here."

"Thought we'd lost you." That was Miya, and her voice wavered then hardened. "You better not be dying on us."

He made the enormous effort of opening his eyes and found himself stretched out on the backseat of Tater's car, tucked under the ork's jacket. "What happened?"

"You got the bastard," said Miya, which was always explanation enough for her.

"We managed to lose 'em. They couldn't track us without the spirit," Tater said. "Miya slapped a stim patch on you and did CPR while I found us a barn to hide in. So now we're ghosts, laying low until we figure out what to do with you. Cheese puff?"

Cody took the offered bag of snacks and tore into it, knowing his body needed the sugar even if his pounding drain-headache made him feel nauseous. "You gonna take me in? Maybe your bosses'll forgive you if you hand me over."

Miya shrugged. "Depends."

"On what?"

"On what you wanna do next," Tater said. "We can say we took the datachip off you before you tricked us into thinking you were dead and ran off, but you'll never be able to come home again. It'll be a long road, with Big A on your ass every moment."

He put a hand on Cody's shoulder and looked down into his eyes. "Or you could stay. Become one of us. We'll change your face, wipe your records, and retrain you. Coyote's magic would be a boon to the Black Wolves."

"We'd push for you to join our unit," Miya said. "We could all be together again, fighting side by side. Like the old days." Then, more quietly, she added, "Please."

It was the "please" that nearly did it. Miya never pleaded, never admitted any weakness. And it would be nice, being home again, seeing his cousins daily...

But.

Cody sat up slowly. Outside the car, snow trickled into the barn from a hole in the roof. "Nah. I'll just get you both in more trouble. If the Council decides to bury this, some sneaky punk's gotta show them they're wrong, and I can't do that if I'm part of the system."

Tater smiled sadly, but nodded. "So what are you going to do?"

Cody showed his teeth. "I'm going to go out there and howl, long and loud as I can, to anyone who will listen."

Miya's smile was sharp as a blade, and he pulled her into a tight hug. "Idiot," she said through her tears.

He just smiled and rubbed her back. "So, the official story is I'm playing dead, huh?" He tried to get to his feet. The world swam, and Tater grabbed his shoulder and held him up. "Sure feels true. But I should get going."

"I think you can be dead for a few more hours," Miya said, smiling down at him. "Long enough to finish catching you up on the gossip from home."

Cody was dead for the rest of the night, and as the cousins' laughter rang out into the darkness, so too did a chorus of coyotes singing their joy to the stars.

THE WASTELANDS SPEAK

Jaym Gates

The glint of sun on metal catches my eye, a shadowed smear in the heat shimmer of the desert betraying the convoy. My eagle floats lazily nearby, looking like nothing more than a scavenger as she gives me a view of my hunters. More than I'd thought. My horse shifts nervously under me, reading my concern. I should have expected the megacorps to pull out the big guns.

We stand longer than we should, staring across the desert until my eyes water. I hear my ancestors sneering at me; even a child knows better than to sear their eyes as I have just done. But it's just me against all of them. A nomad woman, a nobody runner, who got in the way of something too big to comprehend.

I think of my ancestors, sweeping across Asia and Europe in a flood that terrorized the known world, and my pulse settles. My horse flicks an ear at me. I focus on her pale ear, on the shimmer of gold in each fine hair that speaks of centuries of adaptation and survival. I think of my mother, and her mother, their sun-wrinkled faces splitting into brilliant smiles, their gnarled hands calmly raising tents and stroking the sides of the mares they milked. I remember the sound of hoofbeats, the feel of my father's arms around me as we thundered across the rocky hills beneath the sweep of eagle's wings.

In the vast, grand history of my people, I find peace. I may be nobody, but I am not alone. I am merely an indrawn breath in a story older than written history. It does not matter if I live; it matters only that I do not give in to fear.

The sun beats down on us. The wind is picking up, sand sifting restlessly. Unwinding my veils, I taste the air, and a wolfish grin splits my face.

A storm is coming. A storm that will cover my tracks and scramble their sensors.

I tap a code into the digital perch buried in my wristband, directing my eagle to scout ahead for somewhere to camp. Obediently, she leaves off, although she plummets to the earth not far from the convoy for a moment. The readout tells me she has captured a small, furry thing for dinner. With a few beats of her massive wings, she rises up and takes to the sky again. Her wide circles won't betray my position, even if they have outriders.

With a displeased snort, my horse moves out from behind the meager shade of the stone outcropping. She shifts her weight, dropping onto her haunches as we slither down the side of a dune. With my eagle watching above, we'll stay in the shadow of old, dead riverbeds and cliffs to avoid any scouts they may send out.

The wastelands are a tale of grief and anger to my people. Although many of my people fell to the lure of technology, moving to slums in the city, stripped of their horses and ancestral wealth, many still maintained their ancient way of life. They moved with the seasons, following the horse herds across expanses of land that killed the unprepared. They hunted with eagles and raised sheep and the shaggy mountain camels, shared stories around the fire while the women embroidered the huge felt sheets which made up our tents and clothes.

It was not an easy life, as my mother often said, but it was a free one, where a person lived and died honestly. She had no use for the cities, refusing to enter them even to trade.

She, and the rest of my tribe, died when the Harrowing came. Their bones are mixed with the sand, their spirits obliterated. They will never sing to me in the winds.

I swore I would never go back there...and yet.

It literally fell into my lap. I was sitting lookout on a shitty smash'n'grab with a gutter-level crew. Just something to get me back on my feet after my latest trip across the wastes. I don't know what happened, really, but I can guess: Someone makes a noise while infiltrating the burned-out shell of a low-level corp satellite office, a rent-a-guard hears it, there's a fight, someone gets thrown through the window.

The ancient data drive must have been on a desk. Maybe someone got thrown across it.

All I know is I heard shattering glass, a bunch of charred papers fell around me like dead leaves, the body of our "infiltration specialist" hit the pavement in front of me, and a small, hard object went down my shirt. A round of fire from inside, a couple yells, and I figured the job had probably gone as far south as it was going to go.

A few blocks later, having made sure no one had followed me, I stopped and fished it (and a few wayward crumbs) out of my shirt. The thing had to have been sixty years old, at least. Of course, in these parts, it's easier to find the past than the future. Took me a few hours, but I found an old woman with the most eclectic collection of data-reading devices I'd ever seen.

I should have killed her even for knowing the drive existed. I probably should have killed myself. Would have been easier.

But I didn't, and the desert stretches before me, promising answers to the dark secrets I now carry. A forgotten wasteland calls me.

"If you're hearing this, the worst has happened. If you're reading this, I hope I made a difference.

"My name is Vashtai Sorenson. I'm a nobody. Just a low-level researcher at Ares, a corporate 'security' team. What a joke. If the public knew a fraction of the things I've seen…

"Anyway, I'm about to go on the run, so I'm hiding this somewhere safe. Maybe I can come back for it someday.

"I guess, if you're seeing this, I didn't."

The flat, calm voice lingers in my ears. After I decoded the drive, I bought a cheap transcoder and copied it a few times. Hid it around the city.

I've already listened one copy to death. I won't say it's unbelievable, because there isn't a depth the megacorps could sink to that would really surprise me.

Her voice is somewhere beyond terror. The woman speaking across decades had passed the horizon of terror and kept running.

"I don't think they knew I was there when they opened the portals."

When I was a kid, I listened to the elders speak of the past, of their spirits and ancestors. We left gifts for the ancestors, spoke their names with respect, and fed them with prayers and kumiss, but we never spoke of the spirits by name anymore.

When I asked my grandmother, her lips thinned, bloodless against her teeth. *"The spirits we once worshiped don't exist anymore,"* she told me. *"They died when the world broke."*

At the time, I didn't know what she meant.

I think I do now.

"The first few experiments were, I think, failures. People went missing around us. Street people I'd spoken with every day since I started working there just...disappeared. Others moved away. No one would tell me why, but one day I saw Charlie's hat tossed in the incinerator. It was covered in blood.

"That's when I started looking.

"You got used to the scent of blood in the labs. I know we weren't innocent. 'Willing' and 'volunteer' are laughable terms in this world, where high-priced lawyers speak language more dangerous than any black spell, and you're only alive until you get in someone's way.

"I turned my eyes away for a long time. I think I wish I hadn't stopped doing that. Some people are meant to be heroes. I'm not one of them. It's too late now."

The first time I listened to the recordings, her deathly calm voice and meandering story drove me wild with impatience. It was like she was talking in circles, a frightened antelope approaching a watering hole surrounded by nova scorpions.

I didn't know, at first, how accurate that was.

We've stopped twice since entering the desert. I hear my grandmother's disapproving voice every time I set up camp. We're soft, my mare and I. We have been out of the desert too long, out of the blistering heat and the dryness which sucks at your marrow.

She lips a cake of dates and sheep fat out of my hand before beginning the dig. We are following an old riverbed, and although she is tired, she has scented water for the last hour and our thirst drives us. Tossing the eagle into the sky to hunt for our dinner, I pull out my shovel and we dig until a trickle of water wells in the damp sand.

It is wise to drink while we can, if the voice in my ears is to be believed.

"I was doing log maintenance on the servers the first time I noticed the anomalies. My job was to scan for any strange behavior which could indicate sabotage or spying. I'd been recruited from the street, where I'd been counting cards in high-stakes games—my pattern recognition is the best there is. I knew my logs, knew every blip of data and usage.

"I knew something was wrong.

"So I listened. I watched. And I learned something worse than I'd ever guessed."

The wind has picked up, snatching at my veils with greedy, cruel hands. We avoid the worst of it by following old riverbeds and canyons. It's an indirect route, risking that I will be the last to arrive at our destination. I am betting it all that those who hunt me don't know where we're going.

We pause at the mouth of a canyon. I dismount, wrap my horse in the things my ancestors used to protect their horses before steam was discovered, improved, just a little, with modern magics. Her eyes, her ears, her nostrils. She is functionally deaf and blind now in every way which matters to a creature. She trusts me to keep her safe.

I pull my mother's shawl around my shoulders, belting it with the leather my father braided. For a moment, I am cast into a whirlpool of dream and memory. I stand in the wind and sand, reverent. My ancestors speak in the winds; their bones walk in the sands sifting endlessly across the wastes. I hear the pounding beat of cavalries as vast as the sea, the hellish screaming of warhorses. I feel the bones of invaders crunching between my teeth, taste the coppery tang of spilled life.

This is something the foreigners will never understand; the weight of time and history that shifts beneath our feet with every step. I am myself, but I am also the lingering voice of kings and queens feared across the known world. I am a fleeting wisp of ephemeral time, and the scion of endless generations.

It is easy to get lost in fancy and memory, in the embrace of the desert's wrath. Here, there are no superior sneers or dismissive glances. Here, I am not a filthy nomad worthy only of taking out the trash, and eventually dying in a hail of bullets on an equally trashy job.

Here, my ancestors speak to me, and my horse is as fierce as the eagle which perches on her saddle. This is what those who hunt me do not understand: They see only a lone woman; a clumsy fool who gawks at the technicolor chaos of the cities and doesn't know the slang. They hunt me like a wounded bison that runs only on animal terror.

I am not alone here. They cannot see my ancestors, not until it is too late. When my blade cracks their spines and my horse's hooves cave in their skulls, then they will see the tidal wave of the steppes. Then they will understand.

This is *my* desert. *My* hunt. *My* job. *My* story.

The desert beckons. I ride into the wasteland, my tracks swept away by the storm into which I ride.

"They opened a gate to Dis, and what came through to devour them will never leave my memory."

I still don't know how the drive made it all the way across the desert to Samarkand. Not when there is nothing left of the homes my people made.

I don't know how it came to me, one of the few people who can still speak a language that died when death blossomed in the deserts of my people.

"If you find this, I didn't make it. If you've never heard of me, then my plan failed. If you're listening to this, I need your help."

The storm begins to die down as I approach the coordinates the faceless woman left me. I did my research; this was once the corp town of Zarafshan. Now it is just desert. The sand here is coarse. When I dismount and let it run through my fingers, I see it is made of metal and bone and stone, not sand.

There is not a piece of anything larger than my little fingernail. It is as if everything was run through a millstone. My jaw tightens. I know I don't have long before the megacorps show up. By now, they may have figured out where I was headed, and they can travel a lot faster than I can.

Fortunately, it turns out the destruction didn't spread outside the city. I locate the outcroppings of stone quickly enough. Whatever caused the destruction here focused on what was living.

The cave is tiny. I nearly get stuck many times. But, finally, I find a small metal box. There are things inside. That's all the time I have. My wrist unit alerts me that my eagle has seen the corp convoy. It's time to get out of here.

Such a long journey, and I do not even have time to sing my family to rest. I can feel their spirits. My mother's rage. My father's grief. My grandmother's hands on my shoulders. The wails of strangers.

The winds are filled with ghosts and the broken spirits of an ancient people. Zarafshan was ripped into pieces by something. Not long after, the wasteland wiped out everything else.

The voices in my head warn me that any living thing which lingers here will meet the same fate. A grim smile lights my face. The dead will not harm one who can sing with them.

"I came to Zarafshan to make a name for myself. This forgotten outpost in the middle of the desert, a place my people sneered at and refused to enter.

"They disowned me when I told them I was going to work for the megacorps. They had put everything they had into giving me an education. The cities laughed at the backward nomads, but everyone in my tribe could read. Many of them had gone away and gotten degrees. They brought the new science and magic, and married it to the old science of magic and created havens in the mountains the megacorps couldn't touch. If someone wanted to go to college, the women sold their tapestries, the men sold a prize mare to a corp executive as a status symbol, and off to school we went.

"But working for the megacorps...that was a betrayal.

"Now I am trapped here. I have forgotten the ways of the desert. I would not survive there, even if I was not hunted. My people would not lift a finger to help me.

"I'm catching a ride out first thing tomorrow. Told my boss I needed to go to Samarkand to buy a gift for my sister's wedding.

"I've called in the only favor I have left. A friend is hiding copies of all the information I've gathered in a cave. The coordinates are written in the place where the people of the Blue Veil send their women for water.

"I hope you succeed where I didn't."

Later, when this is over, I will remember the sound of my people's anger. The convoy didn't stand a chance. Shamans and the best weapons money could buy, chewed to indiscriminate bits to join the rubble of this cursed city. Zarafshan was wiped from the face of the Earth; my people linger here to ensure it remains dead.

I sang for them, sang as tears ran down my face and my horse quivered in rage and fear beside me; both of us shedding our blood on the sand in offering, in supplication for protection from the inferno. She, too, heard their songs, which echo in her blood as well.

Now we have a mission. The drives and crumbling documents in my saddlebags tell of corporate corruption, of bargains with evil such as we once thought existed only in stories. I sat in the destruction and read the documents to my ancestors, and wept for what we had all lost.

A long desert crossing awaits me. I will not return to the place where I first discovered this path. Instead, I will ride to Ashgabat. I have friends there; people who know where these secrets will do the most good.

It is time for the wastelands to tell their story.

WHERE THE HEART IS
A WOLF AND RAVEN STORY

Michael A. Stackpole

I figured the kid as being seven, maybe eight years old. On the smaller side, that impression aided by his oversized glasses with soiled white tape at a corner. Short-sleeved shirt had cartoon animals on it—probably a pajama top by the look of it. Denims worn at the heels, and slightly oversized sneakers someone had done up in a double knot.

He sat in the office chair, legs crisscrossed on the seat, nose buried in a book. Aside from turning pages, which he did on a regular basis, the only other motions to him were pushing the glasses back up his nose and the nervous habit of tapping a finger against one of his emergent tusks.

The young ork somehow remained focused, despite being in an unfamiliar place. Moreover, he somehow avoided being distracted by the man Dr. Raven had charged with the task of watching over him. Kid Stealth crouched by the doorway on titanium legs modeled after those of a velociraptor, creating the kind of image that haunts nightmares.

I looked away from the monitor playing the security cam's feed and frowned at Plutarch Graogrim. "And this kid asked for me?"

Tark, also an ork, had graduated from Harvard before he underwent his transformation, and joined Raven's crew shortly thereafter. He was our resident genius on pretty much everything this side of murder—Stealth had that covered. He jerked a thumb toward the screen. "Take a good look at the book."

"Oh." The kid had his nose buried in one of the Wysteria novels—a fantasy series featuring Sir Brendan Rake, the Dolorous Knight of the Moon, who had a decidedly wolfish aspect to him. "He's moving right through it, too, but, from the look of him, shouldn't someone be reading *to* him?"

Tark shrugged. "He marched up to the door, book under his arm, and said he wanted to talk to you. That he'd *only* talk to you."

I took another close look at the screen. "I don't know him. I mean, I can't place him."

"Which is why you probably ought to go talk to him."

"That what Dr. Raven thinks?"

"He's incoming—about two hours. Tom Electric is piloting, so could be faster. Doc pointed out, correctly, that if our visitor would only speak to you, that only you can learn why he's here."

The obviousness of that conclusion left me wondering if this was the sort of day when I *wasn't* going to be smarter than a fifth grader.

"To bite and rend only requires courage, Longtooth, not brains."

Another constituency heard from. The Old One—a splinter of the Wolf Spirit that dwelled inside me—was often a great help, especially in dire situations. However, talking to a kid wasn't going to be dire.

He's a child, Old One, biting and rending aren't part of the program here.

"They are always *part, Longtooth. You just need to know when to use them."*

I rolled my eyes and headed upstairs to the office, declining to argue the point with him. The Old One felt about biting and rending the way Kid Stealth felt about plastic explosive: it *could* solve any problem. I didn't wholly disagree, but I really didn't want to be cleaning up the mess.

Stealth cleared the doorway without so much as a whisper, and yet a flicker of an eyebrow let me know our visitor had marked Stealth's movement. Even as I entered the room, however, the kid kept reading until he hit the bottom of a page. Then he slid a scrap of paper in as a bookmark and reverently closed the volume. His head rose and he slid his glasses back up his nose again.

"I'm Wolfgang Kies. Can I help you?"

He slid from the chair, set the book down on the seat, then advanced toward me, extending his hand. "I am Dirk Watts. You have to help my mom."

I shook his hand, my grip swallowing up his hand. "If your mom needs our help, she should be the one here."

Dirk's dark eyes narrowed. "Look, Mister Wolf, I'm only eight years old, but it's kinda obvious that if an eight-year-old tells you his mom needs help, she's not thinking clearly enough to ask herself."

Kid Stealth, who I'd thought would have retreated as far from the office as possible, came and squatted beside me. "I like this one."

The Old One howled in agreement with the Murder Machine, and their agreement sent a cold chill running up my spine.

I grabbed another chair and sat. "Okay, Dirk, you're right. So let's start again. What kind of trouble is your mom in?"

The boy shrugged. "She's upset and she looks at me and she's scared. I mean, not the usual way. This is different. She hugs me, and she promises she won't let anything happen to me." The little guy's voice just shrank and his lips pressed tight together.

I filled the momentary silence. "Okay, it would help a little if I knew your mom's name. Can you write it down?" I offered that so he'd have a moment more to regain his voice.

He nodded, so I crossed behind him to Raven's desk, grabbed a pen and a memo pad. I handed them across and Dirk turned toward the chair. He set the pad on the book and carefully wrote out his mother's name, then handed it to me.

"Jessie Watts." I showed the paper to Stealth, mainly because the camera Tark was watching us through was behind him. "Do you know where you live?"

Dirk's brow wrinkled as he concentrated. "Mostly there's St. Andrew's mission. Sometimes they don't have room. We sleep out lots. She's afraid now."

I jotted down the name *St. Andrew's* and added a couple question marks. The mission *did* provide housing, preferring mothers and children. Sometimes they even had enough to feed their residents, but beds were always on a first come, first served basis. More importantly, however, ork families tended not to stray into St. Andrew's diocese, and humans stayed away from the Seattle Underground and other ork haunts.

"St. Andrew's, got it." I rubbed my forehead. "Anything happen recently to make your mom scared?"

Dirk shrugged, frustration washing over his face. "I didn't see anything. I spend a lot of time at the library, so I don't always know what she's doing."

"Is that where you're supposed to be now?"

"I didn't lie to her." He glanced back at the book on the chair. "I said I'd be reading."

I smiled. "It's okay. Just asked because the library is where we might find her when she comes looking for you. Does she work?"

The boy frowned. "She does stuff to make money, but I don't know."

A gentle knock came at the door, then it cracked open. Tark poked his head in and flashed a tablet toward us. A picture of a handsome woman appeared on the screen. Brown eyes, black hair, tending toward slender. Her expression had that fine combination of boredom and anxiety that marks things like official identification. "Is this your mom, Dirk?"

The boy nodded enthusiastically, with the hint of a smile reaching his lips.

Tark gave him a nod. "We'll find her. Val has already started."

I gave Tark a thumbs-up. "See, Dirk, it will all be good."

"I believe you." The boy walked over and gave me a big hug. "No way the Knight of the Dolorous Moon will fail."

Valerie Valkyrie, Raven's resident decker, wove feeds together from Seattle's surveillance infrastructure into a tapestry that caught Jessie Watts near the Market, heading toward downtown. While Val directed Tark on an intercept course with her, I called up Harry Braxen. An ork like Tark, he worked for Lone Star keeping the peace in Seattle. I asked him if Jessie Watts had a Lone Star file.

He tried to give me some static about how those files were private, and I reminded him that he was just saving Val the aggravation of drilling through Lone Star's IC *again,* so he relented. The kid's mom had had multiple run-ins with Lone Star—petty theft, pandering, public intoxication, and criminal trespass at an estate called *Stonehouse out on the Sound.* That stuck out in a "which of these is not like the others" kinda way, since it would have been quite the hike for her to get out there. The family—the Seaborns of Seaborn Dynamics fame—had declined to press charges, so once she sobered up, Lone Star let her go.

Seaborn Dynamics I didn't know much about, mainly because they weren't a firm that pumped out product for the rabble like me. They made things other businesses used to create bigger things: chips for computers, carbon dioxide for soda, propellant for bullets—the staples of life. The reason they used Lone Star for security was to clean *up* their image with the public, and that right there says a kiloton. Lone Star's being on the job freed up SD's house troops for dealing with more delicate matters, which was an uphill climb, since SD employed people you couldn't be sure were even housebroken yet. Word on the street was that folks working with SD weren't worth hassling. SD's gillettes hit back, tended to be sloppy and, while cruel, oddly inefficient. Every bar in town had at least one souse who had the scars to prove they hadn't listened to that advice.

Other than that, Seaborn Dynamics had the rep of being a typical megacorp. They treated their workers like crap, used lawyers the way Stealth used armor piercing bullets, and instead of doing anything to inspire good stories in the news, just smothered all the bad ones they could find. The CEO ruled with an iron fist and, in this case, apparently didn't bother with the velvet glove.

But she liked dogs, so I guess that made it all okay.

Something else about the family lingered in the back of my head, but was taking its own time to work its way forward.

When Tark brought Dirk's mother into Raven's place, Jessie Watts resembled her ID picture the way a ghost resembles a living person. I didn't know how long ago the first image of her had been made, but life had been hard since then. She'd become stringy—substance abuse, happenstance, or malnutrition, take your pick. Her eyes remained dull and fear shot through her voice—though her answering questions with a single word made the fear hard to pick out.

Then we reunited her with Dirk, and her face brightened for an eyeblink.

"Oh, my baby. I was so worried!" She dropped to her knees before him and hugged her to him, tears beginning to flow. She kissed his forehead, then pressed her forehead to his. Her hair slid down to hide her face. Then her head sank and she began sobbing.

The boy stroked her hair. "It's okay, Momma. It will be okay."

She sniffed and looked up hopefully into his face. "You can't know that."

"I do, Momma." He nodded solemnly and brushed away her tears. "We always make it okay, Momma."

"But it's bad this time, Dirk, real bad."

"We have some experience in dealing with 'real bad,' Ms. Watts." The new voice, deep and warm, brimming with assurance, drowned her soft sobs. "I'm Dr. Raven. My people and I have seen worse and handled it."

Jessie Watts turned, cradling her son to her chest, and looked up at the figure framed by the doorway. Broad of shoulder, clean-limbed, with sharp features and long black hair that cascaded down over his shoulders, Dr. Raven filled the doorway. The pointed tips of his elven ears crested through his hair, but his muscular build and the reddish-brown tone of his skin spoke to his Native American heritage.

Most remarkable of all, however, were the red and blue highlights swirling through his dark eyes, just as the *aurora borealis* played through the night sky.

She gasped.

Dirk beamed. "Now it is *really* okay, Momma. Dr. Raven will take care of everything."

Valerie Valkyrie and Tark took Dirk to the kitchen to get something to eat. He agreed only to go if they would let him bring something back for his mom. He snagged his book from the chair, giving her somewhere to sit and compose herself.

Once he'd departed, Raven dropped to a knee before her and took her hands in his. His gentleness seemed to startle her, but he didn't trap her hands, and she slowly began to relax.

"Your son is a good boy. He is concerned for you." Raven glanced back at the closed office door. "I don't think we have long before he returns. He believes you need some help and I would be inclined to agree. How can we help you?"

"There's nothing..." She shook her head, then glanced up. "I shouldn't have let him read those books. He got it into his head that there are heroes who can... Look, I know who you are, well, who you must be. I've heard stories. Even if I believed half of them, it wouldn't make any difference. You can't..."

"Jessie, problems have many solutions. Just describe yours to us, and maybe we can find a way clear of things." Doc kept his voice even and warm, suggesting it was all a harmless way to pass the time before Dirk returned. "Something happened recently, didn't it? What? I already know it involves Dirk, because your fear is for him. You couldn't bear to lose him, no matter how hard it has been for you."

Her shoulders slumped. "You have no idea."

"I know that being alone in the world is tough. And for you, a single human mother who has an ork child—a very precocious and preternaturally intelligent one—it must be doubly or triply so."

"He doesn't miss anything. I mean, he sees things I don't." She swiped at a tear. "He's really the adult..."

"He does seem very responsible." Raven smiled reassuringly. "People have urged you to give him up, haven't they?"

"I didn't ask for...Dirk, he changed while I carried him. When I gave birth to an ork...it had been bad enough for my folks that I was pregnant without being married but this, this was worse. My dad decided I'd slept with an ork and he threw me out. And the orks, some of them try to help, but others, they're very insistent. They tell me Dirk is one of theirs, and that I shouldn't be allowed to have him." Her head came up, eyes rimmed with red. "But he's all I've got. I can't lose him."

Raven nodded solemnly. "Who's threatening to take him away?"

She looked down again. "I can't."

Two bits of information collided in my brain. "His father. Clifton Seaborn."

Jessie yanked her hands from Raven's and stared at me, eyes enormous and all whites. "No, no, that's not true!" She shouted it as if volume and vehemence could deny it.

Raven looked at me, an eyebrow raised.

"A couple years ago, Ms. Watts paid a visit to the Seaborn estate, Stonehouse. And there was a rumor recently that Clifton Jr. has lymphoma. Not looking good."

"Ah." Raven stroked his chin. "Clifton Seaborn wishes to cure his son through a marrow transplant. He asked you if... no, no Clifton Seaborn *told* you that Dirk would donate, and threatened to take him away from you if you didn't agree, yes?"

"He had a lawyer find me. He said he would sue for custody and I would lose. Or he would give me a million in Seaborn corporate scrip, plus get me placed with one of their plants far away, if I gave Dirk up. But I..." She covered her face with her hands and started sobbing again.

Raven reached out, resting his hands on her shoulders. "You considered that, maybe, just maybe, Dirk would be better off with Clifton. It was a moment of weakness, and then you came to your senses."

"No, Doctor." She sniffed as she looked up. "You make it sound right. I was only thinking that maybe, if Dirk was...I'd have a chance, you know? I was thinking of *me*."

"But you came to your senses." Raven's voice took on strength. "In simple point of the fact, you, as Dirk's parent, decided what was best for him, and that was to keep him away from Clifton Seaborn. Does Dirk have a SIN?"

She nodded. "He's in the system, yes, but I didn't list Seaborn as his father."

"No matter. On birth they would have taken a small blood sample and run the DNA. The database is supposed to be anonymous and for research only, but Seaborn would have the ability to check it for marrow matches for his son."

Jessie pulled a tissue from her pocket and wiped her nose. "I left home young and did what I had to. You wouldn't know it to look at me now, but I was pretty. I worked for a modeling agency...we did events and parties and things. Cliffy was funny and generous. A good time. Married, too, I guess I knew. Then I got pregnant and my world collapsed. But Dirk, he was so..."

She glanced up at me. "The time I went to the estate—it's like a fortress, really—I was in a bad place. I didn't know what I was doing, but Cliffy wasn't having anything to do with a bastard, especially not an ork..."

I seemed to recall that SD employed a lot of orks, but only at the bottom corporate levels. Orks worked there not because they wanted to, but it was a steady shot until something better came along. Didn't surprise me at all that the corporate attitude came straight from the family running it. The fact that Clifton's son would be beholden to an ork had to be driving the boy's father even crazier than he already sounded.

"That bodes ill." Raven stood in one fluid motion. "It appears he has changed his mind. We shall have to acquaint him with the fact that your son is a person, not a therapy. With luck, he will be reasonable."

Dr. Raven and I headed downtown to the Seaborn's Dynamics tower. Surprised me that Doc tagged me for the trip, since Tark knew all the ins and outs of economics and business and such, but given the Seaborn attitude concerning orks, his very presence might have caused an issue. So I tagged along in Doc's shadow, which was fine. With him around, no one was going to pay me any attention anyway.

The corporate tower was something. I'm not exactly sure what the architect had in mind for his creation. The grey cladding had layers, kind of like leaves on the stalk of a flower, but the uppermost floors appeared to be shaped like a giant torch. And the leaves below had a dragon-scale pattern to them. I guessed he was going for some rebirth/enlightenment thing, but the Old One had a different take.

"Looks like a snake vomiting out its own skeleton," he grumbled.

Raven, wearing a khaki-colored suit over a white shirt and light brown shoes, strode across the wide foyer's marble tiles as if he owned the place. Me, trailing in a leather jacket, my second-best pair of jeans and a dark t-shirt, looked as if I swept up around the place.

The woman at the reception desk ignored me and favored Dr. Raven with a smile. "How may I help you?"

"I am Dr. Richard Raven. I am here to see Clifton Seaborn about his son."

The woman's brow tightened. "Do you have an appointment?"

"No, but this is rather urgent."

A plastic smile spread over the lower half of her face. "The Seaborn family really appreciates everyone who is willing to help with poor Junior's condition, but all medical advice goes through his physician. Thank you for your concern."

"You don't understand."

The receptionist's expression sharpened. "Don't make me call security, Doctor—"

"Tell Mr. Seaborn this is about his *other* son. We'll be waiting over here."

Raven steered me toward a very comfortable couch, but I barely had enough time to even think about taking a nap before a big guy in a suit large enough to conceal a bazooka invited us to follow him to the elevator. He used a key and whisked us up to a floor that likely touched the bottom of the flame.

He showed us into a corner office which, given the neutrality of the colors and presence of books purchased by the meter, SD used for impromptu meetings they wanted to give the appearance of importance.

The only exception to that rule was the tall portrait of Seaborn's CEO, Ilsa Seaborn. The artist had made her regal and ageless, despite the steel-grey of her hair. The forbidding look on her face made me wonder if, during a thunderstorm, the flashes of light transformed the portrait's face into a death's-head. Her severe clothes contrasted with a gaudy brooch which looked a great deal like a model of the building. She had a little dog tucked under her arm to humanize her, but near as I could tell she was just bringing her lunch to work.

Clifton Seaborn swept into the room with the false joviality of a doctor who can't remember your name entering the examination room. "You must be...Dr. Raven and...?"

I shrugged. "I pick up his laundry."

Clifton clasped his long-fingered hands together so he wouldn't have to shake hands. "You sent up a cryptic message."

Raven smiled. "I have no desire to waste your time, Mr. Seaborn. Simply put, Jessie Watts and her son, Dirk, are under my protection. I understand the boy is important to you, that he may be the source of a cure for your other son's lymphoma. Threatening him or his mother will cease now. I trust you understand me. Good day."

The Old One howled triumphantly as Cliffy's jaw shot down, further elongating his face. "What did you just say?"

Raven opened his arms, his muscular build a sharp contrast to that of the corporate bean pole. "If you need to hear it again,

I suggest you play back the recordings you're making of this meeting."

His mouth snapped shut for a second, and his expression sharpened venomously. "I've read about you, Raven, you and your band of merry men. You may have bedeviled, in some small way, *minor* corporations, but you're punching above your weight right now. Seaborn Dynamics is a multitrillion-nuyen, multinational corporation..."

"...which your *mother* runs."

Raven's interjection brought a purple tone to Seaborn's reddish face. "This has nothing to do with my mother..."

Raven chuckled. "Of course it does. I've read about you, too. Your mother, Ilsa, the She-wolf of Seattle Sound, took the nearly bankrupt machine-tool company her grandfather started a century ago and built it into this. She is so driven she forced your father to take *her* name when they wed. She produced one heir, *you*, and based on the responsibilities you have here, you're marginally less productive than the janitorial staff *en banc.* According to financial reports, your mother was grooming another executive to take over, but then, twelve years ago, your wife gave birth to your son. You regained relevance because you gave her a new heir for her corporation. But do go on, you were saying, this has nothing to do with your mother?"

Cliffy couldn't look Raven in the eye, so he took a chance on me. I just let the Old One growl through my throat, and what little color remained in his face just quietly drained away.

Raven headed for the door, but turned back toward Seaborn before opening it. "I will allow that you may actually have feelings for your sick son. No one wishes him to die. As I said before, Dirk is under my protection. If you wish his help in saving your son, reach out and arrangements can be made."

"Doc, back there in the office, what did you mean by 'arrangements can be made?' Sounded to me like Jessie wanted nothing to do with Seaborn."

"Correct." The fire in Raven's eyes picked up speed. "She's terrified, and with good reason, so she has not looked at the greater implications of the situation. Her love for her son leads me to believe she wouldn't want any child to die. Getting her cooperation to let Dirk donate might require Clifton's mother to reach out to Jessie. The shared experience of being mothers may create a bond."

"And if it doesn't?"

Raven exhaled slowly. "The Seaborn's resources give them a lot to offer Jessie. They could set her and Dirk up for life. She's certainly furious enough that she might refuse any offers, but a suitable settlement could give a decent quality of life to both Dirk and Jessie. That would be a win all the way around."

"That would be the sensible outcome, wouldn't it?"

"Sensible never comes, Longtooth, when the scent of victory fills the nose."

A shiver ran down my spine. Clifton Seaborn been born at the top of the heap, which he figured made him an apex predator. I had a notion folks would be feeling a lot of pain before we could disabuse him of that notion.

We got back to headquarters quickly enough and brought Jessie up to speed on our meeting. She took it well overall, even giggling when she got told of Cliff's reaction to being told how the world worked.

Tark helped Tom Electric pack Jessie and Dirk into one of our vehicles for a run out to a safehouse we maintained in Issaquah. Once they took off, I made a call to a couple gillettes who worked with us often enough. I called Tiger Jackson and Iron Mike Morrissey, whom I used to refer to as Zag and Zig respectively, and told them to pack enough stuff to stay on-station for a week. I figured Tark and I would spell them, and Kid Stealth would take a shift all by himself, so we'd keep mother and son safe for however long it took.

About five minutes after the two of them had arrived—which would be four minutes into Tiger making googly eyes at Val—Tark caught a phone call. He waved the room to silence, then put it on speaker. "Everybody is here, Harry. Say again."

The ork cop's voice filled with weariness. "Your car got hit. Eyewitness says motorcyclist cut through traffic, slapped a contact explosive on the hood. Shaped charge killed the engine. Airbags blew. Your boy, Tom Electric, got out, got a couple of shots off, but a crew coming out of a big, black vehicle put him down. DocWagon's working on him now. He took three to the chest, one to the neck. Straight into the ICU. Jessie Watts got beat up by the airbag up front. She's on the same transport with Tom. Witnesses said the men snatched an ork child—her son, yeah?"

Dr. Raven stepped toward the phone. "Nothing to identify the shooters?"

"Nothing but the fact they were low-rent. That blast on the engine, pure luck it did anything nastier than shredding the radiator. Stinks of Seaborn's house dogs."

"Thank you, Mr. Braxen. The child is under our protection. We'll take it from here."

"Raven, you don't have any proof—"

"If the child was taken for ransom, Clifton Seaborn will need us to get him back. If not, Clifton Seaborn has the child. We *will* get him back."

"Look, you don't know how nasty Stonehouse is. I've been out there. We do perimeter duty, and it is a fortress."

"I believe you know our capabilities."

"Listen to me, Raven. Being an ork, I have a particular dislike for the Seaborns. Killing them all would be a service, and I'm sure you can do it. Still, it won't be an easy job. How can I convince you how foolish you're being? Wait, I know." Braxen's voice went silent, then something beeped on one of Val's consoles. "There, I've sent you a diagram for the place and the security protocols. Just take a look at it. A man would have to be stupid to go in there."

"Then I guess we won't send *a* man." Raven smiled. "Thank you, Harry."

"Just saving Valerie wear and tear on a keyboard."

"Is there any chance your outside people are going to be called away from the grounds on an emergency?"

"No, but I think there's a retirement party for someone tonight."

"I owe you, Harry."

"Well, after this, I may need a job, so..."

Valerie, smiling, turned toward the phone. "I just covered your tracks for you. Better get moving. You'll miss the party."

"No party for me. I'll be around, so I can be first on scene. You know, in case it isn't entirely clean."

"That will be appreciated." Raven's eyes narrowed as Valerie splashed the plans over the op center wall screen. "You're right, could be quite a mess. We'll have to be on our best behavior, then, and conclude our business as quickly as we can."

The Lone Star service dossier on Stonehouse stacked the odds against our getting in and out completely clean. I mean, the Seaborns weren't getting any points for creativity when it came to naming the place, but they were 14/10 for putting it together.

The whole thing took up a hillside which had been reforested after the Seaborns flattened an old neighborhood that had the misfortune of existing where Ilsa wanted to wake up every morning. They'd imported the manor house from Ireland—some old Jacobean pile rising up five stories with corner turrets that added another two. The old place's stable, kennels, and carriage house had likewise emigrated, being transformed into additional housing for staff, dogs, and guests. A meter-and-a-half-high stone wall surrounded the place, with trenching dug in at the base throughout the woods that added another meter to the wall. Broken glass topped it where folks were likely to see it, with razor wire added in the woods.

Because they'd built over a neighborhood on a hillside, it had three terraces. Highest up lay the garden, along with a small observatory tucked in the corner. The middle terrace handled all the housing and some broad, green lawns for croquet, tennis or lawn parties. The lowest terrace, much of which remained screened from the main house by a hedge, provided for parking, with the garage built beneath the middle terrace. A crushed stone driveway looped up from the gate and back down the other side.

Staff housing mentioned previously didn't include barracks for security troops. While the Lone Star docs mentioned shifts of SD's own corporate gunners, they provided no solid numbers for the same. Assuming they only had a van's worth in residence at any time would be a mistake.

Kid Stealth studied the plans for the garage and shook his head. "Extra guards live down here. Room enough and plumbing hook-ups for a dozen." He touched the display with his flesh and blood hand, dragged and shifted the image into a three-dimensional model. "There, one entrance by the parking area, another into the house toward the back, a third via elevator into the kennels. Bolt hole back to the hill's far side?"

"Could be as many as twenty-four people, armed and dangerous." Raven folded his arms over his chest. "It will be a target-rich environment.

Stealth popped the mag from his carbine, then snapped it back with a *click*. "Want me to call up the Redwings?"

"This is a hostage rescue, not an invasion, my friend. I don't think we shall require their services, but thank you." He nodded gratefully at the Murder Machine. "Val, can you jam their communications and keep reinforcements away?"

The young woman nodded. "I'll need to be close. Put me in the War Wagon and you won't have any interlopers."

"Good. Shoot Harry Braxen a note. See if he'd oblige us by finding Jessie Watts and having her ready to see her son."

"On it."

Raven turned and looked at the rest of us. "Dirk's safety is our prime goal. We'll return fire, but we're not shooting civilians unless they threaten him directly. Use suppressors. Keep your shots on target."

He circled his index finger on the front gate. "The five of us, less Wolf, will hit the front gate, engage, and move forward as far as we can. We want all eyes on us. Wolf, you'll come in at the back. You're going to be Dirk's knight in shining armor."

Tiger frowned. "All due respect, but he ought to have someone winging him."

I smiled and fingered the wolf's-head medallion I wore at my throat. "That's the thing about knights in shining armor, Tiger—we're used to going it alone."

Raven nodded. "Same rules of engagement for you, Wolf, but I leave the particulars to your discretion."

"Roger that." I returned the nod and the Old One sent up a bloodcurdling howl that echoed in my brain long into the night.

Iron Mike and Tiger dropped me off a couple blocks from the back of the estate. As the Seaborns had done with the hill's east side, others had done with the west, razing old neighborhoods and consolidating their new fiefdoms. They raised McMansions, none of which matched each other in style, color, or appearance. I had my choice of a bubbly, geodesic dome ameboid thing, an homage to the Parthenon, and something that looked enough like an antebellum Georgian mansion I was tempted to set it on fire. Given the Seaborn's reactionary attitude concerning orks, I figured they owned that particular property, too, and it was where any escape route would come out.

I crept along the property line between Tara and Ptomaine and paused in the shadows of Stonehouse's back wall. When Doc had told Harry, "Then I guess we won't send *a* man," he wasn't talking numbers. He was talking about *me*, and a certain particular style I have in situations like this.

I'd met Richard Raven at a time when a homicidal maniac had roamed through Seattle. He left a mangled trail of victims during what was known as the Full Moon Slashings; and it just so happened I was pretty sure I was the slasher. Waking up covered in blood, clothes shredded, with a full moon sinking from the sky will leave you with the impression you're guilty of that kind of thing. Dr. Raven convinced me that wasn't so, and trained me to control the Old One. Together we put an end to the Full Moon Slasher, and I learned how to avoid succumbing to lunacy.

Except when it's the only sane thing to do.

My watch told me the festivities at the gate would begin in two minutes. I took a deep breath and exhaled slowly. I turned my vision inside and found the Old One lurking there. Composed of shadow, with his eyes burning scarlet. *It's time, Old One.*

Another howl shook me. *"For the child, I know, Longtooth. For him, we hunt together."*

A shriek torn from my throat eclipsed the Old One's howl. As the magic woven within the Wolf Spirit took me, it snapped my bones. My limbs grew shorter, but the muscles compensated by flowing into new insertions. They granted me greater strength and speed. My muzzle jutted forward as the bones exploded, then reshaped themselves. Fangs grew, as did my ears and pelt. The bony ridges around my eyes thickened and my clawed hands tore at the earth.

The Old One somehow resisted taking me further. Always he whispered to me of the freedom of the wolf, tempting me to join him in our true form. But this time he left me caught between both worlds. Not man. Not wolf. Something else.

Something that can hunt the child.

With a single leap, I cleared the stone wall and the knife-wire strung along it. I landed in the garden, crushed stone under my hands, hidden in the observatory's shadow. I kept low to the ground, haunches bunched and ready to spring at prey. I lifted my muzzle to the sky and breathed in.

"Inhale deeply, Longtooth. So much more than you know as a man."

I'd have snapped back a smart remark, but I caught the boy's scent. Sweet and innocent, yet tinged with that acrid hint of fear.

I started off toward the house, eating up the distance in long bounds. I snarled as I descended to the middle terrace, not a warning, but a promise. I wanted to blame that on the Old One, but it was mine to own. I did not like Clifton and his sour scent marked him as a sick animal.

"We cull the weak, Longtooth."

Then they came. The snarls. The barks. Beasts, four-footed, once noble, the wolf's distant cousins. Lean as greyhounds, but the size of a mastiff. As men are wont to do, they ruined them with their razored claws, glinting ceramic teeth, and glowing eyes that let them see in the dark.

That was the folly of men. They gave great vision to creatures that lived by their noses. Had those dogs been able to scent me, they would not have galloped forward so eagerly. One tiny hint, one wisp wafted to them on the night's breeze, and they'd have fled back to the kennels from whence they had come.

I gave full throat to a growl that should have warned them off, but the way men had warped them left the beasts with no sense. On they came, the three of them muscular and fast, black as night, closing the distance in the blink of an eye.

The first leaped at me, mouth gaping. The Old One lent me his speed. I dipped a shoulder and that dog sailed past, artificial fangs snapping closed on night air alone. I lashed out with my right hand, backhanding the next dog upside its head. Bones snapped and one of the sparking red eyes flew into the night. That dog spun through the air, slamming into the first, tangling with it amid snarls and barks.

The last one lunged at my left flank. I spun away. It caught a mouthful of my leather jacket. The ceramic teeth sliced through it, tearing away everything from the armpit halfway to my spine. Yet before it could land to turn and strike again, I pounded my right fist down between its shoulder blades. I pulverized vertebrae, severing its spine. It hit the ground hard and bounced once.

My spin brought me around to face the first dog again. The Old One gave voice to a snarl that raised the animal's hackles. It bared its teeth, but took half a step backward. Another snarl, a bit more intense, and the beast lay down between its broken comrades.

"It is ended, Longtooth. Let us move on."

I crossed the rest of the central terrace and loped around to the north side of the house. My sharpened hearing caught hushed sounds of fighting coming from the gate direction. The suppressors muffled the gunshots down to whispered coughs, but the *click-clack* of the guns' action came to me loud and clear. Still, no alarm from that direction or the house, which I took as a sign that Val had jammed every radio signal in the area.

I leaped up onto a patio and crossed to a pair of French doors which stood partly ajar. The boy's scent poured out with the light. Likewise Clifton's. Less strong came a number of similar scents, including one spoiled odor I guessed came from Clifton Junior.

"Listen, mister, I'm only eight years old, but I don't think you're doing this right!"

"I am your father. You will do what I tell you." Clifton Seaborn stood in the middle of a room that had to be called a parlor because someone had decorated it as a set for Jane Austen cosplay. Dark wood here and there, floral wallpaper, a bunch of portraits of old folks, and furniture supporting its own weight in lace doilies. Could be the decorations had come with the house when transplanted, but they all smelled too new for that to be true.

Dirk sat on a piano bench and pushed his glasses up his nose again. He started ticking things off on his fingers. "You don't have a doctor here. You hurt my mom. You're not asking me, you're forcing me, and you won't bargain."

Clifton grasped his own head in both hands. "I can't believe I'm losing an argument with a eight-year-old. An ork at that."

"Look, mister—"

"No, *you* look." Clifton drew a snub-nosed .32 from his blazer pocket. "I didn't hurt your mother, but I can."

"I don't think that's a good idea." I spoke from the shadows on the patio, my words underscored with a growl.

Seaborn spun around and thrust the gun toward the French doors. "Stay back, I'll shoot."

"Unless you're packing silver bullets, I'm not really concerned."

Moving a bit faster than I expected, Seaborn grabbed Dirk and yanked the boy over to shield him. He shifted the pistol from me to the boy. "At this range, I can't miss."

I tensed. I could make it to him in a hop and a half. Chances were he'd only register me as a blur. One slash up, one slash down. *Might even take the hand off at the wrist.* I could do it.

"But, Longtooth, can you guarantee the pup remains safe?"

Before I could answer, a hand landed on my shoulder. "You can stand down, Wolf."

My nose full of Raven's scent, I slunk back into the shadows. He filled the doorway, his hands empty and open. Tark, a suppressed Uzi slung from his shoulder, followed Doc into the parlor.

Clifton kept his grip tight on the boy, but directed the pistol toward Tark. "The gun, put it down now."

Tark complied, but Doc ignored Seaborn. "Are you okay, Dirk?"

The boy shrugged, then looked up. "Is my mom okay?"

"Airbag banged her around a little, but she's fine. She's on her way."

Dirk nodded once.

Raven turned his attention to Clifton. "You should put your gun down. We should talk more seriously."

Seaborn shifted the gun back to Dirk. "No, I'm in command here. You and your people leave, right now."

Doc spread his hands wider. "We're just talking, and you know we're not going anywhere. You're not going to shoot the boy. Not here. Not in your home, where your son and your wife can hear. Imagine Clifton Junior having to live with the fact that you murdered an eight-year-old so he could live."

"At least he'll be alive."

I kept my voice low, barely a whisper. "I can be on him, Doc. A heartbeat." Which I could hear, because Clifton's heart was pounding like a trip-hammer.

Doc raised a finger, stopping me. "But, Mr. Seaborn, your son will never look at you again as he does now, knowing..."

The pistol wavered.

Then the parlor door swung open and Ilsa Seaborn strode in, a Pomeranian clutched under one arm. Cadaverously slender, her upper lip curled in a sneer, her gaze swept over the room. Her dark eyes narrowed when she beheld Tark and Dirk, and fury built in those eyes.

The dog, sensing the coming storm, bared its teeth and barked.

"What, Clifton Cornelius Seaborn, are orks doing in my house?"

"They have to be here, mother." He pulled Dirk around to give her a good look at him. "This boy is a match for Junior. He can save him."

She lashed out with her free hand, the slap snapping Clifton's head around. "For him to be a match, it means you have lain with an ork. And then you lied to me about it." Her tone left no doubt that the lie was the greater crime in her mind.

Dirk pulled himself free of Clifton's grip and squared up on Ilsa. "Look, lady, you have a choice. Neither one of us likes your son. But he's right. Your grandson is sick. I can help him. I can fix him."

All the color drained from Ilsa's face and she looked as if she was going to launch her dog at him. I growled from the shadows, which flattened the dog's ears and tucked its tail in tight. "How dare you speak to me thus!"

Raven pressed his hands together. "Out of the mouths of babes comes wisdom. There is a situation here, Ms. Seaborn. Your son kidnapped an ork child for the purpose of performing unsanctioned medical experimentation on him."

"He would never be prosecuted for such a thing..."

"Agreed, but Dirk's story would get out. Word on the street, that sort of thing." Doc twisted, waving a hand toward Tark. "My associate, Plutarch Graogrim, can elucidate."

Tark lifted his chin and clasped his hands at the small of his back. "Seaborn Dynamics and its affiliated companies and partners draw 86.7% of their manufacturing workforce from the ork population. Your relationship with this workforce is tenuous at best, and will become nightmarish overnight. Because of your just-in-time manufacturing and inventory policies, a complete work stoppage will leave you bankrupt in nine months."

"Seaborn Dynamics has survived worse."

"Ms. Seaborn, we both know that is not true. The rich only remain rich if labor allows them to continue their domination. Given the differential in human and ork birth rates—which means a shrinking employee pool for you—you'll see the end of Seaborn Dynamics before Clifton Junior reaches his majority."

"Plutarch's numbers are correct and your future is grim." Raven clasped his hands together again. "Your family legacy is doomed unless..."

Ilsa's face became a steel mask. "I will never surrender control..."

Raven shook his head. "That isn't the question."

"What is?"

"Is your contempt for orks something you feel in your gut, or is it performative outrage so you can fit right in with the other Brahmins in the corporate world? You're too smart to believe racial superiority is anything but a myth. In your world, money from an ork spends just as well as that from an elf or a man, no?"

The woman stroked her dog's head. "Orks are a growing demographic, true. And their money does spend."

Tark canted his head. "You can't be that afraid those in your social circle will ostracize you for changing your view on orks, can you?"

Isla's nostrils flared. "Young...man, if I decide orks are no longer to be shunned, orks will no longer be shunned. And I shall enjoy bending anyone who disagrees to my will. My doctor *has* said I need a hobby."

Tark's eyes narrowed. "Then what's the hold up?"

"The necessary pivot to create the future image you suggest is one beyond the ability of even the finest PR firms to craft. Historically we are a firm that Orks *tolerate*. To think they would embrace a change on our part is pure fancy. They would never believe we had reformed ourselves so radically. The future you suggest dies aborning."

Dirk took a step forward and extended his hand toward her. "No, *Grandmother*, it *will* live. I will save my half-brother. You will have a change of heart."

"A change of heart?" The woman stared down at him. "A *change* of heart. That could work. Which one of them put you up to saying that, child?"

Dirk smiled slowly, with devilish deliberation. "I'm only eight years old, but it's not too hard to figure out."

The Old One chuckled. *"Eight in body, ancient in spirit."*

Ilsa pursed her lips for a moment, then nodded. "You may be of even yet more use, young man. Do you know what it is that Seaborn Dynamics does?"

Dirk shrugged. "You can tell me later. After you take me to my brother, so we can tell him he doesn't have to worry anymore." He took another step forward, his hand still outstretched.

She hesitated, then set her dog down and, albeit stiffly, took his hand. As she turned toward the door, she glanced back over her shoulder. "I trust you will see yourselves out?"

Raven nodded. "His mother is on her way here for him."

"Of course she is. I'll have the servants open the east wing for her." Ilsa looked down at Dirk. "You'd like to live here, wouldn't you? Your mother, too?"

Dirk nodded. "Do you have a library?"

"It is positively huge."

He slid his glasses back up his nose. "Then we'll stay until I've read every book."

"Splendid. Come along."

Dirk twisted back and waved to all of us. "Thank you."

As the parlor door closed behind them, Raven stepped forward and took the gun from Clifton's hand. "So no one gets hurt."

Clifton, slumped on the piano bench, looked up at Doc. "He had this all planned, didn't he?"

Having regained my human form deep in the shadows, I entered the room. "He came to us saying his mother needed help, and she's got it now. Not bad for an eight-year-old."

Raven cracked the pistol open, poured the shells into his pocket, then snapped it shut again. "He used the book to get to Wolf, and Wolf to get to our organization. To get help for his mom, he needed some muscle. Under Dirk's plan, we would have arranged a negotiation, which would have come to the same conclusion, but without quite so much drama and bloodshed."

"Yes, it would have worked that way, wouldn't it?" Clifton clasped his head in both hands. "My God, my mother finally has the heir she wants. I'm no good to her. I might as well be dead."

Raven's voice deepened. "But you are not. Neither is your son, and he needs a father now a lot more than your mother ever needed an heir. Be what he needs and accomplish something good with your life. It may be your last chance."

Clifton stared down at his hands. "My last chance... I have to make it work."

Somehow, I figured he would. Or, Dirk, knowing how much Clifton Junior needed a father, would make it work. He'd play Clifton even more sweetly than he'd played us, and they'd all live happily ever after.

As we headed out across the lawn to where Stealth, Tiger, and Iron Mike had taken control of what few Seaborn gillettes remained breathing, I rested a hand on Doc's shoulder. "We were used by a kid, Doc. I got socks older than him."

"We were, Wolf, we definitely were used." My friend smiled down at me. "But unlike all the other times, I don't feel dirty this time. And in our game, that's a win, and I'm happy to have it notched in our favor."

INCIDENTS, ACCIDENTS, AND CONSEQUENCES

Russell Zimmerman

"Please state your name exactly as it appears in your EvoProfile," the security guard said with the robotic tone of someone who was bored silly. Anyone who worked with the public and had a mandatory line sounded the same, no matter what they were saying. "Failure to comply and/or inaccuracies may be met with violence," he finished by rote.

"Kenjiro Yamatetsu," I said.

"Thank you. Please look into the scanner and prepare for a retinal survey, Mr. Yamatetsu," he said as I passed through the magnetic anomaly detection scanner, giving me the barest of glances to confirm that I matched my EvoProfile's basic parameters: *Homo sapiens sapiens* of mixed East Asian heritage, looking like a male in his early twenties. "Failure to comply and/or inaccuracies may be met with violence."

I settled my chin on the scanner—metahuman friendly, it adjusted itself to match my height and automatically resized itself to fit my skull—and stared into the light as my fine capillary network was meticulously examined.

"Thank you. Please press your hand on either palm scanner for biometric analysis. If you do not have an organic hand, provide supplementary identification as per EvoUnique protocols," he continued, as bored as someone asking if I wanted to megasize my burger combo meal. Our repetitive ordeal was nearing an end, though, the finish line was in sight. "Failure to comply and/or inaccuracies may be met with violence."

I placed my hand—my left, as my right *was*, in fact, not an organic hand. Instead, it gleamed silver-bright, shiny and chrome as was the latest fashion—on the scanner and let the veins in my hand be scanned by an assortment of near infrared beams. Everything about me matched up with my on-record biometrics, apparently, because none of the promised violence was forthcoming. Voice, eye, and fingerprint scans were the extent of my security probes to-date. I had never yet been presented with the more invasive doors openable only to Evo corporation's top-ranked executives and their families.

"Thank you. Welcome to the Excellence Building, Mr. Yamatetsu," was the final incantation in the ritual of greeting and reception, accompanied by an appropriately stiff-backed, deep bow. He was a Seattleite and an Anglo, but he'd been well, if not perfectly, trained. There was probably something on my file that noted time spent working in Evo Asia, so no doubt my security clearance carried some special rider that told them to be appropriately deferential to make me feel more at home.

"*Arigatou*," I said with a nod deep enough to count as a bow in Seattle, unlike what most of my peers would have done. I never took offense to the back and forth. I never showed impatience in the face of their screenings. Evo security personnel were, after all, just doing their job, performing their role, serving their chosen purpose. They had their parts to play to keep our parent corporation running, and I had mine. To do otherwise was to be *amae*, willfully self-indulgent, to put yourself over everyone around you. How could I be frustrated or insulted by our guards keeping us all safe through their routine checks?

So no, I was all pleasant smiles and friendly, American-style head bobs as I walked across the lobby and into the building. "Excellence" was one of a number of Evo-owned properties scattered around Seattle. We hadn't ever gone in for the shining tower in the Emerald City, no gleaming skyscraper all our own, no looming pyramid or arcology branded with our logo and visible from near orbit. We didn't have a "statement piece" the way so many other corporations of our stature did, or, rather, we didn't have one in Seattle. Excellence was one of our regional satellite buildings, given as bland and forgettable a name as possible, an act of urban camouflage, not truly hiding, but easily overlooked.

Dedicated opponents would find us, of course. Those who put in the effort and had the resources would see through the charade quite handily. But, like with most locks on most doors, it was not the dedicated professional we sought to keep out. The idea was simply to make them work for it. To present a smaller target, a less obvious one, to not make it easy for the hypothetical "them."

Reading Chang Yu and Sun Tzu had taught me that a good fighter secured himself against defeat by concealing the disposition of his troops, covering up his tracks, and taking unremitting precautions. I had done all three.

To a shallow extent, the lack of an enormous Evo logo was concealing the disposition of our troops. Whether it was clearly an Evo property or not, our security forces were taking their unremitting precautions, keeping it as secure as any other Evo building. Such was my ideal in discussions like I was walking into, in fact. I was not an unassailable, unstoppable, corporate entity. I had no legend around my name, no half-century of experience building up mystique, I was no Damien Knight, no Hideo Yoshida, no Inazo Aneki. My last name was Yamatetsu because it had been *assigned* to me back when Evo had been called Yamatetsu instead; I had not been raised by a proud executive. I had no family connections or favors to call in.

My supervisors increasingly appreciated how aware I was of that fact, and encouraged me to take advantage of it. A vice president had a name, had face, had a reputation, and had known strengths and weaknesses. I did not. I had nothing but Evo, and a head full of augmentations that made me very, very good at my job. *Any* job. My current department head, Akiko Tanaka—Senior Managing Director, Forensic Accounting—had sent me on this task for just the very reason that, especially in Seattle, I was an unknown quantity. My loyalty was to the corporation, making me an ideal intermediary.

A pattern was emerging in our Neo-Tokyo and other Evo Asia offices, a pattern that had not yet shown itself in North America; things improved after I arrived and had the opportunity to work. Fat was trimmed, employee morale improved, problems were solved. Things *got done* after I arrived. This was my first trip on this sort of assignment to Seattle, though. I was no one to them. I didn't mind.

I went through all the necessary pleasantries on my way through the building and toward the Ambition III boardroom on the second-from-the-top floor. I'd scanned, and as such memorized the building's layout prior to my trip, as part of my usual self-assigned homework. There was no way to take an assignment to Ambition III, not even Ambition I, much less Prestige, their top-end boardroom option, as anything but a snub. The woman I was here to meet was Seattle-based and remarkably well connected. She got the room she wanted. She'd asked specifically for this one, their seventh-or-eighth best, for the meeting with me.

It suited me fine, though. The fact she sought to insult me meant she already underestimated me.

I let my smile shine through as I entered Ambition III, a sincere, friendly-looking greeting. She had chosen to make this an adversarial meeting from the first, brief exchange of emails, and had carried that same negative energy through boardroom selection and even the scheduling of the meeting itself; she'd regretfully insisted it be early, and I knew she had done so to not give me jet lag recovery time. She wanted me off guard and uncomfortable. But I didn't sleep the same way most people did, so that, too, showed me only that she didn't know the extent of my bioware, nanotech, and genetic augmentations.

In her defense, *most* people, even of her esteemed executive rank, didn't know that full extent.

Still and all, the animosity came from her, and I was not obliged to return it. My smile was genuine as I first bowed a greeting (to honor the company's Japanese roots), then shook her hand (to show respect for the North American greeting and my host office).

"Mr. Yamatetsu, welcome to Seattle. It is *such* a pleasure to meet you," Kerry MacSwain lied to my face.

"Ms. MacSwain, the pleasure's all mine," I returned, only half-a-lie. This trip was for work, not pleasure, but I did not doubt I would have a better time during our conversation.

She gestured for me to sit down, and I did so. MacSwain was a stunning elven woman of thoroughly Western European heritage—not a drop of Asian *or* Russian to be found (which was a bit of a novelty for me). Her skin was far fairer than mine, her red-golden hair was pulled back in a simple but timelessly fashionable ponytail, her eyes were gleaming, top-end cybernetic models of the precision engineering possible only on Evo's Industry II satellite. She'd had them colored to look organic, the flashing green that people loved to expect from Tír na nÓg natives, but I knew the signs. With her pay grade and access to Evo upgrades, the eyes weren't quite windows to the soul, but they *were* a giveaway to a whole head full of chrome. My own irises were a metallic silver—showing my hand, a bit, to make people underestimate me.

Let them know I've had cyberoptics installed, and that they very likely connect to a small fortune in headware. Let them assume I have the perception-enhancing package, the full TechnoSage suite of expert systems and analytics programs we improved upon from Saeder-Krupp's comparatively primitive Cyberlogician prototypes. Let them wonder what biogenetic upgrades I have alongside the encephalons, the attention coprocessors, the visualizers, the empathy software subroutines, and who-knows-what-else. I didn't try to hide it like the Kerry MacSwains. I liked to let people know. I would show them, in time, that simply knowing *some* of it didn't do them any good.

She held my gaze without fear or apprehension, her smile threatening to turn to a smirk, through continued small talk, having an administrative assistant bring us ice water, and that sort of thing. My internal chem sensors warned me about the alkaline level in the beverage being outside of the norms I was accustomed to, and my internal *Guru* nanobiomonitor ex-pressed mild displeasure, but there wasn't anything dangerous about it, so I didn't let it show. The gesture of offering water was a primal one, not merely a polite one, whether people knew it or not. It made me a guest. It told me I belonged. It was a sign of hospitality. I appreciated it, sincerely.

Through it all, though, she looked me directly in the eye. A power move. A display. A statement.

I understood her confidence; she'd been in Seattle, in Evo North America, for a very long time. She'd been *high-ranked* here, in fact, for a very long time. I was an upstart. A nobody. I looked young, but was even younger than she (likely thought she) knew. Her overconfidence was natural.

"So, Mr. Yamatetsu, I hope you'll forgive me," she finally began, truly began. Small talk was suddenly a thing of the past, and she adjusted her chair across from me at the polished, real hardwood, tabletop, and steepled her fingers. "But I'm afraid I must have missed something in Ms. Tanaka's emails yesterday.

Why is it, exactly, that Forensic Accounting has sent you here, especially on such short notice?"

My empathy subroutines noticed a *down*-tick in her anxiety level. Her blood level and heart rate lowered as she confronted me. Huh. She was *more* comfortable with an escalation and point-blank demand for information than she had been with small talk. I could appreciate that.

"Oh, *gomen-nasai,* I'm very sorry," I lied, bowing apologetically as much as the table allowed. I played up the Japanese etiquette angle. Let her keep thinking I was a fish out of water, "Tanaka-san must have been unclear, or perhaps it was simply an autotranslation issue. I am certain, however, the fault is not yours. Your welcome, given that uncertainty, is even more appreciat—"

"Before you continue." She pressed against that etiquette to keep me off balance. She was self-defeating. I'd been about to go into the reason I came. Instead, she'd interrupted me. "Let me clarify, Mr. Yamatetsu. I don't want to know why you're here, or, at least, that's not what I'm asking. I want to know why *you* are here."

"I am here because I was sent here," I said, with a meaningless, but mildly pleasant smile. "I'm not certain wha—"

"No, that's why you came. That's not why you're here. Why did Forensic Accounting send you? You, in particular?" She lifted one flawless eyebrow, deeply arched, accentuating her sharp elven features. "Out of everyone available, why did Tanaka choose to send Mr. Yamatetsu to deliver whatever message this is?"

"Ah, I see." I nodded politely. "To be transparent with you, I was sent, and I work for Forensic Accounting, but Tanaka-san was not the one who sent me. As to why *I* was sent? I imagine it is because of my uniqu—"

"...heritage?" She tilted her head just a bit, thinking she'd scored a point.

Ah. That explained it.

She had. I, with all my headware, training, and practice, faltered for a moment. I wasn't accustomed to people being so abrupt with their "gotcha" moment. So much for Irish charm. She had, truly, been in Seattle a long time.

"I am very good at my job, young man," she said, as aware of our age and experience gap as I was, for all that being an elf kept her looking eternally youthful. "I did not get *very* good at my job by not making friends to tell me what questions to ask, and having friends ready to answer, regardless of what question I ask them. I know who—I know *what*, you are, Mr. Yamatetsu—and how you got that name."

I kept a mild smile on my face. It took some effort to do so, but a smile was a shield, and I needed it until, at last, I could counterattack.

"I also know who and what I am, Ms. MacSwain. Yes, I was once designated Subject 301-K. I was, I am, a clone. One of very few to survive to my age, and one of even fewer to do so with a mental capacity greater than a bright Shiba Inu or Border Collie. And yes, I was assigned the corporation's name as my own, when the decision was made to allow me to serve as a citizen."

It had taken years of forced-growth treatments, accelerated-pace virtual reality education simulations, and comprehensive physical and mental examinations, before they decided my ongoing experiment was a tentative success, and that I was a viable, and in fact valuable, test subject.

In the years since that decision, while I had attended universities and began to work off my debt to the corporation I owed literally everything to, Yamatetsu Corporation had changed to Evo Corporation, but I had kept the name. I lifted my chin slightly at the memory, proud of myself because it had been my *choice* to keep my name.

"But that's not what I was going to say, no. I am not here because of my unique...family history." I put it delicately, being a conglomeration crafted from tissue samples of every sitting member of the board at the time of my *in vitro* conception, "But because of my unique *capabilities*. Evo Asia had a problem, and asked for solutions. I, alone, was capable of coming up with the one they decided was perfect. Chief Executive Officer Kirilenko agreed with Tanaka-san's assessment, and transport was arranged. I am here to show you that resolution after explaining to you that problem and, I hope, for both our sakes, to convince you to agree to play your part in it."

She narrowed her eyes, suspicious and mildly disappointed I hadn't been even more rattled. For an elf, she was showing impatience. She *was* confident, confident enough to make her brash. She had played her card too early, and had showed me it was her only ace. She laid another, awkward card on the table, though, as one hand moved flicker-quick near her collar.

Then, with a coy smile, she leaned forward—no business suit, however conservative, can stand up to a posture purposefully showing cleavage and a top button smoothly undone for just the purpose of revealing it—and looked at me through long eyelashes. She *was* notably curvaceous for an elf.

"How do you plan to 'convince' me, Mr. Yamatetsu?" She fluttered her eyelashes at me, and let that oft-practiced crooked smile tug at the corners of her red-lipped mouth. "You know, we have the room reserved for as long as we'd like it. Tell me, despite your...condition...do you have any other 'unique capabilities?' Have you ever tried to find out?"

My *Guru* nanobiomonitor alerted me to a wave of augmented pheromones crossing the table toward me, and my emotion-tracking software politely informed me that I was, yes, in fact, currently the target of a seduction attempt.

My pleasant, blank smile returned. The polite one. The one that was a shield against embarrassment...for her.

"I have no interest in testing those theories, ma'am, with you or anyone else," I said, as gently as I could, refusing to insult her by verbally acknowledging the absurdity of her offer. She knew my age, my actual age, and must have been hoping I was in the throes of some sort of puberty. "This room is a bit chilly. You might be more comfortable if you fixed that button before we begin in earnest."

She sighed, but didn't blush; she'd known it was a longshot, but she was only disappointed, not ashamed, in her attempt's failure. I was accustomed to being found attractive. I could certainly acknowledge that she was conventionally attractive, as well, and out of curiosity a sliver of my attention span ran simulations and showed me the likelihood that a genetic pairing would make children of above-average intelligence, health, and ability for Evo...but that's all it was for me. Idle curiosity. A gene-matching hypothetical. A game. I was entirely capable of acknowledging, even admiring, someone's physical form, while having absolutely no desire for the sweaty, damp, heaving mess most people might enjoy imagining next.

I cleared my throat and took a sip of water, politely looking away until she finally fixed the button.

"The purpose for my visit is threefold, Ms. MacSwain." I gestured with my cybernetic hand and augmented-reality sensors picked up my movement, intent, and concentration, and began to broadcast holo-imagery via the built-in projectors in the room.

"I've been sent here to discuss targeting analysis, Matrix handles, and, finally, the difference between an accident and an incident." I smiled pleasantly as small, zoomed-out piles of documents and supporting files arranged themselves in the holo-display. "Unless you have a strong preference otherwise, I'd like to cover them in that orde—"

"By all means, continue," she cut me off, feeling very American and bold instead of simply rude. She was leaning forward, again, but now openly aggressive with her body language. She thought she was setting the pace. She thought the game was afoot, not realizing she'd already lost. "In that order is fine, please, I'm curious!"

I wasn't going to let her make *me* act rudely in return, no matter how hard she tried. I smiled.

"Before I begin, though, on behalf of Evo employees everywhere, my congratulations on our North American division's profits and consumer confidence garnered from the *CleverShot II* user-firearm interface, or 'smartlink,' launch. In my brief time spent studying smartlink technology as part of my research prior to this trip, even I could see how impressive this product is you've delivered to the market."

My "brief time" had been seven and a half hours, uninterrupted, studying three things at a time, prior to moving on to the rest of my investigation.

"The comparatively low price of materials required and the remarkable quality have made the *CleverShot II* a terrific commercial success, and also Evo's own go-to smartlink not only for all internal security staff, but even for the Marines of Yamatetsu Naval Technol—"

"I'm well aware of our success, young man." She gave me a smug, predatory smile, determined to step on my toes again. "What does this have to do with...anything?"

"Oh, well, as to that, you see—"

"And *don't* tell me Forensic Accounting has spotted any discrepancies." She looked like a cat with a belly full of canary. "I'm quite certain they haven't."

Cover your tracks. She was expecting me to come from one angle, when I was approaching from somewhere else entirely.

I reassured her, knowing she'd never believe me. "Oh, no, Ms. MacSwain, nothing like that, or I'd have been obliged to bring a security detail with me," I attempted a joke that wasn't a joke. If I'd come here to challenge Evo North America and claim embezzlement or the like, we both knew there would probably have been a gunfight. I was ill-suited for that sort of thing, and if the conversation were to be so simple as that, someone else would have been sent.

"I'm not here to make any accusations of fiduciary indiscretion. I swear, on my system identification number."

She leaned back, eyeballing me with open suspicion. It had never occurred to her I might be telling the truth. Another mistake.

"No, as I said, firstly, I'm here to talk about your target analysis code." I thought very hard and pointed with my cyberhand, and my headware flung a three-dimensional approximation of a text window into the air between us, one filled with streaming lines of code, accurate to Evo's internal displays right down to the chosen font. The data scrolled, scrolled, scrolled, and stopped.

"It's this bit here," I gestured, lazily but accurately, pausing the scrolling and zooming in. "Everyone who has seen it appreciates the elegance and cleanliness of most of *CleverShot II's* code in regard to standard smartlink protocols, matters of ideal accuracy, environmental disturbances being factored in, barrel length and the presence or lack of suppressors, user biometric data for recoil management, all of that. But..."

The "but" had her, of course.

"But the code for preventing friendly fire incidents." I wrinkled my nose ever so slightly, as though I'd come across an undercooked piece of meat amidst an otherwise lovely meal. "Here, I found some interesting details."

"What does this have to do with Forensic Accounting?"

Nothing at all, but she'd already told me to go on earlier, so I ignored her and went on.

"The code for target analysis is...*fine*. It works, clearly, or *CleverShot II* wouldn't have made it through trials with acceptable scores, it wouldn't be such a commercial hit, and Evo, certainly, wouldn't have chosen it for our internal use. No, no, the code works. Evo security personnel can't point a weapon at each other without the weapon engaging the safety thanks to instant, accurate RFID recognition. Evo executives and their next-of-kin are all recognized and similarly safety-tagged via a half-dozen facial recognition, gait analysis, and other biometric scans coded in. Grade Beta-Three and above devices will also safety-on a weapon rather than allow crossfires to damage sensitive and irreplaceable hardware, it's all very...very...*fine.*"

"Then what is the problem?" She sounded increasingly agitated, now. She was trying to take the initiative, which I knew meant *she* knew what I was getting ready for.

"It's just that Evo Asia recognized the code, Ms. MacSwain," I said. I didn't gesture this time, just focused, and another perfectly-to-scale text box appeared, with data pouring through it. Semi-translucent, the image hovered just in front of the first one. Line by line, word for word, pixel by pixel, it matched up to the first. "Or, rather, *I* recognized it. More research on my end.

"I know who finalized your target analysis code for Evo North America," I looked at her flatly, eye to eye. "And I know why."

"I'm certain I don't know what you mean." She kept her voice carefully neutral.

"I know that the initial coders for *CleverShot II* were lost in an act of extra-corporate violence." I used the human-resources-approved language to describe a bloody raid from another corporation. "And I know that said attack is why there is such a sharp and sudden cut-off in the quality of coding, and the, for lack of a better term, flavor, or signature, of the programming. I know Ares was concerned about Evo North America's progress, as they should have been, clearly, and I know—ma'am, one moment, please—and I know they attacked, did their damage, and that, in due time, Evo North America's division head, Mary Luce, already had you personally oversee appropriate retaliatory non-financial settlement protocols against Ares."

Which was, again, the human-resources-approved way to professionally say, "I know you hit them back, and made sure to kill more of them than they did us."

"Then *what* is the *problem*, Mr. Yamatetsu?" She sounded impatient, now. Angry. It was hiding her genuine confusion. "What does a cross-town Seattle...spat...have to do with Forensic Accounting and Evo Asia?"

Conceal the disposition of your troops. She was asking me all the wrong questions, because she had made assumptions about who had requested my presence in Seattle, and why.

"Again, Forensic Accounting didn't send me here, Ms. MacSwain." I let myself show a slight smile. Not enough to be rude, just enough to very politely score a point. I wanted her to *know* that she didn't actually have any idea what this was about. "I am currently a registered employee of that department, and it was initially work done for Ms. Tanaka that got this proverbial ball rolling, yes, but please remember it was Chief Executive Officer Kirilenko that gave the green light to my travel and presentat—"

"Fine," she interrupted again, this time with a negligent wave of her hand. A disgusted one. An impatient one. If she had shown just a bit more patience in the first place, she'd have less to be impatient about now. It felt like something Sun Tzu would have written. I know he didn't; I'd have memorized it if he had.

"Are you ready to move on to Matrix handles, ma'am?" I insisted on finishing. "That second point I mentioned?"

She waved angrily for me to continue.

"Evo North America productivity logs, accessed by an approved Matrix intrusion/counter-intrusion specialist," I very politely said 'Evo corporate hacker,' "Show that the coding on the *CleverShot II* program was finalized and signed off by an Evo North America programmer who colorfully uses the corporate-approved sobriquet of 'CoolPro.'"

"Is it not the norm for other divisions to let their programmers and spiders use their Matrix handles?" She glared at me, pretending that *that* was the problem, pretending it was an etiquette thing, pretending ignorance.

"That's not the problem, no, Ms. MacSwain. The problem is that, as I said, I know who that is. I'm not an expert at coding, myself, but I scored well enough in college to notice a thing or two," I half-lied. But only half. It was the closest I planned to go to genuine deception. "And I know that 'CoolPro' has the exact same flair for code, and leaves the exact same 'tells,' for lack of a better term, as one Rodney 'Hot Rod' Chow, who uses, to be clear, 'Hot Rod' conversationally rather than as a Matrix handle, either internally within Evo networks or externally with the Matrix as a whole."

I tried, but not very hard, not to let my disdain drip onto the lovely hardwood table. "Hot Rod." Juvenile. A flick of my fingertips sent another neat stack of images sliding up into the augmented-reality holo-display between us, as visual support for what I was saying. Evo corporate badges and internal human resources reports from a handful of offices.

"I know that our lovely and charming 'Hot Rod' is not an ideal employee—just look at those complaints lodged by female-presenting coworkers, and how long they've been coming in—but I know his skills at programming are how he's skated by, despite his unique disposition and perspective toward women and their opinions." I held her gaze, looking almost disappointed in her, as I let my scorn for him show. "I know that he is, if not a remarkable coder, one that is consistent. Reliable, for decades. Timely. One might say...*fine.*"

His Evo North America file was flagged with CoolPro. Others, though, different. ProCool. CoolProfessional. KoolPro. ProfessionalCooler. ProfessionCool.

"It took some work to track Mr. Chow and his progression from office to office over the years—he's a bit long in the tooth *and* ill-mannered for so much effort to go into 'recruiting' him, isn't he?—but I believe I've got his movements from office to office, department to department, and project to project, entirely mapped out, don't I, Ms. MacSwain? His long, if unremarkable, career, all laid out here, just between you and me? You did your homework on him, too, didn't you?"

My eyebrows lifted in faux-innocence and simple curiosity. I knew she'd done her research. I knew she always did. I knew about her professionalism, her reputation for being thorough, her renown for being good at what she did.

Kerry MacSwain was, after all, Evo North America's well-known expert on corporate extractions. She was Mary Luce's bloody right hand, called upon not merely for routine administrative duties, but whenever a recruitment/kidnapping was called for. So yes, I knew she'd done her homework, and that nothing I was saying about Chow was news to her. There was no way she'd ever send a tactical team in blind, not just regarding the location and security, but regarding their objective itself.

"Do you want him back?" she asked, acknowledging, in a way, everything I'd said, and several things I hadn't yet.

"No," I reassured her with a bit of a snort. "No, we do not. You may retain his services, return him to the job market, or otherwise do with him as you see fit. Though, I suggest you wait until our conversation is entirely finished rather than pass anything along to human resources while we're still talking.

You'll see why he is important as our conversation continues. May I?"

She nodded.

"Then that brings me, ma'am, to the difference between an incident and an accident." Another mental flick, another flurry of files holo-flashed into the space between us. Some were payroll and tactical appraisal files, some were grainy gun-cam operational video logs, some were excerpts from, definitions from, Evo Global's human resources and legal departments.

Some were simply documents this time. Finished, except for the places reserved for her signature.

"You'll forgive me, I hope, if I had my assigned intrusion/ counter-intrusion specialist do a bit more digging. In a detailed examination of internal records following targeted data retrievals and impressive decryption protocols, it looks to *me* that while Evo North America was seeing to those non-financial settlement protocols with Ares, an Evo North America tactical team was *also* assigned to a short-term, long-range task, Ms. MacSwain, to Osaka. The time that team was on assignment overseas coincides, not coincidentally, with an attack on an Evo Asia facility, also in Osaka, where an Evo programmer, 'ProfessionCool,' was working on hardware-side code integration with smartlinks, right up until the night of his extraction/recruitment."

I leaned forward ever so slightly, letting surprise slip into my tone. "Why, it only just now occurred to me, I suppose someone intimately familiar with that hardware-side code could be pretty uniquely qualified to finish the last of that coding for the *CleverShot II* project, couldn't he? I imagine such a coder would need to have plenty of experi—"

"What's this about, if you don't want him back?" she veritably growled this time. "If you want an apology for a blue-on-blue extraction, you're not getting one, kid. It's part of the job."

"I don't want an apology, Ms. MacSwain. I want what's best for the company." I lifted an eyebrow and holograms rearranged themselves, with the nigh-finished documents moved to the forefront of my e-pile of e-evidence. "Two security personnel and one other coder were killed in your, let's say, 'aggressive recruitment attempt.' We've reviewed the security tapes, both on-site and the footage procured from your shooters' own tactical cameras, and it is the firm opinion of Mr. Kirilenko that those deaths were unnecessary."

Her eyes widened, my emotion-trackers noticed, ever, ever, ever so slightly. That's right. The CEO himself, Anatoly Kirilenko, had seen all of it. A military man, himself, he knew what to look for.

"Mr. Kirilenko believes, however, that while Evo North America personnel acted with appropriate restraint and accuracy, which is no doubt why casualties were so low, the Watada-Rengo soldier serving as their local guide, and who decided to have fun and 'go in' with them, very much did not. *He* is the failure point on this op."

In addition to being Evo North America's extraction expert and, not entirely coincidentally, Kerry MacSwain was *also* well known within and without the Evo corporation for her ties to that particular Yakuza organization. Kami only knew *how* her Tír-elven hoop had gotten those connections, but she certainly had them. And they, usually, served her and the company well. Part of why she was so good at her job was that extractions were easier, most of the time, when one had organized crime and other extralegal elements arrayed to assist, run interference, or provide distractions.

Most of the time.

"Let me reassure you, however, that as I speak with you, neither Evo Asia, nor Mr. Kirilenko himself, entertain any plans of direct retribution against," I cleared my throat and looked faintly disappointed, *"Ochinko."*

"Ochinko," the Osaka street tough called himself. A child's term for a penis. He was a razored-out, chromed-up, super-cool criminal who insisted his peers and enemies called him, essentially, *peepee.* Images of him flashed just above the table, and a fresh wave of screenshots and collected spreadsheets. Images of him from mid-extraction security footage, literal smoking gun in hand, an SCK 100 submachine gun taken from a security officer. Images of him spending money, in the loud and brazen way a lucky gangster did. Images of him sleeping, helpless and vulnerable, next to a rented girlfriend that could have easily been an assassin. Documents showing his bank account balances rising just as the slush funds of Evo North America dipped by the same precise amount. Proof of his payment, proof of his attack, proof of their connection.

Take unremitting precautions. I had everything I needed. I had done my research, collated it, translated raw data into actual information, and had wielded it. And then, I had leveraged it.

"In the interest of Mr. Ochinko's ongoing health and safety, however, Evo Asia has asked for a different form of compensation. Mr. Kirilenko agrees with the following conditions, suggested by way of Forensic Accounting, a famously neutral third party in such intra-corporate...spats."

I smiled politely after throwing her own dismissive term back at her.

"At present, the workplace deaths of Mr. Hayashi, Ms. Yamashita, and Mr. Nishimura, are being treated as workplace incidents. As you know, according to Evo policies, incidents... happen. Incidents have no fault, they are caused by forces outside the corporation, they are failures with no clear *point* of failure known. They are acts of fate, the kami, or whatever god or devil people choose to believe in. They are not accidents. As per official policies, accidents have clear points of failure, points where Evo may improve to prevent future accidents. Evo takes responsibility for accidents. Evo cares for the next of kin of accidents. Evo does not, not to nearly the same extent, for incidents."

I leaned forward slightly, aggressively, offensively. I was pushing, really pushing, for the first time. "As per standard Evo protocols, the death benefits offered for workplace incidents are minimal and, in my frank opinion, if I can speak the truth to you, Ms. MacSwain, almost insultingly so. But while minimal, they are, in this case, still an expense absorbed by Evo Asia that it finds...unfair."

A mental flick, and my short stack of unsigned documents slid through the aether to float just a *bit* closer to MacSwain.

"Sign these, and our internal reports will change. We'll fudge a date or two to make things work, or we'll say that they were software testing ahead of the formal launch, but the short form is that *CleverShot II* will be blamed, specifically the portion of code produced by Mr. Rodney Chow. The death of Mr. Nishimura will become the result of Mr. Hayashi's wildly discharging standard-issue Shin Chou Kyogo, or 'SCK,' Model 100 submachinegun. Ms. Yamashita will have perished as she tried to shield him with her own body, and the death of the fortunately single and childless Mr. Hayashi will be a guilt-riddled suicide in the days after his weapon's catastrophic failure. The *CleverShot II* target analysis software will be, internally only, to blame for this tragedy. Rodney Chow, and whatever combination of CoolPro or ProCool he currently favors, will be found to be the reason for the failure. He, and he alone, will be the reason for the...accident."

I *had* told her we didn't want him back.

"After the tragedy is classified not as a workplace incident, but as a workplace accident, with a clear, cut-and-dried, coding flaw to blame, Evo will accept full responsibility, and see to the survivors' families more generously and appropriately. The Nishimura family will be benevolently taken care of as a result of this tragedy, the Yamashita family will be fully compensated and will also rest easy knowing that she died a heroic death, giving her life to save another loyal employee, and Mr. Hayashi's surviving family, however distant, will be comforted by the fact that he was not to blame, but gave his life to express his shame, regardless, as befits a security officer of his rank. Evo will see to all of them, very probably including scholarships for those deemed capable of making the most of them."

I paused, and not only because talking of families almost always made me pause.

"Evo *North America*, that is," I clarified, in case that had been in any way unclear. "Evo *North America* will see to this recompense, and the official statement offering condolences and accepting blame."

She didn't object. I knew when I was winning, so I pressed the advantage. "The *CleverShot II* will take a reputation hit, yes, but only internally. It will be thought of, in-house, as good, yes, but not great."

I knew she wouldn't be happy with that part. I wanted her to take the deal, though. I meant every word of what I was saying. I'd mapped out a hundred different resolutions to the situation, and I was genuinely certain I was offering her the best one.

"But, on the other hand, you can prevent that failure in the future, place blame squarely on someone who hasn't been your employee for long, and who I have no reason to doubt you find personally odious, *and*, hear me out, I have seen to it you now have permission to make up for Rodney Chow's failings with a fresh wave of *extra*-corporate extractions for fresh coding talent. Raid whoever you'd like outside of Evo, however harshly you'd like, with Mr. Kirilenko's blessing and with Evo Global footing that particular bill—within reasonable budgetary bounds approved of by Ms. Tanaka and Forensic Accounting—*and* your relationship with the Osaka Watada-Rengo need not suffer, as Ochinko will be off the hook."

I leaned back, ever so slightly. I had to make it all sound not only reasonable, which it was, but easy. Effortless. The obvious choice, but one that I had lighted upon without much work.

A clever fighter is one who not only wins, but who excels in winning with ease. Sun Tzu would approve. I, I knew, was a very clever fighter.

MacSwain's *Industry II*-quality cyberoptics flicked from the e-documents to me, and back. She was weighing her options. She was wondering if my Kirilenko name-dropping was some sort of bluff. She was wondering if Tanaka-*san* cared about me more than *she* cared about Ochinko or Rodney Chow. She was wondering if she could have me killed, then doctor security records to make it look like I'd never arrived, then offer nothing but confused looks and eventual condolences if anyone asked her about my visit. She was wondering what my hook was, my catch, what I got out of all of this.

She'd die wondering that, because the truth was simple: I didn't have one.

There was no hook, there was no catch. I gained nothing but the approval of my superiors. I wasn't out to trick her, harshly punish her, or steal from her. I meant everything. I wanted our dead employees' families to be better taken care of, and I knew Evo North America had the profit margins to effortlessly support that. I wanted Ochinko's bloodthirstiness and incompetence to be made plain to MacSwain, so she'd leave him out of any future blue-on-blue operations, but I didn't see a value in him being directly punished. I wanted MacSwain to keep her Yakuza connections healthy, because I knew Evo profited from them in the long run. I wanted MacSwain to know her tac-team had performed professionally, so that if future blue-on-blue operations *were* called for, they and their restraint would do the deed. I wanted Tanaka and Forensic Accounting to keep their fearsome reputation, and I wanted Kirilenko pleased with the result, just as much as I wanted MacSwain to leave the boardroom content.

I wanted Evo to improve from all of this; I wanted to finally be rid of the sexist, morale-damaging coder, having finally been given a clear reason to kick him to the curb. I wanted the families of those who'd lost their lives to be fairly compensated for those losses, so they would want to return Evo's loyalty. I didn't want them to know their family members had died by Evo's hand, on Evo's dime, over Evo's troubles.

I wanted Evo to win.

I wanted all of Evo to win.

I wanted all of Evo to win because of me—whether they knew it or not.

His victories bring him neither reputation for wisdom nor credit for courage, Sun Tzu wrote of the clever fighter. I understood. I had known, for my entire short life, that even the open-minded Evo might never quite accept me, never quite embrace me, never quite give me the credit others might get. I had been granted corporate citizenship, and no small rank, but I knew I might never truly fit in with my peers. I knew that, and accepted it.

I didn't care if I got the credit.

I just wanted Evo to win.

Hence a skillful fighter puts himself into a position which makes defeat impossible, and does not miss the moment for defeating the enemy. Sun Tzu had given me the idea for how best to make Evo win.

My enemy wasn't Kerry MacSwain. My enemy wasn't anyone in Evo, ever, unless they betrayed my family. My enemy was, in fact, *not*-Evo. My enemy was everyone outside of the corporation that wanted to see us falter, see us fumble, see us fall apart. My enemy was inefficiency, ineptitude, indiscretion. My enemy was failure itself.

Kerry MacSwain squinted, her cyberoptics flared with green light during a high-security data transfer, and the faintly glowing documents were e-signed, encrypted, and re-uploaded to internal servers.

Done.

I nodded and showed my most genuine smile of the day, overtly feeling pleased.

She stood, reached across the table, and offered me an open hand.

Oh, yes. Of course. Symbolism was important to North Americans.

I stood, reached across the gap, and shook her hand. I was ready, though. Displays of power and attempts at intimidation were important to North Americans, too.

She gave me a tug even as she leaned across the table toward me. She was stronger than she looked, and I knew I wasn't, but I still *chose* to let her pull me awkwardly forward. If this was what it would take for her to feel better, I was fine with letting her think I was off-balance. My dignity was intact, no matter how close her face got to mine, or how grim her expression.

"If ever you fly across the Atlantic to be a pain in my arse again, 'Mr. Yamatetsu,' y'vat-grown bastard," her Irish brogue slipped out and she said my name like it was a trick, a bluster, a power move on my part. It was unfortunate she'd decided there needed to be ugliness between us, despite the amicable solution I'd presented her. "You'll nae be flying back home, and nobody will care if it's an accident or an incident that does you in."

She let go after a too-hard squeeze that my cyberhand pain receptors told me *should* have caused significant discomfort, if only I'd not muted them before reaching toward her.

I bowed politely, thoroughly unphased. "You, also, have a lovely day, Ms. MacSwain, and thank you for your time," I said exactly like she hadn't just threatened to murder me. "I will give Mr. Kirilenko and Tanaka-*san* your regards."

I was not afraid of her. If ever I bothered her again, it would be because I had good reason to, and I would have appropriate protections in place. If she ever did see me again, it would be because she deserved it, because she had hurt the company again, because she was sloppy or spiteful or malicious enough to do more harm than good to the only thing I loved and the only family I had.

I was Kenjiro Yamatetsu. I was a child of the Evo corporation—quite literally—and they had built me for this.

I was consequences.

ABOUT THE AUTHORS

Marie Bilodeau is an Ottawa-based author, TTRPG writer, and storyteller. Her speculative fiction has won several awards and has been translated into French (*Les Éditions Alire*) and Chinese (*SF World*). Her short stories have also appeared in various anthologies and magazines like *Analog Science Fiction* and *Fact* and *Amazing Stories*. She's Chair of Ottawa's speculative fiction literary con, Can*Con and, in a past life not-so-long ago, was Deputy Publisher for The Ed Greenwood Group (TEGG).

Marie is also a storyteller, and has told stories across Canada in theaters, tea shops, at festivals, and under disco balls. She's won story slams with personal stories, has participated in epic tellings at the National Arts Centre, and has adapted classical material. Follow her adventures in mayhem at www.mariebilodeau.com.

Dylan Birtolo is a writer, game designer, and professional sword-swinger. He's published multiple novels, novellas, and short stories both in established universes and worlds of his own creation. Some of the universes that he's created stories in are *Shadowrun, Exalted, BattleTech, Freeport*, and *Pathfinder*. On the gaming side, he's the lead designer at Lynnvander Studios and has created multiple games including *Pathfinder's Level 20, Starfinder's Pirates of Skydock, Evil Dead 2*, and many more to come. He trains with the Seattle Knights, an acting troop that focuses on stage combat, and has performed in live shows, videos, and movies. He's had the honor of jousting, and yes, the armor is real.

Crystal Frasier is an award-winning author and game designer hailing from the fetid swamps of Florida. Beyond running the shadows of the Sixth World, she has spun fictions for the gaming worlds of *Pathfinder, Mutants & Masterminds,* and *Vampire: The Masquerade,* as well as her original graphic novels *Cheer Up: Love & Pompoms* and *Whippoorwills.* Her twenty-year career of fictional adventure has netted her Ennie Awards and a GLAAD Media Award, as well as exciting personal triumphs—including taming a fearsome corgi and punching a dinosaur. Despite all this, her proudest achievement is being the kind of person her amazing wife likes.

Jaym Gates is an author, editor, and game designer based out of Seattle, where she lives with her partner, their three rescued German Shepherds, and their horses. She's written and edited anthologies, board games, video games, mobile games, and academic works, but spends most of her time these days as a technical writer. You can find out more at jaymgates.com.

Jason M. Hardy was honored to win best short-form biography at the 2023 Biobies Awards, a ceremony where he tends to do quite well because he made them up. But maybe he'll let someone else win if a suitable donation to the ceremony is offered. He is the Creative Director of Catalyst Game Labs' RPG Division, which is also something he pretty much made up but it at least has other staff, unlike the Biobies. He has published nine novels (seven in English) and dozens of novellas and short stories. He lives in Chicago with his wife and children.

Ken' Horner is a chemist, father, and writer, somehow managing to sustain all three. Often asked about the spelling of his pen name, pronounced Ken prime, it harkens back to the early days of writing on the formative internet with his friend Ken Petruzzelli and the prime distinguished the two. He resides in Western Michigan with his wife, Cherie, and three boys, Vincent, Liam, and Callan, who are his biggest supporters. He also has dogs, chicken, turkeys, ducks, and a snake which could care less about his pursuits. Any theoretical free time would be split between the family and gaming with friends.

R. L. King is the author of the Amazon-bestselling *Alastair Stone Chronicles* urban fantasy series, along with the *Happenstance and Bron* and *Calanar* series set in the Stone Chronicles universe. She has written two *Shadowrun* novels, *Borrowed Time* and *Veiled Extraction*, along with numerous short fiction pieces and game materials. She lives in San Jose, California with an understanding spouse, four ridiculously adorable cats, and a crested gecko named Lofwyr. She is currently pursuing a Master's degree in Publishing from Western Colorado University.

Andrew Peregrine became a freelance games writer as a side hustle and it's got a bit out of control. He has written for most major companies, most notably Chaosium (*Regency Cthulhu*) Cubicle 7 (*Doctor Who*) EN Publishing (*Judge Dredd*) and White Wolf/Renegade (*Vampire*). He is also the line developer for *Dune: Adventures in the Imperium* (Modiphius) and *My Little Pony* (Renegade). As a side-side hustle he produces his own games as Corone Design including *Cabal* and *Hellcats and Hockeysticks*. His most recent project, *Opera House*, combines gaming with his supposedly 'real job' as a lighting technician in theatre. Andrew has published several short stories in other anthologies but still hasn't managed to finish a novel yet, although he has started at least three. Andrew lives in London with his partner Claire, and owns no cats.

Alina Pete is a nehiyaw artist and writer from Little Pine First Nation in Saskatchewan. They grew up urban but spent summers wandering in the Qu'Appelle Valley with their cousins from Cowessess First Nation. Alina is best known for their Aurora Award–winning comics, but they also write short stories and poems, and their work has been featured in several Indigenous comic anthologies. They are the creator and editor of the comics anthology *Indiginerds: Tales from Modern Indigenous Life*. Alina lives on unceded Kwantlen, Katzie, Semiahmoo and Tsawwassen land with their partner.

Aaron Rosenberg is the author of over 50 novels, including the *Twin Cities Cryptids* urban fantasy/cozy series, the *DuckBob SF* comedy series, the *Relicant Chronicles* epic fantasy series, the *Areyat Islands* fantasy pirate mystery series, and, with David Niall Wilson, the *O.C.L.T.* occult thriller series. In addition to work for *Shadowrun* (including the novel *Shadow Dance* and stories in *Drawing Destiny* and *World of Shadows*), his tie-in work contains novels for *Star Trek, Warhammer, World of WarCraft, Stargate: Atlantis, Mutants & Masterminds*, and *Eureka* and short stories for *The X-Files, World of Darkness, Crusader Kings II, Deadlands, Master of Orion*, and *Europa Universalis IV*. He has written children's books (including the award-winning *Bandslam: The Junior Novel* and the #1 best-selling *42: The Jackie Robinson Story*), educational books, and roleplaying games (including the original games *Asylum, Spookshow*, and *Chosen*; work for White Wolf, Wizards of the Coast, Fantasy Flight, Pinnacle, and many others; the Origins Award-winning *Gamemastering Secrets*; and the Gold ENnie-winning *Lure of the Lich Lord*). Aaron lives in New York with his family. You can follow him online at gryphonrose.com, on Facebook at facebook.com/gryphonrose, and on X (formerly known as Twitter) @gryphonrose.

Michael A. Stackpole is an award-winning novelist, game designer, computer game designer, podcaster, screenwriter and graphic novelist. He's had over fifty-five novels published, the best known of those being the New York Times bestselling *I, Jedi* and *Rogue Squadron*. He has an asteroid named after him (*165612*). In 2023 the International Association of Media Tie-In Writers named him their Grandmaster by presenting him the Faust Award. His most recent novel is *Dark Souls: Masque of Vindication*.

Bryan CP Steele. Forty-seven year old husband, father, producer, author, designer, and painter; if it has anything to do with the gaming industry, Bryan has made it his goal to try his hand at it. He has been a gamer for thirty plus years, industry professional for over two decades, with over two million published words across numerous companies and brands: *Iron Kingdoms, Babylon 5, Conan, Starship Troopers, Pacific Rim, Traveler, RuneQuest, Power Rangers, Transformers*, and more. Bryan calls himself "the professional nerd," and firmly stands by his motto—leave every room at least a little happier than when you got there.

RJ Thomas. A native and current resident of northwest Ohio, RJ is an award-winning game author and the current line developer for the *Shadowrun* TTRPG line published by Catalyst Game Labs. In 2011, he started his professional gaming career as a member of the Catalyst Demo Team. Soon after joining the CDT, he became a freelance writer and later project developer for the *Shadowrun* line. During that time, he's contributed to over forty *Shadowrun* projects across three different editions. His credits include *Hazard Pay, Run and Gun, Street Grimoire, Street Lethal, Cutting Black, Scotophobia, Shadowrun 2050,* and *Dark Terrors* (the latter two he shares an Ennie Award with fellow SR authors) among others. He's also crafted the *Shadowrun* adventures *Battle of Manhattan, Counting Coup, Starving the Masses,* and *False Flag*. Additionally, he's penned several *Shadowrun* short stories such as *Butcher's Bill, My Brother's Keeper, SNAFU, Neon Reflections,* and the *Drawing Destiny* anthology story *One for the Other*. In 2022, he crossed into Catalyst Game Lab's other major product line *BattleTech* with the short story *The Space Cowboys from Quatre Belle,* published in *Shrapnel* (the official *BattleTech* magazine), Issue #11.

Bryan Young (he/they) works across many different media. His work as a writer and producer has been called "filmmaking gold" by *The New York Times*. He's also published comic books with Slave Labor Graphics and Image Comics. He's been a regular contributor for the Huffington Post, StarWars.com, Star Wars Insider magazine, SYFY, /Film, and was the founder and editor in chief of the geek news and review site *Big Shiny Robot!* In 2014, he wrote the critically acclaimed history book, *A Children's Illustrated History of Presidential Assassination*. He co-authored *Robotech: The Macross Saga* RPG and has written five books in the *BattleTech* Universe: *Honor's Gauntlet, A Question of Survival, Fox Tales, Without Question,* and the forthcoming *VoidBreaker*. His latest non-fiction tie-in book, *The Big Bang Theory Book of Lists* is a #1 Bestseller on Amazon. His work has won two Diamond Quill awards and in 2023 he was named Writer of the Year by the League of Utah Writers. He teaches writing for Writer's Digest, Script Magazine, and at the University of Utah. Follow him across social media @ swankmotron or visit swankmotron.com.

Russell Zimmerman is a word-merc, a keyboard for hire, a lone typeslinger wandering the wild frontiers of the Matrix.

A freelance writer for over a decade now, he's contributed to wargames, roleplaying games, and video games, ranging from *BattleTech* to the *Fallout* franchise, from *Warhammer 40k* to his beloved *Shadowrun*, and beyond! Regular Sixth World fans know him for Jimmy Kincaid and Dash Red Clay, and he's excited to use this anthology to kick off his latest protagonist, Kenjiro Yamatetsu, with more Kenji on the way soon! By the time you're reading this, Rusty (btw, you can call him Rusty, it's cool) will be settled in to a lovely new apartment with his lovely (old?) wife, Felicia, somewhere in Brooklyn, NYC. Time for a new adventure!

ABOUT THE EDITORS

John Helfers has been working in branded IP development and publishing for more than twenty-five years. During his eighteen years at Tekno Books, at one time the largest book packager in the nation, he managed several *New York Times*-bestselling novel series, working with such authors as Tom Clancy, Charlaine Harris, Dale Brown, Mercedes Lackey, Stephen Coonts, and many others, as well producing hundreds of anthologies and novels.

Currently he's the Executive Editor at Catalyst Game Labs, where he oversees the fiction lines for *BattleTech*, *Shadowrun* and *Leviathans*, publishing more than 1 million words of original fiction every year. He lives and works in Green Bay, Wisconsin.

Jennifer Brozek is a multi-talented, award-winning author, editor, and media tie-in writer. She is the author of *Never Let Me Sleep* and *The Last Days of Salton Academy*, both of which were nominated for the Bram Stoker Award. Her YA tie-in novels, *BattleTech: The Nellus Academy Incident* and *Shadowrun: Auditions*, have both won Scribe Awards. Her editing work has earned her nominations for the British Fantasy Award, the Bram Stoker Award, and the Hugo Award. She won the Australian Shadows Award for the *Grants Pass* anthology, co-edited with Amanda Pillar. Jennifer's short form work has appeared in *Apex Publications*, *Uncanny Magazine*, *Daily Science Fiction*, and in anthologies set in the worlds of *Valdemar*, *Shadowrun*, *V-Wars*, *Masters of Orion*, *Well World*, and *Predator*.

Jennifer has been a full-time freelance author and editor for over seventeen years, and she has never been happier. She keeps a tight schedule on her writing and editing projects and somehow manages to find time to teach writing classes and volunteer for several professional writing organizations such as SFWA, HWA, and IAMTW. She shares her husband, Jeff, with several cats and often uses him as a sounding board for her story ideas. Visit Jennifer's worlds at jenniferbrozek.com or her social media accounts on LinkTree: https://linktr.ee/ JenniferBrozek.

LOOKING FOR MORE SHADOWRUN FICTION, CHUMMER?

WE'LL HOOK YOU UP!

Catalyst Game Labs brings you the very best in *Shadowrun* fiction, available at most ebook retailers, including Amazon, Apple Books, Kobo, Barnes & Noble, and more!

NOVELS

1. *Never Deal with a Dragon* (Secrets of Power #1)
    by Robert N. Charrette
2. *Choose Your Enemies Carefully* (Secrets of Power #2)
    by Robert N. Charrette
3. *Find Your Own Truth* (Secrets of Power #3)
    by Robert N. Charrette
4. *2XS* by Nigel Findley
5. *Changeling* by Chris Kubasik
6. *Never Trust an Elf* by Robert N. Charrette
7. *Shadowplay* by Nigel Findley
8. *Night's Pawn* by Tom Dowd
9. *Striper Assassin* by Nyx Smith
10. *Lone Wolf* by Nigel Findley
11. *Fade to Black* by Nyx Smith
12. *Burning Bright* by Tom Dowd
13. *Who Hunts the Hunter* by Nyx Smith
14. *House of the Sun* by Nigel Findley
15. *Worlds Without End* by Caroline Spector
16. *Just Compensation* by Robert N. Charrette
17. *Preying for Keeps* by Mel Odom
18. *Dead Air* by Jak Koke
19. *The Lucifer Deck* by Lisa Smedman
20. *Steel Rain* by Nyx Smith
21. *Shadowboxer* by Nicholas Pollotta
22. *Stranger Souls* (Dragon Heart Saga #1) by Jak Koke
23. *Headhunters* by Mel Odom
24. *Clockwork Asylum* (Dragon Heart Saga #2) by Jak Koke
25. *Blood Sport* by Lisa Smedman
26. *Beyond the Pale* (Dragon Heart Saga #3) by Jak Koke
27. *Technobabel* by Stephen Kenson
28. *Wolf and Raven* by Michael A. Stackpole

OMNIBUSES

1. *The Secrets of Power Trilogy*, by Robert N. Charrette

ANTHOLOGIES

1. *Spells & Chrome*, edited by John Helfers
2. *World of Shadows*, edited by John Helfers
3. *Drawing Destiny: A Sixth World Tarot Anthology*, edited by John Helfers
4. *Sprawl Stories, Vol. 1*, edited by John Helfers
5. *The Complete Frame Job*, edited by John Helfers
6. *Down These Dark Streets: The Collected Stories of Russell Zimmerman*
7. *Old School (Sprawl Stories, Volume Two)*, edited by John Helfers
8. *Auditions*, by Jennifer Brozek
9. *Shadow Borders (Sprawl Stories, Volume Three)* edited by John Helfers

NOVELLAS

1. *Neat* by Russell Zimmerman
2. *The Vladivostok Gauntlet* by Olivier Gagnon
3. *Nothing Personal* by Olivier Gagnon
4. *Another Rainy Night* by Patrick Goodman
5. *Sail Away, Sweet Sister* by Patrick Goodman
6. *The Seattle Gambit* by Olivier Gagnon
7. *DocWagon 19* by Jennifer Brozek
8. *Wolf & Buffalo* by R.L. King
9. *Big Dreams* by R.L. King
10. *Blind Magic* by Dylan Birtolo
11. *The Frame Job, Part 1: Yu* by Dylan Birtolo
12. *The Frame Job, Part 2: Emu* by Brooke Chang
13. *The Frame Job, Part 3: Rude* by Bryan CP Steele
14. *The Frame Job, Part 4: Frostburn* by CZ Wright
15. *The Frame Job, Part 5: Zipfile* by Jason Schmetzer
16. *The Frame Job, Part 6: Retribution* by Jason M. Hardy
17. *Tower of the Scorpion* by Mel Odom
18. *Chaser* by Russell Zimmerman
19. *A Kiss to Die For* by Jennifer Brozek
20. *Crocodile Tears* by Chris A. Jackson
21. *See How She Runs* by Jennifer Brozek
22. *Under Pressure* by Scott Schletz
23. *Kill Penalty* by Clifton Lambert
24. *Kings of the Street* by O. C. Presley
25. *Clean Record* by Dylan Birtolo
26. *Unrepairable* by Jennifer Brozek
27. *Mercy Street* by Bryan Young
28. *Corporate Business* by Dylan Birtolo
29. *Best Laid Plans* by Anton Strout
30. *The Kilimanjaro Run* by Jennifer Brozek
31. *Rules of the Kaidō Club* by Katherine Monasterio